"I am at your service, Your Grace."

Wicked little minx.

"I require assistance removing my attire," Wycliff said.

Her blue eyes darkened and the slightest gasp escaped her lips.

"Yes, of course, Your Grace," she whispered. A smile played on her lips, the kind of woman's smile that said, *"You'll pay for this, mister."*

He knew it well. All over the world, from London's ballrooms to harems to the islands of Tahiti, women smiled like that.

The sweet, seductive torture was about to begin.

First, she smoothed her hands across his shoulders and chest. Then her small female hands slid down to the buttons on his waistcoat.

Her eyes met his. Her blue eyes, like the ocean.

One button undone . . .

Romances by Maya Rodale

THE TATTOOED DUKE
A TALE OF TWO LOVERS
A GROOM OF ONE'S OWN
THE HEIR AND THE SPARE
THE ROGUE AND THE RIVAL

MAYA RODALE

The Tattooed Duke

AVON
An Imprint of HarperCollinsPublishers

AVON BOOKS
An Imprint of HarperCollins*Publishers*
10 East 53rd Street
New York, New York 10022-5299

Copyright © 2012 by Maya Rodale
ISBN 978-0-06-208892-5
www.avonromance.com

First Avon Books mass market printing: March 2012

Avon Trademark Reg. U.S. Pat. Off. and in Other Countries, Marca Registrada, Hecho en U.S.A.
HarperCollins® is a registered trademark of HarperCollins Publishers.

Printed in the U.S.A.

10 9 8 7 6 5 4 3 2 1

For my friends at the Rodale Institute.
I miss y'all, but Timbuktu was calling.

and

For Tony,
my very own ~~long-haired, pierced, and tattooed duke~~
brilliant and dashing 'round-the-world explorer.

XOXO,
Your writing girl ~~housemaid~~ wife

Acknowledgments

This author is indebted to Sarah Tormey for encouragement and feedback; to Denise for an inspiring and productive writing trip to Barbados; to my talented editor Tessa for helping me take this book to the next level; to my momma for always encouraging me to do what I love; and to Tony and Penny, just because.

Above all, this book would not have been possible without the amazing care of everyone at Hands On Healing. I was in extraordinary pain and could barely type when I started this book, and now I am writing "thank you," pain-free. I cannot thank you all enough.

Chapter 1

The Duke Returns

London, 1825
The docks

They said he had been a pirate. It seemed utterly believable. The other rumors about Sebastian Digby, the Duke of Wycliff, were equally riveting. It was said that he had charmed and seduced his way across countries and continents; that there existed no law or woman he couldn't bend to suit his whims; that he had lived among the natives in Tahiti and swam utterly nude in the clear turquoise waters; that he had escaped the dankest of prisons and thoroughly enjoyed himself in a sultan's harem.

A gentleman he clearly was not.

And now this charming, adventurous, scandalous duke had returned home, to London.

Miss Eliza Fielding had joined the throngs on the dock to witness the long-awaited return of this duke, as per the orders of her employer, Mr. Derek Knightly. She wrote for the monstrously popular newspaper he owned and edited, *The London Weekly*. In fact, she was one of the four infamous Writing

Girls who wrote for the paper. For the moment, at any rate.

If she didn't get this story . . .

Eliza tugged her bonnet lower across her brow to protect against the light drizzle falling and dug her hands into the pockets of her coat.

"If you don't get this story," Mr. Knightly had told her plainly as she stood in his Fleet Street office just yesterday, "I can no longer employ you as a writer for *The London Weekly.* I cannot justify it if you are not submitting publishable works."

It was perfectly logical. It was only business. And yet it felt like a lover's betrayal.

Knightly didn't need to say that she hadn't been turning in any decent stories—they both knew it. Weeks had turned into months, and not one article of hers appeared in its pages.

Oh, she used to write the most marvelous stories—a week in the workhouse undercover to expose the wretched conditions, exclusive interviews with Newgate prisoners condemned to death, detailing the goings-on in a brothel to show what the lives of prostitutes were really like. If there was a truth in need of light, Eliza was up to the task. If adventure, danger, and the dark side of London were involved, so much the better.

Lately she hadn't been inspired. The words wouldn't come. Hours, she spent with a quill in hand, dripping splotches of ink of a blank sheet of paper.

But this story . . .

Knightly's assignment was plain: to uncover every last secret of the Duke of Wycliff. All of London was panting for the intimate details of his ten years abroad. It wasn't *just* that he was a duke—and the latest in the long line of "Wicked Wycliffs," as the family was known. That alone would have required column inches of ink. But all those rumors . . .

Had he really been a pirate? Was it true about the harem? Had he been made the chief of a small tribe on a remote island in Polynesia? What of mountains scaled, fires started, and lands explored? More importantly to the ton, was he looking for a wife?

The questions were plentiful. The answers were hers to discover. But how?

"But how?" she asked Knightly. "He's a duke and I am quite far from that. We don't exactly move in the same circles."

Julianna, Countess Roxbury—fellow Writing Girl and gossip columnist—was far better suited to the task.

"Do you not want this story?" Knightly asked impatiently. She saw him glance at the stack of papers on his desk awaiting his attention.

"Oh, I do," Eliza said passionately. It wasn't the money—Knightly's wages were fair, but not extravagant. There was something about being a Writing Girl: the true friendship, the thrill of pushing the boundaries of what a woman could do in this day and age, the love of chasing a great story and the pleasure of writing, excruciating as it occasionally could be.

She made a living by her own wits, dignity intact, and she was beholden to no one. She would not give that up lightly.

"Figure something out," Knightly told her. "Become his mistress. Bribe his staff. Or better yet, disguise yourself as one of the housemaids. I care not, *but get this damned story.*"

Knightly didn't need to say "or else!" or bandy

about idle threats to make his point. The truth was there, clear as day: this was her last chance to write something great or there would only be three Writing Girls.

Thus, she was now here, on the docks along with a mob of Londoners vying to see this long-lost pirate duke. All manner of curiosities were hauled off the ship: exotic creatures, exquisite blossoms and plants, dozens of battered crates with words like *Danger* or *Fragile* or *Incendiary* branded on the boards.

Interesting, to be sure, but nothing compared to the man himself.

Everything about him would cause a scandal.

Then she saw him.

His dark hair was unfashionably long, brushing his shoulders and pulled back in a queue save for some windswept strands that whipped around his sharply slanting cheeks.

His skin was still sun-browned. A tantalizing patch exposed at the nape of his neck—which a gentleman would have covered—begged one to wonder how much of his skin had been exposed to the sultry tropical sun. Had he stripped down to his breeches, baring his chest? Or had the lot of his clothing been deemed too restrictive and discarded?

He wore no cravat at his neck; instead, buttons were left undone on his linen shirt, offering a glimpse of the bare skin of his chest. His gray jacket was worn carelessly opened, as if he did not even notice the drizzling rain.

When he moved, one might catch a glimpse of a sword hanging at his side. One would be wise to assume he carried a knife in his boot or a pistol in his coat pocket.

The story. The story. *The story.*

Even on this damp afternoon, Eliza felt like her nerves were smoldering, sparked by equal parts excitement and fear. It was the feeling she always had at the start of a mission, but this time there was something else.

Something that left her breathless. Something that made her feel the heat all over, even in this cool, wet weather. Something that made it awfully difficult to breathe for a second. Something that made it impossible to wrench her gaze away from the man, the duke, *the story.*

Two men, garbed in dark, rough coats next to her in the crowd began a conversation that Eliza freely eavesdropped on as she kept her gazed fixed upon her quarry. She leaned in, the better to listen to their gruff voices.

"I heard that his household is looking to hire, but chits aren't exactly lining up for the job. I know I told my sister under no circumstances was she to take a job there, duke's household or not."

"Aye? Why is that?" This man's posture and tone said he thought it stupid to refuse a job, particularly from a duke.

"Everyone knows the Wicked Wycliffs like to tup their housemaids and then send 'em packing when they're with child," the other said authoritatively. She wondered where he'd heard gossip like that. Probably from *The London Weekly.*

"More than usual?" the man said, thus pointing out that this was hardly unusual behavior.

"Aye, they're legendary for it. They don't call 'em the Wicked Wycliffs for nothing. And this one, particularly—look at him. Would you want yer sister or your missus working under the same roof as him?"

In unison the three fixed their attention on the duke. He boldly paced the ship's deck with determined strides, coat thrown open to the elements and white shirt now wet and plastered across his wide, flat chest and abdomen. Heat infused Eliza's cheeks and . . . elsewhere.

The duke paused to converse with a rough-looking man with one arm in a sling and one eye covered by a black patch. The very definition of disreputable company.

The duke turned to give an order to the crew as they carried off precious cargo. Eliza knew that he was not captain of the ship, but lud, if he didn't act like he was the lord and master of everything around him.

To say the duke was handsome did not do it justice—even from the distance she viewed him at. He was utterly captivating. Danger, indeed.

"No," the man next to her said. "I wouldn't want any of my womenfolk gettin' near the likes of that."

Eliza smiled, because she would dare to get close. She thought again of Knightly's flippant, impatient words: *Or better yet, disguise yourself as one of the housemaids.*

Her heart pounded as she pieced that together with the gossip she had shamelessly overheard: *I heard that his household is looking to hire, but chits aren't exactly lining up for the job.*

Shivers of excitement. The thrill of the chase. Her job on the line.

Get the story. Get the story. Get the story . . .

On the spot, she made a decision. In order to save her position as one of *The London Weekly*'s Writing

Girls, she would disguise herself as a maid in the household of the scandalous, wicked Duke of Wycliff.

The very next day, wearing a plain dress and with fake letters of reference from her fellow Writing Girls, the Duchess of Brandon and the Countess Roxbury, Eliza found herself at work in Wycliff House—dusting the library bookshelves, in particular, while His Grace entertained a caller—where she would have unfettered access to the duke, his household, and his secrets . . . and to the shocking story she needed in order to remain a writer at *The London Weekly*.

Chapter 2

In Which There Is Nudity

Wycliff House

Within four and twenty hours of his return to English soil, Sebastian Digby, the new Duke of Wycliff, had a caller. His idiot cousin Basil had come to visit. Worse, Basil brought a decade's worth of gossip and a deplorable inability to discern the interesting from the mundane.

Sebastian—still not used to the name Wycliff applied to himself—had once been held in an Egyptian prison with a man who insisted on telling the long, excruciatingly dull history of herding cattle in the desert. Basil's company and conversation rivaled that for sleep inducing properties.

Nevertheless, in proper English fashion they took tea before the fireplace on another damp, gray March afternoon.

A maid dusted the bookshelves. She had a very nice backside. Such was the saving grace of the afternoon.

Basil rambled on. He reported all the major scandals—marriages, a divorce, duels and deaths—and briefly mentioned news regarding Lady Althea

Shackley. At the mention of her name, Wycliff shifted uncomfortably in his chair.

Basil then mentioned the creditors plaguing the household and loitering in front of the house. News that the duke had returned spread like the plague, and hordes of merchants crawled out of the woodwork to demand payments owed for services rendered by the previous duke, or that had accumulated whilst Wycliff was adventuring on the far side of the world.

Wycliff knew he would have to do something about them. Pay them, presumably.

Or swiftly depart for lands unknown. He was leaning toward the latter. Timbuktu, in particular.

"We had all given you up for dead," Basil began. "Though rumors would float back every now and then."

"We?"

"Myself, my missus, the rest of the ton," Basil explained. "But then we all heard rumors of your adventures and whereabouts. Is it true that you spent a week in a harem ravishing a hundred concubines of the sultan?"

Gossip apparently was not much troubled by distance.

Nearby, the maid with the lovely bottom slowed with her dusting, as if she were eavesdropping. He assumed so; anyone would be. Dull as Basil might be, he was far more interesting than dusting.

Wycliff grinned at the memory of the one exquisite night of unbridled passion kindled by the grave threat of discovery. Some things were worth risking life and limb for.

"It was only one night," he clarified. The maid

coughed. Aye, she was listening. And doing the math.

"That's the sort of rumors and gossip that will have the ton matrons in a tizzy," Basil remarked. He bit into a biscuit and brushed the bread crumbs from his puce-colored waistcoat.

"That's what I do, Basil," Sebastian replied. He always had. It's what the Wycliffs had done for generations. There wasn't a more outrageous, debaucherous, devil-may-care clan in England's history. The men were notorious for dallying with the household maids, for spending fortunes on mistresses, and for generally being a drunken, undisciplined lot. Oddly enough, they tended to marry stern, practical, cold wives. The sort that *might* manage to impose some order and civilizing behavior. None had ever managed to do so.

His own parents were no exception. By some miracle, he had inherited his mother's rigid self-control, and it warred constantly with his Wicked Wycliff blood.

"I suppose it doesn't take much to upset the ton," Basil conceded. He clearly took after the other side of the family. The dull side. "Now what about those rumors that you were a pirate?"

"What about them?" Wycliff asked, lifting his brow suggestively just to provoke his cousin. He ought to invite Harlan to join them. Basil would surely be aghast at the man's eye patch, injured arm, and pirate charade. He wondered if the parrot had survived the journey from Fiji to London to Wycliff House.

"Will you not deny it?" Basil asked, his voice tinged with glee. "And do tell about Tahiti. I heard that's where they found you."

"Warm crystal blue waters sparkling on white sand beaches, incessant sunshine, loose, barely clad women. It gets a bit boring after a while," Wycliff said with a shrug. Monroe Burke, friend and rival, had found him there with the news of the previous duke's passing. Or, the news that he had a reason to return after a decade abroad.

"You were bored in a tropical paradise and returned to England to claim your dukedom," Basil stated. "Hmmph."

"Such is life . . ." Wycliff mused. He was supposed to feel guilty about his travels and adventures, but he had refused. He knew he was supposed to thank his bloody stars he'd been born a duke, but more often than not it felt more like a burden than a blessing. Instead, he went after what he wanted in life, dukedom be damned. Was that such a crime, or was it a well-lived life?

The maid glanced over her shoulder, and even with her face in profile he could see her scowl. That, and her delicate English features and a creamy complexion. A little pink rosebud of a mouth. Her hair was dark and pulled into a tight knot at the base of her neck. Wycliff wanted to see more. He wanted to see her eyes.

"Well, best of luck to you upon reentering society," Basil said, casting a critical eye on Wycliff's appearance. "You'll have to cut your hair, of course. And you will never get into Almack's with . . . with . . . that *earring*."

Little did Basil know, the small gold hoop—a sailor's traditional burial funds—was the least of the decoration he'd picked up on his travels.

"Of all the placed I've traveled to, from Africa to Australia, and Almack's is the one that's inaccessible to me," Wycliff drawled. "Pity, that."

The maid couldn't restrain a bubble of laughter. Definitely listening.

"If you want a wife and an heir, you'll have to venture to Almack's. Brave that, or else everything shall go to me!" Basil said with a touch of glee. "Sure would please my missus."

Wycliff glanced at the maid, who lifted her brow, silently suggesting that he'd do best to take a wife rather than leave an entire dukedom to *Basil*, for Lord's sake.

"Not that there is much to inherit, given the bothersome creditors by your door," Basil added. "Still, my missus would fancy herself a duchess."

Wycliff's expression darkened. Then he reminded himself that he wouldn't care about Basil inheriting because he himself would be dead. Quite frankly, that was the Wycliff tradition: worry not, for the heirs shall sort out the mess with the mortgaged estates, rampant debt, rebellious tenants, etc, etc.

Bastards.

The maid kept dusting—had it not been done in years?—moving on now toward his desk. Being bored and women-starved, Wycliff freely ogled her bottom and the hourglass shape of her hips. Her eyes, though—he wished to see her eyes. A man could tell so much about a woman by her eyes.

"But you must take a wife, if only for the fortune," Basil continued, and Wycliff did not disagree with him. "First, you'll need to cut your hair, visit Saville Row for proper attire—"

Wycliff wore plain buckskin breeches and a shirt that was open at the collar and rolled at the sleeves. His boots had carried him through Africa, pounded the decks of dozens of ships, waded through swamps and seas alike. Frankly, his clothing looked like it had suffered all that and worse.

"I thought it was enough to be a duke," he interrupted rudely.

"Sometimes it is," Basil replied. "But if you are desperate . . ."

"I am not desperate."

In fact, he had no intention of shackling himself. He had other plans for his time in England—namely, to plan and seek funding for the expedition of a lifetime, before he set sail once more. But Basil would not accept this, so he didn't even bother to try to persuade his cousin otherwise. Instead he allowed him to carry on.

"Well you ought to find a wife," Basil said. "I'd be delighted to assist you, introduce you around, etcetera."

If he was planning to take a wife, Wycliff mused, telling his idiot cousin would be the first mistake. That was the path to matchmaking disasters and other high society atrocities.

"Thank you, cousin. So very kind of you."

And with that Basil slurped one last sip of tea, set down the cup, and stood to go. Finally, this visit would be over and he could get on with reacclimating himself to his native country. Beginning with the brothels.

Basil ambled through the study, slowing as he neared the desk. Wycliff swore under his breath.

"Don't look," Wycliff muttered. Basil looked. Of course he looked.

"I say, are those drawings of your travels?" his cousin exclaimed. He then took the liberty of lifting one up for a better view.

"Blimey, cousin! What the devil—" Basil's eyes nearly bugged out of his head.

It was a portrait of a girl named Miri; she had graciously allowed him to draw her, including the tattoos that covered her hands, which were clutching her full, luscious breasts. She was laughing in the picture, and he couldn't recall why; he would never know now, unless he sailed back to ask her.

He ignored a pang of longing, like homesickness.

"Tattooing," Wycliff explained. "It's a Tahitian custom that involves sharp bone tapping ink under the skin. It takes days. It's excruciating—" He stopped when Basil's skin adopted a greenish hue, matching his waistcoat.

The maid was angling for a look at the drawing, too, and he grinned, and allowed her to see. He watched her eyes widen and look up to him, searching for answers.

The look knocked the smile off his face and kicked his breath away. Blue. Her eyes were gray-blue like the ocean, where he longed to be.

"I suppose one would expect such customs from the savages," said the idiot cousin. Wycliff rolled his eyes.

"They're not savages, Basil, they are people who happen to live by a different set of cultural practices," he lectured.

"Of course, given your travels you may have a different perspective, but really, no one on earth surpasses the British," Basil replied, rifling through more sheets.

Of someone else's private property. Idiot. Cousin.

The maid bit her lip. She wanted to speak, and Wycliff was very intrigued.

"Well that one is quite a stunner," Basil said, referring to a watercolor of Orama, a lovely woman with soft lips and a warm embrace, who had allowed him to sketch her nude form as she rose like Aphrodite from the ocean with the turquoise water lapping around her hips. She was breathtaking, and it was some vile mistake that his idiot cousin Basil should be able to look at such raw beauty.

Out of the corner of his eye Wycliff saw the little maid's cheeks turn pink. He'd forgotten how adorably prudish and modest English women could be.

Wycliff took the sheet away from Basil, and the other sketches, "For all your talk of civilized behavior in England, it seems quite uncivilized to sort through a man's personal papers."

"Indeed, indeed. I say, my apologies. One just has such a curiosity for all things exotic. You'll have to join me at my club, cousin, and tell my friends of your travels," Basil offered. Wycliff muttered something like agreement, even though he had no desire to sit around a stuffy old club with stuffy old men.

Finally, after much ado, Basil was gone and he was alone with the maid. She curtsied awkwardly before him, murmured "Your Grace" and asked if there was anything she could provide him with. All with that little pink mouth of hers. Wicked thoughts crossed his mind, but he would not give voice to those, even though it would be such a typical Wicked Wycliff thing to do.

"If you can, I'd like that hour of my life back," he said frankly.

"If I had the ability to turn back time, I'd have no need of your wages," she replied tartly as she gathered up the tea things. It ought to have been a simple affair, but china cups clattered against sauces and silver spoons clinked across the tray and she spilled the milk. She also swore under her breath, which delighted him. She must have met Harlan already, he thought, or had some unsavory past of her own.

Thus far this little maid with the sea blue eyes and salty language was the only thing of interest in England.

"What is your name?" he asked.

She hesitated before answering. "Eliza."

With her arms laden with the tea tray, she managed a short, awkward curtsey on her way out, treating him to a splendid view of her backside, again.

Once she was gone, he pulled the key from the leather cord he wore around his neck and used it to unlock and open the door leading from the library to a room otherwise cut off from the rest of the house. It was here that he kept those things he wished no one to see. Not yet.

Chapter 3

In Which the Nudity Is His Grace's

Later that day, dusk

Eliza stood outside the door to His Grace's bedchamber, summoning the gumption to walk in unannounced while His Grace was in a bath. Naked. It wasn't as if she'd never seen a naked man before. She wasn't some sheltered missish thing.

The protocol for a situation like this eluded her: a naked duke, in the bath, without a drying cloth. She probably shouldn't go in. Or should she? Having never grown up with servants, nor having been one herself, Eliza was learning everything about her new job the hard way.

She had filled that damned bathtub—hauling heavy buckets of boiling water up three floors—with the help of another housemaid, Jenny. The task required moving fast enough to keep the water warm, but not so fast that they'd spill it. It had been excruciating. The duke had better enjoy his damned bath.

In Eliza's haste and inexperience, she had forgotten to leave a drying cloth. She did not yet know if he was the type to roar and holler in anger, and she did not care to find out, because he was an imposing, intimidating hulk of a man and because she was the type to roar and holler back. That spelled trouble. That spelled *fired,* and she could not lose this position or her story for *The London Weekly.*

Get the story. *Get the story.*

Thus, she debated. Leave him without a drying cloth? Or interrupt?

He hadn't arrived with a valet, or hired one yet, which meant there was no one else to attend to him . . .

Such was the life of a writer, undercover and in disguise. The things she did for Mr. Knightly, and for *The Weekly*! If she had to go to such lengths to get a story published—employed as a housemaid in the most scandalous household in town—then by damn, she would. She would *not* lose her position. Not over this.

She ought to go in, she reasoned. She would not pay attention to him, and he would do the same because she was a servant and thus utterly beneath his notice. That much she knew about master and servant relations. Yet she had a feeling it would not be so simple.

Eliza recalled the way His Grace had looked at her in the study this afternoon, and how his gaze felt like an intimate caress. The man left her breathless.

"Bother it all," she muttered, and entered his chambers. Then she stopped short.

She saw the duke in the bath, as expected. But it was no ordinary sight. His hair was wet and slicked back from his face, showing off strong, hard features. His mouth was full and firm and not smiling. Even in this pose of relaxation, he put her in mind of a warrior: always aware, always ready.

The water lapped at his waist, his chest a wide, exposed expanse of taut skin over sculpted muscle. As Eliza stepped toward him and saw more of the man illuminated by the burning embers in the grate and the flickering of candles, she noticed that his chest was covered in inky blue-black lines. Tattoos, like the drawing.

She gasped. His eyes opened.

"Hello, Eliza." The duke's voice was low, smoky, and sent tremors down her spine. The window was slightly ajar and the cool breeze made the candle flames dance wildly, casting slate-colored shadows, making the room seem like some strange, magical, otherworld.

"Your Grace," she murmured, and bobbed into a curtsey.

"Have you come to join me?" he asked in a rough voice, and she could not tell if he was serious or bamming her.

"My wages don't cover that, either, Your Grace," she replied, not yet having mastered her subservience, but she was rewarded for her impertinence when his mouth curved into a grin.

Eliza's gaze inevitably drifted back to his nudity. The tattooing covered the broad expanse of his muscled chest, wrapping up over the shoulders and generously covering his upper arms, even inching onto his forearms. A million questions were poised on the tip of her tongue. Yet her mouth was suddenly too dry to form words.

"Tattoos," he confirmed, reading her mind. "It's a Tahitian custom. When in Rome . . ."

"You mentioned that it was painful," she said, referring to the exchange earlier. "It seems like it must."

"Like the devil."

"Why would you do it, then?"

"Because to not do so is considered cowardly," he explained in a low voice.

"That's all? Because you do not wish to be seen as weak in front of men on the far side of the world?"

The duke laughed. "You don't understand men, do you?"

"Apparently not," she replied dryly.

"The sketches are one thing to see; this is another entirely. Wouldn't you agree?" Eliza nodded yes. "It's a record of my travels, and one of many artifacts that I have collected and brought back to England. There's a whole world out there, beyond London. People should know that."

"Can I look closer?" she asked in a whisper, because it seemed too illicit to ask a duke for an intimate glimpse of his person. But she had to see the tattoos up close. If she could touch them, she would. This was the sort of thing *The Weekly* would love. But also, her own curiosity impelled her to seek satisfaction.

Eliza knelt by the tub to see the tattoos, but her attention was also drawn to the scar she noticed on his upper lip, and the stubble upon his jaw. He had a clean, soapy scent that was at odds with the air of danger around him.

His head was close to hers, his mouth only inches away.

She wanted to touch his skin, to know if the tattoos left it rough or smooth. To feel the hard muscles of his arms and his chest underneath her palms. For *The Weekly*, of course.

As if the duke could read her mind, he took her

hand and rested it on his bicep, just above where the tattoo began.

With a glance at him for permission, she traced her fingers along the lines—some straight, some jagged, some swirling up and around the curve of his shoulder and leading her down to the expanse of his torso. She splayed her palm across his chest and felt his hot skin and pulsing heartbeat.

The duke's hand closed over hers.

The candles were still wavering, throwing shadows. Steam rose up from the water, making the air hot and humid between them. His lips parted—to kiss her or rebuke her for being so forward?

Her own lips opened to tell him that she was not that kind of girl. Yet Eliza was in the habit of ignoring common sense and better judgment when it came to satisfying her curiosity, chasing a story or embracing adventure. Or men. She had secrets and stories to prove it.

Jenny, the other housemaid, chose that moment to enter the room. There was a sigh of relief—hers, or the duke's? Eliza snatched her hand away. The duke leaned back and closed his eyes as she stood and moved away from him to speak to the other maid.

"I was just checking if His Grace was finished," Jenny said in a whisper. "We'll have to remove the tub and water tonight." Then her eyes widened as she noted the Duke's tattoos as well. "And you'll need to turn down the bed, and all that. And have a care . . . you know his reputation."

Chapter 4

The Writing Girls

Offices of The London Weekly
The following day, Wednesday

Eliza dashed down Fleet Street. Her heart boomed in her chest. It hurt to breathe.

It had been a trial to sneak out past Saddler, the butler, and the lot of footmen that stood about. Mrs. Penelope Buxby, the housekeeper, was easier to avoid once she started with the whiskey. It was late afternoon; she had begun at luncheon. Jenny agreed to cover for Eliza's absence, saying that she was sweeping in the attic. No one would look for her there.

Eliza arrived at 57 Fleet Street, breasts heaving and heart pounding. She nodded to Mehitable Loud, the enormous and terrifying-looking but friendly giant who protected the offices and all those in it, particularly Mr. Knightly, the owner-editor-proprietor of London's most widely read, gossiped-about newspaper.

Eliza had not fully composed herself when she finally dashed into the weekly meeting of the writers of *The London Weekly*. Late. Damien Owens and

Alistair Grey stopped talking and heads swiveled to look in her direction. Knightly noted her attire with a lift of his brow.

She wore a plain gray dress, with her white apron still pinned to the front, and a little white bonnet over her hair. There hadn't been the time or place to change. Her hands were pink and raw from a morning spent scrubbing floors.

It was Annabelle who gave voice to the question: "Eliza, why are you dressed as a servant?"

"I have recently taken employ in the household of the Duke of Wycliff," she answered, biting back a smile as the room erupted into murmurs and she noted the gleam in Knightly's eyes and the grin tugging at his lips.

They knew what this meant: a spy in the house that all of London was gagging to know about.

Eliza had always written stories that took her undercover, often in disguise, to explore a side of London most never saw—and certainly one that other papers rarely covered. She wrote about the penny weddings of lower classes, or quack medicines, and once even spent a few days in the workhouse in order to alert Londoners to the real conditions.

It was nothing new for her to immerse herself so fully, to put her body and soul on the line for the paper. But this time it was different, because there was a scandalous, mysterious, unconventional duke involved. Even more pressing, this time her every column submitted could be her last.

But not this one. She grinned. The one in her hand was *gold*.

" 'The Tattooed Duke,' " she added, and *The Weekly* staff exploded with questions. Her heart was still beating fast and she felt light-headed. It wasn't just the mad dash to arrive, but the novel sensation and heady feeling of being the center of attention.

Eliza handed the sheet to Knightly, wincing at how it had become damp and crinkled during her race to the offices. He began to read.

> *It was the best of times and it was the worst of times for the new Duke of Wycliff, recently returned to London to reclaim an old, notorious title. He looks nothing like a duke ought to. His hair is kept scandalously long; it is not the fashion now, nor was it when he quit England ten years ago. Like a common sailor, this duke wears a small gold hoop in one ear.*
>
> *But those are trifling things in comparison to the duke's tattoos . . .*

Knightly skimmed ahead, settling on one line to read aloud: " 'His appearance is that of some wild, heathen warrior,' " and Eliza realized that her face surely took on fiery hue. Had she known Knightly would read the story—written feverishly late last night—she might not have written those words.

She glanced at her friends. Dear Annabelle's blue eyes were wide with shock, and Julianna's delight was unmistakable. Julianna possessed an insatiable taste for gossip, and this was undoubtedly quenching it. Sophie was listening with obvious interest.

"This is wonderfully scandalous," Julianna murmured. She was the author of "Fashionable Intelligence," the best gossip column in London. And she was Lady Julianna Roxbury, née Somerset.

"Scandal equals sales," Knightly remarked automatically. It was the phrase upon which he had built his ever-growing publishing empire.

"Scandal equals published," Eliza whispered under her breath. Annabelle Swift, advice columnist and the sweetest girl in the world, sympathetically nodded her head.

"Scandal equals tell me more," Julianna said when the meeting concluded a short while later.

"Yes, everything," Sophie added. Since her marriage to the Duke of Hamilton and Brandon, Sophie occasionally wrote about weddings, which she hated, in her column "Miss Harlow's Marriage in High Life." But she more often wrote about fashion, which she loved.

"Thank you both for your letters of reference," Eliza began, and her rich, titled friends both laughed. The letters had been a necessary part of her application for the position of household servant. Eliza continued, "The housekeeper was shocked that someone of my impeccable qualifications would wish to leave your households to work for Wycliff."

"Little does she know . . ." Sophie murmured.

"I am a terrible housemaid, but no one else is lining up to take my place," Eliza said. " It seems the duke's reputation scared off all but the most desperate applicants; the rumors of his debts scared off the rest. How lucky for me."

"Good help is so hard to find," Julianna said wistfully.

"They will be lining up after your story about the tattooed duke is published," Sophie said.

"Which begs the question, dear Eliza, of how you know about those tattoos," Julianna asked pointedly.

"I'm sure everyone was perishing with curiosity but would not dare ask in front of the group," Annabelle added.

"I might have encountered His Grace in the bath," Eliza said, realizing that those words didn't quite explain it at all. They didn't capture the candlelight, for instance, the steam rising from the hot water, or how she knelt by his side and traced her fingers along the inky swirls of his tattoo.

"Oh my goodness," Annabelle gasped. "Did he try to take advantage of you?"

"No," Eliza said hesitatingly. But their lips had been close enough for a kiss. "I merely slipped in to leave a drying cloth for His Grace."

"It's only a matter of time," Julianna declared. "The Wycliff dukes are notorious rakes, and known to enjoy their housemaids."

"I have so many chores that I haven't the time for that," Eliza deadpanned. "At night I'm too exhausted."

"Spoken like a wife," Sophie said, grinning.

"What's he really like?" Annabelle asked. "Is he nice?"

"Nice is not quite the word," Eliza answered. "Given that he was rumored to have been a pirate. His idiot cousin said something about him ravishing an entire harem in one night."

"Ah, so he is not your average gentleman," Julianna remarked with a gleam in her eye, which Eliza matched.

"Is he handsome, then?" Sophie asked wistfully. "He sounds handsome. There is nothing quite like a handsome duke." He certainly wasn't beautiful—there was something too sharp in his cheekbones, too rugged in his unshaven jaw and long hair roughly tied back in a queue. Eliza recalled that scar on his lip, suggesting all his adventures. And then his gaze—so very aware, so very bold.

"In a way . . . a way that leaves a girl breathless."

"I daresay the Wycliff tradition will live on another day," Julianna murmured.

"Or night," Sophie added.

"I told you both, I'm too busy and too tired," Eliza said, though it was only partially true. The thrill of chasing and capturing a story like this kept her up writing at all hours. As for the Duke himself . . . the word *yes* burned on her lips.

But *nothing* could get in the way of getting her stories printed. Not when it seemed she had written pure gold with this one. Not when every column could possibly be her last.

"When do we get to make the acquaintance of this duke?" Julianna asked. "This oh-so scandalous duke."

"I haven't noticed a swarm of invitations. But I'm sure he'd take your call," Eliza answered. No one came to call, other than his idiot cousin Basil. He didn't receive many letters either. She'd thought there would be a swarm ready to make his acquaintance—he was a duke, after all—but it seemed word had already traveled that he was . . . unusual.

"We cannot call upon him," Sophie said morosely.

"Rules. Scandal. Angry husbands, etcetera," Julianna explained.

"Ah, yes," Eliza said, reminded of that vast gulf between her friends the duchess and the countess, and herself, the daughter of an actress and playwright.

There were so many pesky social rules that she never bothered with. "Pity that. I should enjoy watching the exchange."

"We shall throw a party and invite him," Sophie suggested.

"He does not seem inclined to socialize," Eliza said. Thus far he had spent most of his hours in a locked room—*whatever did he do in there?*—or in his private study with maps and books and journals, which she was eager to obtain. He took meals with his one-eyed, one-armed friend Harlan, but otherwise kept to his work.

"A brooding, tattooed, recluse duke," Annabelle said breathlessly. "The housemaid with a double life. It's a Minerva Press novel come to life."

Eliza laughed and said, "Except for all the scrubbing of floors, which is not anyone's idea of romance."

Chapter 5

In Which Scrubbing Floors Is Romantic

The following day found Eliza scrubbing the foyer floors and eating her words. Saddler, the butler, was nearby in his pantry obsessively polishing the silver. The door was ajar, so he could hear if her work went idle for a moment. The butler, she discovered, also had an unnerving habit of silently appearing behind her and giving her a horrible fright just in those moments when she paused to let her mind wander from her work.

But it was not the butler on her mind.

His Grace had strolled by, and Eliza spent the next hour reliving all seven seconds that it took him to stroll through the foyer from the drawing room to his library and ogle her shamelessly.

When the duke appeared, she had been on her hands and knees, in a position of utter supplication, and vexed with the strands of hair falling in her face. Her cheeks were flushed, due to steam rising from the bucket of hot soapy water.

He did not ignore her, as he ought to have done. She'd heard that servants in some households were required to turn and face the wall when their masters appeared.

Instead, the duke indulged in a look that would have been horribly rude for the liberty of it. If she'd had a daughter and a man looked at her that way, she would have called him out for the hot, fierce gaze that freely swept slowly over her breasts, the dip in her back, and the rise of her bottom. It was so brazen, so bold, that she could feel it.

An hour later she was still feeling it—the heat of it, the shock of it, the mock outrage and secret pleasure.

Chapter 6

In Which the Duke Curses His Fate

The following evening

Wycliff pulled a sip from his tankard of ale and muttered a stunning array of curses. "Oh damn. Oh bloody hell. Oh Lord above and Lucifer in the heavens. Shit."

Timbuktu had always been far away, but not far like this. He'd dreamed of being the first European to make it there—and back. It was a challenge that had stayed with him through the years as he ambled around the world, taking advantage of opportunities that came his way. He had been a reckless wanderer in the manner of a Wycliff, but the discipline he inherited from his mother—*where else would it have come from?*—was boldly asserting itself.

Wycliff wanted to lead a proper expedition. He wanted to accomplish something—especially something that had nothing to do with the circumstances of his noble birth.

He had a dream, a plan. He would have to let it go.

He took another long sip of his drink.

Beside him, Harlan appraised the serving wenches

and barmaids of this pub just off St. James's street and said, "Now there's a fetching lass."

Wycliff followed his gaze and concluded that Harlan was very deep into his cups or utterly desperate after long, chaste months at sea. The chit was fine. But he wouldn't have classified her as "a fetching lass" by any stretch.

"Are you quite sure? Because you've had a few, and you only have one working eye," he pointed out.

Harlan adjusted his eye patch with his one good arm, the one that wasn't wrapped in a sling made out of an old bedsheet.

"Oh, I'm quite sure that I've had a few and have been at sea for a few months," Harlan replied.

To which Wycliff raised his glass and said, "Cheers."

She wasn't a looker; Harlan could have her. Not like that maid, Eliza. Now *she* was a fetching chit. Every time he encountered her around the house, he noticed something about her, like the perfect, pert shape of her bum. Or her breasts, which promised to be a good handful. Or a figure that made a man ache and think extremely ungentlemanly thoughts.

But it was her eyes that affected him most, and not because they reminded him of the sea and the sky and other lovely blue things. She really looked at him, searching, curious—when she ought to turn and face the wall whenever he passed.

Wycliff had no interest in rebuking her for that. He was a terrible duke in that way. Mrs. Buxby ought to have, if she wasn't so drunk all the time. But she'd been the housekeeper since before he was born, and he wasn't about to reprimand her. Besides, the Wycliffs were never ones to keep a conventional household.

He sipped his ale again. Like all the Wycliffs before him, he was hankering after the maid, when he had real problems to face. Bloody hell and damnation. He was thinking with the wrong organ.

"I'll be back shortly," Harlan said. "Actually, I hope I'm not back for an hour at least. Maybe longer," he added before downing his ale and sauntering across the room to chat up the barmaid who had caught his eye.

They were drinking because Wycliff had received awful news that day. They were also drinking because he could not tolerate the confines of Wycliff House with that information looming over his every breath. And especially not with that housemaid, Eliza, sauntering from room to room, hips swaying, pink lips smiling and tempting him with racy thoughts. And then her breasts . . .

He wanted to bend her over the dining table and ravish her. Or the desk, or one of the twenty beds, or any piece of furniture, really. The sooner the better, too, since every last stitch of furniture would likely need to be sold.

That was the news he had received today, from a pipsqueak solicitor and a banker who resembled a whale: There could be no expedition. At least not one he funded himself, because His Grace, the eighth Duke of Wycliff, was broke.

Chapter 7

In Which There Is a Midnight Interlude

The hour was late. The sheet of paper before her, blank. Eliza bit her lip, lost in thought. Her first column would be published tomorrow and she awaited it eagerly, like Christmas or her birthday. In the fast-paced world of newspaper publishing, however, she had little time to savor her success before the next column was due.

Thus far she had written *The Tattooed Duke* on the page. That was all.

What else to detail? His household was unconventional and haphazard. His possessions were unusual and almost contradictory: skulls and seashells and weaponry and exotic plants. And those were only the items she'd glimpsed. There remained the matter of what lay behind that locked door in the library. Or of his journals, which lay scattered upon his desk.

She ought to read them.

The page was still blank before her. It was this paralyzing panic, leaving her unable to string words together, that had caused her downward spiral at *The London Weekly*. Every column now was her last chance, and she felt it like a lump in her throat. She could not afford unwritten pages.

She ought to go see about those journals. Or that locked room.

Perhaps tomorrow, Eliza thought, daring a longing glance at her bed. But the risk of discovery in daytime was too great.

She ought to go now, even though it was nearly midnight.

No, she might encounter the duke. Her pulse quickened.

Or, she thought, a smile playing at her lips, she might encounter the duke in a dark and quiet house. Either way, she would find something to write about.

Impulsively she grabbed her wrapper and blew out the candle in her bedchamber. Under the cover of darkness she made her way down the stairs and into the library. Fortunately, the fire had not died down completely.

Eliza crept over to his desk, heart pounding and breath held.

Get the story. *Get the story.* The words were never far from her mind.

But . . . was that a pang of guilt? She had not missed the duke's irritation when his idiot cousin freely explored his personal papers, as she was about to do now.

Or was that excitement upon discovering the Wicked Duke of Wycliff's personal journal detailing his travels and the devil only knew what else? She lifted the cover and saw rows of the duke's scrawl.

Get the story. *Get the story.*

Eliza took a moment to light a candle. The words now appeared before her.

Tahiti, 1823.
Miri enlightened me to some exquisite positions, the
likes of which no English maiden would ever dare . . .

Eliza's cheeks burned hot as she continued to read.
Had that been a pang of guilt? It was no match for her
curiosity, especially about relations between a man
and a woman that she would never have imagined.
She flipped the page.

Lord above, there were illustrations, too!

What she experienced now was certainly not guilt
and far surpassed curiosity. She felt an awareness that
was new to her. A new heat, a new intensity, in places
she'd never really felt before. The dusky centers of
her breasts were suddenly exquisitely sensitive. Suddenly every part of her was begging for attention.

All of this warred with jealousy for this girl, Miri,
who had experienced some sort of rapture with the
duke *under an unfathomably starry sky with a warm and*
sultry island breeze stealing over our naked, heated skin.

Eliza fanned herself. She continued to read of
their passionate encounters and the outrageous pain
from the tattooing; of learning the native language,
the social rules, and plant-hunting expeditions far
inland; of gloriously lazy afternoons swimming in
the turquoise surf.

She flipped back to the very vivid illustrations. She
turned the book sideways. She tilted her head. And
then she dared to dream . . . dared to imagine herself
with the duke in these positions no English maiden
would ever try.

A gasp escaped her lips. Her heart was thudding
hard and fast in her chest. She felt positively strangled by her dressing gown. This was becoming too
much.

Eliza slammed the journal shut, placed it back on his desk and blew out the candle. She had not read much that could be used in her column—unless she wanted to ruin every maiden in London, and perhaps a few marriages, with some very graphic descriptions of outrageously pleasurable lovemaking.

Such were Eliza's thoughts and she tiptoed down the hall and crossed the foyer, barely concealed by the sconces that had been left burning. The duke. His pleasure. Her writing. The pangs of guilt returned, but still they were no match for the hot spark of desire that, tonight, had been nurtured into a slow, smoldering fire.

She was halfway across the wide expanse of the marble foyer when the duke entered through the front door. Apparently, he had been out.

"Eliza." His voice was low, but lud, did it carry in the vast, empty hall.

"Your Grace," she whispered. How did one greet a duke in the middle of the night, whilst in her dressing gown? Well, she knew how Miri would greet him . . .

She haphazardly bobbed into a curtsey instead.

Slowly, Wycliff crossed the foyer, with those long, determined strides of his, and she had every opportunity to admire the power, barely restrained, in his every movement. He stood before her.

It was dark. Late. She'd just been reading the very intimate details of his passionate lovemaking and found herself breathless.

"It's late for a housemaid to be scurrying through the halls," the duke remarked. "And in her dressing gown, too . . ." His voice dropped to a whisper and trailed off. That awareness she'd felt earlier she felt again now, in spades. Her every nerve was at attention, awaiting something, anything, from him.

"I had forgotten something," she managed.

"What would that be?"

My wits, Eliza thought. My sense of decency. My respect for other people's private property and privacy. And a bit of maidenly virtue, too, she realized, given the tantalizing descriptions and images she'd just read and seen.

"I wanted to check on the fires . . ." she said, like a practiced actress. Or liar. It was definitely pangs of guilt that she was experiencing, and they were growing stronger now, overtaking any feelings of curiosity or desire she'd felt earlier.

He was a man—albeit one who'd led a fascinating life and who was devastatingly handsome. He was a man who deserved his privacy, his reputation. And he was a man who made her heart skip beats just with a glance, who made her feel breathless and light-headed with every knowing smile he threw her way. A man who intrigued her, set her aflame, a man who . . .

. . . was clasping her waist with one, warm hand. Who knew that the curve of her hip possessed such sensitivity?

Eliza tilted her head back to look up at him. His eyes were unbelievably dark in this light, but there was no mistaking the spark there—desire, or mischief, she wasn't sure. Did not much care at the moment.

His mouth closed down on hers. His lips were warm and she was hot and melting under their gentle pressure. With his tongue, he lightly traced the seam of her lips, urging her to open to him, and she did. He tasted of drink—but also danger and experience and power and the sort of wicked pleasure that had never occurred to her before tonight.

Wycliff clasped his hands on her cheeks, his fingers threading through her hair. That heat was overwhelming now. She wished for a sultry island breeze to pass the foyer, to cool her outrageously hot skin. But that thought lead to the book, to the pictures, to the wrong she had committed by reading his private papers.

Still, she kissed him. How one said no to this Wicked Wycliff was beyond her. One probably did not, hence the name. It was impossible for her to utter that little word, *no*, when he kissed her like it was the first time and last time all at once, not when he held her so possessively. And she liked it. *Like* was perhaps not the word. She would think about that later . . . for now, she tentatively placed her hands upon his chest and felt his heart pounding hard beneath her palms. The clock inconveniently ruined the moment. One loud chime broke the silence and signaled the hour was very late indeed. The kiss was over.

He said one word, "Go," in a rough voice, and she hurried up the stairs, all the way to her tiny chamber on the third floor.

The sheet of paper was still there, blank. The good news: she had discovered delicious information for her column. The wretched part: after that kiss, he was no longer mere fodder, but a hot-blooded, passionate man, and it tore at her heart to think of committing his secrets to print.

Chapter 8

Introducing "The Tattooed Duke"

Saturday morning

To his surprise, Wycliff had company for breakfast—other than good old Harlan, who never missed a meal. Harlan was attempting to eat with one arm, thanks to that ridiculous sling he insisted upon wearing, all for an injury that had occurred ages ago.

Wycliff had picked up with Harlan somewhere around Zanzibar, and never quite lost him. They'd battled sharks, pirates, and other disasters. They'd taken turns saving each other's lives.

Harlan had moved into the ducal residence without asking and had taken to scheming about future adventures "in places with better weather" and flirting with the housemaids and taking whiskey-laced tea with Mrs. Penelope Buxby.

Wycliff thus far had resisted the urge to pump Harlan for information about the delectable Eliza of the heart-stopping midnight kiss. What had he been thinking? He hadn't, of course, drunk and morose as he'd been over the bad news about the dukedom's finances. But damn, had that kiss been worth it.

Harlan glanced at Eliza and back at the duke, who carefully adopted a blank expression. Wycliff knew that if Harlan had the merest inkling that he harbored even the most fleeting, passing fancy for a girl, he would be mercilessly and relentlessly taunted for it. Harlan was probably just past his thirtieth year, but his maturity had not advanced much beyond thirteen.

Eliza presently attempted to serve them breakfast; it involved a clattering of glasses and plates and curses under her breath. She was a terrible servant (but did that chit know how to kiss!), though Mrs. Buxby swore that she came with glowing recommendations from a duchess and a countess. That, and he was given to understand that applicants were not exactly lining up to serve such a notorious family.

In a better household, a footman might have done her job. But funds were limited, and staff as well. Jobs that must be done by men were done by the few footmen, leaving housemaids to serve meals in their place. But Wycliff was not a man to stand on ceremony.

He caught a glance from Eliza's ocean blue eyes. She took it as a request to refill his coffee—a habit he had acquired in Turkey.

He didn't really want any. But as she stood to pour, he noticed that her breasts were exactly at his eye level, thanks to his seated position and her standing position. He would be drinking an exorbitant amount of the stuff this morning.

"Your Grace," Saddler intoned from somewhere just behind his shoulder. Wycliff swore under his breath and fought the urge to jump in shock. The butler had the damnedest habit of moving silently and just *appearing*. It was unnerving.

"You have callers," he intoned, holding out a silver tray bearing the card of Mr. Monroe Burke, who shortly after entered with a newspaper folded in hand.

Splendid. More mouths to feed.

"Where have you come to whisk me away to today?" Wycliff asked dryly. The last time Burke had just dropped in on him had been in Tahiti. That was about a year after Burke had deliberately stranded him there. Ah, friendly competition.

But then Burke had sailed back with news of his inheritance and a "free" passage back to England. Wycliff hadn't realized what he was inheriting. He might have stayed on those warm white sands, under cloudless skies and a hot sun.

"Good morning to you, too, Your Grace," Burke replied. "I've come to see how you're settling in."

"Plagued by creditors, annoyed with the weather, longing for sunshine, and already bored with the title," Wycliff answered, sipping his coffee. Things were worse than he had anticipated. His hope for a quick visit in his native lands was fading.

"And missing the free, easy, and much more naked women of Tahiti," Harlan added, with a wink of his good eye.

Burke grinned and said, "Let's start a club."

He saw Eliza's eyes widen. With another day or two in the Wycliff household she wouldn't be shocked by anything.

"Why are we here, then?" Wycliff asked. "I see no advantages to life in England."

"We're here because you've become a duke," Burke pointed out. "You have responsibilities."

Harlan pulled a face.

"But that doesn't explain what either of you are doing here." Wycliff caught Eliza's eye, and she sauntered over with the coffeepot. He attempted to glance discreetly at her breasts. They were round and heaving and lovely, and he'd just been at sail for far too long. He was a man, a Wycliff. He couldn't help but look.

"I like to balance my adventures at sea with adventures in London," Burke answered.

"Cheers to that," Harlan added, raising his glass, and Wycliff turned away from ogling Eliza's breasts to join in.

"Is it not bad luck to toast with water. Or tea?" Burke wondered. "Or all that coffee he's drinking?"

"Who says there's nothing stronger in this?" Harlan replied, grinning. "The housekeeper keeps quite the stash."

"That's where all the money is," Wycliff muttered, but only Eliza heard him. He delighted in the soft rush of her breath; laughter, restrained.

"So, have you forgiven me yet, Wycliff?" Burke asked. It was strange to have his childhood friend address him by this new name of his, the title. He thought about saying something, but knew that he was lucky to be addressed as such and not some horribly insulting appellation that served to highlight friendship.

He didn't feel like Wycliff yet either. But that didn't signify.

"Forgiven you for tracking me down in paradise

and returning me to cold, rainy, responsibility laden England? Never."

"It's growing on me," Harlan said.

Wycliff turned to him, appalled. "Yesterday you had a list of seventy-three places to travel to that were far better than England."

"Hadn't hit the town yet," Harlan remarked. "Did last night. English lasses are quite something." Wycliff glanced over at Eliza.

A coy suggestive smile played on her lips. His own romp last night had done nothing to satiate his desire, and it was the housemaid he kept thinking about.

"Complete sentences are also 'quite something,'" Wycliff remarked.

"Well excuse me, Your Graceship, not all of us attended Eton," Harlan retorted, purposefully mangling the form of address.

"I see the bickering continues," Burke cut in with a smirk. "You two are like an old married couple."

"Aye, all bickering, no bedding," Harlan quipped and Wycliff scowled in annoyance . . . and noted a gleam of amusement in Eliza's eyes.

"Thank you for clearing that up," Wycliff drawled.

"I don't think those are the rumors you need to be concerned about," Burke stated ominously.

"Yes, I know, with this earring and my long hair I'll never get into bloody boring Almack's," Wycliff said, utterly sarcastically.

"Bugger Almack's. I mean *The London Weekly*," Burke said, holding the issue up.

"It's a newspaper," Wycliff stated plainly, sipping his coffee.

"*Au contraire.* It's not just any newspaper," Burke contradicted, and his lips curved into a smile . . . the same one Wycliff had seen just before towering waves crashed down on their ship, or before he uttered the news about his father and the dukedom, tainting that beautiful day in Paradise. It was the smile reserved for unpleasant information.

He sipped his coffee and waited. He looked at Burke, and then shifted his gaze to the left where Eliza was pouring tea with a faint smile on her lips, and then back to Burke for his explanation of the *special* newspaper.

Damn right, it's not just any paper, Eliza thought as she poured more tea for this Burke fellow. Was it from the regular pot, or the one for Harlan with Mrs. Buxby's special blend of whiskey tea? She couldn't recall.

Oh well, a little whiskey in the morning never hurt anyone. She caught the duke's eye and moved to refill his coffee cup. He drank an excessive amount.

"And just what is so special about this one?" the duke asked, clearly skeptical.

"The Writing Girls, for one thing," Burke answered, and she tried not to smile.

"Ah, it's written by women? I suppose it contains the latest reports on hair ribbons, hemlines, and face paint. I can assure you that is of no interest to me," the duke said.

Eliza considered allowing the steaming hot liquid to overflow from the cup to his lap. She hated such typical comments about women's interests. But then again, that was similar to the hotheaded letter she had written to Knightly, demanding he hire a woman writer—herself— covering Serious Issues instead of weddings, gossip, and love advice.

And now here she was as a maid, for Lord's sake, reporting gossip about a scandalous, handsome duke. She was tempted to sigh.

Get the story. *Get the story* . . .

"It's not hair ribbons, you dolt," Burke replied. "I doubt even girls in the schoolroom are interested in that. This paper is full of tawdry news and gossip, always veering on the salacious and the scandalous. *Everyone* reads it."

Eliza's heart fluttered with pride. For his passionate description of *The Weekly,* this Mr. Monroe Burke would see himself flatteringly portrayed in her next article.

"Everyone?" Wycliff lifted one brow questioningly.

"One cannot have a conversation in the ton without having read it. Both high- and lowborn alike follow it avidly," Burke explained. It was true; the rest of the staff was poring over it in the kitchens this very minute.

"Another caller, Your Grace," Saddler intoned, and Eliza nearly jumped from the surprise. How a man could move so silently was beyond her.

The duke's idiot cousin bounded in behind him.

"I say, are you talking about *The London Weekly*?" He asked. Today he wore a violet-colored waistcoat that clashed violently with his complexion.

"Even Basil knows about it," Burke pointed out.

"Well, now *that* is saying something," the duke said.

"Did you read the story about you, cousin? I say, I expected you to be in a roar of a temper, but since you are not, I reckon you hadn't seen it yet."

"Is that why you're here, too? To witness a scene?" the duke asked Burke.

"In part," Burke answered. "That, and Timbuktu."

"Timbuktu?" Wycliff echoed with interest.

"It's warm there. And dry," Harlan added. "No English lasses, though."

"Are we going to read *The Weekly* or not?" Basil interrupted.

Wycliff snatched the paper from Burke, who said, "It's on the second page."

The second page! Her stories usually appeared on, oh, the seventeenth or eighteenth page, in the back next to the ads for magical cure-all creams for unmentionable conditions and the corset maker—for men.

" 'The Tattooed Duke,' " Burke began with a devilish grin, reading the title. Eliza wanted to explain that subtlety did not sell, but she kept her mouth shut. In fact, she bit down on her lip to keep from bursting into a smile. Her story, on the second page!

"How'd they find out about that?" Harlan asked, eyes wide and leaning forward.

The duke glanced at Eliza. She made a herculean effort to appear blank and thanked the Lord she had grown up in the theater.

"Anyone on the crew of my ship would have seen it," Burke pointed out. "Many of whom have wives or exchanges with loose women, all who are prone to talk."

"Oh, the tattoos!" Basil exclaimed, and the duke wearily rubbed his eyes. "Like in your drawing with the naked girl. I confess I did feel compelled to share that with the gents at my club. Was it a secret?"

That seemed to explain everything to their satisfaction. She dared to exhale a sigh of relief.

"Keep reading," the duke demanded, shoving the paper back to Burke.

"Very well, Your Grace," Burke replied, "Or should I say 'Your Tattooed Grace'? Doesn't sound quite right, does it?"

"Isn't it interesting that something so common-place on one side of the world should be such a novelty elsewhere?" Harlan mused.

"Keep reading," Wycliff demanded, and Burke did, reading aloud the details of the duke's wild, foreign appearance and the tattoos.

> "The native artwork covers His Grace's broad chest, shoulders and upper arms. With his hair pulled back and the extensive, inky black tattoos, he appears to be a dangerous, heathen warrior.
>
> The women also endure, as witnessed by sketches in His Grace's collection that depict tattooed hands strategically placed to cover some particularly feminine charms. Other illustrations depict strange flora and fauna that would be of great interest to the gardeners at Kew. More interesting to the bucks of the ton are the duke's drawings of native women with their tattoos, long jet hair, sultry smiles, and an utter lack of corsets, dresses, stockings, and the other frippery with which young ladies deck themselves. Does His Grace now expect such free behavior from England's belles?"

"So they're *all* naked?" Basil asked breathlessly. Eliza cringed.

"It's too bloody hot to wear clothing," Harlan answered.

"What happened to your eye? And your arm?" Basil asked.

"Pirate attack," he answered gravely. The other

day, Eliza overhead him telling Thomas the footman that he'd been wrestling with a shark. And before that, that a sacrifice to the gods had gone awry.

Burke continued to read: " 'The duke did not even deny ravishing hundreds of women in one night in a harem. Ladies of London, beware! This duke appears to possess exotic and unquenchable tastes.' "

"I'm not particularly bothered by this," the duke said. "Although, it doesn't mention my achievements for the crown."

"Such as spreading citizens all over the world?" Harlan added.

"Like father, like son," Burke dared to say, to the duke's glare.

"Promoting England abroad. Facilitating the exchange of cultures," the duke answered smugly.

One of the gentlemen snorted.

"The ton is in an uproar," Basil stated. "My missus took callers *before noon* for the sole purpose of discussing this. One of them even fainted. I heard them screeching for the smelling salts."

"Really?" Wycliff asked.

"Indeed. It's the tattoos. And the earring. And the piracy," Basil added. "And the naked women. All those marriage-minded mama's are the ones to watch out for, and right now they're deciding if the fact that you are a duke is reason enough to overlook everything else about you."

The duke was silent, and Eliza wondered if he did plan to marry. She felt a fluttering in her belly at the thought, which she dismissed as ridiculous.

"If you are *not* inclined to marriage, then I have news for you," Burke said, and the duke gave him his full attention. "The French government has offered ten thousand pounds to whomever reaches Timbuktu first."

Eliza wanted to laugh at the range of expressions from disgust at the mention of "French" to wide-eyed wonder upon "Timbuktu."

"And returns, I presume?" Wycliff clarified.

"I'm thinking of preparing an expedition myself," Burke said calmly, but the duke looked like he was about to spit poison. The men's gazes locked, tense, vicious.

"What is Timbuktu?" Basil asked, and Eliza was glad of the idiot cousin for asking such questions that she also wished to know.

"It's a city in Africa, where the streets are paved with gold, where it rains diamonds, and all the women are naked and free with their affections," Burke answered.

"Don't listen to him, Basil," the duke contradicted. "It's a legendary city in Africa that is probably nothing more than a pathetic collection of mud huts. But no European has ever been able to get there, and certainly no one has ever returned from the attempt."

"Until the great Monroe Burke," said the damned Monroe Burke.

"Or the Duke of Wycliff. You know it's always been my intention to take up this challenge. To Timbuktu. I believe I informed you of that on the return from Tahiti. At length, and in detail," Wycliff replied tensely. Eliza watched the flash of annoyance cross Burke's features before they settled into something like amusement.

"And the great rivalry between us continues," Burke said grandly, attempting to dismiss the duke's quiet fury. "From the privies of Eton to the golden mud huts of Timbuktu."

Eliza cleared the plates, and when she arrived with them in the kitchen, the cook and the maids were all huddled around their own issue of *The London Weekly*. They were reading "The Tattooed Duke." She fought hard to keep her smile sly, but a giant grin tugged and broke through. She had, at last, arrived.

Chapter 9

In Which the Duke's Reputation Precedes Him

Later that evening

The name had not left him all day, tripping off the tongue in three melodic steps. Tim ... buk ... tu. Like a poem, or a song, or a prayer.

Wycliff had always wanted to go, ever since hearing stories as a lad and aching to escape the confines of Wycliff House or school. He thought about it in Tahiti and talked about it on the way back to England. In fact, he retuned only to plan for this expedition. And now the French dangled an incentive other than glory. Ten thousand pounds! Pity he couldn't get that up front.

Pity Burke was after it as well. Some *friend*. But then again, theirs was a friendship based on rivalry—forever attempting to outdrink, outsmoke, outfight, and outwench the other. The whole world was a stage upon which they enacted a constant battle for superiority. Burke had abandoned him in Tahiti for a year. Wycliff once stranded Burke in a leper colony for a week.

Now both had set their sights on Timbuktu.

Even after ten years abroad, the wanderlust had possessed Wycliff the minute he stepped off Burke's ship onto the London docks. There was something so stifling about England, and the rain and the history and the shadow of his father and all the other Dukes of Wycliff who had drunk, debauched, and died before him.

He did not want to live like that. Nor do it with his hands tied and manacled by debt.

Timbuktu was his chosen destination.

And this—this ballroom, this society affair, this orgy of wealth and decadence and gossip—this was some circle of hell he had to pass through on his journey.

"I hope to God they still serve brandy at these routs," he said. It'd been an age since he attended a society function.

Burke grinned. "No one would come if they didn't." They pushed through the crowd, accepting nods of greeting (Burke) and stares (Wycliff). No one greeted him or remarked on how long it had been or inquired about his travels. Apparently he was too bizarre to even converse with. A frown tugged at his mouth.

Wycliff hadn't thought how strange he must appear with his long hair and the earring. It occurred to him now, as he sauntered through the ballroom, that they must be imagining his tattoos and thus picturing him in some state of undress.

No wonder all the maidens and matrons seemed flush and flustered as he passed. He couldn't help it; he grinned.

While sipping his brandy, he savored the memory of explaining a London ball to the women in Tahiti.

Then he taught them to waltz on the white sand beaches, right into the surf.

But now, in the ballroom of Lord and Lady Something-or-Other, he likened it to shark-infested waters.

They circled slowly, in tightly controlled circles. They eyed him through narrowed eyes, with their long pointed noses sniffing for weakness. Occasionally one would bump up against him in warning.

One particular shark already had a taste for him, and Wycliff saw her glide through the swarms in his direction. The other guests stepped aside to allow this man-eating lady clear access to her prey.

Her hair gleamed, golden, in the candlelight. Gold, like Timbuktu. He'd do well to remember that.

That crimson pout, scowling at him now—he it knew it intimately. Once upon a time that mouth had alternated between begging for his touch and insulting him with name-calling. She was a fiery one. She was all the churning, roiling energy of an ocean storm fiercely contained in a corset and silk.

"Lady Althea Shackley," he drawled when she paused before him. Her green eyes were bright and her cheeks flushed pink. "It's been an age."

She smiled, and stripped off her gloves. With her bare hand she slapped him soundly on the cheek.

The ballroom immediately fell silent.

She turned on her heel and stalked away with a swish of silk skirts and her head held high.

The crowd, en masse, fixed their attention upon him. With a mocking smile, the Tattooed Duke of Wycliff raised his glass in toast.

"To England!" he called out. Many were forced to raise their glasses with him in toast to their country—

even though he was the most foreign-looking and -acting one among them, title notwithstanding. He was a duke, so anyone who gave a whit about titles and rank could not refuse.

In that moment, Wycliff understood: he wasn't just unfashionable, he bordered on treasonous. For a man of his stature to adopt the customs of another culture suggested that England wasn't supremely superior after all. He had betrayed his country and it could not be tolerated.

"To the King," he stated, raising his glass again. The ballroom guests followed in kind. A smug smile tugged at his lips—how it must pain them all to show solidarity with the treasonous duke who kept his hair long, wore an earring, bore tattoos across his sun-browned chest, and drove scorned women to public acts of violence in his presence. He was that kind of man.

They didn't call them the Wicked Wycliffs for nothing.

His cheek actually tingled, still. Lady Althea had not held back. It was a well-deserved, exquisitely timed slap. It reminded them all of the scandalous circumstances in which he had fled the country.

Lady Althea paused in her exit to look scornfully over her shoulder.

"And to the Queen," he said, raising his glass to her. Lady Althea turned and walked away.

Chapter 10

Starry Night

After his short-lived foray into high society, Wycliff returned home. That, too, depressed his mood. The evening had been trading one gilded cage for another when every inch of him craved wide-open freedom.

He took a bottle of brandy up to the roof, where he might lean over the railing, gaze at the stars, breathe fresh air and otherwise pretend that he was at sail on the ocean. But the house was still below him—no gentle rolling, as on the sea—and the damned London smog ruined the view.

He could not leave. Because . . .

One required funds to launch an expedition. He was utterly without funds. He had even stepped over a creditor sleeping on the front stairs. In the morning he'd have a word with Saddler about at least pretending to lend some dignity to this unconventional household.

If he were a typical duke, Wycliff thought idly, he would marry a wealthy bride and be done with it. Upon consideration, a rich wife was the answer to his problems in one neat little female package with a bow on top. She would provide money for him to leave and mind the estate while he was gone.

Yet between *The London Weekly*'s outrageous column and Lady Althea's public and violent attack, a rich wife attaching herself to the likes of him was a remote possibility.

Or, he could purchase a one-way ticket and gallivant from port to port, trading one adventure for another with no grand plan and nothing to rely on but wit and charm, as he had done all these years.

He could be at sea this time tomorrow night. His heartbeat quickened.

What stopped him? His desire was for something greater than merely being on a boat, much as he loved the salty sea air and crashing sound of waves. It was time for a real challenge to put him to the test. It was time for a success; to make his mark on the world as his own self, not just "one of those Wicked Wycliffs."

Timbuktu. Undiscovered, dangerous, and with a promised prize of money and glory. An uncharted land to claim. It was the perfect adventure.

There was, possibly, the option of begging passage along with Burke's crew. But that wasn't what he wanted either: Wycliff wanted to lead, not to follow. He wanted to forge his own damned path in the world.

He could be the first man to make it there and back.

Wycliff turned at the sound of someone else joining him on the roof. The door's hinges were not well oiled. Another problem for the list: debt, decay, squeaky roof door.

"Your Grace?" A female voice cut through the darkness. He knew it belonged to Eliza, the maid he'd been ogling at every opportunity. The other day, he'd seen her bent over on all fours, scrubbing the foyer floor. He had to review the account books for an hour to get himself back to rights.

Riveting stuff, the account books.

And the other night . . . He'd been drinking that evening, but hadn't been truly intoxicated until his lips touched hers. It was a reckless, impulsive, idiotic thing to do, kissing the housemaid in the foyer at midnight. He'd do it again in a heartbeat.

She should not be there, on the roof, in the dark, with him.

"What are you doing here?" he asked, his voice rough to his own ears.

"I heard something. It was you, I presume. But I thought I ought to investigate," she explained, coming to stand beside him against the railing.

There was always one little moment—blink and quite possibly miss it—when everything just shifted and the whole course altered. This was that moment. Wycliff dukes and their maids were notorious through the ages.

Part of him argued that it was all the permission required for him to bend her over and take his pleasure.

But he craved more than that—to make love rather than spend himself with any warm and willing female body. He also was desperately trying not to be a typical Wycliff, actions of the other evening notwithstanding.

And yet, this pretty, sassy girl ventured up to the

roof to investigate a strange noise in the night. Even alone up here with a notorious scoundrel like him, she was perfectly poised. She was either a complete ninny or the kind of woman he could fall in love with.

The moment. When everything changed. Because he was a Wycliff, and a reckless adventurer, he handed her the bottle of brandy.

"Thank you, Your Grace," she replied so primly. Then she took a proper sip from the bottle and handed it back to him. No coughing, or sputtering, or tears. Remarkable.

"I take tea with Mrs. Buxby every afternoon," she explained.

"Glad to hear some things never change," he remarked.

"What brings you up to the roof, may I ask?" she said to him, rather boldly. Then again, he had just invited her to drink with him. The boundaries were already blurred.

"You're very inquisitive for a maid," he replied. "Impertinent is more like it. It's really none of your business what I am or am not doing on the roof. I could fire you for such insubordination."

"I know, Your Grace. I am horribly forward." She appeared to be contrite, but he couldn't shake the feeling that it was an act. Yet he found he enjoyed her company and did not care to spoil this moment. Fine night air, good brandy, a pretty girl. A man could do worse.

"I am going to tell you anyway," Wycliff said, "because I've been drinking and because you will probably never find employ elsewhere after working here, so I'll probably have to keep you."

"Yes, Your Grace." A smile played on her lips. Adorable.

"I came up here so that I might see the stars and be reminded of my time at sea. But this damned smog is in the way."

She looked away from him and up at the night sky.

"There are a few," she pointed out. He followed her gaze up, over the rooftops, in the direction of the moon.

"Yes but out on the ocean you can see a million. Ten million. Have you ever been outside of London, Eliza?"

"Once, to Brighton," she said flatly.

"Was it a pleasant trip?"

"I was swept away by the splendor of the pavilion, the sea air, the romance of holiday . . . The whole thing was a mistake."

"I confess I am intrigued," he murmured, leaning toward her. Women often commented on how he towered over them. Some found it intimidating, others irresistible. Eliza did not pull away.

"You shall remain intrigued," she replied pertly before hastily adding, "Your Grace."

He grinned and held out the brandy bottle to her. "More?"

"Please."

After she drank, he took the bottle back and had another swig himself. They fell into a comfortable silence, both looking over the city or up at the few visible stars. Wycliff was acutely aware of her lithe female form just there, beside him, on this secluded rooftop.

She broke the silence to ask what he was thinking.

"I do not make it a habit to confide in my housemaids," he said, mainly to remind himself that this was not done.

"Of course not," she agreed. "But you've been drinking."

Seeing as he did not put much stock in ducal this or ducal that, it seemed ridiculous to stand on ceremony and refuse to have a pleasant conversation with a pretty girl who could drink brandy like a man.

"The crux of the matter is that . . . I know that I belong here, as Wycliff. But I want to be out there." He gestured grandly to the rooftops and the sky and the whole wide world on the outskirts of London.

Eliza followed his gesture and knew that he meant the farthest corners of the world. She knew, too, how he paced the floors of Wycliff House and rattled the bars on his cage—lovely as it was—in search of a way out.

"You are remarkably self-aware," she said. He was trouble and a bit spoiled, but he wasn't stupid. And he was handsome, ridiculously so. She did her best to act collected and calm, as if she sipped brandy on rooftops with dukes all the time.

But she was acutely aware of the intensity of her heartbeat. Her gaze kept returning to his mouth. Her thoughts kept imagining her lips against his.

"As we've said, I've been drinking. But I can't go out there, because I haven't the funds."

"That is a problem," she agreed. One he would hopefully tell her more about. She heard Knightly's voice in the back of her thoughts: Get the story. *Get the story.*

"The dukedom is wasted on Wycliff men," he carried on. "Look at me: drinking, wishing and plotting to leave the country, and confiding in a housemaid."

Eliza took the bottle from his grasp and took another sip, hoping the burn of the brandy would keep her from blurting out that she was more than a mere housemaid. She was a writer—a *published* writer. She was a good friend to her fellow Writing Girls, she kept secrets and dealt with problems and had her own wishes and dreams.

She was more than a woman with a broom and an apron. But because the duke thought that was all she was capable of, it lessened any regret she might feel for what she wrote about him.

But still, it begged the question of why she cared what he thought of her. That was something to be considered another time. Unless it was fodder for her articles, it wasn't worth her attention.

Get the story. *Get the story.*

"You wish to avoid your fate," she summarized.

"I suppose that is one remarkably accurate and succinct way to put it," the duke answered. Again, she wished to point out that she was a writer, that she had a way with words.

"But I want . . . what I'm not supposed to want," he said, and sipped from the bottle. "Tonight, at the ball, Lady Althea slapped me clear across the face in front of everyone."

"The audacity," Eliza murmured, when instead she wished to ask what he'd done to deserve it.

Julianna probably witnessed it with unabashed glee and had already written an entire installment of "Fashionable Intelligence" relating the scene for those who had missed it—the Elizas of the world, the housemaids and the working class and the ones who were never on the invitation list. Being friends with a duchess and a countess who never missed a party and who always had new dresses was hard sometimes.

But then again, they could never do this: go off in disguise and spend the evening looking at the stars and drinking brandy with the most intriguing, handsome, scandalous duke in town. She found herself leaning closer and breathing him in.

"I deserved the slap, of course. But that incident, coupled with that scathing newspaper column . . ." If he saw her shrink back, he did not show it. " . . . has made it impossible for me to stay, and impossible for me to escape. I feel as if I do not belong here, yet England and the dukedom own me and I cannot leave."

"Why did you even return?" Eliza asked.

"Honestly? I was bored of Tahiti and another option presented itself."

"I am tempted to slap you myself," Eliza remarked.

"Burke had stranded Harlan and myself there a year earlier with some noble idea of teaching us a lesson about being careful what we wish for. I knew that the time was coming for me to own up. I just didn't expect it so soon, so suddenly. I still remember laying on the beach and seeing Burke's ship on the horizon . . . and then him delivering the news that my father had died and I was now Wycliff. I thought I ought to return."

"You are redeemed. Slightly."

"How kind of you to say so. I do have a sense of duty," he said. There was a slight smile on his lips, and it reached his eyes, too. He reached out to push a wayward strand of hair back from her face. His fingertips brushed across her cheek then, and she couldn't help but close her eyes and savor it.

"We should go before I ravish you on the rooftop," the duke stated.

Eliza's eyes widened and she could feel a coy smile forming on her lips. When had she ever been coy? Or a flirt? That one week in Brighton, perhaps . . .

"Go," he commanded, sounding very ducal. She had been dismissed. "And do not open your door if I knock."

Chapter 11

In Which the Writing Girls Visit the British Museum

Sunday

It was Sunday afternoon, Eliza's half day off, and she was spending it at the British Museum with her fellow Writing Girls and Sophie's younger, troublesome sister-in-law, Lady Charlotte. They all paused before a particularly chiseled stature of a man—a god, surely—who was utterly unclothed save for one strategically placed leaf. A very large leaf, one might add.

"Oh my goodness," Julianna murmured. Her lips curved into a delightfully wicked smile.

"Indeed," Sophie agreed in the same tone, and then she admonished her sister-in-law: "Charlotte, close your eyes."

"Good Lord above," Annabelle whispered, fanning herself furiously.

"That is nothing compared to Wycliff," Eliza remarked truthfully, as she walked away from the statue and moved on to the next, leaving stunned companions in her wake.

It was a far cry from their usual Sunday afternoon activity: lolling about sipping tea and flipping through issues of *La Belle Assemblée*. Eliza knew it was vexing for Annabelle to see all those gorgeous dresses that she could not afford nor had occasion to wear. She felt the same.

After her week of hard labor, she wouldn't have minded slouching on a settee, being served tea and cookies, and idly gossiping. Though she had to admit, gaping at nude male statues wasn't altogether bad.

"I thought it would be pottery," Annabelle said. Her cheeks were bright pink.

"Over here," Sophie indicated. They all crossed the room to admire the pottery. Which, of course, had nude men chasing after nude women. And lutes.

"Who knew pottery could be so interesting?" Lady Charlotte mused. "And who knew the ancients were so . . . *naked*."

"Charlotte!" Sophie hissed.

"Oh, when did you become such a stick in the mud, Sophie?" Julianna asked.

"Since I became responsible for the virtue of a young trouble-prone lady," Sophie muttered.

"Imagine if we adopted this tendency toward nudity," Lady Charlotte carried on.

Annabelle blushed furiously. Eliza's face also took on a pinkish hue. Every image of an undressed male brought Wycliff to mind. He was so much more impressive than this collection of marble men. And that wasn't even considering his tattoos, which made him so much more forbidden and wicked.

"Pray tell, Eliza, what has your cheeks burning?" Julianna prodded. That was the vexing thing about having a particularly observant friend.

"Oh, you know," Eliza said airily. She couldn't quite say it aloud. But could it be anything else?

"The duke. You must be smitten," Sophie said, grinning.

"Of course she is, if he is anything like how he used to be," Julianna added. "And, naturally, given how he is reputed to be of late."

"What had he been like before?" Eliza asked. It was a fair question; any reporter ought to inquire about her subject's past. She just happened to be interested for her own reasons as well.

Julianna explained in a hushed but excited tone: "Well, all the Dukes of Wycliff were utterly wicked and notorious rakes. Ballroom legend has it that no Duke of Wycliff has ever been reformed. They have married—and they tend to pledge their troth to the most stern and strict women, oddly enough—and they have produced heirs, but none has ever surrendered his wicked ways."

"Doesn't that sound like a *challenge*?" Lady Charlotte asked. "A delicious, tempting, splendid challenge?"

"No, Charlotte, it does not. At least not for you," Sophie admonished.

Eliza wasn't thinking of reforming him. No, her thoughts strayed to matters far less noble and much more wicked.

Wycliff hadn't knocked on her door last night, as he warned he might. Would she have answered if he had? She felt a shiver of danger, because she would have opened the door—and not for the story.

"The duke mentioned an altercation with Lady Shackley," Eliza began as the group strolled through the galleries, idly gazing at more nude statues and pottery. She couldn't ask Wycliff about the slap heard 'round the ballroom, but she could ask Julianna.

"Oh, that was thrilling," Lady Charlotte gushed.

"Did he mention it to you?" Julianna asked. "Are you conversing with the duke? Is the duke confiding in you?"

They were curious. Rightfully so. Dukes and housemaids tupping was one thing; confiding in each other was quite another.

"It's nothing," Eliza said with a shrug, because she didn't know if in fact it was something or nothing. At the moment she was more interested in what existed between Wycliff and Lady Shackley. "I confess I am curious about her. And him. It might be useful information for my column. And I can't possibly ask the duke."

"Well, I presume the slap was a long time coming, and in response to the manner in which Wycliff left Lady Shackley years ago."

"They had been sweethearts?" Eliza inquired.

"Lovers," Julianna said, and Eliza felt it like a fist to her belly. "Wycliff was caught in bed with Lady Althea Shackley, by her husband. I have it on very good authority that Lord Shackley heard them all the way in the foyer—from behind closed bedchamber doors. On the third floor."

"How shameless," Eliza said. But she felt a shiver of . . . danger? Excitement? Craving?

"Lady Shackley was promptly sent off to the Outer Hebrides. She returned when her husband died, a few years ago, and has since refused numerous proposals. Everyone is of the opinion that she was saving herself for Wycliff's return," Julianna informed her as they continued their stroll. It was tremendously useful having a gossip columnist as a friend.

"A slap across the face is a curious way to greet one's long-lost lover," Eliza remarked.

"I can understand it perfectly," Julianna said. But then again, she had shot her husband, before they married. "Because here is the other part of the story: the late Lord Shackley, upon discovering them, paid Wycliff one thousand pounds to leave the country. His friend, Burke, offered him a place on his ship. And the rest, they say, is history."

"I'm not sure that I would forgive him if I were Lady Shackley," Annabelle said thoughtfully. "But if he was forced by circumstances beyond their control . . ."

"If Roxbury accepted money to leave me, I would hunt him down and really make him pay for it," Julianna said passionately.

"Ah, young love," Lady Charlotte said with a sigh. They all laughed.

"I actually made the acquaintance of Lady Shackley yesterday," Sophie said. "We met during Lady Walmsly's calling hours. She was very well versed with your column, Eliza."

"Her long-lost lover returns," Annabelle said, "and she is now unattached. She must be tremendously excited."

"And she is fueled by Eliza's stories," Julianna said. "It's a wonder she stopped with the slap."

"Oh, Eliza, your column was just delicious," Sophie said with a smile. "I cannot believe the ruse you are up to."

"I am enjoying the experience, other than the chores," Eliza said. "I feel that I learned things about other cultures."

"Yes, that's why we enjoyed your column. For the educational benefits," Lady Charlotte said primly—but with a wicked gleam in her eye.

"Not at all because of her lengthy descriptions of his lengthy—"

"Julianna, you are a lady," Annabelle hissed.

"Oh Annabelle, you know how she is," Sophie said, laughing.

"Scandal monger," Eliza said, grinning.

"Yes, but now you are as well!" Julianna added, linking their arms together. "What shall be the subject of your next column?"

"The duke!" Eliza exclaimed in a strangled whisper.

"Of course it will be the duke," Sophie said, looking puzzled.

"He's *here*," Eliza hissed before frantically dodging behind the nearest statue, ever mindful of her disguise. Housemaids were generally not in the habit of museum strolls with duchesses and countesses.

"What are you doing?" Sophie asked.

"I can't let him see me here," Eliza whispered. "That would ruin everything."

From her hiding place, she watched as Wycliff conversed with an older, gray-haired bespectacled man. He fit in perfectly with the museum, and Eliza wondered if he worked there. He and the duke shook hands firmly before the duke took his leave.

After an hour of strategic loitering, eavesdropping, and inquiring, Eliza managed to learn that the duke had come to visit Professor James Warwick, of the British Museum. But why? That, she would have yet to discover.

Chapter 12

In Which Our Heroine Discovers Timbuktu

Monday

It was ridiculous, but she did not know where Timbuktu was and she very much wanted to. Eliza cursed her girl's education, yet was still thankful her father, a playwright, had taught her to read and to write. Her mother had taught her very creative household accounting and acting. Her geography lessons didn't cover much beyond stage right, stage left, or the city of London, which she knew extraordinarily well.

In the duke's private study there were dozens of maps scattered across the table and a blue-green globe that spun on a stand. Armed with her feather duster as an excuse, Eliza slipped in when His Grace was out with Harlan in the garden, tending to some of the bizarre creatures they'd brought back.

While Jenny daydreamed, whistled, and stared out the window she was cleaning on the other side of the room, Eliza spun the globe around fast. And then slowly, inch by inch. She found England, France,

Australia, Africa. Tahiti was much harder to locate, and Timbuktu . . . where the devil was it?

She hadn't noticed the duke's arrival until he stood behind her and whispered in her ear: "What are you looking for?"

Eliza shuddered and gasped, *"Oh my lord."*

"No, merely your lord and master," Wycliff replied, stepping back and grinning.

"Oh for Lord's sake," she retorted, turning around and biting back a smile. She noted that Jenny was still washing the windows and humming to herself, and only mildly interested in the duke's presence. "I was dusting. And curious. Where might a girl find Timbuktu?"

"If it were easy enough that a girl could find it, it'd already have been discovered and colonized," Wycliff remarked.

"And there wouldn't be a ten thousand pound prize for finding it," Eliza added.

"Considering the venture yourself?" Wycliff asked. He leaned against the bookshelf that had been stocked with leather-bound volumes and all sorts of curiosities from his travels. She would have to dust those later, too.

"Well now that you mention it, Your Grace, I daresay it'd be more exciting than cleaning."

"That, you could be assured of. And much, much more dangerous." There was a devilish spark in his eye that made her think there was plenty of danger right here.

His Grace stepped uncommonly close to her and pointed to a spot on the globe. His hands were riddled with scars, which did not surprise her in the least.

"Timbuktu is here, in northern Africa. Or it's rumored to be."

"It doesn't look too far. What is the great challenge?"

"Mainly surviving disease, the extreme heat, crossing the desert, and the vicious, murderous tribes that live here and want to keep Europeans out."

"And why do you wish to go and endure all of that? You could live so comfortably here, ordering around your staff and taking hot baths every morning, afternoon, and night."

"Tempting," the duke said in a low voice that warmed her up. "But Timbuktu is a challenge. It will test the limits of my wits and ability. Then there is glory, when I succeed. It's something I could accomplish and be damned proud to have done so."

"Being a duke isn't glorious and challenging enough?" Eliza asked. From her vantage point, it seemed so.

"All I did was get born; I did nothing to deserve it," Wycliff said. "The challenge is surviving the tedium of balancing account books."

"Not as thrilling as exploring," Eliza agreed. And she could see his point, though empathizing was another matter entirely.

"The life of a peer does not appeal to me, really. Sitting around at Parliament, at the club, in the library with accounts. Going to the same old parties with the same old people. It is not exactly my idea of a life well lived," Wycliff said.

"You should try dusting and mopping the floors. It will give you an appreciation for it. Or at the very least, sitting," Eliza remarked.

"Aye to that," Jenny muttered on the other side of the room, reminding them that they were not alone, even though it felt like there was no one else in the world.

Wycliff smiled at her. "Touché, Eliza." He pushed a strand of hair behind his ear, and the gold hoop glinted in the afternoon sunlight.

"But what about your duties here, Your Grace? The tenants on your estates, or the wages of your household staff . . ." Left unspoken was the question, *How can you just dash off around the world and leave those that depend upon you?*

That grin of his vanished. His jaw tightened and his eyes clouded with anger. She had offended him. Surprisingly, he didn't make her suffer for it.

Before her eyes, she saw the transformation—the flash of feeling, and the overpowering self-control that allowed him to process and store that emotion and then smile lazily at her.

"You're a bold, impertinent thing, aren't you," he drawled.

She decided to play along. "I take my excitement where I may, Your Grace."

"Until I am off on the next wave of my great adventures, I suppose you will have to be my amusement. I find you infinitely more entertaining than the account books," he said, grinning down at her in a way that made her knees weak.

"Well now isn't that a compliment, if ever there was one," Eliza said dryly. But she knew her cheeks were pink with pleasure, and that he saw.

"I've cavorted around the world on my charm alone," he remarked.

"If that is the case, then what is keeping you here?"

"Besides some sense of duty to my noble station,

even if I wish to leave it?" he asked dryly. "I want to lead my own expedition and I lack the funds to do so." The duke spoke quietly, so low that Eliza knew that Jenny cleaning the windows on the other side of the room could not hear. So low and rough that she suspected he was saying it aloud for the first time. To her.

The globe spun lazily between them. They fell silent. She thought of Lady Shackley and her riches. She would have wagered the duke was thinking about that, too.

He stopped the globe and pointed to another spot in Europe.

"I started my explorations in Paris, particularly women's boudoirs. Circumstances forced me to flee to Italy and then it was onward to Greece," the duke explained, identifying the countries as he spoke. "My valet refused to travel further, so I went off on my own, through Egypt, Turkey. Down to Zanzibar, where I met Harlan. Tahiti is here—that's where Burke had abandoned me and then came to collect me with the grim news about my father."

He pointed out all these foreign places on the map to her. He'd covered so much of the globe and she had only left London, that once, for the disastrous and ill-fated trip to Brighton where she'd acted stupidly and paid the price for it.

Some things, some people, were best kept in the past, and some adventures were not worth having. She shuddered at the thought of that disaster. The duke placed his hand on the small of her back.

"Are you alright?" He ducked his head to be close to hers.

"Just fine. Thank you."

Her heart had begun to race, and it had nothing to do with fear. It felt like pleasure.

"What is the most beautiful place you have been to?" she asked. It was the perfect opportunity to collect stories from His Grace. He was talkative, and she was absorbed by the lovely sensations of such intimacy and proximity to him. Best of all, Jenny was on the other side of the room, listening and whistling while cleaning the windows, so the duke couldn't concretely blame her if one of his travel tales ended up on the pages of *The London Weekly*.

He spun tales of warm ocean water, stormy seas, cannibals and strange customs, brightly colored birds, battles and wild escapes from certain death. All the while, he kept his palm on the small of her back, hot and possessive.

Chapter 13

In Which There Is a Rivalry

Monday Evening

Being a destitute peer and social outcast meant that Wycliff had no club to turn to. Instead, he indulged in the classic activity of brandy, cigars, and cards with Harlan and Burke in the library. It was almost like being back on the ship.

"I heard you were at the British Museum yesterday," Burke said as he sorted his cards.

"Where did you hear that bit of news?" Wycliff asked.

"The newspapers," Burke answered.

Those damned papers, Wycliff thought. He couldn't so much as sneeze without it being reported that he was suffering from a foreign plague that would decimate the population of England.

"Why they must record my every breath, I know not," he said, sipping his brandy.

"You are strange. You can't do anything without it being remarked upon. You were seen at the museum. It was discussed. No one knows the purpose of your visit," Burke said pointedly. He glanced across the table at Wycliff.

A long silence ensued. A deliberately long silence. Wycliff didn't know how the papers were getting their information, and until he did, he wasn't saying a word about anything, especially something important. His visit with an old professor was no one else's business.

"This is the part where you explain yourself," Harlan explained to him.

"I don't think I will," Wycliff said. He took a sip of his drink. His look challenged his companions to press further.

"Then could you tell us what is behind that locked door?" Harlan asked casually, nodding his head in the direction of the ornately carved doors that led to a private room off the library.

"No," Wycliff said shortly. He fought the urge to check that the key was still around his neck.

"A man with secrets. The ladies must be all agog," Burke said dryly.

"You've seen that they are not, thanks to that damned column in *The Weekly*," Wycliff replied. "Other than, perhaps, Lady Althea."

"Ah yes, Hades' Own Harpy," Burke said, grinning.

"That housemaid, on the other hand . . ." Harlan said, lifting his brow and exhaling a steady stream of cigar smoke.

Wycliff looked up sharply.

"Just because I have only one eye . . ." Harlan said, shrugging and sorting his cards. Burke laughed.

"There's nothing to discuss," Wycliff replied, even as his thoughts strayed to Eliza, and what tasks she was performing at this hour. Probably turning down the beds. God, the thought of his delectable Eliza leaning over a bed made his breeches tight.

"I also heard you have made an appointment to see the Royal Society. What for?" Burke asked, glancing up from his cards.

"Was that in the papers, too?" Wycliff questioned.

"No, gossip at the club," Burke said, and surprisingly, it stung. White's and the other gentlemen's clubs were dull and populated with pompous old windbags and idiotic second sons. But it rankled that there was a place he could not go.

"What else are they saying at the club?" he asked, careful not to let any feeling into his voice.

"That you'll never receive funding from the Royal Society," Burke replied. He puffed on his cigar.

"Why ever not?" Wycliff asked sharply.

"Because you are too scandalous. Too wild. To unpredictable," Burke said frankly. Wycliff scowled. Because he was a Wicked Wycliff.

"You mean I'm not easily controlled," he retorted.

"You're not," Harlan and Burke said in unison.

"They're also saying that someone ought to go to Timbuktu," Burke said. "That we cannot let the French claim it." His every word landed like a gunshot. In an instant, Wycliff understood.

"Who is being suggested to go?" he asked, his voice clipped.

Burke refused to meet his eye, keeping his gaze on the cards in his hands. "Myself," he said quietly.

"You are a sea captain. Timbuktu is in the middle of Africa," Wycliff scoffed. Burke kept focused on his cards. Harlan smoked and avidly watched the conversation.

"I am not a walking scandal," Burke replied. "I

have a sterling reputation for carrying out orders. Successfully."

Wycliff raised his brow. It was the only movement he would allow. Otherwise, he'd have been tempted to violence. Burke was the navy's darling, and he was the black sheep, the rogue. But an experienced one.

"Do my accomplishments not matter?" he challenged. "The languages I have learned, the documentation I have compiled, the cultures I have studied, the plants and other specimens that I have accumulated?"

"You have a collection of stuff," Burke said dismissively. "Which I carted back in the precious cargo space on my ship. You're welcome."

"I have knowledge of the world that will immensely benefit England," Wycliff replied sharply. "Must I cut my hair, remove the earring, and dress up like a dandy to win their attention and favor?"

"It's too late for that," Burke said. "Everyone already knows about your tattoos. They know you've gone native. But if you really wish to change public perception of you, *The Weekly* is the way to go."

"Am I to take out an advertisement? Write an article defending myself?"

"You could. Or you could discover who authors the Tattooed Duke column and give him something to write about, other than all the shocking, intimate details of your life. That's what I would do."

"And exact some revenge for what he already wrote," said Harlan, the bloodthirsty wretch.

Wycliff sipped his drink thoughtfully. This idea had some merit. He ought to put a stop to it before it went further.

"*After* he publishes something flattering," Burke added.

"Or she," Harlan added.

She sucked in her breath from the other side of the library door where she shamelessly eavesdropped, extremely grateful the gents had left it ajar. Rivalry. A mysteriously locked door. Secret plans . . .

. . . and beds that needed to be prepared before His Grace turned in for the evening.

She was bent over the mattress, smoothing out the pillows, when he found her later that evening.

Chapter 14

In Which Attire Is Removed

The duke's bedchamber

Later, after tucking away a cigar and a few brandies, Wycliff entered his bedchamber to find his maid bent over the mattress.

Housemaid. Housemaid. Housemaid.

He would do to remember that.

"My luck has changed," he drawled from where he stood in the doorway. She peeked over her shoulder at him, and he saw her blue eyes coolly assessing the facts: a drunk duke in a doorway. Her fetching self bent over the bed.

"Whatever do you mean?" she asked, unfortunately straightening up into a significantly less compromising position. Alas.

Wycliff lifted one brow. She replied in kind.

He grinned, and groaned. The thing about avoiding one's fate was that occasionally one wanted to accept parts of it. Like dallying with the maids in the grand tradition of the Wicked Wycliffs. This one maid, in particular.

But what did that one lift of her brow mean? He

could not tell if it meant *Yes, Your Grace* or *Dare not, Duke*.

He'd seen—and stopped—men who hadn't heeded a woman's *no*. He didn't want a reluctant woman, he wanted a passionate and generous lover. And that was the thing about a maid—how was he supposed to know she was surrendering because she wanted to or felt she ought to please her lord and master?

Damned luck being the Wycliff that cared about a chit's feelings. That was a first. There were ways to tell, though, how willing and wanton a woman could be. He smiled slightly. Anticipation.

Wycliff pushed off from the doorjamb and sauntered into his room.

"Is there anything else I may assist you with, Your Grace?" Eliza asked ever so properly and politely. Funny, that, when he had such wicked thoughts.

"Since I have returned, I have not yet hired a valet," he told her. In fact, he hadn't had one since that sissy, Alderson, quit Greece and returned to England. He'd taken care of his own attire and shaving for so long, he hadn't quite gotten around to hiring another valet. Besides, one didn't take a valet to Timbuktu, and he hadn't given up on that venture yet.

"I am aware of that, Your Grace." It was so strange to be addressed as *Your Grace*. Or *Wycliff*. It didn't feel like his name yet.

"The lack of valet means the burdensome task of removing my attire is left to me," he explained. She crossed her arms over her chest, which did marvelous things to her breasts, and gave him a look of utter contemptuous disbelief. He grinned and pressed on.

"Given my lofty stature, I can't possibly be expected to perform such a menial task myself. To answer your question, yes, there is something that I require your assistance with."

"I am at your service, Your Grace," she said smoothly. Wicked little minx.

"I require assistance removing my attire," he said, feeling like such an ass until her blue eyes darkened and the slightest gasp escaped her lips.

"Yes, of course, Your Grace," she whispered. A smile played on her lips, the kind of woman's smile that said, *You'll pay for this, mister.* He knew it well. All over the world, from London's ballrooms to harems to the islands of Tahiti, women smiled like that.

The sweet, seductive torture was about to begin.

First, she smoothed her hands across his shoulders and chest. He didn't wear a cravat because he couldn't be bothered with tying a scrap of fabric in an elaborate nooselike knot around his neck. He'd left his jacket in the study, reeking of cigar smoke.

Then her small female hands slid down to the buttons on his waistcoat.

Her eyes met his. Her blue eyes, like the ocean. He could barely tell in the light of a few candles and the moon, but he knew from memory.

One button undone.

Never breaking his gaze, she made short work of the other two. Her fingers delicately brushed against his stomach, and the look in her eyes promised wicked things. His breath hitched in his throat and the corners of his mouth tugged up into a grin.

He lowered his mouth, but after only the briefest touch of his lips upon hers, Eliza gasped and ducked her head away. For a moment he tasted her. For a fleeting second he knew her. Then she pushed back the fabric of the waistcoat, over his shoulders and off. Bold little thing.

Like a good valet, she carefully folded it and set it aside. He wanted to rip it from her hands, drop it on the floor, and proceed with her ravishment.

Next, she grabbed handfuls of his shirt, untucked it from his breeches and gently tugged the damned thing overhead. Again with the bloody folding. He groaned in frustration. She smiled with all the patience of a saint and the wicked designs of a vengeful, seductive goddess.

This housemaid was not just some young chit. But who was she? Wycliff stood before her with his torso bare—and his tattoos black, bold, and undisguised. She eyed the key, tied to the leather cord around his neck. He shouldn't have allowed her to see that. But he was too far gone with lust to think clearly.

His breeches strained to contain him.

She was not unaffected. He knew, because he saw the heavy rise and fall of her breasts. He held her by the waist, his palm open, urging her close enough to kiss. He needed to. He needed to know her. He needed to feel her heart beat and taste her and breathe her in.

"Your Grace . . ." Her breath was but a whisper.

"When it's just us, call me Sebastian. Wycliff is . . . something else. Someone else." And that was the distinction, wasn't it?

He, Sebastian, wanted to be with her, Eliza.

But to the world it would look like another roué Wycliff duke seducing the housemaid.

"Sebastian," she said, tracing her fingertip along

the waistband of his breeches, which unbelievably became even tighter. He was so damned hard, it was becoming impossible to breathe, and his heart pounded heavily in his chest.

That tantalizing trace of her fingers continued, but lamentably up and not down. She was entranced by his tattoos. For the first time since arriving in London, he was glad of them, if only because they intrigued her.

When he could tolerate it no longer, Wycliff claimed her for a kiss. In that instant he knew that her desire was real. He knew that she kissed him because she wanted to, needed to, as he did. Not because he was lord and master.

And he knew, because her kiss was tentative and teasing at first. He urged her to open to him; she tasted so sweet. She kissed him harder, and he liked it. He nibbled her lower lip. When she did the same to him, he was almost undone.

She kissed him truly, passionately, not with the practice and coldheartedness of a seductress. And like that, she had managed a small claim on his heart.

Eliza wasn't just some housemaid to him.

She was, in fact, the most luscious, heady, intoxicating woman, and with her warm and willing in his grasp, he started toward the bed.

After all, she had just murmured his name with unmistakable longing. She was melting under his touch, he could feel it. Her every sigh and moan, every inch of her hot flesh against his, told him one truth: she wanted him.

Must go to the bed, he thought . . . Where he would act like nothing more than the typical Wicked Wycliff he was trying very hard not to be.

A Wycliff would take her now.

He refused to be a Wycliff.

Sebastian let her go.

Only later, when Eliza was safely upstairs in her own narrow chamber with the door locked behind her, did she pause to exhale. Her dress felt too tight, too hot. She wanted to rip it off. She wanted Wycliff to rip it off. But that was impossible.

Sebastian . . . the pleasure she felt at being given that intimacy of using his true name hit her like a heady rush. She told herself it was a professional accomplishment to be so intimate with her subject.

The story. The story. *The story.*

This would not grace the pages of *The London Weekly.*

Because that kiss wasn't for the story at all but for her own pleasure. A man hadn't made her feel this way since . . . well, ever. Not even with L— Not even in Brighton.

Chapter 15

In Which the Duke Does Some Sleuthing

Wycliff wasn't such a fool that he thought a visit to *The London Weekly* would produce anything other than frustration. At best, the editor, proprietor, and publisher of such inflammatory, slanderous, libelous content might slip up and reveal a clue about the author. He might even be intimidated enough to tone the rubbish down for subsequent columns.

He wasn't such a fool to think that the editor would cease publication of what word on the street said was the most popular thing in town. But something had to be done to keep the scandal under control, especially with Burke sniffing around his expedition. Wycliff would not roll over and surrender his lifelong dream so easily. He wasn't French after all.

The offices of the newspaper were remarkably easy to find, thanks to the sign hanging over the door declaring THE LONDON WEEKLY in capital letters decked in gold leaf. The source of all his ills was clearly marked, right there on 57 Fleet Street. He could see it from a block away.

The entry was blocked by a man of gargantuan proportions.

"What's your business?" he asked gruffly, with a faint accent that Wycliff placed as somewhere far to the east of Europe. His arms, thick as logs, were folded over his whiskey barrel chest. The man's skin was swarthy, his brows thick and his eyes black. Wycliff estimated him to be of Turkish origin.

"I'm here to see Mr. Knightly," he stated.

"Are you now?" the man asked. Listening closely, Wycliff was now quite sure of his Turkish roots. The giant grinned, and not in a nice way. "Do you have an appointment?"

"Mr. Knightly can't possibly be surprised by my arrival." A few of this massive man's teeth had gone missing. Wycliff's options were clear: attempt battle and likely lose; attempt to negotiate and likely lose.

"Are you the Tattooed Duke?"

"The very one. I hope proof is not required. At least not on the street," Wycliff said. And then he added a line in Turkish.

"You know my language," the giant said, awed.

"I know a lot of languages," Wycliff replied. "When one's life depends upon the good graces of a foreign host, the least a man can do is learn a few lines in their native tongue."

"You are not like regular Englishmen," the giant observed.

"I should hope not. And you, too, for you wouldn't sell nearly as many newspapers if I was."

"I'll let you in to see Knightly, but I won't do anything to stop that column. We've all seen an increase in wages since it started running."

"An interview with Mr. Knightly is all I ask."

"Upstairs, second on the right. Tell 'em I've let you through." Then the giant grinned, and it was a terrifying thing.

It was easy enough to find Knightly behind his desk. That Wycliff had gotten past the beast guarding the door seemed sufficient reason for everyone to let him carry on with his business.

"You must be Knightly," Wycliff said, standing in the open doorway. The man put down his pen. He reached casually for the top of his desk drawer, where most editors kept a good assortment of weaponry, starting with a loaded pistol. Let him be afraid. Wycliff looked down at the newspaperman.

"And you are?" the man asked coolly.

"Wycliff. Perhaps better known as the Tattooed Duke."

"Ah, I see," Knightly said, leaning back in his chair.

"Your beast of a man at the door let me through."

"Really? I hope you haven't extracted much damage. I'm fond of Mehitable." Knightly had piercing blue eyes, black hair, and a manner that seemed at ease, though Wycliff could tell that the man was tense and aware.

"Mehitable and I came to an understanding," Wycliff explained. "I'm here so that you and I might do the same."

In another part of the office he heard the low hum of male voices punctuated by the chatter of women. Wycliff turned his head to look up the hallway but didn't catch a glimpse of those infamous Writing Girls.

Since an invitation did not seem to be forthcoming from the editor, and he was the higher ranking of the two, Wycliff ambled into the room and looked around. It was a richly appointed chamber, designed to intimidate and impress.

Knightly stood up from his chair and walked over to the sideboard. "I should find it much more tolerable with a drink. Would you care for one as well?"

"Yes, thank you. You are in the habit of angering people, I presume."

"The threat of irate lords and ladies keeps Mehitable employed. And the rest of us as well, for that matter," Knightly said, handing Wycliff a glass of brandy. "I know why you're here. You're upset over your portrayal in my newspaper. However, the next issue is already off to the printer, and I shan't stop the presses on account of anyone, even some mad, bad duke. If you wish to argue or protest, please do go on. Know that I won't change a thing and I thank you for at least allowing me the courtesy of alcohol whilst I must endure your complaints."

"I feel so special," Wycliff deadpanned. Knightly choked on his drink. "I never met a problem that was solved by complaining about it. I don't expect that any sort of outburst, angry threat, or emotional plea will change your plans to mine my private life for your public gain."

"Then what brings you here? If you wish to duel, you need only say the word. We can schedule it—I believe I am free next Tuesday—and I can return to my work," Knightly said, then sipped his drink.

"I thought this issue was already at the presses," Wycliff said, trying to catch him in a lie.

"My work is ongoing, relentless," Knightly replied. There were faint lines around the corner of his eyes; he probably wasn't lying.

"However do your authors keep pace?" Wycliff inquired.

"It's a weekly, not a daily," the editor said plainly. "If they can't handle it, there are a hundred more waiting to replace them."

"You don't put much stock in your writers," Wycliff remarked. One of those authors, perhaps, might feel underappreciated by this Knightly fellow. They might then feel motivated to betray him.

"I actually employ an exceptional collection of writers. But I'm not in the business of handholding or warm tender feelings—not even for the women. My writers are expected to write, and write well. And, frankly, cause a scandal whenever possible. It does remarkable things for sales. Without fail."

"And what of those chits you have writing for you? They must have had tongues wagging all over town. And from what I hear, the allure of scribbling females hasn't worn off."

"Scribbling females," Knightly said with a laugh. "You best not let them hear you say that, although I daresay they've heard it all."

"It's a pretty remarkable thing, hiring females to write in this day and age."

"Exactly. Anything that has the ton in an uproar is bound to be good for sales. My Writing Girls do not disappoint. Neither do your tattoos."

"Is that all you care about—sales?" Wycliff asked.

"Yes," Knightly said, sipping his drink. Wycliff did the same and found it was a fine French brandy.

"I understand. So long as my scandalous self sells your newspapers, I can count on your writers to devote their attentions to drivel about myself. You will make a fortune off of me. But what is it you do with all the money?"

"I have it," the editor said with a shrug. Wycliff understood the security of having money in the bank.

"Tell me, Mr. Knightly, how did you come to employ the chits?" It was an easy, obvious question to get the man talking about his writers.

"If you knew them, the question would be how could I not? A bolder, more brash, more meddlesome collection of females I don't know. Well, most of them, anyway," he said, and Wycliff was immediately intrigued by the quiet ones, whoever they might be.

"And your other writers? Pardon me for asking what may seem to be inane questions, but even given all my travels, I have yet to explore this dark, underbelly of London's publishing world. Duke's usually do not, after all."

Knightly's jaw clenched tightly. Wycliff knew he had hit a nerve. So the upstart news rag proprietor was sensitive about class, was he? Well, he rebounded quickly.

"You do a lot of things dukes do not usually do. Yet I have managed to profit from your exploits, while you do not."

Wycliff said nothing, only finished his drink. The mark was well placed. Knightly knew it.

"Money, or a title? Is one any good without the other?" the duke mused. Honestly. The man across from him was probably flush with cash, yet there it was again—the tightening of the jaw. Even a flash of irritation in his eyes.

" 'Deep Thoughts from the Duke of Wycliff.' Won't

that make a splendid new column for *The Weekly*," Knightly retorted.

"And which writer would I be replacing? One of the chits or some bloke?"

"Nice attempt, Your Grace. I shall not reveal that, not so you can attempt to intimidate the author into writing something more to your liking. Though I doubt you could. After all, I wouldn't send a coward to the den of lion."

Wycliff took that to mean the author was a man. When phrased like that, no decent man with any pretense to calling himself a gentleman could possible send a female into the most salacious and dangerous household in London.

" Well, I can't be bothered to author it, though. Not as a duke," he said, allowing condescension to infuse his tone. And then with a laugh he added, "You could send one of those chits around to take notes as I dictate."

"Yes, I bloody well could," Knightly murmured as he downed the last of his drink.

Chapter 16

In Which the Seeds Are Sown

Conservatory of Wycliff House

Eliza heard the ringing from the drawing room, and because she had not yet learned the distinct tone and pitch of each bell and its corresponding room, she had to dash madly to the butler's pantry to see which one was ringing. And then she had to dash madly to the conservatory, since that's where His Grace was awaiting a maid.

She arrived breathless, which she seemed to do a lot lately. Running here or there, arriving late and worried about being caught and discovered wherever she was. For a spot on the second page of *The Weekly*, though, she wouldn't complain.

Golly, if that didn't make her heart nearly burst with pride.

And then, when summoned by the duke, it mattered naught if she arrived breathless for it would only be a few moments before a look or a caress had all sorts of deliciously unsettling effects upon her.

Just setting her sights upon him did it. She caught a glance of him through the tangled, heady forest of plants. The conservatory was hot, heated by a large stove. It was stuffed with large, luscious plants and trees, obscuring a clear view. As she wandered through, she caught glimpses of Wycliff as he worked, who was as yet unaware that he wasn't alone.

His hair was pulled back from his face, tied roughly with twine. She caught the glint of sunlight on his small gold hoop earring. And his lips were parted slightly as he worked, his gaze utterly focused on what he was doing.

Eliza walked around a potted orange and some other large green plants she didn't recognize until the duke was in full view. He stood at a high table with an assortment of pottery and his hands in the dirt.

His sleeves were rolled up to the elbow, exposing the snaking black lines of his tattoos, which seemed to move as he flexed his muscles. She was transfixed. In fact, she stood there watching and ogling his forearms, like a ninny, until the duke took note of her presence.

"You rang?" she asked, reminding them both what she was doing there.

"I require assistance," he said, stepping aside to make room for her at the table. She had a feeling this was not a typical task of London housemaids. But she wasn't one to stand on ceremony when it could yield material for her column.

Get the story. *Get the story.* Knightly's voice was forever in the back of her mind, urging her on.

She saw dozens of pots and small paper packets with what must have been the duke's scrawl. She could make out Latin names and descriptions.

"I haven't much experience with planting, being a born and raised London girl," she said. "All I know of nature is Hyde Park. And this conservatory."

"It's not difficult. I'll show you." Of course he had to say this with the kind of smile that made a girl go hot all over. The kind of smile he'd given her the other night. That couldn't happen again, much as she might hunger for it.

Eliza pushed up her sleeves like his, and it didn't escape her notice the way his gaze lingered on the bare skin of her hands and arms for just a beat longer than necessary or proper. But he quickly looked away.

Did he desire her? Why did that give her such pleasure?

"It's as simple as making a small hole in the soil and placing just a few seeds before covering them up." The soil was cool and soft on her hands; a welcome change from hot, soapy water or a thin coating of dust.

"Where did you learn to do this?" she asked, not because she was a writer on a secret mission to uncover his secrets, but because she was genuinely curious about him. How many dukes puttered around their conservatories? Probably not many, she'd wager.

"The gardeners at our country estates. My governesses often neglected me and my studies, as they were engaged in other pursuits," Wycliff explained. And the hot, mischievous glance he flashed her told Eliza exactly what kind of pursuits he spoke of. "Like any boy, I wandered outside and did my best to get dirty. I often succeed admirably."

"I daresay most dukes wouldn't have been able to run wild like that." She thought of Brandon, Sophie's double-duke husband, who was the very epitome of a straitlaced, dutiful duke who never, ever neglected anything. Or mucked around in the mud.

"We all know that I am not most dukes," Wycliff replied, which was the understatement of the century, in her opinion. Not that she knew many dukes. She just knew that there was no one like him.

"You've enjoyed more freedom than most," she said.

"Or I've been sadly lacking in discipline, as are most Wycliff men. But it depends upon whom you are asking," he added, and then asked casually: "Would you hand me the *Gardenia taitensis*?"

Eliza hesitated. In order to keep up her ruse as an innocent, simpering, unthreatening housemaid, she shouldn't reveal that she could read—and in Latin, too.

No, she had to act stupid. Just this once. It pained her to do so, because she was a proud woman, particularly when it came to her talents with the written word, and she wanted to impress him.

Why did she care to impress him? she wondered. There could only be one reason . . .

His gaze rested on her face, watching her intently.

And that's what suffused her cheeks with a pink blush, like the desert rose blooming nearby. She felt something . . . she cared about what this duke thought of her, which could only mean . . .

While she stumbled and tripped over these feelings, he reached past her for the *Gardenia taitensis*. He brushed against her as he did so. She felt it everywhere.

"What is all this for, anyway?" she asked.

"While I could walk into the Royal Society and impress them with my haughty, ducal demeanor in a plea for funds, I'd rather show them what they could gain by funding my next expedition. I have accumulated an extensive collection of seeds, among other things, that could be tremendously useful to England."

"When you were not ravishing all the women in a sultan's harem, that is," she teased.

"It's important to explore and engage with the local flora, fauna, *and* females," he added. And there it was again—a mischievous flash in his eyes, a quick grin. She could live off flirtatious looks like that.

"All in the noble name of research," she remarked, returning to planting seeds as he'd shown her. He hadn't just been wandering or idling away the days. He'd been doing something important. She should put that in her column.

"Precisely," he agreed. "I'm glad to see you're a woman of sense. Like some rare blossom."

"I'm not sure if I should take that as a compliment or an insult," she responded, but her heart was beating hard with pleasure, because he didn't think her some idiot female after all.

"Take it as a compliment. You'll find life much easier if you do."

"Is that how you take newspaper columns about you?" The words were out of her mouth before she paused to consider if she ought to give voice to them. This was treading on dangerous conversational territory. But she had been starting to feel little pangs of *something*. Was it guilt? Was it pangs of decency?

"Are you reading those?" He treated her to a questioning, sidelong glance. He was probably an excellent interrogator. She ought not have mentioned this at all. *Must keep wits about self.* She cautioned herself even as she could see the outline of his well-muscled chest through his white shirt, and the vee of tattoos at his neck. Even as she thought about another kiss—a glorious, melting, exquisite kiss that tempted her far too much.

"Your Grace, all of London is reading them—or being read to—including your staff. You'll find life much easier if you accept gossip as inevitable." She tried to laugh it off, but he didn't join her.

"I am unconventional, and that is remarkable. That makes me threatening. I understand this. I'm not too bothered by it. However, were it to start affecting my work, or my chances to secure funding for the Timbuktu expedition . . ."

Was that a warning? Her heart beat hard. He couldn't possibly suspect her, his illiterate housemaid with her hands in the dirt.

"I understand. Idle gossip is one thing, until it begins to wreak havoc upon one's life," she said. Could she walk that line?

"What is it about you that makes me talk so much?" Wycliff questioned. She didn't know, but she was tremendously grateful for it. His confidence in her made her bold. As if she weren't just a housemaid, or the lowly, unknown Writing Girl with the articles in the back of the paper, next to the cure-alls for revolting maladies.

She was now a star writer, falling for her subject.

"Are you trying to impress me, Your Grace?" She dared to flirt with him. But how could she not? It was a warm, lovely day in the conservatory, and this intrepid, worldly explorer was spending the hours with her.

"Impress you?" he repeated, laughing a bit. But he placed his hands on either side of her, blocking her in. She couldn't move if she wanted to.

It went without saying that she did not want to.

"Or perhaps win my favor?" she asked pertly, tempting him to take it further.

"Or just a kiss?" he asked as he gently brushed his lips across hers.

Eliza thought of the reasons they should not kiss as his hot, tempting mouth pressed upon hers, urging her to open to him.

The story. This was not part of the story. *To hell with the story.*

She entwined her arms around his neck, running her fingers through the soft locks of his hair and shamelessly pressing the length of her body against his. She felt his taut chest against her breasts. The duke groaned and his broad hands caressed her all over, leaving heated skin in their wake.

Eliza tilted her head back as he pressed hot, open kisses upon the sensitive skin of her neck. She clasped the fabric of his shirt in her hands. She felt the leather cord he wore, with the key that surely opened those taunting, locked doors.

Get the story. *Get the story.*

She ought to slip it off. But more than that, she wanted, needed, ached to feel his hot bare flesh against hers.

But she shouldn't. She had her reasons, and they had nothing to do with the story and everything to do with that mistake she made years ago in Brighton.

Chapter 17

The Tattooed Duke Strikes Again

"It appears that I've joined you in infamy," Harlan said, tossing a newspaper onto the great oak desk, where they joined an assortment of Arabic texts, journals from Wycliff's travels, and maps.

It was another issue of *The London Weekly*.

Wycliff stared at it for a moment, as if Harlan had tossed a dead fish onto his desk. He asked, "Am I going to need a drink?"

"Likely. But then again, doesn't one always?" Harlan mused.

Sometimes Wycliff wondered if whiskey ran through the man's veins. He picked up the paper, saw the familiar title, "The Tattooed Duke," and began to read as Harlan sauntered over to the windows and looked out into the garden, a makeshift home for some of the creatures they'd brought back.

The Duke of Wycliff, of number four, Berkeley Square, is proud to say he is not perfectly normal, thank you very much. While the ton is aghast at his oddities, and readers of this paper avidly devour the details, the duke cares not for their gossip or their opinions.

There is a room in Wycliff House that remains locked at all times. The duke is the only one with the key and he wears it on a leather cord 'round his neck. His desk is covered with unusual texts: the Muslim holy book, maps, handwritten journals in foreign languages. Hardly the stuff of a typical English gentleman.

Also in the duke's possession are journals describing extraordinarily passionate intimate relations with native women in such vivid detail that any maiden would be ruined to read them. And if she were to glance at the detailed illustrations? There would be a run on smelling salts.

As befitting such an avowed unconventional man, His Grace keeps company that would make a ton matron pale. His faithful companion is a sailor of unknown origins, with only one good eye and one good arm. The stories are wildly inconsistent and devilishly enthralling: wrestling with a shark, a duel with a foreign king, a pagan ritual gone awry, a pirate attack.

One waits with baited breath to see what this tattooed duke will do next. There are rumors that he is planning an expedition to the ever-elusive Timbuktu. So is his rival, mere mister Monroe Burke. This author, intimately acquainted with the facts, would put money on the Wicked Wycliff. To fund Burke Monroe is to surrender to the French. Perish the thought!

Wycliff set the newspaper down. The stuff about Burke was just splendid. It almost made the rest of it forgivable.

He was now portrayed as a heathen, friend of the

devil, author of naughty diary entries, and owner of a locked room that contained God only knew what. Wycliff sighed, oddly curious as to what the gossip would claim the room contained.

Harlan handed him a glass of brandy and asked, "Do you think it's someone in this house?"

He'd been wondering the same thing. Was it Jenny? No, she didn't seem to think of much other than Thomas the footman. Mrs. Buxby was too drunk; Saddler not clever enough. There were all the other maids and footmen that he didn't know.

And then there was Eliza.

It couldn't be her. She couldn't read and write. In fact, he'd seen the hot pink flush of her cheeks, like an African sunset, when he'd unthinkingly asked her to. He'd felt like such an ass.

Even if she were acting as an informant, he couldn't pinpoint anything to her—or any other staff member. The salacious details that made their way into print were all items that many had heard, or overheard, or that could be gleaned merely by snooping around.

He had half a mind to cross the room and test and inspect the lock on the door to his private room.

"I don't know, Harlan. Any ideas? You fraternize with the household help more than I do."

"I go where the whiskey flows freely and companionship is to be found. That is most often Mrs. Buxby's parlor. But no, it's not me. You're my ticket out of here."

"Or Burke. Can you believe his plot to launch a Royal Society funded expedition to Timbuktu? How many hours have we all discussed my intentions to do exactly that? I didn't think he would blatantly steal my plans."

"Well, you're not the first person to consider making the trip. I'm sure he is not planning his travels just to vex or to spite you. Not when there's ten thousand on the line. He doesn't have a title to fall back on," Harlan remarked, oddly supportive of their rival. Wycliff decided not to press the point, but he filed that information away.

"The lot of good this title has done for me. It's money that's required. Or at least a title that isn't tainted by scandal, going back seven generations. But damn, Harlan, of all the places in the world . . ."

Harlan shrugged. "You ought to make your pitch to the Royal Society sooner rather than later. The account books will wait . . ."

Wycliff thought of the maid's simple question— *What about the tenants and your staff?*—and he felt duty tugging at conscience. He thought, too, of adventure, and Timbuktu, and the wide-open plains of Africa and the pride of discovery. The past he inherited, or a future he forged for himself?

"Let's go, then," he said. "We have work to do."

There were papers to write, to detail the customs of other cultures. There were more seeds to plant, specimens to catalogue, wild animals to feed. All in preparation for his proposal to the Royal Society. The funds had to go to *him*, not Burke, who was a ship captain with no scientific background or exploration experience to recommend him.

This was something he deserved, Wycliff thought. Not because he was a duke, but because he'd spent the past ten years roaming, collecting, detailing, accumulating experience. Timbuktu belonged to him.

Chapter 18

In Which His Grace Suffers Rejection

Something bad had happened; it was clear to the entire household. Saddler kept to his pantry, Mrs. Buxby nervously sipped her whiskey-tea, and the others made themselves scarce. The duke bellowed and raged, he stomped and stormed. When something shattered, Eliza was the only one brave enough to venture forth with a broom and dustpan.

She had an ulterior motive: details for her column. That was the only reason, of course. It had nothing to do with concern or care or a simple desire to be near him, especially after their heated moments and scorching kisses.

It certainly had nothing to do with wanting to clean up whatever unholy mess His Grace had made. She had never cared for housework before, but she loathed it now.

She found him in the second floor gallery, stomping across acres of once-polished parquet floors. Furniture sat covered under white sheets, like odd, misshapen ghosts.

Along the east wall, windows overlooked Berkeley Square. On the opposite wall hung dozens of portraits of previous dukes, their homes, dogs, wives, and mistresses. Eliza thought portraits were always supposed to be dour, but these dukes looked jolly. And naughty. Their wives, on the other had, looked so very sober.

The live duke in her midst, however, was glowering and prowling like a caged beast in a rage. He fixed his eyes upon her, and she felt herself shrinking back and stepping behind what seemed to be a chair under a sheet.

The duke stalked toward her, collected the chair and heaved it across the room, where it crashed against the wall, cracked, splintered and collapsed.

His dark hair had escaped its tie and tumbled wildly around his shoulders. He looked like a towering, enraged warrior capable of anything he put his mind to, whether it be violence or passion.

Eliza's heart began to pound and she thought perhaps the cleaning of broken glass could wait.

He growled at her: "What are you doing here?"

She took a deep breath. She had survived two days in Newgate for a story, spent time in a brothel—as an observer—and investigated factories. One angry duke was nothing to her. She straightened her spine.

"I heard something break. I came to tend to it," she explained.

The duke folded his arms across his chest and glowered at her. Tattoos peeked from the vee in his shirt, which any proper gentleman would have covered with an elegantly tied cravat.

"The whiskey bottle could not withstand the excitement of meeting the wall suddenly, and with great force," he explained.

"I see," she murmured. Much like the chair.

"I am in a terrible temper," Wycliff stated, and she bit her lip. He continued: "And I can see that you are holding back some impertinent quip. I really don't give a damn."

"I'll just see to the broken bottle before you injure yourself upon it, Your Grace." Eliza proceeded to locate the broken bottle on the far side of the room while Wycliff followed behind her, sputtering in rage. With her back to him, she dared to smile.

"Injure my— I'm not going to— Don't be ridiculous. You just wanted to see what all my hollering was about."

"I'll confess to a curiosity." She peeked over her shoulder at him; he was still glaring.

"Well, I will tell *you*, Eliza."

"If you wish," she said, and then began to sweep shards of glass into a pile. The fumes of the spilled whiskey were intoxicating on their own. Mrs. Buxby would be livid to see it wasted thus.

"Apparently, I am thoroughly disreputable," the duke stated dryly, and she only murmured "Mmm" as he continued. "So very disreputable and scandalous that I cannot be trusted with an expedition. Or the funds for one."

"According to whom?" she inquired. Besides, of course, nearly everyone.

"The Royal Geographical Society of London."

Eliza kept her head bowed low.

"They—those old, gray, overweight and overbearing old oafs—" the duke muttered.

Esteemed men of Science, Eliza thought to herself.

"They said that I demonstrated a lack of discipline. They could not, in good conscience, use the King's

money to send one reckless and scandalous peer gallivanting debaucherously around the world."

"Gallivanting debaucherously?"

"Exactly. One of them actually accused me of
wenching and thieving my way across continents.
That is apparently an unsuitable use of resources."

"What of your quest to Timbuktu? What about
your collection, and your papers? Did you not explain all of that to them?"

Here the duke's smile turned bitter and his eyes
darkened considerably. Her heart ached for him, for
he was continually denied what he wanted. Yet he
defiantly searched for another way. He refused to
give up.

"They were not interested in hearing more about
that because they already have their man to claim
Timbuktu. He's been settled with a ship, a crew, a
veritable army, a princely sum, and the well wishes
of the King. Damn him!"

"Who is it?"

"My good friend, Monroe Burke. And not because
he's more qualified than me—which we can all agree
he is not. He may be a captain in the navy, but I'm
the one with the scientific knowledge and experience
that will make the expedition useful and not some
bloody, conquering free for all that serves only to
make more enemies. Do you know, Eliza, what rec-
ommends him over myself?"

"I couldn't venture a guess."

"His reputation. Or rather, it is my reputation
that's the issue. Whatever dregs of it are left, thanks
to those damned, bloody news rags. They're the
damned thorn in my side," the duke muttered. Eliza

thought she might have actually heard him growl under his breath.

"The newspapers?" she echoed lightly. By now all the glass shards were neatly contained in one pile of clear, sharp daggers. Nevertheless, she continued to sweep with her gaze firmly focused on the floor.

"Though they claim to be men of science and learning, the Royal Society relies on extremely questionable sources of information. Nevermind my work, or my decade of experience. Because *The Weekly* has detailed the more salacious aspects of my travels, they think I'll take the King's money and spend it on trollops and rum while sailing carefree around the globe. It was that damned column in *The London Weekly* that did me in."

"Which one?" she asked, and was appalled at the hollow sound of her own voice. She was raised by an actress, she ought to be better at acting through scenes like this.

"The Tattooed Duke. I am assured that everyone in England is reading it, from the King himself to the lowest scullery maid."

"Oh yes, that one," Eliza said, recovering herself. "The one that mentioned the harem."

"Idiot Basil spreading that gossip all over town," Wycliff grumbled. "The lot of it."

"Was it not true?" she asked.

"It wasn't *hundreds* in a night. Good God, you can't make proper love to a woman in just a few minutes, which is all you'd have in order to ravish hundreds from dusk till dawn."

"How long does one need to make proper love to a woman?" Eliza asked. "Just out of curiosity, of course. Scientifically speaking."

That teased out a harrumph of laughter from the sullen duke.

"At least one entire night from sunset to sunrise," he answered, not missing a beat.

Wycliff caught her gaze and held it, with an intensity so strong that she couldn't break it. For that moment, she couldn't breathe. There was something so wild and reckless about him; she ached to throw caution to the wind and join him in mad, passionate pursuits. But her position—in his house, and at *The Weekly*—depended upon her restraint.

"You could write your corrections in to the editor of the newspaper," she suggested, once she'd recovered herself. "I've heard that is sometimes done."

Wycliff gave her an incredulous stare, punctuated with bitter laughter.

"Are you truly suggesting that all I need to do to right some egregious wrongs is to *write a letter to the editor*?"

"It most likely wouldn't solve anything, other than soothing your temper," she said, and resumed her sweeping. Amazing things resulted from letters to the editor; that's how she came to write for *The Weekly*. But she couldn't mention that to the duke.

"Darling," Wycliff purred like a practiced charmer. "My darling Eliza. Shooting things soothes my temper. Shooting living things is even better. Hurling furniture and whiskey bottles against the wall also has mollifying qualities. Writing a letter to some low-life hack news rag editor is . . . well, let's just say it would soothe my temper if I could also stab him with the quill and gag him with the letter."

Eliza stared at him, horrified. He just shrugged.

"I am merely a housemaid, Your Grace," she said once she had collected herself.

"A tempting, intriguing, and impertinent housemaid," he corrected.

She curtsied, cheeks flushed, heart racing. "At your service."

"I do need to do something about that newspaper, though," the duke mused, and began to pace around her. "Especially that damned Tattooed Duke column. It's scandal mongering and it's ruining things for me. The Royal Society has been spooked by it, and the haute ton is gob-smacked. Left unchecked, I suspect it will only get worse.

Never had a patch of floor been swept so thoroughly. Eliza couldn't look at him. She could only see, in her mind's eye, all the things that she'd written about him thus far. Every outrageous, damaging word.

"If they won't stop writing about me, the least that malicious and vile writer could do would be to compose something decent . . . let alone flattering. I have done great things, mind you. It wasn't all just whoring my way across continents."

"I would be curious to know of your adventures, Your Grace," Eliza said, pausing in her sweeping.

"I have liberated slave ships in the Indian Ocean," he began. Eliza glanced around in the vain hope that anyone was around to hear this. Because if she was the only one to know it, then she could not publish it.

All alone with the duke, she listened to Wycliff's *noble* adventures, wretchedly aware that she could not print one glorious word of it without ruining her disguise.

"I have survived shipwrecks and captained a purloined pirate ship around Cape Horn. I collected strange plants now prized by the King at Kew Gardens, and now planted all over England. I rescued a woman or two from an unfortunate marriage, sunk a French warship or two, negotiated the liberation of Burke's crew from a pack of cannibals, and I saved Harlan from a shark attack, or most of him, at least. I did spend a night in a harem and enjoyed myself considerably before liberating a kidnapped English maiden *before* she lost her innocence. And above all, I have represented my country with decency, diplomacy, and dignity, which is more than can be said for most of the Royal Navy."

Awe did not begin to describe what she felt . . . Neither did supremely vexing. Neither did adoration or mesmerized, though all these words and phrases crossed her mind. Her heart beat hard and her conscience rang bells of alarm.

The duke was an amazing adventurer. He was a reluctant duke, and an outrageous scandal, but this was a man who had really lived. She was acutely aware of her own little misadventures in this small, albeit bustling, corner of the world. She'd enjoyed more excitement than most women. But it did not compare to the duke's travels. What marvelous fun it would be to join him . . .

"There is an entire world out there, far beyond the skyline of London, and I have seen it and sailed it and learned it. I can't fathom how someone like Basil can live going from his home to his club to some party and not feel like he is wasting precious moments, precious years, of his life."

"At first I didn't quite understand why you were so reluctant to be home," she said. "To be a duke. But now I think I am beginning to."

"Have you not traveled?"

"Once, to Brighton." Damned, damned Brighton trip. If there was one thing she regretted— Other adventures might have happier endings, she thought.

"That's right," he remembered. "And it didn't give you a taste for adventure and travel?"

"It quite nearly ruined me," Eliza said, but the duke seemed to miss the flat note of her voice, thank goodness. It wasn't something she wished to explain. Or even think about it.

"Yes, that's the beauty of it. When you know how wide and blue and wonderful the rest of the world is, London seems like a dank dungeon in comparison. Staying here becomes impossible. Ruined. As if I could be content going from party to party . . ."

She could see how one might become bored with that . . . eventually. But when the duke prattled on about the chains of his charmed life, she did not feel so guilty about what she wrote. She boldly interrupted him.

"Some of us, Your Grace, would love the opportunity to become bored with fancy dresses and glorious parties and champagne and waltzes."

"I'm an ass," he said flatly, suddenly realizing that he was complaining about wealth and privilege to a housemaid. "Please accept my sincere apologies."

"Very well," she said, to be agreeable, and because her point had been made.

"I'd take you to a ball, but you wouldn't want to go with the likes of me," Wycliff told her, taking the broom from her and setting it against the wall.

"Instead . . . Eliza, would you care for a waltz?" he asked, sweeping into a grand bow before her. She gave a little laugh. Fancy that, a duke, requesting a dance with her, a mere housemaid as far as he knew.

"Now?" She laughed nervously again.

"Is there somewhere else you need to be?" Wycliff asked, obviously expecting the answer to be no. She was his servant, and expected to be at his beck and call every moment of the day. What other business could she possibly have, other than his?

She was immensely glad for the lessons from Sophie and Julianna, because this was an offer a girl was mad to refuse.

Wycliff pulled her against him, pressed his large, warm open palm into the small of her back and clasped her hand in his. He tilted his head down so they could see eye-to-eye. His brown eyes, dark, with a spark of mystery and mischief.

"Are you ready?" he asked with the velvety smooth voice of a practiced rogue.

Before she could say yes or no, he swept them into a waltz around the gallery floor. There was no music, but they didn't need it. *One, two, three. . .*

The duke waltzed her around a settee covered in a white sheet, and then around a table and set of chairs, also covered, and then she stopped paying attention to her surroundings. *One, two, three. . .*

His shirt was open at the neck. She looked at his exposed sun-browned skin and was struck by the urge to press her lips to it and taste him. She bit down on her lower lip instead.

And then she made the mistake of closing her eyes.

She felt his touch more intensely—the heat from his skin and the possessiveness of his grasp. She breathed in his scent—just plain soap and whiskey and something indescribably him that made her light-headed in a lovely way. She dared to imagine that she was not a housemaid, or the writer betraying him, but a woman he could love passionately.

When she opened her eyes, Eliza saw a hungry look in the duke's dark eyes. She felt it, from the sudden flight of butterflies in her belly to the ever quickening of her pulse.

She stood corrected: a waltz with Wycliff was an offer a girl was mad to accept because . . . she might do stupid things like think he wanted her. Or that she could have him.

They waltzed on, with no sound other than their footsteps and the thudding of her heart. She heard the duke's breath catch and then they stopped suddenly. She stumbled into his hard, tattooed chest, and his arm clasped her against him protectively.

"Your Grace," Saddler intoned. Eliza dared a glance at him and saw that his face dripped with disapproval. Weren't butlers supposed to maintain a stony, inscrutable expression at all times?

"An urgent missive has arrived for you, Your Grace. From Lady Shackley."

Chapter 19

A Visit from Mr. Monroe Burke

The library, late

Wycliff stood with his hands clasped behind his back, glaring out the window. Harlan sprawled in a chair, smoking a cheroot. A card game lay abandoned, for they had a caller. Wycliff had been winning.

"Mr. Burke," Saddler intoned before vanishing just as silently as he appeared. Wycliff thought of refusing to see him but he was too curious.

"Aren't you going to congratulate me?" Burke asked, sauntering in. He had called, uninvited. Presumably gloating was on the agenda.

"The thought did cross my mind that a gentleman would," Wycliff said, turning from the window to face his traitorous friend. "Then the newspapers reminded me that I was not a gentleman. So no, I don't think I will congratulate you."

"Oh, come now, Wycliff. Don't be a sore loser." Burke attempted a laugh that fell flat. Harlan exhaled a gray slip of smoke.

Wycliff stepped forward and said, bitterly, "I had thought you were a friend."

"You thought you were the only adventurer with his sights set on Timbuktu? With that offer of ten thousand pounds, everyone and their mother is angling to go."

"I hadn't realized it was in *your* sights. But then, it's not as if we had discussed *my* plans for my trip. Extensively. In detail. Over the course of months." They had done exactly that. From his seat, Harlan nodded in agreement.

The voyage from Tahiti to London was a long one, and the three of them had shared meals, drinks, card games, and smoked together under the brilliantly starry skies over the ocean. And they had talked. That Wycliff intended to be the first to arrive at Timbuktu and return had been a subject of many conversations. As had the details—the routes to take, the supplies required, languages, strategy, customs, tribes one would encounter. Burke had taken this knowledge and this dream.

The thief.

"Yes, we did talk about Timbuktu. On *my* ship," Burke added, leaning against the mantel and looking pointedly at the decanter of brandy that Wycliff purposely had not offered to his guest.

"Your point?" Wycliff challenged.

"I am the one with a ship. A crew. Experience," Burke said, and when Wycliff opened his mouth to protest, Burke kept going. "Experience *leading*. You skipped from here to there, frolicking and debauching, one thing to another with no determined course of action, and responsible for no one but yourself."

"You've been reading the papers, too," Wycliff said, strolling over to the sideboard to pour himself a drink. He did not offer any to Burke.

"I was there, Wycliff. I saw and heard more than I cared to."

"Funny how that detail—*you* up to your neck in debauchery with *me*—never makes it to print." Perhaps he could make it happen by bringing it to Knightly's attention. Now that was a letter to the editor he would like to write. He smiled bitterly at the thought.

"Yes, but who would believe it, to look at me?" Burke asked, looking every inch the perfect, polite gentleman who was on time for church, decorous to women, and never indulged in vices.

"You look like a stuffed-up prig," Harlan chimed in.

"Exactly," Burke beamed.

"Duplicitous. On so many counts," Wycliff remarked. He sipped his brandy and made a great show of savoring it. Burke scowled.

"You weren't going to be funded anyway, and for reasons that have nothing to do with me," Burke pointed out. To what purpose other than to rankle, Wycliff knew not.

"I don't find that remotely consoling. However, I hope it assuages your guilt. Which, needlessly to say, I hope is eating you alive."

"This conversation is proceeding exactly as I expected it would," Burke said calmly, but color was rising on his cheeks.

"It's the money, is it not? The lure of ten thousand pounds has you ready to throw your old friend under the carriage wheels. What do you even need the funds for? Is your father no longer paying your bills? Do you have secret gaming debts that your captain's salary won't cover? "

"I would like to marry." He said this quietly, in such a painfully honorable manner that it simply annoyed Wycliff more than anything.

"Ah, a noble quest to win a lady's hand," he remarked dryly. There was nothing worse than a deceitful friend, except one who deceived for a noble reason like love.

Burke shrugged. "That, and to be in a position to afford her."

"Who is she?" He had to ask. There was no way he could not ask.

"She is my reason for everything. My north star. My secret," Burke answered.

Wycliff rolled his eyes. For some reason, he thought of Eliza, and downed the rest of his drink.

"I see that you are in no mood to converse about this—" Burke said shortly.

"I am shocked you thought I would be," Wycliff stated dryly.

"My expedition will leave in a fortnight. I will need a crew," Burke said, with a pointed look at Harlan, and then his gaze settled on Wycliff.

"You've come to the wrong place, if that's what you're looking for," Wycliff told him.

"Then I'd better be on my way," Burke replied evenly. He took his leave, and Wycliff loudly wished him the *best* of luck as he quit the library.

"So the trip is off?" Harlan asked, still puffing away at his cheroot.

"No. I will find another way," Wycliff said, scowling. "There is always another way."

His glance fell on his desk. Particularly on a certain letter amidst all the maps, travel accounts, drawings, and account books. It was from Lady Shackley. The lovely, lively, and evil Lady Althea Shackley. Temptation called like a siren song.

"I hope you think of something, because all I can think of is resorting to highway robbery," Harlan said. It wasn't the worst idea ever. But Wycliff had a better one. The siren song tugged at his heart, his brain.

"Or marrying money," Wycliff said.

"I'm not really the marrying kind," Harlan said flatly.

"I could be. Especially if I shall be spending the honeymoon en route to Timbuktu. Sans bride."

"How are you going to go about getting a rich bride, given your reputation? If the old windbags at the Royal Society are gossiping about you, just imagine the chits in this town. Their jaws must be hurting," Harlan said with a naughty pause, "from all the talk."

Wycliff grinned. The letter from Althea was just there on his desk, requesting that he call upon her.

"Your concern for my reputation and marriageability makes you sound remarkably like Basil. But this title has to be good for something. Surely one could overlook my unsavory, scandalous aspects for the prospect of being a duchess."

"I think we need Basil's help. Where is he now, when we could use him?"

"Likely at his club losing vast sums of money at card games. But we needn't call him in just yet," Wycliff said. There was another option. A risky, dangerous possibility. One that had worked before. He held up the letter. "Shackley money?"

* * *

Never, in the history of the world, had a doorknob been so thoroughly polished. Never, since the flood, had a spot of earth been so meticulously dusted, cleaned, shined, and otherwise tended to. Eliza stood outside the library door, conveniently left ever so slightly ajar, cleaned and eavesdropped. Shamelessly.

It was almost too easy.

She saw an opportunity for her column to make amends. Or possibly avenge the duke. Or perhaps she might throw a wrench in his plans to marry Lady Shackley. *Why* did that affect her so strongly? It made her stomach positively knot up.

Her heart hurt for him, with all of these setbacks: first the Royal Society's rejection, and now Burke's usurpation. The staff gossiped during the late hours in which he wrote papers detailing the cultures and customs he had encountered, among other things—and all the late hours in which she was unable to sneak back into the library to illicitly read his journals. All the hours he spent cataloguing the strange items he'd brought back. The sunny afternoons when he stayed inside with his account books, determining what could be sold to raise money to cover the estate's debts—ones not even of his own making, but his cross to bear nevertheless. And the blasted hours he was locked away in that room . . . doing what?

Her efforts at lock picking had been unsuccessful. As much as the duke confided in her, he did not take her beyond that threshold. It was one of the thoughts that kept her up at night. She didn't dare sneak out again, not after that kiss that awakened all sorts of desires and feelings that did nothing but complicate matters.

Eliza knew, too, that he often escaped to the roof after hours to look for stars and breathe in the cool night air. It tortured her: should she go to him? Sometimes she did. Should she stay away? Absolutely—that way lay danger in so many ways.

Would he knock on her door? She hoped not, as often she, too, saw the far side of midnight. Her column didn't write itself, and "writing scandal-mongering newspaper columns" was never listed among her duties as housemaid.

But the truth was: she wanted him to knock on her bedchamber door. She wanted it with an intensity that was unbecoming in a lady. She feared it and craved it in the same breath. It came down to one thing, really.

She wanted to be near him, with him. So long as she could write her column, she could stay here. The minute her disguise was revealed, it was back out on to the streets of London, and the loss of the story that made her writing career.

It made sense to her in an odd, tortured way. Because she craved him, she had to betray him. And yet . . . perhaps she could use her column for his benefit instead. Burke and the Royal Society ought to brace themselves, she thought.

Especially if the duke was thinking long and hard about Shackley money. Particularly, marrying it. This affected Eliza in a most peculiar manner: her stomach literally ached at the prospect and she dared not examine why.

Later that evening, she feverishly composed another installment of "The Tattooed Duke." She wrote with half a mind to salvage his reputation. She wrote with jealously of Lady Althea gnawing at her heart.

She wrote, desperate to hang onto her position at *The Weekly* and desperate to stay in the duke's employ. She wrote as if she might somehow make him forgive her this betrayal and possibly love her. She wrote, eager to again experience that sweet triumph of success, and dizzy at the prospect of more. She wrote as if the words *scandal equals sales* were tattooed across her heart.

Chapter 20

Bittersweet Success

Offices of The London Weekly

"Ladies first," Knightly said as Eliza slipped into the last empty seat. Her heart was pounding, and not just because of the mad dash to arrive on time. She had seen a ghost, just outside the pub across the street. The long-lost Liam whom she had not seen since Brighton, all those years ago. What was he doing here after all this time?

"Ladies late," Grenville muttered. What an old crank. She would have said something, if she weren't gasping for breath. Instead she gave him the same disapproving look Saddler tended to dole out to the servants.

"Eliza, all of London is on tenterhooks for the latest installment of your column on the Tattooed Duke," Knightly began. "Myself included."

"It's true," Julianna cut in. "At all the parties, it's the only thing anyone talks about. It pains me that I cannot boast of my connection to you and *The Weekly*."

"But there are major issues facing the nation,"

Grenville cried. "Does not the aristocracy concern themselves with pertinent matters?"

"Not at parties, dear old Grenville," Julianna said sweetly. "It's where all the lords and ladies gossip about each other and prowl about for husbands, wives, and lovers. There is no speaking of anything serious. That's what Parliament is for."

"Apparently, our members of Parliament are whoring and roving around the world and tattooing themselves like heathens and savages. It's a disgrace," Grenville grumbled.

"It's sales," Knightly stated.

"Scandal equals sales," the entire staff recited obligingly. It was the governing principle of the paper, and it had made Knightly's fortune and served them all well.

"As you are all aware, *The Weekly* outperforms all the other London papers. But last week's edition . . ." Knightly paused, so obviously proud and at a loss for words. "We had a second printing by Monday. By Tuesday afternoon there wasn't a copy to be had. And today the presses are churning out more copies."

All eyes turned to Eliza. In her hands was the only copy of the third and next installment of "The Tattooed Duke."

Eliza handed over her copy. The room fell silent, save for the crackle of the pages as Knightly unfolded the installment. And then, he began to read aloud.

" 'It is a truth universally acknowledged that a man in want of a fortune must be in search of a wife. The new Duke of Wycliff has his eye on the marriage mart, in the quest for a rich spouse. One in particular, in fact. His debtors and creditors no doubt are of the same inclination.' "

"Oh, *Eliza*," Julianna murmured.

"Why 'oh Eliza'?" Annabelle asked. "All she wrote was that he is looking for a wife. That's not tremendously remarkable. Or is it?"

"While it is true that many peers are poor, and many a marriage is simply a transaction . . ." Julianna began, and the men in the room took this time to think other thoughts. But Knightly paid attention. ". . . one might be given to understand that a dowry is a factor in a contracted nuptial. But one does not just say it aloud."

"Or print it up for all of London to see," Sophie added.

"We do. *The Weekly* does." Knightly was firm.

"He will never find a bride, then," Julianna replied, just as certain. "The duke has almost nothing to recommend him."

"The title isn't enough?" Eliza asked hopefully. She had just assumed that somewhere there was a girl who would overlook anything to be a duchess. And while she did not intend to destroy his chances at marriage, she knew this column suffered from her petty jealously. And longing.

"It's his saving grace, no pun intended," Julianna replied. "That, and that he is not hideous. But he looks strange, and keeps odd company. We are given to understand that he has gone native." *The Weekly* expert on High Society continued with her deconstruction of Wycliff's dire social situation as the Writing Girls listened avidly. The rest of the staff idly paid attention. "His attire is not at all the fashion, and his appetites, shall we say, seem insatiable and unusual. How is any London belle to endure? Who would hand off their daughters—and their dowries—to a scandalous, possibly savage recluse?"

"His best hope was for a love match, when anything may be forgiven," Sophie explained.

"But who can fall in love with a known fortune hunter?" Annabelle concluded.

"So this shall ruin him?" Eliza asked, vainly hopeful the answer was no. She didn't want him to marry Lady Shackley, that was all, but she didn't want to ruin things more either. This column was supposed to help him!

"Well, what is the rest of it?" Julianna inquired.

"The bit about Lady Shackley," Eliza said, cringing. "And Monroe Burke's mission on behalf of the Royal Society. And how the duke wishes for funds to outfit an expedition to Timbuktu."

"Shall we make him respectable, Julianna?" Sophie asked. "We'll invite him to balls and waltz with the Tattooed Duke. Our husbands can take him to White's, where they can respectably drink, complain about Parliament and their wives, and generally not do anything scandalous."

"Your husband could do that," Julianna replied, and then in a far lower tone, "Mine is delightfully incapable of proper behavior."

"Does respectable sell?" Knightly asked. And that answered that.

Next to her, Eliza practiced her inscrutable expression, while inside she seethed with something . . . because her friends had wonderful, loving husbands and popular newspaper columns of their own, and lots of pretty dresses and the ability to just make someone respectable. She had tried, with this column, but apparently it would backfire. She was such a fool.

The meeting continued. Grenville led a passionate oration about parliamentary issues, probably to make them all suffer some intelligent conversation after the passionate, frivolous debate about the Duke of Wycliff's matrimonial prospects. The other writers reported on the latest accidents and offenses: a madman escaped from Bedlam terrorizing young ladies all over London, the theft of a diamond necklace from Lady Mowbry's home at Berkeley Square, a fire at a bake shop in High Holburn.

All the while, Eliza thought about leaving. She was *mostly* sure she had seen that devil from her past, Liam, lurking outside. Had it been her vivid imagination, coddled by a lifetime in the theater? Or could she trust her own senses? After all this time, she'd thought he would be dead. Or hoped he was, that ruthless, thieving bounder.

But there he was, loitering outside the pub. It must be a coincidence.

But his eyes had met hers. She had seen him. *Why?*

She knew she would have to find out later, for Knightly called her into his office for a private interview after the meeting. The last time she'd been here . . . she shuddered. Knightly had put the fear of God into her that day—or to be more precise, the fear of life without being a Writing Girl, life without the work she loved.

"Eliza," Knightly said briskly. "Sit."

She took a seat on one of the large upholstered chairs before his desk. They were of a proportion more suitable for a man, and thus made her feel unbelievably small and insignificant. It was probably unintentional, she thought, for Knightly likely hadn't decorated his office with the intention of doing business with women.

Then again, he was a man to employ every advantage.

"I want to discuss your column," he said.

She waited a beat for him to continue.

"I should let you know that I have decided to make 'The Tattooed Duke' a regular column. 'Miss Harlow's Marriage in High Life,' 'Fashionable Intelligence,' 'Dear Annabelle,' 'The Tattooed Duke.' All by Knightly's Writing Girls."

The news left her speechless. A wave of relief surged over her—she would not be fired! She would not lose her livelihood! And then her heart might have ceased to beat for a moment. In fact, her heart felt like it might explode with pride.

"You ought to have an increase in your wages as well," Knightly continued, and at that, Eliza beamed. She smiled so hard, so true, so wide, that her cheeks ached. She was back from the edge. She had written herself out of disaster and back into success. All it took was a good story—*Get the story, get the story*—and a good disguise. And the right subject.

At the thought of Wycliff, her smile faded slightly. Her success had come at the expense of his.

Still, she was so proud of herself. And relieved, frankly. And speechless.

Absolutely. Utterly. Speechless.

Knightly continued as if this were just another business transaction instead of the hopes and dreams of a young female writer coming true against all odds: "I'm not quite sure what to do about the byline, given your situation. Have you used your real name with the duke?"

"Yes." It was the only real thing about her and the duke . . . other than her desire for him.

"We'll think of something. Now that settles everything. Regular column, byline, raise. I feel unusually charitable today, but really, Eliza, you've earned it. This story has taken the town by storm."

"Thank you, Mr. Knightly."

Eliza stood to go, but instead strolled over to the large windows overlooking Fleet Street. He was still there—Liam, that ghost—looking like trouble. What was he doing there? Was it a coincidence, or had he come looking for her?

One thing was certain: she did not wish to know.

"Is something the matter?" Knightly asked.

"Would you escort me back to the duke's house?" The words tumbled out, and she felt absolutely ridiculous to give voice to them.

"Is the duke harming you?" Knightly's voice was hard, low, and she made note to always stay on his good side.

"No. He isn't. But I can't say why." One answer would bring up too many questions she was not prepared to answer.

Knightly stood and collected his hat and coat from a hook on the wall.

"Shall we be off, then?"

She nodded yes, and watched in amazement as Knightly removed a loaded pistol from his desk drawer. So much for pens and paper. But it made sense; newspaper editors often had to defend themselves from angry readers upset with their portrayal. Even Wycliff had come to see him, she had learned.

At Knightly's request, Mehitable Loud joined them, too. All six feet six inches of towering muscle and brawn that made up Mehitable. One was surely safe with him on her side.

The unlikely trio stepped out of *The London Weekly* offices at the last moments of dusk. And lo and behold, there he was—Liam, smoking and loitering in front of Garroway's. She felt something akin to relief that she hadn't imagined him. But it was exceedingly disconcerting to see him there. Still.

However, he took one look at her companions and vanished into the crowds.

She was glad that he saw her with Knightly and Mehitable, especially. Perhaps that might scare him off permanently.

Knightly flagged down a hired hack and they all clamored in for the ride to Wycliff House. They dropped her off one block away so that she might not be noticed in questionable—or identifiable—company.

All she had to do was slip into the house and hope her absence hadn't been noted.

Chapter 21

In Which Her Absence Had Been Noted

Wednesday evening

Eliza had gone missing for a few hours that afternoon. Wycliff was annoyed to discover he noticed her absence. He didn't believe she was sweeping the attic or busy with linens because, strangely, the house felt different—like the atmosphere had shifted, or the pressure dropped or the mood was more subdued.

Wycliff did not love the house, but he liked it even less without her in it.

Worst of all was the gossip that reached him from belowstairs: she had returned to his house accompanied by not one, but two men. He was curious—what business outside of his household could she possibly have? Something like jealousy gnawed at his gut and he didn't like it.

Mrs. Buxby, lovable old drunk that she was, hadn't paid the slightest attention to Eliza or the other maid, who was fornicating with the footman. But after over thirty years on the job, why should she? From what he could gather, save for Saddler, his entire household was one den of sin.

Typical of a Wycliff household.

Yet that did not explain where his maid, Eliza, had gone or with whom or why, or, most vexing of all, why he gave a damn.

Over dinner, Harlan needled and prodded as he was wont to do. Wycliff would have taken supper alone in his room, except it would have looked like he was avoiding something, which would only make matters worse.

"I heard one of the housemaids vanished for a few hours this afternoon," Harlan began as he tucked into the beef and potatoes.

"Gossiping with the servants again?" Wycliff asked, trying to sound like a bored aristocrat. His *something*—whatever it was—with Eliza could not be discovered by Harlan. But he still wanted to know all the gossip, especially if it concerned that lithe little maid with the jet black hair and ocean blue eyes that intruded on his thoughts and aroused his desire.

"Always," Harlan said with a grin. "I reckon she wouldn't have gotten caught, but for the other one inquired to Mrs. Buxby about her whereabouts and then it was discovered. It was an exciting afternoon belowstairs."

"You two are drinking us out of house and home," Wycliff grumbled.

"Can't be helped. Not with this weather. Not with Timbuktu nothing but a faraway dream," he said wistfully, and Wycliff rolled his eyes.

"Did she say where she had been?" Wycliff asked.

"Who?"

"Eliza."

"The missing maid? You know her name." Harlan's brows shot up high on his forehead. He sipped his wine and stared fixedly at Wycliff with his one good eye. It was damned unnerving.

"Naming is a simple technique for distinguishing one thing or person from another. It makes life immensely easier," Wycliff said loftily.

"I haven't been in England long but I do know that ducal sorts don't much bother learning the names of anyone, let alone their housemaids," Harlan countered.

"I'm unconventional. You can read all about it in the newspapers."

"Can't be bothered to read it. Not when the entire staff is discussing it."

"Are they?" Wycliff said, to encourage Harlan to say more. Of course the entire staff was discussing it. That's what they did: gossiped about the master of the house.

"Aye, when they're not reading *Pamela* or some other romantic rot about lordships ravishing their female staff. It's what they do every afternoon while sewing and mending. I suppose you are not unconventional after all," Harlan mused, and sipped his drink.

Wycliff sipped his wine. Suddenly this conversation bothered him. It was so very typical—a Wycliff duke, his maid. It was precisely the kind of behavior he was trying to avoid. He did not want to be typical. He wanted that cool self-possession and control from his mother's side to win over the wenching ways of his father.

And yet, his thoughts strayed to Eliza. His senses seemed finely attuned to all things her: he was primed to detect her voice, her laughter, evidence that she had swept through a room. More than once he thought of things he might request her to bring to him, only so he might see her.

Wycliff sipped his wine, thinking these troubling thoughts. Then he noticed Harlan, far too observant, looking like he'd been mind-reading.

"Harlan, do you remember that time you were bound and gagged by cannibals?" Wycliff asked.

"Indeed I do. And yes, before you ask, I also remember how you single-handedly saved my life with naught but a pocketknife and a palm frond."

"Kindly do keep that in the forefront of your mind. And Thomas," Wycliff said, turning to the footman attending their supper, "I know about you and Jenny, so I expect this evening's conversation to remain between us blokes."

Chapter 22

In Which a Housemaid Finds Herself in Trouble

The study at Wycliff House

You called for me, Your Grace?" Eliza asked meekly. She stood before his desk nervously smoothing out the aprons on her skirts. All he could think of was lifting those skirts, exploring, bringing her to unfathomable pleasure . . .

Focus, man, he commanded himself. Mrs. Buxby should have been reprimanding this errant housemaid, not he. But the housekeeper was deep in her teacups and wouldn't suitably impress the seriousness of the situation concerning Eliza. Mrs. Buxby also would not dig for information and then remember to relate it to him afterward.

And because he had been bewitched by the girl, Wycliff took every advantage to be in her company.

Eliza stood before him expectantly. He pushed his fingers through his hair and tried to recall his father for some guidance on how to act ducal, but he could only remember the occasion—he must have been only ten—when he burst into the study and found one of the housemaids giggling and perched on his father's knee. She then gained weight in her belly, and left to visit her family in Shropshire shortly thereafter. Many a maid had suffered the same condition.

Wycliff cleared his throat. He was born to act like a bloody lord and master, and many a man and woman had told him he knew perfectly well how to do so. If he wanted to lead an expedition he would have to deal with insubordination properly.

Starting with Eliza.

Whom he wanted to ravish.

On his desk.

"It has come to my attention that you took leave of your duties yesterday afternoon. Without permission." He summoned the voice he used with recalcitrant animals and potentially hostile tribes. The tone itself was effective at crossing language barriers.

She said nothing, as she was deeply fascinated by an invisible spot on the carpet. In her silence, he wondered: Was he asking as her lord and master who expected her at his beck and call at all hours? Or as a would-be lover or jealous rival for her affections?

"You do not deny it," he stated. Where the devil had she gone? And with whom? Why did the ignorance and curiosity burn in his gut? Had it been Jenny in her place—he couldn't have cared less. But Eliza . . .

"I am sincerely sorry, Your Grace," Eliza burst out. "My mother had taken ill and I had gone to visit her."

Bollocks, he thought. More hand-wringing. He'd wager an elephant that her mother was right as rain.

"I'm deeply sorry to hear that," he said consolingly, and all the more intrigued. Was she with a lover? Was she in trouble? He had to ask: "What ails your mother?"

"Consumption. It's very tragic." Eliza batted her long lashes. He nearly groaned. She was spinning falsehoods like a practiced stage actress—fine. But did she need to look so bloody adorable as she did?

"Will you need more time away to spend with her?" he asked. When she seemed surprised at the offer, he carried on, "I'm not an ogre, Eliza. I may be unconventional, but I am human and I do care for my fellow man. And woman," And then he smiled and went in for the kill. "That is why I was so glad to learn you had chaperones for your return journey."

Her head snapped up, eyes blazing. He smiled like a cat with a mouse. She, brazenly, smiled in return.

"Brothers?" he inquired politely.

"Cousins," she corrected. The audacity. Lying through her teeth, too. And then she had the nerve to smile again.

Funny, that. Because the gossip said that one of the men accompanying her had been unusually large. Wycliff's mind wandered to the giant guarding the door at *The London Weekly*. A coincidence? He did not believe in coincidences. But he also believed in evidence and proof, not gossip.

His heart began to pound, and this annoyed him.

Wycliff drummed his fingers on his desk and looked her over well and good. Silky jet black hair pulled back in a tight, spinsterish bun. Made him want to give a little tug and watch it tumble down.

She wore a plain gray dress with a white apron pinned to the front reminding him of her place in his world. A maid. Naught but a maid. *Or . . . ?*

Her hands, clasped sweetly in front of her, were telling. They were rough and red; they were the hands of a woman who worked. More telling they were *not* covered in ink stains. And she could not read or write. He'd seen her blush of mortification when he had asked her to. He still felt like an ass about that.

She smiled sweetly at him.

But she could be an informant for a *Weekly* writer? A few extra coins each week to supplement the meager wages he could afford to pay her . . . it was possible.

It would behoove him to tread delicately. Observe. Test.

"While I am greatly sympathetic to your consumptive mother, I do need to make an example of you for the other staff," he told her.

"Are you going to sack me?" she asked breathlessly, and it was nearly his undoing. Her eyes widened with terror, her skin paled, and the hand-wringing intensified. This anguish struck him as actually genuine.

The urge to consol her was great, as was the urge to take her in his arms and . . . Thank God the desk hid his lap from her view. It wouldn't do to let her know the power she held over him because of this illicit, constant attraction.

His Wycliff blood ran true. There was no denying it.

"No. However, there will be some form of punishment," he said smoothly, letting his voice drop a register, just to watch her eyes widen and her lips part. Did she think he was going to beat her? Or enact some deviant sexual act upon her unwilling person? Good Lord. He had something much less dangerous and more bizarre in mind.

"I will require assistance cataloguing some of the insect specimens from my travels. It is immensely tedious work. You will suffer through it, under my supervision."

He would get to be near her. Just to torture himself.

Feed her details he'd like made known to London, just in case she was an informant.

And perhaps he might emerge wiser. More tempted and tortured but wiser. And the insect catalogue would be finished faster.

"Yes, Your Grace," she all but whispered.

"We'll begin later this afternoon," he said, and by way of ending this torturous meeting, started shuffling the papers on his desk. She bobbed a little curtsey and sauntered out. Wycliff watched the sway of her hips and his breeches tightened in response.

When she was gone, he returned his attention to the papers spread out before him. In his shuffles he had unearthed a letter from Lady Althea that arrived days ago and that he had not yet responded to. The lure of Shackley money called like a siren song. She had asked for him to pay a call upon her; there was a personal matter to be discussed in person that could not be committed to print.

Chapter 23

In Which Cataloguing Insects Is a
Romantic Endeavor. Yes, Really.

Later that day

In truth, Wycliff could not wait another moment to
be *near* Eliza. Lately it seemed he lived only for the
moments that she was in his proximity. He yanked
hard on the bellpull. While he waited, his thoughts
strayed to another troubling female . . . Lady Althea.
And her letter. He couldn't decide if he would pay her
a visit or avoid her.

Eliza finally arrived.

"Insects," he said gruffly, because he was glad to
see her, more than was respectable. And Lady Althea
. . . Maddening females. He took one look at Eliza's
ocean blue eyes and pink mouth and was irritated all
over again. Just in a different way.

"Yes, Your Grace." She was meek because he had
to punish her, or make some ridiculous show of pretending to. He hoped she got over that deference
soon.

"What are you waiting for?" he asked. She was

just standing there, timidlike, as if waiting for him to ravish her. Or was he just suffering from wishful thinking?

"I am awaiting direction, Your Grace. I have never catalogued insects before. Usually, I just kill them." Spoken like a city girl, he thought.

"Well these are already dead. Please don't squash them. It would be a tremendous loss to science if you did."

"Yes, Your Grace." He scowled. There was nothing quite so irritating as an excessively agreeable female. Especially when he was in a mood for sparring.

"We'll need paper. And pens. And there are boxes labeled 'Insects' over there that need to be brought to the table. Do not drop them or you'll be sacked."

"You have made great improvements in your ducal demeanor," she said, finally showing some backbone.

"Are you saying that I'm being overbearing, tyrannical, and generally disagreeable?"

"Yes, Your Grace," she said, this time with a smirk.

"That's what I thought," he replied, and a smirk to match hers tugged at his mouth.

He watched as she crossed the room purposefully. And then she stopped. There were many boxes. Some were labeled *Insects* and some were not.

She hesitated. So did he.

There were two sides warring within him: end this awkward moment and tell her what was what, or wait and somehow prove that she was a spy for *The Weekly* because she guessed which box said *Insects*. He was ridiculous. She was a lovely chit, a tempting minx, and really, what grounds did he have to suspect this illiterate and beautiful woman of such treachery?

With a sigh, he said, "The ones on the top, to the left."

Then she began to move boxes and he collected paper and quills, and the moment had passed. But he felt bad to doubt her. It felt wrong to test her thus. She'd been a damn fine confidante, and he lusted after her tremendously. Yet a part of him suspected her of a massive betrayal.

The tyrannical, ducal demeanor would have to smooth over the rough moment.

"Start unpacking the boxes. It's full of glass jars. Kindly refrain from breaking them."

"I have experience sweeping broken glass, Your Grace." It was marvelous, really, how calmly she said things like that. But nevertheless he gave her a look of shock, simply *shock* that she dare refer to the brash introduction of the whiskey bottle and the wall.

If she were an informant . . . she'd be clinging to this position and not risking a firing by leaving for hours, unexplained, or speaking so freely with him. This logic satisfied him.

"And I can give you more experience, but not with these things that I've hauled halfway around the world." Wycliff towered over her to supervise the removal of glass jars from the box onto the tabletop, as if his proximity and generally overbearing demeanor would keep his treasures safe, when he knew perfectly well it was more likely to rattle her. She was steady. Quite steady. Admirable.

"Why did you haul them halfway around the world?" she asked.

"Contrary to popular belief, I was not whoring and slaughtering my way across nations. I like to observe the natural order and immerse myself in other cultures."

"Like the tattooing."

"It's the obvious, painful example, yes. The scandalous thing, really, is that I do not believe the English are the most superior beings to ever breathe air. Do not dare repeat that to anyone or they'll revoke my title and execute me for treason."

"Yes, Your Grace."

He wanted to bet the house that he would see those words in *The London Weekly* come Saturday's issue.

"And stop saying that. I told you to call me Sebastian when we were in private."

"Is that a family name?" she inquired.

"Of course. I was named after the previous duke, who was named after the previous duke, etcetera, etcetera. And yours?" he asked. From his travels, he learned what significance and meaning went into a name.

"My father named me after Eliza Hayward. She wrote novels and edited a newspaper. He's a playwright."

"Do you go to the theater, then?" It was pleasing, this working side by side, conversing freely. But it was so dangerous to learn her, to know her. Egad, next he would see her as a woman with hopes, and dreams, and *feelings*, and go right on and fall headlong in love with her.

Housemaid, he told himself. *Housemaid. Housemaid. Housemaid.*

Wycliff focused on the task at hand so he might keep himself under control. He would not ravish her here, now. They might damage the specimens that he had hauled halfway around the world.

"When I am able to, which isn't often," she answered. Her housemaidness hung awkwardly in the air between them. This was why one just romped with the servants and didn't try to engage them in conversation. But he *liked* talking to Eliza. It wasn't like Althea, which had him feeling like he was crossing fiery hot coals, and was a very good reason to ignore the summons she had sent. Or like other women, who were content with inane chatter about nothing in particular.

"The theater is one thing I did miss while abroad," he said. "Although, stories told around campfires out in the bush can be just as captivating." He missed those stories of local gods and goddesses, and mythical explanations for the natural phenomena or historical battles.

Eliza glanced up at him, smiling shyly, and it just did something to the region of his heart.

"All the jars are unpacked," she said. An array of insects and butterflies were spread before them, along with paper and quill.

"Can you write?" he asked, because still, he needed to test her. He needed to because he could, quite possibly, experience a prolonged state of intense attraction and emotional attachment for her. Some might call it love. But not he.

When Eliza hesitated yet again, he wanted to kick himself. She was a housemaid, for heaven's sake. Of course she could not read or write. Last time he checked, most daughters of the peerage could barely sign their names on their calling cards. And here he thought some lower class girl was a writer for a newspaper in 1825. It was ludicrous.

"My apologies. That is insensitive and idiotic of

me. Just hand them to me and describe them, and I'll write the name and some notes and then they all go back in the box for some exhibit I may or may not present to the world. If my reputation doesn't scare everyone off."

They worked in a pleasant, easy rhythm. Eliza would pick up a jar and describe the creature in it—blue wings with an iridescent sheen, shiny brown with hundreds of legs—and it made sense to him that she had been raised in the theater. She had a way with words. He wrote down everything.

Their hands kept touching as she handed the jars to him. Her hands were not those perfectly butter soft hands of a lady. Hell, his hands were rough, too. They worked, he and Eliza.

He was nagged by the urge to set her up so she didn't have to work, other than cataloguing insects with him. But that would make her his mistress . . .

And the problem with that was . . . what? He didn't have the funds, for one thing. And that reminded him, again, of Lady Althea's letter. The damned thing kept intruding. He would have to visit her and put this matter to rest.

"There, that is the last of them," Wycliff said, for they had finished up with this batch. The work had gone quickly and pleasantly with her company. "You were a good assistant," he told her.

"Thank you, Your Grace," Eliza replied cheekily. She glanced up at him with a sparkle in her eyes, like sunlight on a calm sea. His heart tightened hard in his chest. For a second he couldn't breathe.

"What did I tell you about that . . . ?" he asked in a pretend growl that broke into a grin and then devolved into a kiss. He caught her off guard. She was still smiling when his lips touched hers. For one scorching second she returned his passion in spades. For one brilliant moment in time all was deeply and unshakably right.

And then, glory to the gods, one second turned into another. The kiss deepened. Her tongue tangled with his, in a devastating combination of innocence and pure passion. Wycliff cradled her cheeks in his palms; they were warm to the touch.

She ran her fingers through his hair. His heart began to thud, hard and heavy like a tribal drum. He kissed her more, savoring her sweet taste. If his life had depended upon it, he couldn't have stopped.

He wanted to explore her, to know more of her. Slowly he slid his hands lower, to her breasts. Eliza gasped and arched her back. Minx. His groin tightened and he closed the last little distance between them.

"Sebastian," she whispered.

"Mmm . . ." It was imperative that he feel the warm, bare skin of her breasts. He wanted to take her in his mouth and lavish attention on her breasts until she was gasping with pleasure. The duke did just that.

"Sebastian," she said in breathless whisper. His mouth closed down upon hers. He was aware, dimly, that she was trying to tell him something. But talking meant not kissing, and in the moment not kissing was akin to death. And then she slid her arms under his shirt, pressing her small palms against the naked skin of his chest.

If that small touch gave him so much pleasure, he would likely explode were they to be utterly nude, together. In that instant he wished for that intimacy with her more than he'd ever wanted anything. More than Timbuktu.

He broke the kiss, shocked by that thought, unbidden.

Her mouth was gorgeously swollen from his kisses. Her eyes were dark in an immensely seductive way. Her attire was a bit askew.

More than Timbuktu . . .

Chapter 24

In the Den of the Lioness

Drawing room at Lady Shackley's residence

I wasn't sure that you would come, Wycliff," Althea purred as she swept into the drawing room where he waited for her. He wasn't sure that he would either. And yet one devastating kiss and shocking, unbidden thought had driven him here. Wanting something—someone—more than Timbuktu, his lifelong dream, was utter madness. The more he thought about it, the more he confirmed that yes, his heart beat for this adventure.

He pictured Burke leading an army across the wide-open African plains. It burned.

He imagined himself discovering the city under a hot and fast African sunset. He could not give that up for a woman. For a housemaid.

Thus, he called upon Lady Althea. She had written, requesting he come, for there was some matter that could not be committed to print. He was curious, of course. And then there was the siren's lure of Shackley money.

Wycliff was shown to the drawing room, and

avoided the settee where she might slink up against him and work her wiles upon his person. He wasn't in the mood to rebuff her advances, or to discover he did so out of some misguided notion of loyalty to his housemaid. Instead, he sat in some dainty, rickety, spindly leg chair and prayed it wouldn't collapse.

He was surprised to find himself there, too, because until the other day he was content to take that slap and leave it at that. But Burke and the Royal Society changed his mind. He had shockingly thought he might earn his way through his own merits.

Lady Althea ought to thank them, truly.

"And here you are. Here we are together, again. Mmmm." Althea tapped one dainty finger against her rouged lips. There was nothing worse than kissing a woman with a painted mouth. He declined to mention this. They would not be kissing. But at one point in time . . .

Wycliff smiled politely at her. So much had changed since they were lovers. He had changed. He'd gone from being a wild and reckless rake to . . . a wild and reckless but *wiser* adventuring duke. The self-control and brains he'd inherited from his mother were asserting themselves on his Wicked Wycliff self.

"How long has it been?" she purred, lasciviously eyeing him from her perch on the settee opposite. He was glad to be risking the chair, rather than her.

"Just about a week or so," he said, being deliberately obtuse and referring to the ball where she had slapped him, and not their violent parting ten years ago. He added: "Sufficient time has passed for your temper to have cooled enough to offer me an apology."

She bristled openly. That was the problem with

them: he could not resist provoking her, and she had a temper like a keg of gunpowder.

Perhaps nothing had changed at all.

"You deserved it and you know it," she retorted.

"Aye. You are right," he said, because it was true and because judging by her dress, jewels, and home, she seemed exceedingly wealthy and he was in the market for a rich wife. He ought to have sat next to her on the settee. There were worse ways to earn an expedition.

"You did. But my manners were deplorable," she said, which was likely the closest thing to an apology he'd get. In a softer, more reasonable tone, she continued: "But to see you again after all these years brought back such strong memories, especially about the way you left . . . I was angry, Sebastian."

He'd taken one thousand pounds from her husband to leave the country. He deserved the slap. Especially since he did not regret his actions.

"I am sorry to hear about Lord Shackley," he said consolingly. The old codger had done him a favor he could never begin to repay. That one thousand pounds set him up for the life-changing voyage and the fresh perspective on the world he had needed—and that his own father could have never supplied. Not the wisdom, or the cash.

"You are not, neither am I, and we both know it," Althea replied sharply, revealing that her understanding of life, or anything, really, was as shallow as ever.

"Tell me how you really feel, Althea. I've come all this way." He risked leaning back in the little chair.

"I myself have also returned to London after an

extended stay . . . elsewhere. The Outer Hebrides, in fact." She had practically draped herself across the settee. Her long, birdlike arms stretched along the back, her back arched and bosoms thrust forward. It looked deuced uncomfortable—but tremendously flattering, he had to admit.

She wore a necklace with a small, gold, heart-shaped locket that nestled perfectly between her breasts. He looked, of course, and looked away.

"That must have been a peaceful holiday for you," he said politely. The Outer Hebrides had to be one of the duller places on earth.

"Oh, it wasn't a holiday, Wycliff," she said, laughing bitterly. "Shackley sent me away, just after we were caught. While you've been cavorting all over the world on an expedition my late husband funded, I've been serving penance."

His jaw fell open. He quickly shut it. A worse punishment for a social butterfly like Lady Althea he could not imagine. She fed off of the energy of soirees, of social intrigues, and off the lust of men.

In South America, one had to be wary of blood-sucking bats. In England, there was Althea.

"In the *Outer Hebrides*," she repeated for emphasis. Or had she gone a touch mad? Solitude could do that to some people.

"You must be thrilled to have returned to the social whirl."

"With one yearly visit from Shackley," Lady Althea said, and she punctuated it with a delicate shudder. The sleeve of her dress slipped off her shoulder.

"What would you like, Althea? An apology?" He was suddenly irritable. He wanted to be back at

Wycliff House, of all places, so he could catalogue insects with his maid. The implications of this strange desire were not to be examined at present.

"To start, yes, I would like an apology."

"I'm sorry things did not work out as you'd have liked them to, Althea, but that whole damned mess between you, me, and Shackley was the best thing that ever happened to me."

"But I have waited for you all this time, Sebastian. Does that not mean anything to you?" Her lips formed a pout. Her eyes glistened. She fingered the locket she wore around her neck. It was a cheap trinket, at odds with the rest of her. It seemed familiar . . .

"What did you wish to tell me, Althea? What is the grave matter that could not be committed to print?"

"The Outer Hebrides, Sebastian," she said again, and he sighed impatiently. But his heart started to pound. The air crackled with danger, with warning. His skin tingled hot, then cold.

"We have established that, Lady Althea, and I'm assured your banishment was no secret."

She treated him to a scowl. *Dolt,* her look seemed to say.

Viper. His look betrayed his thoughts of her.

"Why do you think Shackley sent me there?" she asked.

"To punish you for loud, blatant adultery in the marital bed," he said flatly. It had been a magnificent afternoon. All her wild, evil passion was unbearable out of bed, but in bed . . . he had the memory. He felt no desire to relive it. But it had been glorious.

"Yes, Wycliff. But there was *something else.*" Her lips curved into the kind of smile that foretold doom.

She told him what that *something else* was. His heart

stopped beating. He had sought her out in search of an expedition, when this news she delivered all but assured him he wouldn't leave England for quite some time.

He thought of Eliza, too, and how it all was a tangled knot he could not possibly unravel. His Wycliff blood rang true, and fate had snared him despite his best efforts to avoid it.

Chapter 25

Sensational Novels

The housekeeper's parlor

"**P**lease keep reading, Eliza. It makes this sewing less tedious," Jenny said, heaving a sigh and looking at the endless yards of white fabric gathered on her waist and spilling to the floor. All of it required hemming and sewing to turn it into bedsheets for the household.

Eliza was more than happy to read, rather than sew. She despised sewing.

"The reading and the tea livens things up," Mrs. Buxby said, happily taking a break from her sewing and sipping her special afternoon blend. Jenny and Eliza shared a smile. They too indulged, but not to the same degree as the seasoned housekeeper. Who could blame her after all her decades in service?

"The tea certainly makes things . . ." Jenny held up a sheet with a row of crooked stitches. "Well, I'm not quite sure what the word is."

"'Tis perfectly straight, my dears," Mrs. Buxby said, squinting at the sheet in question. Eliza and

Jenny shared appalled glances. "But do carry on with the reading," she said with a wave of her hand.

Eliza was reading from a tattered old copy of *Pamela; Or, Virtue Rewarded*. It told the story of a maid who was relentlessly pursued by the lord of the manor. Virtue prevails, and he marries her. It was one of those novels that had been devoured voraciously by ladies for decades, in part for the love story, and likely in part for its more titillating aspects.

The parallels to her present situation were not lost upon Eliza.

She found her page and began to read in a calm voice, hoping not to betray her own tortured feelings:

"'He has a noble estate; and yet I believe he loves my good maiden, though his servant, better than all the ladies in the land; and he tried to overcome it, because he knows you are so much his inferior; and 'tis my opinion he finds he can't . . .'"

Jenny sighed. She, Lord help her, did as well.

"Skip ahead to the part where he ravishes her," Mrs. Buxby urged. "It's much more exciting than this romantic nonsense."

"Very well," Eliza said, turning only a page ahead. When she skimmed the words, heat suffused her cheeks. A fortifying sip of whiskey-tea was most certainly in order. She continued reading.

"'I screamed and ran to the bed and Mrs. Jervis screamed, too, and he said, "I'll do you no harm, if you forbear this noise, but otherwise take what follows." Instantly he came to the bed; for I had crept into it—'"

Jenny paused in her sewing and looked up with a frown. "If his lordship is about to ravish her against her wishes, why does she run to the bed?" she asked.

"That seems like the worst possible place, if one is so very concerned about her virtue."

"It is remarkably stupid. But the housekeeper is there to protect her," Eliza pointed out.

"Aye, but later in the book the housekeeper is a wicked procuress," Mrs. Buxby said, calmly sipping her tea.

Jenny and Eliza paled.

"Oh, lords above, ladies," Mrs. Buxby said, exasperated. " I'm no evil Mrs. Jewkes. I've been with this family a long time and if anything I've spent countless hours protecting my girls *from* those Wycliff rogues. Now what happens after they're in bed? I've read this before but I can't recall, although if I suppose if virtue is rewarded, nothing much occurs." The housekeeper's disappointment was clear.

Eliza took a deep breath and slowly exhaled before continuing to read about the late night ravishment of virtuous Pamela by the nefarious rake, Lord B.

" 'I found his hand in my bosom, and when my fright let me know it, I was ready to die; and I sighed, and screamed, and fainted away. And still he had his arms about my neck. I knew nothing more of the matter, one fit following another, till about three hours after, as it proved to be . . .' "

Good Lord, she thought, pausing to sip her tea. *Three hours?* Looking up from the pages, she happened to see that Harlan was leaning in the doorway, with a patch over his right eye, one arm in a sling and the other holding a book.

"Shocking behavior, ladies," he said. "Whiskey. Tales of debauchery. This is absolutely the place to be."

"Have you come with more respectable and morally improving literature?" Eliza asked.

"If you did, you can do us all a courtesy and not make us suffer through it," Mrs. Buxby ordered.

"Fear not. I overheard you reading *Pamela* and was inspired to bring, instead, *Shamela*."

"What is that?" Jenny asked.

"It's the parody of *Pamela*, written by Henry Fielding. Any relation?"

"None that I am aware of," Eliza answered.

"I thought writing might be a family pursuit," Harlan said pointedly. Thanking the Lord that she was born to an actress and raised in the theater, Eliza merely sipped her tea and asked, cool as you please, "Whatever leads you to that conclusion?"

But her heart was pounding.

"Wycliff enlightened me about your family. Your father, I believe, is a playwright." Harlan's one eye was trained intensely upon her.

Her heart was now booming like one of the tribal drums Wycliff had shown her.

She forced a smile and replied, "He is. A very fine one, too."

Harlan shifted his weight and stepped further into the room. The interrogation continued. Or was it polite conversation? It felt like an interrogation.

"And your mother is an actress. It seems your family has a talent for theatrics."

The insinuation was bold and unflattering on so many levels.

"They do," Eliza said, adding pertly, "And I have a knack for dusting."

"While that is all rather fascinating," Mrs. Buxby cut in, "I should like to hear from this *Shamela* book."

"I shall oblige you, happily, as thanks for this exceptional tea you provide every afternoon," Harlan said, with a wink at the housekeeper, who harrumphed in return. Then he began to read.

"'The young squire hath been here and as sure as a gun he hath taken a fancy to me . . .'"

All eyes shifted to settle upon Eliza. She merely shrugged and focused intently upon her stitching. But inside, her insides were all aflutter. They had noticed! That made it real, somehow. She wasn't prone to flights of fancy, but with matters of the heart, one could never be sure.

"'He took me by the hand and I pretended to be shy. Laud, says I, sir, I hope you don't intend to be rude; no, says he, my dear, and then he kissed me, till he took away my breath—and I pretended to be angry, and to get away, and then he kissed me again and breathed very short and looked very silly, and by ill-luck Mrs. Jervis came in and had like to have spoiled sport. How troublesome is such an interruption.'"

"How clever," Eliza remarked. "Shamela's virtue is a sham."

"Oh, that's a handy old trick," Mrs. Buxby said. "I like this version of the story much better."

"I as well," Jenny added. "Please do keep reading."

Eliza carried on with her sewing, burning up inside as she listened to Harlan read about Shamela's affair with the parson while feigning virtue and decency to claim the hand in marriage of the idiot Lord Booby, as he was called in this version.

Even with her focus intent upon the fabric, and tight, taut stitches in her hand, she stole glances at Harlan, reading with his one good eye and holding the book in his one good hand.

"'Young gentlemen are taught that to marry their chambermaids and to indulge in the passion of lust at the expense of reason and common sense is an act of religion, virtue, and honor, and indeed the surest road to happiness,'" he read in a gravelly voice, pausing to level a stare at her. "'All chambermaids are strictly enjoined to look out after their masters; they are taught to use little arts to that purpose. And lastly, are countenanced in impertinence to their superiors and in betraying the secrets of families.'"

The revelation struck her suddenly, clearly, undeniably: he knows.

Chapter 26

The Tattooed Duke Returns

It was not yet ten o'clock, the duke had only just sat down to his breakfast and Eliza had already broken one glass, one coffee cup, and dropped a plate of bacon. To say she was nervous was the understatement of the nineteenth century.

The London Weekly lay just to the left of Wycliff's plate, freshly pressed and ironed by Saddler himself, who muttered biblical verses while tending to "Satan's own news rag."

Within moments the duke would agree.

She set a plate down before him. He held her gaze for a moment before she looked away. Harlan sauntered in with his eye patch covering his left eye. Basil arrived, presumably uninvited but tolerated.

Eliza busied herself pouring tea and coffee, and at the ready to fetch brandy.

"Well let's do get on with it, shall we?" the duke said grandly as he snapped open the crisp pages of the paper. "This is the show you've all come for, right?"

"How bad could it be?" Harlan mused, sipping tea. The duke glared meanly at him and began to read.

" 'The Tattooed Duke by W.G. Meadows.' "

"Oh, we have a clue," Basil exclaimed. "A name!"

Eliza spilled the tea right over the edge of the teacup. But who cared? She had a byline! A column of her own! She had known about it—Knightly's word was good—but there was *nothing* like hearing it aloud. And from the duke's own voice, too. This was a long-awaited, hard-earned moment—for which she was surrounded by the people least likely to share her joy.

Did the glory matter, then, if there was no one to share it with?

Suddenly, she felt deflated.

"The author just made another grave mistake," Wycliff muttered, and carried on: " 'It is a truth universally acknowledged that a man in want of a fortune must be in search of a wife. The new duke of Wycliff has his eye on the marriage mart, in the quest for a rich spouse. One in particular. His debtors and creditors no doubt are of the same inclination.' "

"Bad," Harlan said. And to Eliza, he said, "We'll need Mrs. Buxby's special blend this morning."

"I thought you were *not* looking for a wife?" Basil inquired, blinking quickly.

"That was before my 'friend' stole my funding from the Royal Society," Wycliff stated dryly.

"Well, I suppose I could introduce you around . . ." Basil said. But his offer was not as enthusiastic as it had been a few weeks earlier, before all the gossip sheets spilled oceans of ink detailing the duke's every shocking secret.

"Keep reading," Harlan requested. "I want to know if it gets worse."

It does, Eliza wanted to tell him. But she bit her

tongue and hoped no one noticed that she hadn't gone to fetch Mrs. Buxby's special blend of tea.

" 'His debtors should be so lucky to see a farthing if some wealthy chit comes up to scratch to save His Grace. The adventurous duke has his sights set not on domesticity with his English bride, but the dangerous, heathen wilds of Africa, of claiming that mythical city: Timbuktu. In spite of the Royal Society's refusal to fund his expedition.' "

"Why would you go to Africa if you marry a wealthy chit? You could get a new curricle, a membership to White's, a box at Covent Garden," Basil said, showing how little he understood his cousin.

"That is one option," the duke said diplomatically. But Eliza knew it wasn't an option for him. Then he continued to read.

" 'The Royal Society already has its man for the journey: Monroe Burke is set to depart within a few weeks. But is he really the best man for the task?' "

The duke laughed. Eliza couldn't enjoy it, not when she knew what came next.

"Coffee?" she asked the duke in a hollow voice just above a whisper.

"Brandy," Wycliff said, holding her gaze for a hot second before she had to turn away. She did not deserve to look at him. Not when the worst was yet to come.

" 'Ten years previous, the duke first set sail with funds from the late Lord Shackley. Could Shackley money be the ticket again? After the infamous slap the lady bestowed upon His Grace, one might think not. And yet, she has been corresponding privately with this long-lost tattooed Duke. One wonders: is it for love, or for money? Is she aware of what would become of her fortune and her husband?' "

Eliza's stomach was in knots; it had been ever since she wrote that paragraph. It was the workings of a jealous would-be lover, an underhanded tactic against an unwitting competitor. She wanted the duke for herself, but she couldn't offer him anything. Lady Althea could. Unless . . .

It was selfish. And shameful. And too late to retract it.

"How can anyone love a madwoman like Lady Althea?" Harlan inquired.

"She's turned down numerous proposals since her husband died," Basil said. "So clearly some people find it possible."

"Don't speak of her like that," Wycliff growled, to raised eyebrows all around. Eliza swore her breath caught harshly in her throat. Worse, Harlan seemed to notice. With his one eye.

"You have been known to refer to her as 'Hades' Own Harpy,' " Harlan said carefully. They all watched as the duke slowly and methodically crumpled the newspaper into a tight ball of paper and ink and rage.

His features were tense. Just yesterday he had laughed with her and swept her into his arms for a kiss, Eliza recalled. And now he was grimly defending *Lady Shackley*. Hades' Own Harpy!

"And you have also referred to her as your narrow escape from the bloodsucking clutches of Satan," Harlan added. The duke stood and stalked around the table. His movements were tight, controlled, taut, like he would explode at any second.

"What happened?" Basil asked. Wycliff sneered in response. Harlan added a sincere "Aye mate" that was ignored.

The duke looked directly at *her*, brazenly treating her to a long, heated gaze from the far side of the room. Her heartbeat slowly faded, and the room dimmed and everything seemed to fade but the duke, Sebastian, and whatever was troubling him, and the way he looked at her with an intensity she could not understand. *Did he know?*

She couldn't breathe.

What happened with Lady Althea yesterday? She longed to ask. But it was the words *I'm so sorry* that burned like the fires of hell on her lips.

She dared not say a word.

"Just don't speak of her at all," the duke said flatly. He tossed the paper into the fire.

Wycliff didn't notice the way she flinched. But Harlan did, even with just one eye.

Chapter 27

Sunset Over London

Later that evening

The duke had gone up to the roof after breakfast, and at sunset, when he still had not returned, Eliza prepared a tray of food for him, with a bottle of wine. For a moment she wavered over placing two glasses on the tray, but she couldn't imagine she'd be welcome. One glass it was, to accompany his meal. And brandy. And a cigar.

She was very sorry for the things she had written. So sorry that she thought of confessing everything to the duke. But that mad thought drew a bitter laugh.

Did she want to give up her newfound raging success?

The paper hit the stands and the breakfast tables just after dawn that day. By noon Knightly sent her a letter that merely read, *Excellent, Eliza*. Annabelle would probably give her right hand, *her writing hand*, to gain such favor and attention from him. As far as Eliza knew, no one Writing Girl had received written praise from their single-minded employer.

By the time afternoon tea had come and gone, Julianna had also dared to send a note that simply read, *Talk of the town, darling.*

And this was all in addition to her hopes and dreams: a column of her own. A measure of security in her position. Were the byline and increased wages enough to compensate for the growing ache in her heart? Each column had become more difficult than the last to write, as she tried to please Knightly and the duke.

This was what she had always wanted. A column of her own—a sensational column of her own. She was no longer the Writing Girl in the shadows. Today, she was likely the most read and talked about writer in London.

And she could only enjoy it alone, which seemed to mean that she couldn't enjoy it at all.

There was no purpose in confessing to him, she thought bitterly. What did she have to gain by telling him? He would cast her out, surely, and she'd lose her livelihood *and* her heart.

She paused there, on the servants' stairs, precariously balancing the tray.

Her heart. She was falling for him.

And not because he was her ticket to all of her wishes and dreams.

Ridiculous. Perhaps she might admit to being intrigued by him. Attracted to him, even. But she wasn't in love with him. Love made one do utterly mad, reckless, idiotic things. This . . . she shook her head and everything on the tray rattled. Whatever this was, it wasn't love, and it could not be. It wasn't allowed.

Oh bother it all, she was falling head over heels for him.

"Your Grace," she called out to him. How to open the door with both hands full? *Oh blast.*

He didn't answer, and after several minutes of extreme awkwardness, she managed to fling the door open, trip on the final stair, and fall to her knees onto the roof. With some satisfaction, she noted that she still held the tray aloft. She was improving at this housemaid business.

The duke snapped to attention at the disruption, and a smile tugged at his lips when he saw her thus.

When she set eyes on him, she forgot about everything else.

He sat on the far side of the roof, bare forearms resting on his raised knees. His dark hair was pulled back from his face, and in the sunset light his sun-browned skin seemed warm and aglow. The sun was a fiery orange orb sinking low in the sky and lighting up London in a strange colorful light.

The duke's shirt was open, his bare, tattooed chest absorbing the last rays of the sun. Beside him, a *full* brandy bottle. Really, the man was magnificent.

"I thought you might want something to eat," she said, setting the tray beside him.

The words *I'm sorry, I have ruined everything* tingled upon her lips. She was sorry, but she was also proud. The duke was not the kind of man who wanted her pity, though. She sighed and pushed the matter out of her mind.

"You're a treasure, Eliza."

She bit her tongue, and turned to go. There was something immensely troubling on his mind, and she didn't want to know because then she would have to decide whether to detail it in her column. Or not. She would be forced to choose between her own success or his. Curses.

"Stay," he commanded. "Sit."

She smiled wryly because it was exactly what she wanted him to say. In her imagination, though, it didn't sound much like the commands one gave a puppy. She could tell, though, that he was too tightly coiled and troubled to have much of a care. So she told him: "You are improving at this duke business."

"Well, a man has to do what a man must do."

"You sound so weary." Because she wanted to, and because he said so, Eliza took a seat beside him and arranged her skirts and apron around her legs.

The duke pushed his fingers through his hair. A few strands fell around his face, and those were tucked behind his ear. The sun glinted hard on the gold earring. It wasn't big at all, quite discreet, really, and not worth all the fuss.

But she knew it wasn't the thing itself, but the proud show of a duke's past as a common sailor that had everyone in an uproar. Because the lot of them cared so much about stations and titles, and he—a duke—did not. It was impossible to reconcile, so they tried to make it go away.

She understood that her column fed the flames, but it didn't start the fire.

Then the duke said, "I feel I can confide in you, Eliza."

She imagined that if her beating heart were ripped from her chest while she watched, it would feel similar to what she experienced now.

"Was it the newspaper column this morning?" she ventured.

"As damning as it was, that's the least of my problems now," he replied cryptically.

"Oh." It sounded too much like a sigh of relief. She couldn't look at him. Instead, her gaze fell on his forearms. He always wore his sleeves rolled up to his elbows; tonight was no exception. He really had marvelous arms—all muscled and strong and sunkissed, and wickedly tattooed, and she ached to have them hold her again.

But that was not allowed.

"I'd still like to find the writer, W. G. Meddling."

"W.G. Meadows," she corrected softly.

"I would still like to find that malicious, Grub Street hack and string him up by his—"

Eliza lifted one brow coolly, reminding him that even if she were not a lady, she'd still appreciate the same courtesy.

"String him up and hack him to bits," Wycliff said. "I think I'd use my machete, which I won in a wrestling match from a dwarf in Zanzibar."

Eliza smiled wanly.

"But no, as I said, that's the least of my problems. It certainly complicates everything, though," he said, easily uncorking the bottle of wine she'd brought. "You didn't bring two glasses?" he questioned as poured a glass and handed it to her.

"I am a housemaid, Your Grace, and could never presume to share your wine," she said, even as she accepted the proffered glass. It was not every day that dukes drank and conversed with their maids, all alone up on the roof with the sun setting and the moon rising. How could she possibly refuse?

"I'd like to be sharing something else. Your bed." he said softly, and heat suffused her cheeks. She could feel his desire, but to hear it aloud was another thing entirely. And the thing was: she felt the same. Wildly, wantonly, up all night, distracted all day—she felt the same. She wanted him in her bed like she wanted a column of her own in *The London Weekly*.

But it could never be. Never.

"My bed is a tiny, narrow cot in the attic," she replied, being deliberately obtuse. "Sharing it would be deuced uncomfortable."

"Very well, we'll share mine. It's one thing I did miss while abroad. After a certain age, sleeping on the ground begins to lose its appeal and one wishes for a large feather mattress."

The duke drank from the bottle and entwined his fingers with hers. She thought of his taut, muscled, tattooed body hot and hard against hers in his massive feather bed, and she felt things in places she'd never really felt before.

"Lady Shackley—" he began. And then stopped. "No, I don't want to think about it anymore."

Eliza turned to him, her face just inches from his. "Then do not think of it, Wycliff."

And then his mouth closed upon hers.

We shouldn't, she thought. But nagging thoughts were nothing compared to the exquisite sensation of being claimed by Wycliff. He cradled the nape of her neck with his hand, slid his fingers into her hair which she was dimly aware of tumbling down around her shoulders.

I want to. That's what her heart said. Her every nerve, which was on high alert. Every inch awaited his touch. Eliza gave into this kiss without a fight. Her mouth loved his in return. She kissed him because she wanted to, because she couldn't resist, because she was falling for him, and because . . .

While she was desperately curious about whatever Lady Shackley had done to trouble him so, she did *not* want him to tell her. Knowledge was dangerous, and he made the mistake of trusting her.

If his mouth was otherwise occupied, he could not tell her and she could not betray him.

It was the lesser of two evils.

And she wanted to kiss the duke. Wycliff. Sebastian. She *needed* to, like she needed air to breathe.

So she kissed for all those reasons, even though she knew she shouldn't. Those really good reasons to restrain herself rudely intruded on this kiss, but she had become remarkably adept at ignoring them. So she did.

Her heart thudded in her chest—like a warning of danger. This was the way to trouble. And yet kissing the duke felt so unbelievably good, and right, and a million other lovely things jumbled together all adding up to *pleasure*. He tasted like wine, like wanting. It wrenched at her heart, that wanting, because she didn't think anyone had ever wanted her so much that she could taste it.

Tears stung at her eyes, shut tight. Eliza slipped her fingers through the locks of his hair, urging him closer to her so he could not see how this kiss affected her.

Sebastian cradled her face in his strong hands and urged her to open to him. His tongue tangled and sparred with hers for a deliciously wanton kiss. That desire she tasted? She felt it, too, now.

Liar, her conscience whispered at her. She was deceiving him with her every breath, except for this kiss. Her passion was real, her desire true. In another world, veils of deception wouldn't hang between them.

And then there was that business about her heart beating hard, sending waves of warmth coursing through her. She might be falling for him.

She was definitely falling for him.

He tugged her into his lap, straddling him. Her skirts hitched up around her waist and the duke took full advantage.

Wicked Wycliffs, indeed. She laughed gently into his kiss, and felt his grin against her lips. That was intimacy. That was a beautiful thing. That was a moment that would always be theirs alone.

The sunset was now little more than a simmering glow, swiftly fading to darkness. The night air was cool on her heated, bare skin. His shirt, already open, came off. Once again she was able to indulge in his exotic tattoos.

All of London knew about his tattoos, but she was the only one to touch them, to know them so intimately. It was a gift she would keep locked up close and treasure forever. She traced her fingertips over the inky lines and the ridges of his chest. His skin was smooth, and hot to the touch. A wicked smile played on her lips.

Pent-up desire was a dangerous thing, Wycliff thought vaguely, and Eliza's touch just unlocked the gate. He could not get enough, and greedy man that he was, he grasped at her hair, tugging gently. She moaned softly.

He needed her close, closer. He really wanted to bury himself deep inside of her. For the moment, he forced himself to be content with learning the contours of her body: the dip in her lower back, the curve of her bottom, which he'd been ogling for weeks now. Her full breasts fit so perfectly in his hands, it seemed criminal to let go.

He'd been ages without a woman, thanks to that long sea voyage, and he realized now he hadn't spent much time in the brothels since returning to London. He hadn't given much thought to any woman at all, other than Eliza. This stunned him, made his breath hitch.

It had been a lifetime since he was with a woman like her, his mysterious confidante with the soulful, wicked kiss. He had the feeling that he couldn't get enough. Like he'd been held underwater too long and had to have air or die. Like he had to have Eliza, in every earthly sensual way, or he would die.

Time passed. Night had fallen. And he wasn't aware of it happening, but it did: he was lying on his back on the roof, looking up at Eliza straddled above him and the moon and few paltry stars behind her.

His cock was hard, throbbing with wanting, and Eliza, tempting minx, moved slowly against him. He groaned.

"I do believe I was saying something about a feather bed . . ." he said. He could see it now—could feel it now—Eliza, a feather mattress, and himself.

"My bed is closer," she murmured wickedly. And then she drew back. "My goodness, that was unbelievably forward of me."

Her dark hair fell loosely around her shoulders. Her lips were red from his kiss—that's how a woman's mouth should look, he thought, not like Althea's painted lips. That thought jolted him back . . .

"Eliza, you may have noticed I'm not exactly a stickler for propriety," he replied with a faint grin.

"I may have heard a rumor to that effect," she answered cheekily.

"But I have to marry Lady Shackley."

Chapter 28

Why the Duke Must Marry Hades' Own Harpy

Still on the roof

There, he said it. At the worst possible moment, too. In fact, the *last* possible moment before he totally and completely lived up to his Wicked Wycliff heritage and ravished the maid on the roof, for God's sake.

He had now given voice to that awful thing that had been nagging him all night and all day. If he thought he was reluctant to assume the responsibilities of his title, well, now he knew a dig-in-the-heels, lean-back-with-every-inch-of-force-he-could-harness kind of reluctance. Because it wasn't a duke's duty that was calling for him now. He ought to do what a man ought to do.

He might be tattooed, and all kinds of scandalous, but he was a good man. He knew what mattered, what was right.

Sailors told stories of waves one hundred feet high that simply swallowed ships whole. How anyone lived to tell after witnessing such a feat was never answered, but Wycliff had known of ships that just vanished. That was how he felt upon hearing Althea's news that could not be committed to paper.

"Is it for the money?" Eliza asked.

"It's not about the money, although that will be a great consolation," he said. The only consolation.

"Oh," she said softly.

"I have referred to Althea as Hades' Own Harpy and a hundred other awful things that are all true," he said, referring to the breakfast conversation that he knew she had listened to avidly. "But one cannot say such things about the mother of their child."

If Eliza felt anything upon that revelation, she did not show it. Well, other than the way her hand wavered as she took a sip of wine. He took some satisfaction in that. He didn't want to be the only one walloped by the news. And he wanted some indication that she cared for him—although what the devil he could do with her affection, he knew not.

As she coolly and calmly absorbed the news and drank her wine, he relived the moment in Lady Althea's drawing room when the earth shook everything off balance, the heavens opened up to rain down curses, and life as he'd known it came to a grinding, screeching halt.

Lady Althea had smiled so warmly with her fiery red mouth.

"A baby, Wycliff. Your baby." He couldn't breathe.

"Where is it?" he asked. He looked around stupidly, as if it might be tucked in a corner somewhere. But by now it wouldn't be a baby, but a small brat of ten years.

"*He*. He is away at boarding school," she said, smoothing out invisible wrinkles in her silk skirts.

"Send for him at once," he had said in the clipped

tones of an angry duke. He wanted to see this child that was supposedly his. Not that he could do anything about it, for it would have the Shackley name.

His child. Another man's name. How many Wycliff spawn were alive and kicking in England? Many more than the Digby family Bible recorded.

A child that was his but not his. Such a typical Wycliff thing to do, but had it burned and rankled the other dukes thus? He had scowled so violently even Althea was taken aback

"I cannot send for him now," she said, recovering. "It's in the middle of the school term and the headmaster is quite strict."

"Then I'll go to him," Wycliff answered testily. He'd never bothered with the rules of headmasters before. Now wasn't the time to start. "Apparently, I have a son, Althea. That means something."

A son. The dukedom was this inanimate thing. A son—that was his own flesh and blood.

"You cannot go to him, you'll embarrass him before his friends," she said pleadingly, placing a hand on his arm. By God if that didn't wallop him like a cannonball in the gut. He didn't give a damn what other small-minded peers thought of his eccentricities, but he'd always sworn he would not mortify his children as his father had done to him.

He knew in that moment that he was not afraid of being the Duke of Wycliff, but being like every other duke who had preceded him: all the wastrels that embarrassed their children and squandered their lives and fortune. Unlike the others, he had learned a thing or two about the world, and a thing or two about duty, and a thing or two about himself.

"I'll write to the headmaster at once, and have

him sent back to London," Althea said. She rubbed that gold, heart-shaped locket between her fingers. Opening it, closing it. He remembered now, why it was familiar. Once upon a time he had given it to her, complete with a lock of his hair. A silly thing, he thought, but she had asked him for it and it seemed easy enough to comply . . .

Althea still kept it. Althea still cared. Althea had been waiting. For him.

Yet he had taken the money from her husband, boarded a ship, and never looked back. He thought he had escaped. Apparently, he had not.

"Send word when the child arrives," Wycliff said, his tone sharp.

"Fine," Althea replied, pouting.

He showed himself out.

What the devil had happened? *A child?* He would have to marry her now. Yet, he felt a duty to do it. Responsibility. Mainly, though, he felt pity for the child. How could he leave a child to be raised by the likes of her? A pack of wolves would provide more maternal, affectionate care.

Why did his insides revolt at the notion of marriage? She had the money he needed. He could marry her and promptly leave on an expedition. And then another and another . . .

He should be relieved. Tremendously. But why did his chest feel so tight, like he couldn't breathe, and sore, and like he'd been trampled by a team of oxen?

The entire situation was troubling and he did not know how to make sense of it. Hence, the brooding.

"A child?" Eliza echoed, and he was brought back from that damned scene, back to the present, where he was on the roof with a very disheveled maid perched upon his lap. One who he'd quite nearly ravished. She slowly untangled herself and her skirts.

"Don't go," he said. Commanded.

"I'm merely removing myself from your person," she replied.

"Don't go." He said it again, employing the Ducal Voice so she wouldn't know how he desperately wanted her company, especially tonight.

"You didn't have to tell me," she said, and she seemed almost annoyed that he had done so. As if she wanted a tumble with no strings, nothing serious, attached.

"I know. And yet I feel that I owe it to you," he said, and she glanced away.

"Your Grace, I am only a housemaid. I wouldn't be the first or the last to dally with my lord and master. I wouldn't be so foolish as to think it means anything."

"You needn't be cruel," he said. He didn't know what it could mean, or what it might be. But he knew with utmost certainty that it wasn't just some tumble.

"I am merely being practical," Eliza told him, pushing back a lock of her hair.

"I'm not." He reached out and grabbed her wrist. "I couldn't make love to you without telling you. I feel something for you, Eliza."

"You really shouldn't," she whispered, devastatingly.

"Too damned late for that," he murmured, and lowered his mouth to hers. As if that last hour hadn't happened, Eliza turned away.

Chapter 29

Inconvenient Truths

Wednesday

Days passed in which Wycliff existed in an extended state of tension. Althea. Eliza. Duty. Pleasure. England. The world. The wild, wicked recklessness of his Wycliff blood, or the cool, self-control of his mother's family.

He'd spent days poring over maps of Timbuktu, as if to remind himself why he would not indulge in an affair with his maid, and why he must marry Lady Althea. Money for his expedition, for one thing. His duty to the child, for another.

A child. He couldn't fathom it.

Frankly, he couldn't keep his thoughts concentrated on any subject, unless the subject happened to be Eliza's eyes, or her breasts, or her mouth, or what she might look like naked, how she might feel writhing in pleasure beneath him, the softness of her hair, the delicate sizzle when she gave him a wicked look, and the explosion when their lips touched.

Damn. His breeches were tight again.

No woman had ever preoccupied him so relent-lessly and incessantly.

The good news: he had taken to reading the ac-count book in order to cool his heated blood and restore himself to rights. Riveting stuff, that was. It read like a tale of lovesick idiocy. There were pur-chases of jewels and rents for rooms in fashionable (read: bloody expensive) neighborhoods, followed by a cease in the rent payment and the purchase of mas-sive quantities of wine, brandy, and snuff.

So that's where the Wycliff fortune had gone. It was some gaudy bobble around the neck of a whore. Or it was literally pissed and snorted away.

Any shame he might have felt about using ducal funds for an expedition to Timbuktu just evaporated. There were stupider, more useless things to fritter money away on than enriching experiences, scientific expeditions, or bold conquests for his country.

"Knock, knock, Your Graceship," Harlan said as he strolled into the study, uninvited.

"I'm busy with account books," Wycliff told him.

Harlan snorted and tossed a newspaper on the desk before sauntering off to pour a brandy for himself.

"Really, Harlan, more damned newspapers?"

"This town is awash in them. They all seem to be fixated upon Your Graceness, too. Oddly, I don't find you nearly as interesting as they."

"I don't find myself that interesting either," Wycliff muttered.

If only Eliza did . . .

Dear God, he was becoming besotted. He had kept his wits about him while in a sinking rowboat travel-ing through crocodile-infested waters in an African river. But now he couldn't manage a conversation on any subject without thinking of his housemaid.

Housemaid. Housemaid. Housemaid . . . whom he wished to ravish. *Damn.*

"You were saying, Harlan?"

"I was saying, read the sodding gossip column and then tell me what's really happening."

With an annoyed frown, Wycliff read the sodding gossip column, entitled "The Man About Town."

> *All of London is humming over reports that the Tattooed Duke was seen calling upon Lady Shackley for an extended, private visit. Might they be discussing a new venture? Perhaps it is one in which Shackley money once again funds the wild wanderings of a Wycliff, as the mysterious W.G. Meadows reminds us. Or do they have a joint venture in the works, otherwise known as marriage?*
>
> *Our best hope for the truth lies in W.G. Meadows, that unknown author of "The Tattooed Duke" in The Times's rival newspaper that shall go unmentioned. But who knows who W.G. Meadows is? Lords and ladies alike are frothing at the bit to discover his or her true identity. The supremely wealthy Earl of Alvanley has offered the enormous sum of ten thousand pounds to the person who uncovers the true identity of W.G. Meadows. Dissolute rakes, debutantes with lamentable dowries, the poorly, the greedy, and dare we say the Tattooed Duke himself ought to leap at the opportunity.*
>
> *My sympathies lie with W.G. Meadows, but this Man About Town is on the hunt.*

"Oh for the love—" Wycliff muttered. Each day,

the storm and drama surrounding him became more ridiculous.

"God, anything holy, etcetera, etcetera. You have assumed epic proportions," Harlan said dryly, but then his voice turned earnest. "But what is the truth, and what are you going to do?"

"I might marry Lady Shackley," Wycliff said, strangling the urge to spit after saying such a horrible sentence. "Probably."

"If you marry Hades' Own Harpy, then you'll have no need to ferret out W.G. Meadows."

"And if it weren't for the child, I could ferret out W.G. Meadows and wouldn't need to pledge my troth to Lady Shackley."

"What are you going to do, Wycliff? What of Timbuktu?" Harlan asked plainly. He began to pace, always the sign that he was agitated. Wycliff settled in and wished for a brandy. His one-armed friend had only poured one—for himself. "You have ties here, Wycliff. I do not. Do you know what that means? I am free to go anytime."

The truth of the matter hit Wycliff in the gut, hard. Harlan had every reason to go, and no reason to stay. There was a flare of jealousy, and then a question: why did he stay? Or was this the part where the old comrades in action and adventure parted ways?

He caught himself grinding his jaw and forced himself to stop.

Harlan carried on: "You want to *lead* an expedition. You need to find the money for that and solve all the problems. I just want to go along for the ride, Wycliff. I merely need to enlist in another outfit . . . like Burke's."

The truth of that landed on Wycliff like another

blow, too. Had he not the noble and selfish goal of being a leader of men, he could just tag along with anyone else. Perhaps, after all, he was more ducal than he previously thought.

But what did that have to do with this betrayal? It felt like a betrayal. Reason intruded, told him Harlan had just as much a right to that feeling. For years, Wycliff had been content to see where fate, luck, and opportunity took them. They had no plans, no destination.

That wasn't enough for him anymore. For Harlan, it still was.

When had this gulf between them developed? Had it been there on the open seas, or crept up while he was obsessing over the housemaid and cursing his ill luck?

And for God's sake, where was a drink when a man needed one? He stood, crossed the room and poured one for himself, and Harlan continued pacing and spewing gut-wrenching truths.

"Yes, yes. I know that you have saved my life. But I have also saved yours, Wycliff, so it's really a wash. Do you understand what I am saying?"

"You are leaving," Wycliff said coolly. But his skin was hot. This was a sea change, the shifting sands, etc., and he had not prepared for it. He had not even seen it coming. What a blind idiot he'd been.

"You have ties here," Harlan said, standing still by the mantel. His one eye was a dark brown, almost black. "I do not."

"This damned dukedom, I know . . ."

"You left it once before and haven't exactly been thrilled to assume the responsibilities, though I see you have taken to perusing the account books,"

Harlan said, with a jerk of his head toward the open book on the ducal desk. "And whatever it is you do behind that locked door for hours on end."

Then Harlan's voice lowered and his gaze intensified, and Wycliff almost couldn't stand it. "You are developing ties, Wycliff, the kind that cannot be disentwined or broken. The kind that make a man stay on dry land and give up on reckless pursuits."

"Frankly, the only way I could tolerate marriage or ties to Althea is if I am engaged in reckless pursuit on an ocean far, far away."

"Not Althea, you scurvy cork brain. *Eliza*."

Chapter 30

In Which Our Heroine Experiences Utterly Devastating Public Mortification

Offices of The London Weekly

The meeting began as it always did, with Eliza dashing in at the last possible moment. It had been difficult to escape her chores and quit the household before being caught last week. Today it was well nigh impossible. She had actually shimmied out of the window in the music room, where she ought to have been dusting and sweeping. That was after spending an hour unsuccessfully attempting to break into that locked chamber.

Knightly strolled in, dark-haired, and blue-eyed, and utterly remote. To her left, Annabelle sighed. On her right, Julianna smartly mouthed the words along with Knightly as he said, "Ladies first."

It was like any other meeting, until it wasn't.

"There is a bounty on your head, Eliza," Knightly said, bemused, as if not sure to take the threat seriously or to take it as an indication of spectacular success.

"Ten thousand pounds," Julianna whispered. "From Lord Alvanley."

"Can he afford that?" Eliza asked. It was an unthinkable sum to her.

"He once wagered three thousand pounds on which raindrop would trickle to the bottom of the bow window in White's," Julianna explained to the appalled gathering.

"Eliza, you could have ten thousand pounds!" Annabelle exclaimed.

"If she turns herself in," Knightly said flatly. "Which she would not do if she wishes to remain a writer at this newspaper."

And then Eliza understood: she was suddenly worth ten thousand pounds. A shiver of excitement raced up and down her spine.

If the earl's word and finances were good, and if she never wished to darken the door of *The London Weekly* again.

Ten thousand pounds would make her an heiress.

The duke was looking for a rich wife.

Ten thousand pounds! If she had it, Wycliff wouldn't need to marry Lady Shackley and off to Timbuktu he would go. Although there was the matter of the child, which would not be so easily resolved. And as for herself . . .

It wasn't as if he would take her with him. One did not take women to Timbuktu, and dukes did not marry their housemaids. They especially did not do so when the female in question was authoring a scandalous, traitorous newspaper column. Even if her intentions were pure and her heart was true.

Ten thousand pounds could change *everything*.

Or she could find herself penniless, unemployed, and loveless.

"How many printings were there last week?" she

asked. The gentlemen turned their heads to face her, instead of scribbling on scraps of paper as they usually did when the Writing Girls took their turn in the meeting.

"Four printings, twenty thousand copies sold," Knightly answered, his blue eyes narrowing as he understood her point. A typical good week was ten to twelve thousand.

The question now was not, *What was she worth to the Lord Alvanley?* but, *What was she worth to Derek Knightly?*

"Let's see what you have for us this week," Knightly said. She handed over the latest, in which she tried to salvage the duke's reputation.

> *Two houses, both alike in indignity. The debaucherous past of the Wicked Wycliffs is well known. The scandalous past of Lady Shackley has been detailed in the gossip pages. Something is brewing between them.*
>
> *Yet the duke is not a man to be constrained, not when there is a wide world of adventures awaiting him. He has sunk French ships, battled and outwitted cannibals, survived shipwrecks. As he traveled, he did more than slaughter and whore his way across continents—he kept detailed records and collected specimens of various flora, fauna, and (shudder) insects, all for the advancement of Science. The duke would not just claim a territory like Timbuktu, he would know it and return all of its secrets to England.*

"Interesting . . ." Knightly said when he stopped reading, which meant that it wasn't.

Grenville was more direct: "Where's the bits about the weapons on the women?"

"You're painting him as a hero," Julianna stated, and Eliza saw her friend's green catlike eyes brighten with understanding. If the duke elected to use his intellect and was not obtuse, he would see that Eliza had given him away. She used his own words, told stories of him.

Why?

So he would not have to marry Lady Althea. So Timbuktu could be his for the taking. Eliza thought redeeming his reputation—or attempting to do so—was the least she could do.

Knightly said flatly: "It needs more . . . salacious and scandalous details that make ladies blush and gentlemen jealous. Less noble hero, more rogue. This is not up to *The London Weekly* standards. You'll have to rewrite this."

And then he dismissively held the page out to her. Didn't even look at her. It was a moment of excruciating silence before Eliza managed to reach out and take the offending sheet.

She saw Grenville watching the exchange smugly; he did not like working with women, and this proved his point that they should not write. Alistair stared intently at the hem on his sleeve. The Writing Girls were mute, though Annabelle made an effort to clasp Eliza's hand. But she could not accept it, not now when the eyes of her fellow writers were pityingly fixed upon her.

It was wretched enough that they should watch this shaming. It was cruel of Knightly to put her in this position! Eliza knew her cheeks were scorching, and her heart was thundering in her ears. She wished it would stop. Entirely.

Every other writer for *The London Weekly* watched this unprecedented failure. Knightly's outstretched hand, the pathetic sheet of paper, Eliza rigid with horror.

He might not have always published her work, but he had never rejected it so publicly before. Implied, but unspoken: if she was worth ten thousand pounds, she had better spin tales of pure gold. She had just handed in rubbish.

"Yes, Mr. Knightly," she said, and her voice cracked. She took the page and found herself rooted to her spot.

"Oh, and Eliza," Knightly said. "You have a column to rewrite. The presses will not wait. I suggest you go."

Chapter 31

In Which Something Bad Happens

Eliza might have stayed in the writers' room. In hindsight that's what she ought to have done. But how was she to write under the cold eye of Knightly, or with her peers watching her, knowing her first attempt had failed? How was she to betray the duke, as her fellow writers looked over her shoulder?

No one had ever been rejected in that manner and dismissed from a meeting. How mortifying and horrifying that it should happen to her!

That's how it now felt to her: a matter of betrayal. When had her heart become a part of the story?

Get the story. *Get the story.*

She'd never felt much sympathy for her subjects before. Did she still want this story, or did she want the duke?

What the devil was she to write?

Her thoughts turned inward, attempting to rationalize the matters of her heart. She stuffed the page into her bodice and set out. Nodding goodbye to Mehitable, she stepped blithely into the street. A long walk back to Berkeley Square might clear her mind, and give her an idea of what the latest installment of "The Tattooed Duke" might comprise that would please Knightly, impress the duke, and ease her conscience.

It was a beautiful day. Eliza gave no thought to who might be following her, watching her, copying her every last step. She proceeded along Fleet Street, past the banks, printers, and pubs.

There was always the matter of Wycliff's child with Althea. She could write about that; it was the sort of thing that would explode like fireworks. But then the duke would know for certain—or would he? Lady Althea could have told anyone. Eliza nibbled her lower lip thoughtfully. Knightly or the duke? Which man was she to please?

At a corner, she paused while a team of chargers with a shiny black carriage thundered past. Pedestrians thronged around her, street vendors hollered. She crossed the street, stepping around horses, carriages, children, dodging carts, and other impediments.

She ought to reveal the existence of the child. But then she thought of the poor thing, growing up with everyone knowing what scandalous parentage he had. School would be awful; the ballrooms even worse. And then there was the matter of—

A crowd surrounded her, the usual loud, hot mass of humanity all jostling on their way from here to there. In the midst of the mob, a hand clamped down on her wrist. Eliza yanked free and proceeded briskly. Her heart began to pound. She dared not lose speed and look behind her.

Again she felt whoever it was grasping her skirts, her wrist, her trailing bonnet ribbons. Her heart thundering in her chest, she picked up speed. That

damned knife she brought for a moment like this
was neatly tucked away in her boot, where she might
never reach it in time.

It had to be Liam—had to be—even after all this
time . . . She'd seen him here last week, by some
stroke of ill fortune. They had business to attend to.
She tried to run instead.

In the ducal residence

Wycliff was aware of the damned issue of *The
London Weekly* or *Times* or *Chronicle* or whatever the
hell it was called, which just sat there on the ducal
desk for a torturous hour in which he attempted to
carry on with his accounting. He was perpetually
distracted by the newspaper. If it wasn't one, it was
another. Newspaper, that is. Damned gossip. The
worst of it was, those columnists weren't wrong. That
begged the question of how they—whoever they
were—obtained the information. The private, personal details of his life.

Wycliff closed the account book and set it aside.
How did they know?

It meant those around him—in his house, or who
had been on the ship with him—had been talking.
But to whom?

He leaned back in his chair, kicked his boots up
on the desk and rubbed his jaw pensively. Outside,
the sun was shining, the birds were singing, and the
temperature was actually in the realm of pleasant. He
ought to go out. Do something.

He rang the bell, and when Saddler appeared but

a moment later, Wycliff refused to voice the question on his mind. Where is Eliza?

Good Lord, he was besotted.

Or as Harlan said, tied up and tangled and entwined and destined for dry land. The thought gave him pause, but he shoved it aside and requested horses to be brought around. Then he hollered for Harlan.

"We're going to *The London Weekly* offices," Wycliff explained. "I'd like to do more investigating."

"That sounds more interesting than sitting around the house listening to the maids read *Pamela*," Harlan said by way of agreement.

If these gossips could find out so much about him, could he not discover their identities? He had explored volcanoes, become fluent in tribal languages, wrestled with a wild boar. He could figure out who the hell that damned Man About Town was, or, even better: the real identity of W.G. Meadows. And then, he thought with a proud, eager grin, he would make him—or her?—pay.

On Fleet Street

Eliza sprinted through the crowds as best she could. Shouts and hollers followed in her wake. Clutching her skirts in one hand, her bonnet in the other, she peeked over her shoulder.

"Curses!"

How had Liam known to find her at *The Weekly*—twice?

She bumped into an orange seller, and the bright

fruits went flying into the air and onto the street. *Oh blast.*

Liam paused to pick one up, the thief. Eliza took advantage of the moment to step off into a narrow alley near St. Bride's church and remove the knife from her boot.

It was broad daylight on the street, but this narrow alleyway was dark thanks to buildings that towered over it, blocking the sunlight. She hoped the darkness would work to her advantage, not her detriment.

There was a slick sheen of sweat on her chest and the back of her neck. Stuffed into her bodice was the rejected version of "The Tattooed Duke" by W.G. Meadows. That mere sheet, upon her person, was damning evidence indeed—and worth ten thousand pounds.

Eliza held her breath, hoping to see Liam pass by oblivious to her, tucked in the alley as she was. She held the knife, hidden in the folds of her skirt, just in case he saw her.

He did, craning his neck to peek into every nook and shadow. What did he want from her after all these years?

She held her breath. When he saw her, she tried to let it out but it just caught in her throat. Like smoke from a fire, hot and burning and making it impossible to breathe.

Liam sauntered toward her, and Eliza gave up thoughts of running. She would brazen out this meeting. It had been years since she'd seen him last. Years since he said he was going 'round to the pub and never returned—having taken her every last penny with him. She had assumed Liam either died or was up to no good. Either way, she had decided to forget about him.

And yet here he was.

Liam wore a roughed-up version of a gentleman's attire. The boots were caked in dirt and God only knew what. The breeches were not new, to put it politely. His shirt was wrinkled, his jacket well-worn. His sandy hair was a touch longer, and he was no longer clean-shaven. In spite of all this, he still managed a certain charm, a certain swagger. Eliza knew better now. The man was dangerous, and she'd do well to overlook that rakish grin and that glint in his blue eyes.

Instead she tightened her hold on the knife as best she could, given the sweatiness of her palms.

"Eliza," he murmured. "Fancy meeting you here. It's been a while."

"What do you want, Liam?"

"Perhaps after our chance encounter last week, I thought we might renew our acquaintance." Liam placed his palm on the wall behind her, effectively boxing her in.

"So that was you outside of the pub," Eliza muttered. She had hoped it was a hallucination.

"After a lucrative visit to Sutton's and Robertson's, I stopped to enjoy a pint," Liam said, referring to the pawnbroker a few doors down from *The London Weekly* offices. "And I so happened to see you dashing into the offices. But I waited, just to be sure. Not every day you see a chit at a place of business like that. Just happened to follow you back to the duke's house," he added. Eliza's heart sank with every word. This was not good.

"What a coincidence," she said flatly. What blasted bad luck.

"Didn't think anything of it," Liam carried on, "Until some gossip I learned. About you. And ten thousand pounds."

Leave it to her to be followed by the only madman who followed the news and could read.

Eliza tightened her hold on the knife, or tried to. Her palms were sweating.

"You've already gotten a pretty penny off me. What do you want from me now, Liam?"

He reached into his pocket for something.

"Eliza," he drawled, and smiled in a way that made her stomach lurch. "Would ya kindly tell me if this rag smells like chloroform?"

The sign declaring THE LONDON WEEKLY in capital letters decked in gold and carved into a massive piece of wood was visually demanding. Wycliff could see it from a block away.

But it was a scuffle with an orange seller just to his right that caught his attention. The cart had been disrupted. Oranges rolled all over the street. The seller hollered, gesticulating wildly. Kind pedestrians assisted her, although most stormed along. One, in particular.

One young woman darted away determinedly as she held her skirts in one hand and her bonnet in the other.

Wycliff glanced at Harlan, who nodded in agreement. Wordlessly, they urged their horses to a trot and deftly maneuvered them through the traffic in pursuit.

A more high-strung horse shied at the oranges in its path, causing sudden stops, awkward turns, and more shouts, further complicating his quest to follow that girl.

He saw the girl, whoever she was, slip off the main road into a little alley near St. Bride's church.

"Stupid chit," he muttered. A man forged through the crowd, looking this way and that, as if after the girl who had been rushing along. He was large, rough, and everything about him suggested nefariousness. It was all too clear to Wycliff from where he sat, high above them on his stallion, that the one was after the other.

He guided his mount closer and left the reins with a newspaper-hawking youth. Harlan did the same, with just a little less grace, given his one arm in the sling he had worn when leaving the house. Wycliff flipped the brat a coin and went off to be heroic.

Eliza did not hesitate. She swiftly raised her knee to Liam's groin and connected solidly. Her triumph was short-lived, as he doubled over and fell onto her. She thought about stabbing him, and then about explaining the blood on her dress to Mrs. Buxby and Jenny and Wycliff.

So, instead she kicked out again and elbowed where she could, finally letting out the scream that had been caught in her throat.

She'd hardly gotten it out before Liam managed to clamp the chloroform rag over her mouth, tugging her down with him. As she fell, Eliza's head cracked against the brick wall behind her. She knew she hit hard because she immediately started hallucinating. Before the blackness closed in entirely, a vision of Wycliff flashed before her eyes.

* * *

Eliza.

His heart stopped.

Eliza. Here. Hurt.

Wycliff roared. And then he attacked. He grabbed hold of the disgusting, thieving, rotting cretin and hurled him with the force of a deceived, enraged lover and a righteous man to the other side of the alley, a mere ten feet away. The man slammed into the brick wall with a crack and a thump before slumping to the ground in a thick, distorted, tangled mass of limbs.

A dirty red rag fell from his unfurled fingers. Wycliff could smell the sickeningly sweet stench of chloroform.

"I got that one. Go to her," Harlan said, appearing at his side, and Wycliff didn't need to be told twice. This was how they had worked, he and Harlan: it didn't take a lot of words for them to communicate. It was how they had managed to get around the globe relatively unscathed. One watched out for the other and they worked together.

And Harlan was quitting! An hour ago it was the worst thing Wycliff could have imagined. That was before Eliza lay at his feet, unconscious.

In the region of his heart, he experienced a tightening so intense he lost his breath. His heart beat hard after that, pounding out a truth he could not acknowledge in the moment; not with words, at any rate. But he knew then . . . oh, he knew. She was no mere housemaid. Not to him.

Slowly, he bent down, gently feeling for a pulse in her limp wrist. It was there, faintly. Her breaths were shallow. She had struggled, but still suffered a dose of the chloroform. There was nothing to do but take her back to Wycliff House and let her sleep it off. And pray.

Chloroform could be fatal. He fervently hoped this was not the case.

"What do you want to do with this one?" Harlan asked from across the alley.

"Kill him."

"Really? Because I've got some questions I'd like to ask him," Harlan said coolly. "Namely, what business he has with our little housemaid."

"All right, take him back, then. It's probably time you lost that sling, since you'll need both arms for a beast like that one. I'll have my arms full with her."

"Pity. I was enjoying the ruse. The maids were so much more obliging because of it," Harlan remarked. Then he removed the sling, used it to bind the wrists of their captive, and proceeded to haul him out to the street. He paused.

"Your Graceness, it's going to be a trick getting these two back on our horses. Don't think there's any way to be discreet about it."

Wycliff swore. The last thing he needed was to be spotted removing an unconscious female from a dark alley. His one-eyed friend Harlan hauling the bruised and bloodied body of a street thug wouldn't appear much better.

"We could wait until nightfall," Harlan suggested. "Employ the cover of darkness . . ."

"Harlan, it is a good five hours before it grows dark. I for one am not about to sit around in this squalid alley with that stinking creature. And Eliza needs to be taken home immediately."

"Eliza." Harlan lifted his brow, curious.

"What's your point?"

"Ties." And that was all he needed to say to explain everything.

"Speaking of ties, your captive is waking up and undoing his."

"Bloody hell," Harlan swore, and turned to bind the man tighter.

Resolutely, Wycliff strode to the mouth of the alley, flashed some coin and obtained help—no questions asked—and hired a hack to transport his quarry back to Wycliff House.

When he clasped Eliza, drawing her into his arms, a knife fell from her hand. It was one he recognized, because it was one of his. Time stopped for a moment, as he put two and two together. Housemaids did not carry knives upon their person just because. Eliza had a reason. And he didn't know what it was.

Why did that *hurt*?

There was no way around it: people stopped and stared to watch the Tattooed Duke in the flesh carry out an unknown limp female body from a dark alley. Murmurs erupted in the crowd, though no one moved to stop him. When Harlan followed, urging a now conscious but resistant man, bound and gagged, the din of the crowd grew louder.

It was the sound of everyone assuming the worst.

Of stories being blown out of proportion.

Of rumors starting and accumulating impossible details at such a dizzying pace that within an hour strangers would be saying the Tattooed Duke had murdered a man with his bare hands, in cold blood, in the bright light of day while the man pleaded for his life and the duke laughed wickedly.

Wycliff kept his head high. He dared them, with a

look, to keep at bay. They could talk—fine. But they must not get in the way of his returning Eliza to safety, so he could care for her.

Holding her in his arms, he climbed into the carriage. His heart beat hard with not one, but two truths.

She kept secrets from him.

And he was falling in love with her.

Chapter 32

Discovery

Upon their return, Wycliff barked orders to the staff: tie up this cretin and lock him in the basement, draw a bath, brew tea, prepare his bedchamber for her, and above all move faster, dammit. In the back of his mind he could imagine Eliza pertly commenting that he was perfectly demonstrating how to act like a powerful, commanding aristocrat.

But it wasn't an act: He was the lord of the manor and his lady had been injured.

Wycliff carried her up the stairs to his bedchamber, straight to his bed.

Eliza. In his bed. This wasn't how it was supposed to be.

He lay her down gently, atop the blankets.

Why had she taken one of his knives?

Clearly, she had anticipated the attack. She wasn't a brazen thief, excited by the thrill of pilfering from others. She would have taken one of the nicer ones, then. No, Eliza must have been in trouble and she hadn't confided in him. He frowned, because that bothered him tremendously.

He had confided in her, and she had not even alluded to problems of her own. But had he ever asked? No, because he'd been trying to see her only as a servant—not a woman with a history and thoughts and feelings. And now he'd failed at that by going and falling for her, yet he did not know anything about her, really.

Next, her plain gray woolen dress was carefully peeled off. Jenny helped while the footmen brought up hot water for the bath.

"What should I do with this, Your Grace?" Jenny asked, holding up the dress. It was dirty and bad things had happened to it. Off to the fire it ought to go, he told her, and he would buy her new gowns. Pretty ones. He'd find the money.

Her muslin underthings were plain, white, pristine.

For days, for weeks, Wycliff had fantasized about seeing her in a state of undress. For all their kisses, he'd only caught a glimpse here or there. He hadn't seen her uncovered and unadorned. He had imagined it, at length and in great detail. But not like this.

Frankly, he didn't even want to go further. When he saw her pure and naked for the first time, he wanted it to be in the throes of passion, and part of a grand seduction. Not like this.

Wycliff traced his finger along the edge of her bodice, wishing this moment were different, with her awake, eyes bright with passion, lips parted slightly awaiting his kiss.

His finger caught on something tucked into her bodice.

She moved, slightly, and her lips moved, too, though she was still in a slumber.

In that little wriggle Wycliff heard the unmistakable sound of a sheet of paper trapped in the bodice.

He learned that from bedrooms and boudoirs from London to Zanzibar.

"I never said I was a gentleman," he told her.

Eliza did not respond because she was unconscious. The lady did not protest when he extricated a folded page from her corset. Then he unfolded it and began to read.

The Tattooed Duke

In the wilder days of his youth, Wycliff had climbed a gnarly old oak tree with branches that conveniently brushed against a certain lady's bedchamber on the second floor. He'd slipped, thanks to the wine that suggested this was a good idea. When his body hit the ground, it knocked his breath out and his world went black. He felt like that now.

He couldn't breathe for a minute as the full force of these damning words hit him.

Eliza lay before him, blue eyes closed, lips parted, skin too pale. She wasn't talking. She didn't need to.

The Tattooed Duke by W.G. Meadows

Eliza Fielding = Writing Girl Meadows. Fielding, like meadows. How obvious.

It made perfect sense. What a thick-headed idiot he'd been not to suspect.

No, he had suspected. The thought had crossed his mind once or twice and he'd ignored it, simply because he wished it wasn't true. The things he had told her . . .

Everything.

Everything.

For a minute he ceased to breath. It seemed his heart ceased to beat. For all he knew, the earth ceased to spin and the sun quit shining. This was betrayal.

All those hours on the roof when he had confided in her—when he told her things he'd never said aloud before, could never imagine voicing to another person. He had trusted her with his hopes and plans she had gone and written for Londoners to feast upon.

He had thought her naught but a housemaid, when she was, in fact, one of those damned Writing Girls.

Wycliff felt the hot flush of a fool, and then the scorching fire of anger.

She had lied to him, to his face. She lied, and then she kissed him. He recalled the time they had categorized insects together and he thought she couldn't write. And the time on the roof when he noted her way with words and Eliza only smiled. She must think him a fool. And to think, he'd been on the verge of falling in love with her.

Wycliff laughed bitterly from where he sat at her bedside, then Wycliff continued to read.

Two households, both alike in indignity?

He scowled.

The debaucherous past of the Wicked Wycliffs is well known. The scandalous past of Lady Shackley has been detailed in the gossip pages. Something is brewing between them.

Wycliff swore. He gazed at her now, through the narrowed eyes of an angry, suspicious man. She lay in his bed, nearly lifeless. He'd kissed that pale pink pout of a mouth that had lied to him. That pink mouth had turned away from his, too, which now made a certain amount of sense. How could she kiss her subject?

Why did she have to draw the line *there*?

Unless this *something* was one-sided—his side— and her interest went only as far as what could be printed. It didn't go to her heart.

Wycliff began to burn, smoldering with a potent mixture of mortification and rage and, yes, heartache. He had fallen for her. She'd betrayed him every step of the way. Nevertheless, he continued to read. How could he not?

> *Yet the duke is not a man to be constrained, not when there is a wide world of adventures awaiting him.*

So she listened to him, he thought with a scoff. That was some small crumb of consolation.

> *He has sunk French ships, battled and outwitted cannibals, survived shipwrecks. As he traveled, he did more than slaughter and whore his way across continents—he kept detailed records and collected specimens of various flora, fauna, and (shudder) insects, all for the advancement of Science. The duke would not just claim a territory like Timbuktu, he would know it and return all of its secrets to England.*

As Wycliff read these words, he experienced queer

twinges in his chest. If he didn't know better, he might have thought it the feeling of his heart breaking.

This wasn't the usual rubbish W.G. Meadows— Eliza—wrote each week. She was attempting to build him up in the press after weeks of tearing him down. It was a boring column. But it was full of praise.

Eliza showed no change, no sign of life. Her skin was a ghostly pale. Her breath was faint. She did not look like a traitor or a spy or evil. In fact, she looked like nothing more than a pretty young girl.

The footmen were taking forever with the bathwater. Jenny was probably snogging Thomas the footman in the hall.

Time moved slowly, it seemed, when one's world was cracking and disintegrating. This paper in his hands wasn't what he had expected. He didn't know heads from tales anymore.

Wycliff continued to read: rubbish about him and Lady Shackley and some outrageous yarns Harlan was known to spin to impress women.

He read it all the way to the end, and then again, and again and again. Not once was there mention of the one thing that would have the ton in a collective fit of hysterics: the child.

Eliza had taken his wages, shared his wine, his roof, and nearly shared his bed. But she had lied to him, deceived him, and must have thought him a fool the whole time. While he panted over his housemaid and gave her every consideration, she'd just been taunting him with her feminine wiles. For his secrets.

Good God, he wanted to throttle her. But then he remembered—with a rush of something like relief or excitement or hope—if the Earl of Alvanley was to be trusted, Eliza was worth ten thousand pounds. He needed money. He held proof in his hands.

And she wasn't the only one who could use seduction to obtain secrets.

With great care, Wycliff folded the page along the same lines.

Jenny returned, ready to give her a bath.

Wycliff decided he would feign ignorance of Eliza's secret . . . until he learned all of hers. Why had she taken the knife? Did she know her attacker? What happened in Brighton?

These things he wished to know, and he deserved to know.

And then he would turn her in to Lord Alvanley, take the money and set sail for Timbuktu, leaving behind that ocean-eyed beauty with whom he'd *almost* fallen in love.

Chapter 33

Awakening

When she woke a few hours later, Eliza fervently wished she had not. Her mouth was dry, as if she'd slept with cotton scraps stuffed in her cheeks. Her head throbbed viciously. Moving her arms to rub her temples required strength she simply did not possess.

She drifted off again, awakening to the soft, muted light of morning. The duke sat on a chair beside her bed. *His* bed.

Her room was a narrow garret in the attic, with one small pane of glass and a narrow cot. There was no room for a man in a maid's bedchamber. This was most certainly not her room, or her bed. It belonged to the duke.

Her eyes widened in alarm and she opened her mouth, but no sound came out. What was she doing here? What had happened to her?

Wycliff helped her to a seated position—moving was excruciating and nearly impossible on her own. He even fluffed the pillows behind her for support. He cradled her head in his large, open palms and held a cool glass of water to her lips. She drank thirstily.

As she did, her senses and her memory returned. Realizations dawned upon her, like the sun rising to illuminate awful truths that the night had kept hidden. As her awareness brightened, so did the blood in her veins turn cold.

The last thing she recalled was that devil, Liam. They had been in the alley . . .

What was she doing in the alley?

Escape. Why had she been out and about?

The London Weekly's usual meeting. Yes, the meeting where Knightly had cruelly rejected her writing and callously handed it back to her *in front of everyone.* The pitying glances of Grenville, the other Writing Girls and the other writers. And then she had been dismissed.

She choked on a sip of water as the truths burst upon her like a firing squad given the command to shoot.

The page that contained her column had been folded and pressed into her bodice. Where was it now? She wished to reach up and check, but she did not possess the strength and she could not give him ideas. And Wycliff was watching her. *He couldn't know. . . .*

Eliza sank back into the pillows, willing herself to faint for the first time in her life. Willing the earth to open up and swallow her whole. Willing herself to fall asleep and wake again, in another time and place. But this moment was real, and she had to live it and all the ones that followed.

What did Wycliff know?

If she had been out there and now she was here, something must have happened. But what? And how had she made it home? And when did she begin to think of Wycliff House as home?

All these questions burned upon her lips. It mattered not that she was incapable of voicing them; she most certainly would not like the answers. Instead she was left to wonder *What now?* in mute, punishing silence.

"How are you feeling?" Wycliff asked.

Like a liar. A thief. A criminal. A sinner. An utter wretch.

She was glad she could not speak.

Instead of answering, she looked closely at him, taking note of dark circles around his eyes, inadvertently confessing to a lack of sleep. Had he been worried? Or furious?

Eliza glanced around for signs of his rage—shattered glass, empty brandy glasses, broken furniture—but there was nothing to suggest his anger. Except, perhaps, a tension in his unshaven jaw and a hardness in his gaze.

Yesterday she'd seen the heat of passion in his deep brown eyes, for her.

She managed to croak the words "What happened?" She might have been asking about whatever horrible situation she'd encountered yesterday, but her heart wished to know what had caused the heat to vanish from her eyes. She felt cold without it.

"It seems you were attacked, Eliza," he replied, and there was a world of sensation in the way he drawled out the syllables of her name, as if he doubted them, or tested each one for its veracity. Funny how his doubt hurt. But she deserved it.

"Oh," she whispered. She could remember that, mostly. But that didn't explain anything.

At the moment, she would have given anything to know what the duke knew. But to ask was to admit that there was, in fact, something worth knowing. It was a risk she dared not take.

"I shall leave you to rest now," he said. "And then I have questions for you later."

Later

It turned out that by *later* the duke meant not the following day or evening, but even later than that. *Later* meant that Eliza suffered through two days on tenterhooks, desperately trying to glean any information from him.

In that time, as the minutes passed, she had dusted, drawn baths, cleaned bedchambers, and performed other chores while wondering what lay behind that locked door. And now, as she swept the great foyer, she wondered . . .

What did he know?

The question burned in her belly. The questions buzzed around her head like mosquitoes, always humming and nagging and never letting her forget. She had learned from Mrs. Buxby that the duke had brought her unconscious self back to Wycliff House: "Carried ya in his arms like a princess, he did. All hollering and stomping and commanding and the like."

She assumed Liam had gotten to her. Evil, hateful man! But why had the duke been there to rescue her? This troubled Eliza enormously.

She made short, swift motions with the broom, gathering all the dirt from the marble floor.

He had to know.

Did he care for her? Perhaps, but did he care enough to overlook her deceit? No, they had shared naught but a kiss or two—though kisses that set her soul aflame. They had shared plenty of conversations, small intimate touches and smoldering gazes. They had *something* between them, something more than a man and his maid.

But it seemed that *something* was gone. Wycliff now locked himself in his mystery room, avoiding her entirely.

Fair enough; she had ruined his life with her writings. If love strong enough to overcome that existed on God's green earth, then she did not know of it.

And yet, nothing soothed her like immersing herself in the vexations and drama of others. That, and sweeping. That, and she had a column to *rewrite*. Mrs. Buxby, Harlan, and ample amounts of whiskey-tea provided some intelligence that was more scandalous and salacious than her attempt to portray the duke's noble deeds. Unfortunately, she simply didn't have the time to set pen to paper. Someone asked for this and rang for that and there was one errand or chore after another. Still not fully recovered from her attack, at night she collapsed into a dreamless slumber.

With horror, Eliza watched the moments fly by until she knew it was too late. The paper would be at the presses, and it would be the end of her career as a Writing Girl. First, the rejection of something poorly written, and now the plain failure to write *anything*.

She pushed hard on the broom and her neat little dust piles went flying into the air, scattering and falling, and awaiting her broom again.

Even now, two days later, Eliza's cheeks flamed hot at the recollection of Knightly handing her column back to her in front of all the other *Weekly* writers. It had never been done! Mortifying did not begin to describe it. Perhaps she had not been attacked—perhaps she had merely fainted with embarrassment.

But no, the memory of that altercation was scratched hard into her memory, like rude comments carved into pub tables by drunken wretches. Liam's cold blue eyes and the pound, pound, pounding of her heart, and the sickly sweet smell of the chloroform—these things she now remembered clearly.

The soft swish of the broom's straw against marble was constant and swift. Perhaps it was not a matter of what the duke knew, but what she would confess to.

She could never have the duke as her own, never be with him. Some things were never meant to be. Perhaps, if there had been even the most remote chance that she could allow her heart to feel fully without fear, if there was a speck of opportunity for them to be together . . . then she might tell him the truth and hope for his love and forgiveness.

Swish, swish, swish.

She might even confess . . .

But he could not have her, would not have her . . . thus she, as ever, would need to make her own way in the world. Eliza rationalized that it was a matter of a roof above her head, food in her belly, and clothes on her body.

That reminded her of the ten thousand pound bounty on her head. Ten thousand pounds could set her up for life. Ten thousand pounds could send the duke and his envoy to Timbuktu, and back, in gold-plated ships. Ten thousand pounds could restore the

Wycliff coffers—and all without His Grace needing to chain himself to Hades' Own Harpy, Lady Althea.

Swish, swish, swish. . .

The soft tinkle of the servant's bell cut through the foyer. Footsteps approached.

The duke wished to see Eliza.

Chapter 34

In Which There Are Questions

Eliza found the duke in his private study on the second floor. A fire smoldered in the grate, giving just enough light to throw a burnished glow on Wycliff's impossibly high cheekbones. He sat comfortably behind the large oak desk. The surface was covered with maps of the wide, wide world, thick account books, the skull of a creature she did not recognize, a marvelous shell with a glossy pink interior and white spikes on the outside.

It was dusk. A soft violet light entered through the windows.

Wycliff's hair was pulled back tightly in a queue. The gold of his earring glinted in the firelight. The white shirt he wore was opened at the neck, showing off a vee of tanned and tattooed skin.

Eliza swallowed, hard. Every nerve was thrumming. She wanted him, desperately. Never had she felt so far away from him.

He did not ask her to sit. So she bobbed into a curtsey, out of deference. She clasped her hands behind her back so that he wouldn't see her wring them if she failed to restrain the urge to do so.

Buck up, she told herself. She was raised on the stage. She had made her choices and now had naught to do but brazen through.

"Eliza," he drawled. She loved the sound of her name on his lips.

"Your Grace," she murmured. He did not invite her to sit. Their familiarity was gone. He had to know everything. But even if he knew only the half of it, she was still in trouble. Big Trouble.

"It's time we had a talk, you and I." He gave her a torturous, knowing smile. Eliza tilted her chin higher.

Outside, the wind rattled the windowpanes.

The duke stood and strode toward her.

Her heart beat hard.

He brushed past her; she did a slow turn and watched him stop at the sidebar and clink the cut-crystal brandy bottle against two glasses. He meant to get her drunk, did he? Well, she'd been keeping her secrets for a long time now, and it would take more than alcohol to ply them from her lips.

But, lud, did her heart beat intently in her chest, especially when he turned toward her. Was that a glint of mischief in his eyes, or a trick of the light?

The duke handed her the glass, fingers brushing hers, setting off sparks—or so it felt. His head tilted down toward hers . . . a kiss? No, just temptation. His eyes were dark, his expression inscrutable. Her gaze fell on that exposed patch of skin at the base of his neck. The inky black tattoos swirled beneath, peeking out, taunting her.

If this wasn't the beginning of the end, then she wasn't a Writing Girl.

The duke grinned and raised his glass. "To the truth."

"To the truth," she echoed, aware that her voice didn't waver or sound hollow. Her mama would be proud.

"Where to begin?" he mused, thoughtfully sipping his brandy and standing close to her—much too close, as if he might intimidate her with his size and proximity. It worked. "I'm concerned, you see," he said, and she felt her stance soften. "I'm not bothered that you took my knife."

And suddenly there it was in his palm—silver blade flashing, the wooden handle gleaming. When she pilfered it from his collection, it had been worn, dirty, and dusty, which is why she took that one in particular. But now it appeared shiny and new, which meant that the duke had spent hours with that knife in his hands. The thought was unsettling.

He circled around her, knife in one hand, brandy in the other. He spoke in a low, velvety, voice. The lot of it was intoxicating.

"I might have thought it petty thievery, or even carelessness, but clearly you required it for protection."

"Mmm . . ." she murmured noncommittally. She would say nothing unless absolutely necessary.

"You knew, Eliza, that someone was after you." He was smart, this duke.

She bit her lip, perplexed. This was not the line of questioning she had expected. He was supposed to be livid that she was the author of his demise and sack her on the spot. He wasn't supposed to discover she was in danger, and he certainly couldn't be expected to care.

Around he paced, while she concentrated very much on remaining still.

"Who is he?"

Eliza paused, considering her options. It was damned hard to think with Wycliff nearby, gazing at her with his velvety brown eyes, and with those tattoos tempting her, reminding her of the muscled contours of his chest. The duke sipped his brandy. She ached to taste it on his lips.

Think, Eliza, think. What to tell him? That she was a Writing Girl . . . or should she tell the truth about Liam? Both secrets would ruin her in the duke's eyes. If she hadn't lost him already, then confessing either secret would do the trick. But if she wanted that ten thousand pounds Lord Alvanley was offering—and Lord, did she ever—then she'd have to tell the duke about Liam.

"His name is Liam," she said.

"He's a mean bloke," Wycliff said, then sipped his drink as if to wash away the thought of him.

"Oh, I know," she agreed passionately.

"What I'm interested in is what the likes of such scum could want with you?"

"I do not know . . ." Eliza answered. She didn't want to lie anymore. Like a knitted shawl with a loose thread, one hard tug could unravel everything. If she answered one question, it wouldn't be long before she was confessing things that she'd never told anyone.

The duke drained his brandy and set it on the desk, along with the knife.

"It was not a random attack," he stated flatly. "No one carries around cloth soaked in chloroform just in case they might be beset upon by young ladies in the street."

In other circumstances, she might have cracked a smile at that. But not when he was hammering away at the truth of the matter. Knowing him, he probably knew everything already and was just playing this cat and mouse game with her for a spot of amusement before he pushed her out on the doorstep. Someone was probably packing her things now.

"I wonder how you knew to expect him," the duke said, leaning back against the desk.

So politely worded. Yet it was a command all the same.

He waited.

Eliza gazed at him hard, searching for answers or at least some clue as to what he knew. His mouth was set, his jaw tense. But his eyes . . . perhaps it was wishful thinking but she thought she detected concern and care. Or she had before, and she wished it was so again. Perhaps it was the scent of the brandy and the pleasure of being near him, with his attention fixed upon her. Perhaps it was the fear of being chased again and the lingering remnants of a chloroform haze. Perhaps he did care, and maybe he would come to her rescue. A girl could dare to dream.

"It was not the first time," she said plainly. She was resolved; she would tell him everything about Liam. But nothing else.

Wycliff's hand tightened around the glass of brandy, clenching so hard he thought the thing might shatter in his grasp.

She was a lying, scheming vixen.

He was not supposed to care. God above, he did. She was so slight and delicate, which made him want to gather her in his arms and never let her go. Except perhaps to fight off her foes.

She was ridiculous with her chin tilted so defiantly. Especially when she bit her lip nervously. That little quirk nearly undid all his resolve to ferret out her secrets. But he had to know. He lifted his glass of brandy to his lips to clear his head and toughen him up, but he scowled to find it empty.

He reached out and took hers, again touching her fingertips, which made him think of her fingertips caressing the lines of his tattoo, which made him think of her betrayal, and the lot of it reminded him of his plans for this interview.

"Tell me, Eliza. I want to help you," he said, because he wanted her to confide in him.

"It started at . . ." she said, and faltered. "I thought I saw him the week before the attack."

"What does he want?" Wycliff asked. He thought if he focused on a specific problem, he wouldn't think about her and his feelings, dear God.

"I think he wants money. I don't know. But I haven't any money . . ." Eliza let the words trail off, and he wanted her to finish them with *because I am a housemaid* or *because newspaper writing pays rubbish*, or both.

As far as he knew, this was all true. Although, she was now worth ten thousand pounds. She would have to confess to everything, or start spinning an intricate web of lies that would only catch her in the end.

He handed the brandy back to her. Nefarious, yes. Tried and true method for gleaning information? Yes. She took a sip.

He reached out to her, cupping his palm at the curve in her waist. With only the slightest pressure of his fingertips on the sensitive small of her back, he urged her toward him. One, two, delicate tripping steps across the carpet and into his arms.

She returned his smile. They were of one mind, he was sure of it: a good, deep kiss would put an end to this excruciating conversation. It was about a villain who had attacked her. But it was really about the big lie she kept from him—the one about ruining his reputation and prospects with her writing—the one that made any future impossible.

All they had was this moment. And a relentless, all-consuming desire that knew no reason.

She took from him. He wanted her. She was warm and pliant under his palms.

Wycliff lowered his mouth to hers.

She returned his kiss, hesitant at first. Then he teased her open, teased her into being bolder. He tugged her flush against him and slipped his fingers into her hair, cradling her head so he could kiss her thoroughly and improperly. Eliza tasted of brandy, of secrets, of passion. He kissed her hard and she kissed him back with the same intensity.

They went on like that for a moment, or an hour or however long—he knew not—but some time had passed and he could feel her defenses lowering. Unfortunately, he could also feel that his determination to remain hardhearted was fading. Instead, his cock was hard and he wanted to ravish her right there on the carpet.

So he tugged his mouth away and whispered in her ear, "Who is he, Eliza?"

"Mmm," she murmured into his kiss. His tongued teased and tangled with hers. *Mmm indeed.*

He slid his hands down to her bottom. It was the perfect fit in his palms. Pity that she was such a traitor, because he could really fall in love with her.

She gasped as he pressed her against him; she had to know, to feel, that he was aroused.

He nearly groaned. If his plan was to seduce her into spilling secrets, he would have to take this further. There were worse things, he supposed. She was going to get it in a deliciously wicked way.

With a tantalizing slowness his hands explored her. He felt the rise and fall of her breasts against his chest, and he felt the pace quicken as his hands inched higher. He leaned in to whisper in her ear: "Who is he?"

A simple question. A world in her answer, should she deign to voice it. While Wycliff waited, he kissed her, savoring these last precious moments before she confessed and everything changed irreparably. He wanted as much of her as she was willing to give. He closed his palm around her breast, thumbing the peak. He felt it harden through the fabric.

"Oh, Wycliff," she said with a sigh.

Why did she have to lie and keep secrets? If she didn't, they could have *this.* Always.

"Tell me," he urged, still playing with her, to her pleasure. She grasped the fabric of his shirt hard in her palms. The little minx better hold on, for he had only just begun. God help him, though, he loved how it felt to have her hold onto him as though she was about to be swept away.

"He's a mistake. A youthful mistake," she told him, mumbling into his mouth as they kissed. Wycliff tugged at her skirts, inching the fabric up higher. With the tips of his fingers, he explored the soft flesh of her inner thighs, slowly, teasingly, temptingly inching higher and higher.

Eliza tilted her head back, eyes closed, lips parted in pleasure. Beautiful. He pressed his lips at the hollow of her throat.

With his fingertips, he gently caressed the bud of her sex. She moaned.

"Who is he?" Wycliff growled. His frustration was mounting. Seducing answers out of her had seemed a devilishly smart idea an hour ago, but now the worst sort of torment—unsatisfied curiosity and unsatisfied desire—was raining down on him, and he'd brought it upon himself.

She clenched hard on the fabric of his shirt, twisting it in her grasp as he nibbled and sucked at that lovely spot where her neck curved into the shoulder. Through their labored breathing the sound of tearing fabric was unmistakable. She ripped his shirt.

"Wycliff, I want you," she whispered. The words hit his heart like daggers. He wanted so badly for them to be true. He thought they might be, but he knew she was keeping secrets from him. How could he trust her?

"I want to tell you everything," she continued, her hands grasping at his shirt, pulling it open. The tables had turned.

In spite of himself, he grinned. But then his smile faded and his breath hitched as her hot little palms pressed against his bare chest. Oh so slowly she caressed the bare skin, lingering over his tattoos and playing with his nipples with just her fingertips. He hissed from the pleasure of it. His hands grabbed hard onto the desk behind him. It was either that or rip her dress off.

She pressed her sweet, pink little mouth to his naked chest.

No, it was not a bad idea at all.

English women made it harder to get them naked than Tahitian women, but he was a practiced bloke at such important life skills. Not that she made it easy. No, she writhed away from his attempts to separate her from her dress, even as her skirts were hitched up higher. He resumed that gentle caress, there, and she writhed against his hand.

Modesty? He could feel the intensity of her wanting.

Concern for her position? Ridiculous.

Again, his mouth claimed hers. She moaned and sighed like a woman in the throes of pleasure.

"Oh Wycliff, I . . ." Eliza began, but said nothing to him about stopping. He continued to tease her. Her breath was heavy now, and when he pressed his mouth to her throat for a kiss, he felt her pulse pounding and racing like mad.

"Tell me, Eliza," he murmured low, like a command, as he again sought that sweet spot between her legs. She groaned, and tightened her grasp on his arms. She was feeling it, he knew. But she wouldn't let him in. This was a dangerous game.

"I . . . I . . ."

"Tell me," he urged her. He traced his fingertips along her inner thighs. She shuddered. He restrained himself from more, even though his cock was throbbing and he wanted nothing more than to bend her over the desk and bury himself inside her. But he also wanted to know her secrets—why, and who, and what the devil was going on—so he ignored his desire and concentrated on hers.

Eliza's kiss turned hotter, stronger, and he liked it. He knew that she wanted him. Once more she moved against his hand, and he knew she was almost there. She was wet and wanting. His touch intensified and he slid one finger inside of her. Stopping was impossible now. Secrets be damned.

He felt her becoming more pliant, leaning against him a little more, softening her spine. His touch never let up. Little sighs turned into a loud cry of pleasure and he felt her tighten around him. He had brought her to the brink, and then over the edge.

Wycliff pulled back to gaze at this luscious female in his arms. A pink flush colored her cheeks, and her lips were parted so slightly. She was so beautiful, like that, in the throes of pleasure.

"Tell me, Eliza," he urged.

"Oh . . ." she gasped. She slipped her fingers into his hair and pulled him to her once more.

"Eliza . . ." He murmured her name, kissed her mouth, and kissed her hard, with a staggering amount of passion, in search of answers, but reveling in the pursuit of them. He tasted her secrets, felt her reticence, knew that she ached for this and was inches away from abandon. He could feel it all.

And then she wrenched away and said the thing he least expected.

"I am married."

Chapter 35

In Which There Are Answers

Married?" Wycliff echoed. Eliza watched the color drain from his face. Very well, hers was likely pink enough for them both. That pleasure . . .

. . . she'd never known it before. Not even with her—shudder—husband. Yes, she had married, once upon a time and long, long ago.

There, she had said it aloud. Those words kept tucked away all these years had finally slipped out. That secret of hers that not even her fellow Writing Girls knew was now known—by the Duke of Wycliff, of all the people in the world.

Married.

Very well, the words didn't slip out. She said them deliberately so that he might know why their passion could go no further. Lord above, if she hadn't said those words—or if they hadn't been true—she would have been on her back on his bed, a very satiated woman. Or bent over the desk. Either way, she would have made loud, long love to the duke and they would have liked it.

As it was, she'd already been swept away by his

touch. Lud, her heart was still pounding. Her limbs felt positively liquid. She wanted to curl up against him and drift off, surrounded by his strong tattooed arms.

Since that was not to be—and here she heaved a most woeful sigh—she confessed to the marriage. She'd rather explain about the marriage than reveal herself as the author of all his misery.

Which he probably already knew about, anyway.

"Married." He said it again.

"In a way. It's rather complicated. Or perhaps it is not, but nevertheless—"

"You are married," he said flatly. A drink was apparently in order. He stalked to the other side of the room and poured a generous amount. He took a sip and stood there a moment, thoughtful.

"Yes," she said. She had taken a vow before God to love, cherish, honor, and obey. And she had done none of those things, but neither had her husband. It was a youthful mistake, and she had been fine pretending it never happened.

Until Wycliff. Until she met a man she could love. Until she went and fell in love with that man.

And as much as she neglected those vows over the years—as Liam had too, she felt entitled to add—she couldn't toss them away now. The funny thing was, she cared more about the duke's feelings than Liam's.

"Married. To whom?" Wycliff asked, turning to face her.

"Mr. Liam Fielding. A mean man if there ever was one."

Wycliff poured another drink, this one for her.

"I really ought to see to the evening chores," she said evasively.

"As your lord and master, I relieve you of those duties for this evening."

"You're too kind," she replied, inching toward the door. It was a strange battle within her—wanting to be in his embrace, yet desperate to leave to avoid this conversation.

"I'm curious, more to the point," he answered, stepping between her and the door.

"What would you like to know?" she asked. She did owe him the truth. It was just hard for her to say it.

"Why don't you start at the beginning? I suspect this story might begin in Brighton."

"You listen. A marvelous trait in a man," she remarked. "Yes, this story begins in Brighton, seven years ago. I was visiting with my parents; they were putting on a play for Prinny. Liam was performing in the play. It was one of those whirlwind romances, and youthful idiocy. I was seduced. We were married. I quickly regretted it. We parted ways." She added a little shrug, as if to say, *That's all, nothing to see here.*

"There must be more than that."

"I thought I might travel with him—he was in a troupe of traveling players—and see the world, or at least England. Instead he expected me to stay in London where he would visit from time to time. Our different expectations of the marriage were quickly apparent. We fought. He did not hit me, but I knew it was only a matter of time. One afternoon he went out for a pint, taking *all* of my money, and until the other week I hadn't heard a word from him."

Unspoken: she, too, wished to see the wide, wide world. And she had married for all the wrong reasons. Liam was an escape ticket, a hot fleeting young passion. It hadn't been companionship or real love.

"Any children?" Wycliff asked with a lift of his brow, trying to make light of it. But she knew the hows and the whys and the intensity of that question for him.

"None whatsoever," she assured him.

"And he is the one who attacked you?"

"Yes," Eliza said, holding his gaze. The fire snapped on the far side of the room. A gentle rain lashed at the windows. The duke sipped his brandy, and oh, how she wished to, but she needed her wits about her.

"Why?"

Because I'm worth ten thousand pounds in some stupid wager.

"I'm not quite certain. We didn't exactly converse," she said instead.

"And what is your plan for dealing with this situation?" Wycliff went over to the desk and began to light candles. Darkness had fallen.

Eliza laughed. "I thought that I might hide, ignore it, and hope it goes away."

"Brilliant strategy," he said dryly, and something flared within her—irritation, she supposed. With herself. Wycliff plotted and planned. But he wasn't a lone female being stalked all over London. Then again, he'd probably faced worse and defended himself far better than she had.

"What am I supposed to do? Venture all over London in search of Liam?" she asked hotly. "And then what?"

"Why not?"

"Aye. But what if I don't want to find him?" And there it was, the truth. She merely wished to be free of him, though she certainly did not wish him dead. Until recently everything was fine because it'd been easy to pretend it had never happened. Yet, now with Liam on her trail, she couldn't forget.

Every time the duke kissed her, she could not forget that it was so wrong, even though it felt so very right. Though she wanted to give herself to him completely, she belonged to a loathsome man who didn't even want her.

Chapter 36

Another Edition of "The Tattooed Duke"

Married. It wasn't the secret he expected her to confess. He thought she might reveal what she didn't know he knew: that she was the author of "The Tattooed Duke."

Married? He had not expected that.

Harlan had questioned the man, who shared no information of any interest whatsoever. He'd given a false name—Wycliff knew as much now. And then within hours he got away. Wycliff believed Eliza when she said he'd gone off and she didn't keep track of his whereabouts. Why would she want to? He didn't make it easy, and he wasn't exactly desirable company.

Once, he had seen a native tribe rip the still beating heart out of a downed gazelle in Africa. He felt a deep sympathy—nay, empathy—with that little animal. First, the stunning blow of the spear piecing his skin and taking him down—that was the discovery of Eliza's secret writing career. And then to learn that this beguiling, mysterious, dangerous woman he'd fallen for was married . . . to learn that he could never make her his . . . which he shouldn't want to do anyway, given her deceitful ways . . .

The heart wants what the heart wants, even if it's been ripped out of one's chest, still beating hard in the hand of a warrior.

He had not slept. Obviously.

The household was out of brandy.

And it was Saturday, which meant another edition of that damnable newspaper, *The London Weekly*.

Only Harlan joined him for breakfast this morning; Burke knew better, and Basil was likely experiencing the aftereffects of excessive alcohol consumption from some ton soiree.

Eliza calmly served them, quietly pouring coffee and tea as needed.

She might not warm his bed because of those damned wedding vows, but she could unwittingly relate information he'd like all of London to know. Thanks to Alvanley's offer, she could be worth a fortune to him. Thus, she would stay on as housemaid for a few more days.

It was decided.

Even if it tortured him to have her so temptingly close.

Wycliff caught Harlan eyeing him, and then Eliza, looking for evidence of those ties he had mentioned.

He lifted this week's freshly ironed edition of *The London Weekly*. Just to vex his company, he took his good old time reading the article on the first page, something endlessly dull about Parliament. Then he discovered a deep interest in the latest foreign intelligence. Oh, and then, there it was—"The Tattooed Duke."

It wasn't entirely an act when he heaved a sigh and

began to read quietly to himself. He knew what it would say, for he had read the handwritten version stuffed in Eliza's bodice. But then it didn't say what he expected.

Not at all.

This one was different.

Happy Dukes are all alike; every unhappy Duke is unhappy in his own way. We know that all the Wycliff dukes have been scandalous in their own, rakish way, and we know that none have managed the unique, strange scandal of the current duke's bizarre, foreign proclivities. Adventure seems to follow the duke no matter where he goes, be it in Turkey or Fleet Street. He was seen Wednesday last emerging from St. Bride's Lane with the limp form of a female, helpless and unconscious in his arms. Had she been ravished? Murdered? What has become of her?

The duke's partner in crime revealed that the sling he wore was naught but a disguise. When the time came to pull a battered man from that same alley, both of the partner's arms were in good working order. The battered man had been bound and gagged. Sources suggest he's kept captive in the basement dungeon of Wycliff House, tied in chains, and tortured daily with strange implements the duke procured on his travels.

The Tattooed Duke's activities have taken a darker, violent turn. Perhaps among the lawless tribes of his travels this is how it's done. But the duke ought well remember this is England, where women's virtue is protected, the courts protect even the criminals, and dukes frequent clubs and ballrooms, not the underbelly of London.

When Wycliff allowed himself to lift his eyes from the page and look across the room at Eliza, it took everything in him not to roar, or to hurl the coffeepot in her direction. This one had gone too damn far.

This was such a stunning reversal from the version she had penned, the one he had discovered. She must have written it after he had saved her, cared for her, let her sleep in his bed. After he stayed up all hours by her bedside, helplessly clasping her hand so that on some level she might not feel so alone.

Later, he would consider the effects of this on his heart, but for the moment he could feel it hardening in his chest. With great care he began to rip the paper apart in neat methodical shreds of long strips.

"Oi, I didn't get to read it yet," Harlan protested, "and it seems especially interesting this morning."

Wycliff looked meanly at him as he ripped those strips again, into neat little squares of confetti. And then he scattered those bits of paper like poisoned petals in the wind.

"See to that mess," he told Eliza as he stalked out of the dining room. She had gone pale. He didn't care.

Chapter 37

In Which There Is Treachery

Later that afternoon Eliza pleaded illness and retired to her attic bedroom, where she painstakingly reassembled the torn pieces of *The London Weekly* until the awful truth emerged. This version of "The Tattooed Duke" was not one she had written.

"Knightly." She said his name like a curse.

Given her accident, she'd been unable to revise the nice, noble depiction of the duke. Given Knightly's ruthless quest for more sales, more profits, more renown, he had clearly written what he wanted for his paper—never mind what this might to do to her, or the duke, or anything like the love that might have once existed between them.

Eliza thought of that look he gave her this morning after he had read this. She had felt it like a hot knife to her heart.

Did he know?

He must think that she wrote this. But how could she declare her innocence without admitting that she had written all the others, just as damaging?

"Knightly." Again she spat out the name. The lengths she had gone to in order to please him!

Giving up her days and nights for this story, giving up her heart for it! And it wasn't enough. He had to go and write it himself.

So he thought he didn't need her, did he?

A gentle gust of wind blew through her open bedroom window, scattering *The Weekly* bits all over her room. One little scrap tripped on the wind and settled in her lap.

> *The Earl of Alvanley still has no takers on his offer to unmask W.G. Meadows for the princely sum of ten thousand pounds.*

Chapter 38

Confrontation

Eliza found Knightly exactly where she suspected she would: at his desk, in his Fleet Street office. Did the man *ever* go home?

His head snapped up in surprise when she entered and proceeded to scatter one handful and then another of the shredded issue of *The London Weekly* over his desk. The little gray scraps floated down onto the desktop like paper snowflakes.

"Eliza." He said her name by way of greeting. There was no pretense that this would be a cordial meeting.

"Knightly," she responded coolly.

"I trust you have seen today's column," he remarked, setting down his pen and leaning back in his chair.

"Bits of it," she retorted. He didn't crack a smile.

"But enough to ascertain that it was not one you wrote," he said. The man was not an idiot. Even though he did stupid things, like print that pack of lies and put her name on it.

"You made a mistake," she told him bluntly.

"No, I made a calculated decision that it was in my best interests to run my most popular story, rather than feature some empty column inches."

Eliza was glimpsing the coldhearted, ruthless businessman Knightly was reputed to be. Usually, they saw a rakish gent who began meetings with a grin and a cute quip. She didn't like this one; she knew he would be hard and immovable. But then again, so could she.

"I had handed something in," Eliza said.

"Something unsuitable," Knightly countered. "It was still fawning all over the duke, spewing about noble deeds and other dull sales. Scandal—"

"Oh hush about your silly saying!" Eliza cried. "This column you wrote went too far. And the duke thinks I wrote it, because he knows I have written the others."

"So?" Knightly coolly lifted one brow, punctuating the question of why he should care.

"So? So?" Eliza echoed. "Just how am I supposed to keep my position if he knows that I am the one writing such damaging things?"

"This wasn't an issue before."

"He didn't know it was me before."

"Are you absolutely certain he is aware now?" Knightly challenged.

"Have I been accused? No. Has he asked? No. But I am certain that he is aware of my deception." Even the memory of the hateful, hurtful look Wycliff threw at her that morning made her stomach ache. He had to know.

That he had found her on Fleet Street with a hand-written column in her bodice was highly suspicious. He must have known then, if not before. Wycliff was no fool, and she'd been ridiculously optimistic to take him on.

All those questions Wycliff asked the other night,

in that heated seductive interrogation, had likely been driving at this one awful point: that she was W.G. Meadows. Yes, he must know.

"Look, Eliza, it's not the end of the world," Knightly said. "All you need to do is quit your position and take to bribing the other staff. How do you think I gained the information for this column? Drunken louts gossiping at Garroway's after the scene on Wednesday provided most of the content. And the butler hasn't been paid in quite some time; he was willing to talk."

"That's not the point, Knightly."

"We can still get the story," he said, as if he hadn't heard her. "What on earth could possibly be the problem?"

"There's more to life than this damned newspaper, Knightly!"

"So I've been told. Women, in particular, like to harp upon this point. How I choose to spend my time is none of your concern."

"I'm not in the slightest bit interested, since it seems you do naught but sit behind this desk. My point, Knightly, is that this was *my* story. *My* name. *My* work. I have put my life on the line for it, and you don't seem to care one whit."

"Life on the line? While you were dusting bookshelves and polishing the silver? Really?" His skepticism practically dripped from his voice.

"Do you know why that column wasn't extensively rewritten? Because I had been attacked and dosed with chloroform. Because I spent the better part of two days unconscious. *I was the lifeless female he carried out of the alleyway.*"

Knightly's expression became grim, but he remained unmoved.

"The duke found me, you know. With a handwritten version of 'The Tattooed Duke' in my bodice. And I hadn't wondered until now what brought him down to Fleet Street, but I can only conclude that he already suspected me. And from the look he gave me this morning—well, I think he knows. My disguise is ruined."

"I agree it's a series of unfortunate events, but I don't see what the problem is. Yes, you may not be able to carry on in your current disguise, but the story can still continue," Knightly said, stroking the stubble on his jaw.

Oh, it was all about the story, the story, the story!

"The problem, you thick-headed man, is that I have fallen in love with him!" Eliza cried out.

She hadn't realized the words were there, just on the tip of her tongue, until they burst forth. The feeling, though, had been growing for days, weeks now. Her heart had known what her head had not, thus the words spilling out, with Knightly hearing the plain truth at the same time she did.

"I am in love with him, and now he thinks I have told all of London he ravishes and murders young girls in alleyways and keeps beaten men as captives in his basement dungeon."

"I can see how this is a problem for you. However, it is not a problem for me," Knightly said coolly. What a heart of stone this man must have! Poor Annabelle, for having fallen in love with him.

Eliza gasped at the cold, hard truth of it.

"Just you wait, Knightly," she told him. There was a fierce edge in her voice she'd never heard before. "I will *make* this a problem for you."

Chapter 39

A Writing Girl's Revenge

Sunday afternoon

Eliza spent her afternoon off from His Grace's employ—for he still, oddly, had not relieved her of her position—with her fellow Writing Girls at Sophie's home. Well, home was not quite the word for the massive structure that was the London residence of the Dukes of Hamilton and Brandon. There were 107 bedrooms. She and Sophie had counted them one restless, rainy afternoon.

On this particular afternoon, the Writing Girls were sprawled around the duchess's private sitting room, taking tea, reading periodicals and gossiping.

Annabelle flipped through *The Ladies Journal*. Sophie perused *La Belle Assemblée*, and Julianna regaled them all with the latest ton intrigues—so-and-so had accepted a proposal, Miss Something-or-other had declined yet another one.

"And then, of course, there is the latest about Wycliff. Is it true he keeps a man locked in the basement?" Julianna asked. Eliza had been brooding, and was caught unaware by this sudden turn in the conversation.

"Honestly, I do not know if there is a man in the basement," she said. "Or if there even is a basement in Wycliff House. That is the domain of footmen, and I have not gone."

She hadn't yet given thought to this detail of the column—that the captive was likely Liam. He'd likely sung like a bird when questioned. Damn the man.

"How can you not know, when it is plainly written in your column?" Annabelle asked, looking puzzled. "You did write it, did you not?"

"I did not write it," Eliza stated plainly. "Knightly did."

The girls gasped.

"But how? And when? And why?" The questions tumbled out all at once, and Eliza was not sure who asked what, or which question to tackle first. Instead she sipped her tea in an effort to buy time, for she knew that the minute she opened her mouth the entire story would come spilling forth: about Liam and the chloroform, and her argument with Knightly, and falling in love with the duke.

And that is precisely what happened.

"Married?" Sophie echoed.

"In love?" Annabelle asked.

"You quit *The Weekly*?" Julianna gasped.

Eliza decided to answer the easy question first. "I did not quit *The Weekly*, I simply said that I would make my problem Knightly's problem."

"He didn't know you were in love, otherwise he would not have done it," Annabelle said in defense of the man she loved. In her starstruck blue eyes, Knightly could no wrong—even though in Eliza's opinion—and Julianna's, too—he most certainly could. And did.

"I'm sorry, Annabelle, but I'm afraid there's little he cares for, other than his newspaper," Eliza said, trying to be gentle. "He would have done exactly the same, even if he had known."

"He might have added in a dash of romantic intrigue," Sophie said, "hinting at your affections. If he had known," she added.

"True. And that wouldn't have helped either," Eliza said. "He is just like a meddling mama." There were a few giggles at that, even in the midst of the heavy conversation.

"But he didn't know how you felt about him. None of us did," Annabelle said. "You're so quiet about it."

It was true that she didn't wear her heart on her sleeve, like Annabelle or the others. But that didn't mean her heart didn't beat as hard, or that she loved any less. That she hadn't tossed and turned on her narrow cot in her tiny bedchamber in the servants' quarters, thinking of the duke. Sleep eluded her in that hot room, with the bedsheets tangled around her and incriminating writings tucked under the bed.

"Oh, please. Of course she was going to fall in love with him," Julianna said. "He's a breathtakingly handsome man and it was her job to gain his confidence, become intimate with him. Love was inevitable."

"The question is, does he feel the same?" Sophie asked.

"I can't imagine that he does," Eliza replied. And then to change the subject from one problem to another, she said, "He must know that it is me. And he must know that what I have written has ruined his chances of traveling to Timbuktu, and saving the estate from utter ruination. I have destroyed his life's dream. It's unforgivable."

"I did some quite unspeakable and unforgivable things to Roxbury," Julianna said, "and now we are revoltingly in love. You'd be surprised what love can overcome." It did make Eliza feel a bit better, since it was the truth, plain and unsweetened. If Roxbury could forgive Julianna, then perhaps she and Wycliff had a chance—

"That is, if he loved me enough to begin with," she said. "And how can I know?"

"I can't believe Knightly wrote your column . . ." Annabelle said, still fixated upon it.

"I can. He's done similar before," Julianna replied with a scowl. She and Knightly had their own rocky past, since they didn't always see eye-to-eye and neither were shy about it.

"He's only done it when it's the best thing for the paper," Annabelle stated.

"Annabelle," Eliza said, "imagine that you advised a young couple in love to have a heartfelt conversation to work out their difficulties. And instead, for better sales, Knightly rewrote your column to say they should marry other people with all possible haste."

"That would be morally wrong," Annabelle conceded, with a frown tugging at her lips.

"He cannot keep doing this," Eliza said passionately, "not when people's lives depend upon what we write. It's not meddling with newsprint, but fate!"

"That's very dramatic of you," Julianna said, sipping her tea.

"Can we please discuss the fact that you are

married?" Sophie interjected. "Secretly married!"

"This happens all the time in Minerva Press novels," Annabelle said, now smiling. "And now it's actually happening in real life . . ."

"I live to entertain," Eliza said dryly. "Liam was my Matthew Fletcher—but instead of dodging the bullet as you did, Sophie, I married him. That was a mistake I quickly realized."

"Like Somerset and I," Julianna added, mentioning her own first husband, who had been a reckless philanderer.

"Yes. But what can one do? I pretended it never happened. I was glad when he left. Oh, I was spitting mad because he took all my money, but even then I thought, 'Good riddance.' I did not wish to suffer in a loveless marriage."

"What a lucky—or unlucky—break that he should see you at *The Weekly* offices, just as Alvanley's wager is presented."

"But *married* . . ." Sophie said, still awed at the secret.

Annabelle's brow was furrowed again, which meant she was thinking something unpleasant.

"What is it?" Eliza asked her.

"If you are married, that means it doesn't matter what happens with the duke . . ." she said softly.

"Because nothing can happen with the duke," Sophie concluded.

"You could be his mistress," Julianna said bluntly.

"I did consider it," Eliza confessed. "Lord knows I had chances that I turned away from. But I did make a vow. I did give my word, even if it was only to that damned lout, Liam. That, and I'm sure Wycliff wants nothing to do with me."

"Oh dear; this really is quite impossible," Annabelle said. She sighed, poured herself another cup of tea, and liberally dosed it with sugar.

"If Annabelle, ever the optimist, says it's impossible—" Eliza began.

"I'm so sorry," Annabelle said.

"Nonsense," Julianna said briskly. "Annabelle doesn't have the inclination to wicked, scheming thoughts that you and I have, Eliza. We shall come up with something. "

"This is true," Eliza agreed. They had come up with some great things together—like dressing Julianna as a boy and sending her into White's, or spying on Roxbury's duel with Knightly.

"Hello?" Sophie said. "Do I not have a talent for scheming and wicked thoughts as well? I feel so dull otherwise."

"You will have a wedding to write about, I promise," Julianna said to Sophie.

"Let's list the problems at hand. That's how Brandon solves everything," Sophie suggested, speaking of her extremely capable and organized husband.

"Are you truly saying we shall solve all my insurmountable problems by making a list?" Eliza questioned.

"I know," Sophie said, in response to the skepticism in Eliza's voice. "But it's remarkably effective."

She was already rummaging in her desk drawer for writing things.

"I see Brandon has failed to cure you of your cluttered habits," Julianna remarked. They were old friends who once lived together at 24 Bloomsbury Place in quite the bachelorette abode.

"To his eternal frustration," Sophie answered

cheerfully before reclaiming her spot on the settee. "Now, where were we?"

"Listing my problems," Eliza said. "I can already see you do not have enough paper or ink."

"I shall ring for more if need be," Sophie said brightly in the face of her darkness.

"To start, I must find a way to make the duke forgive me," Eliza said.

Sophie wrote that down.

"You must do something about that husband of yours," Julianna added.

Sophie wrote that down as well.

"I may need vengeance upon Knightly. Or at least, I must make things problematic for him," Eliza said bitterly. He had gone too far. He must be made aware of it.

All eyes turned to Annabelle, for her approval.

"My heart beats for him," she said dramatically. "But he mustn't be allowed to block the path of true love."

"Hear hear," Julianna rallied.

"Any other problems?" Sophie asked, pen poised above the paper

"Well, I could be a few inches taller . . ."

"Now you are just being ridiculous," Sophie said. "So we have forgiveness, vengeance, and debt, and that pesky matter of the husband."

The girls fell silent.

The clock ticked, loudly. The clink of a china teacup upon a saucer was suddenly so very loud. Sophie sighed. Eliza bit her lip, as she did when thinking. Julianna twirled a lock of her auburn hair around her fingertips, and Annabelle smoothed out invisible wrinkles on her skirt. The silence was loud, and it struck Eliza like trumpets blaring the hopelessness of her situation.

Four bright girls, and not one of them could think of something that might solve at least one of her problems. Let alone one thing that would fix everything in one fell swoop.

Eliza picked up the most recent issue of *The Weekly*. She had not read the story in one piece, only those dozens of little pieces of confetti painstakingly assembled until the wind blew them all over her room and—

"I know!" she cried out. In a rush of breath she continued: "I know what to do to solve everything."

"Well, do tell," Julianna said, leaning forward eagerly.

"The Earl of Alvanley's offer for ten thousand pounds to unmask W.G. Meadows," Eliza said.

"Oooh," Sophie gasped as she understood.

A mischievous smile played on Eliza's lips, and she said, "I shall turn myself in."

Chapter 40

Introducing Lord Alvanley

The following morning

Are you certain of this?" Sophie posed the question to Eliza for the hundredth time that morning. They were in the carriage now, on their way to call on the Earl of Alvanley so that Eliza might turn herself in and claim his offer of ten thousand pounds. It was decided that Sophie would go along to the Great Confession, as they had taken to calling it, as a way to lend proof. A duchess known to write for *The Weekly* would grant Eliza the kind of authority the earl would probably require.

"Yes, I am certain," Eliza replied. It was the logical course of action. She needed money. So did Wycliff. Out of pride, and a dash of spite, she no longer wished to write for Knightly. This wasn't just a logical thing to do, but perhaps her only choice.

Just wait until London learned it was a housemaid who had unearthed and reported Wicked Wycliff's secrets!

"We shall miss you," Sophie said, and Eliza clasped her hand affectionately. There was a lump of emotion in her throat that couldn't be spoken. The truth couldn't be denied: she was wretchedly sad to be, in essence, quitting her position as a *London Weekly* Writing Girl.

She would still have her friends, of course. Theirs was a bond that wouldn't be broken, and Sophie, Julianna, and Annabelle were the best friends she had ever known. Eliza loved them fiercely.

She would miss their weekly meetings, and all the occasions when they gathered together for tea and gossip. She might still join them, but it wouldn't be the same. They would go on and laugh over Grenville's latest tirade against anything pleasant. Or Knightly. And Eliza would hollowly laugh along, or worse, wait until they could explain to her what she would have experienced with them if she had been there.

Suddenly, she felt so very alone.

"Are you—" Sophie asked again.

But a nervous Eliza said, "Yes, I am sure."

"Very well," Sophie answered, folding her gloves in her hand. Lovely kidskin gloves in the most delicate butter-colored leather. Within hours she'd be able to buy her own expensive gloves, Eliza thought. And send Wycliff to Africa.

"I am nervous," she said, to soothe Sophie. And she was, in truth. What if he did not believe her? What would she do if this plan fell through?

"You don't have to do it," Sophie offered.

"I don't see any other way."

"You can wait until some other opportunity presents itself . . ."

"If I wait, he'll likely marry Lady Shackley. Although, I'm not sure that will make any difference to me." He still might, anyway, because of the child. But she wanted the duke to have options. She knew what it was like to not have choices—any woman did.

"I hope the earl is at home," Sophie said. "I would be vexed if he weren't. I couldn't sleep a wink last night."

"Neither could I," Eliza agreed. She couldn't sleep, for all her heated, wanton, longing for the duke. She wanted his kiss, his touch, his love. Should she have gone to his chamber? The thought crossed her mind, more than once. Courage failed her, and instead she waited for his knock on her door. It never came.

"If Alvanley is the rake that Julianna says he is," Sophie said, "then he should likely be sleeping now, which means that we have a chance of catching him."

"Albeit before his morning coffee, which is a dangerous time to ask a man for anything. I still think we should have called later."

"Technically, we shouldn't be calling at all," Sophie remarked. "But then what's a little breech of propriety when ten thousand pounds are at stake?"

"Goodness, I'm so far beyond the bounds of propriety that calling upon a known bachelor before noon is the least of it," Eliza said, and she even laughed.

"Well at any rate, here we are," Sophie said as the carriage rolled to a stop. "It's too late to turn back now."

The Earl of Alvanley's home was large but not massive. It was in excellent repair. Even the door knocker was polished to such a high shine that Eliza could see her distorted reflection in it. Her expression was cool, collected, which was a miracle considering all the knots in her stomach.

The butler opened the door before they had a

chance to knock. No wonder it stayed so shiny.

His eyes widened, almost imperceptibly, upon seeing two women on the doorstep at a bachelor's residence. Before noon.

Nevertheless, he admitted them into the foyer. Eliza bit her lip to keep her jaw from dropping. Like everything else, the green marble floor was polished to a high shine, and it reflected a large crystal chandelier. Her knees ached, just imagining having to keep that marble in such a state. The walls were covered in a forest-colored paper and hung with huge landscape paintings in massive gold leaf frames. Everything was impeccable and of the highest quality. One could tell, just with a glance.

"We would like an audience with Lord Alvanley," Sophie said grandly, sounding very duchesslike.

"I shall see if he is at home," the butler answered flatly, clearly not impressed. He probably thought them both actresses or some other strumpets. "Who shall I say is calling?"

"W.G. Meadows," Sophie said with a delicious grin. The butler's complexion paled, though his countenance remained unchanged. "And I am the Duchess of Hamilton and Brandon."

"Ah," the butler said dryly. "Then perhaps you would like to wait in the drawing room. A maid will bring you refreshments while you wait."

"Thank you ever so much," Sophie replied, tugging at the fingertips of her gloves as she strolled after the butler. Eliza followed.

They waited for a quarter hour in the drawing room. Everything in it was expensive, Eliza could tell. All the chairs and settees were upholstered in thick green velvet and blue damask. The occasional tables were all of some high quality wood, and polished so they gleamed almost as bright as the door knocker or the foyer floors. A massive portrait of an incredibly buxom woman hung above the mantel. Her attire was a whisper of fabric so sheer and worthless as a garment she might as well not have worn it. The room was definitely the domain of a wealthy bachelor—neat, impeccable, free from the traffic of family or the little warm touches of a woman.

A maid brought a tea tray. Sophie poured, and seemed right at home among the fine things. Eliza thought she herself was far too likely to break something, particularly of the priceless heirloom variety. Nevertheless, she bravely sipped tea from a delicate porcelain cup. They waited.

She opened her mouth to suggest that perhaps they ought to come another time, like never, when the paneled oak doors swung open.

It was the earl. He was tall, with sandy colored hair and brown eyes still heavy lidded from sleep. Julianna had told them he was approaching his fortieth year. Like many a man in London, the earl was a sworn bachelor. But he had long ago inherited, and seemed free of the nagging relations that pressured one to marry and produce brats. The earl entertained himself with drinks, cheroots, and wagers. And, apparently, ordering his staff to polish everything to a ridiculous shine.

"Duchess," he drawled by way of greeting. Sophie inclined her head.

Then his gaze came to settle on Eliza, coolly assessing her. "You must be W.G. Meadows," he said at last. "I wasn't expecting a woman, and yet I'm not surprised. That is, if you are who you say you are."

Eliza nodded yes.

Sophie returned to sitting on the settee, and so they all sat and the earl gratefully accepted a cup of coffee brought in by a maid. He took a sip, ahhed, crossed one leg over the other and said "Where to begin?"

"I suppose you won't simply hand over a bank note for ten thousand pounds," Eliza remarked dryly.

"Which is why I am here," Sophie added. "To provide proof."

The earl sipped his coffee before replying.

"With all due respect, Duchess, while I do take your word for it, you must understand that I cannot give away such a great sum over tea in the morning. Dear God, it is morning," Alvanley said, glancing at the clock resting on the mantel. "There are not many things I arise before noon for. This had better be good."

"We couldn't call at regular hours and risk being seen," Sophie explained.

"Indeed," the earl agreed, sipping his coffee with pleasure.

"What kind of proof are you looking for?" Eliza asked.

"To start, I would love to know how you did it," the earl said. "You are not some society miss, of that I'm certain, even though I make it a point never to pay too much attention to those silly young fools. Present company excluded, naturally. You might be his mistress, but I hadn't heard that Wycliff kept one. Then again, he is a Wycliff so how could he not?"

"I took employ as a housemaid in His Grace's residence," Eliza explained.

The earl's eyes lit up, and not just from the coffee either.

"Brilliant," he said in a clipped but awed way. "Absolutely brilliant."

"Thank you," Eliza answered primly. It was a devilishly good disguise. She just had to ruin it by falling in love with her duke.

"Household gossip is a gold mine. There are no secrets belowstairs, from what I understand. It seems from your writing, though, that you also managed to gain the duke's confidence. That is also not surprising, given that he's one of the Wicked Wycliffs. They have a taste for their household help, more so than the average peer, which is really saying something."

Eliza wanted to blurt out that he wasn't a regular old Wycliff, and that there was so much more to him than anyone ever saw or that she was allowed to relate. That reminded her why she was here.

"Eliza has kept the Writing Girls entertained with news of the duke," Sophie said.

"Yes, the Writing Girls. And now it turns out there is a fourth. I don't suppose either of you care to confirm the identity of the Lady of Distinction?"

"Not even for another ten thousand pounds," Sophie answered, smiling mischievously.

"Some secrets are meant to be kept," Eliza added.

"I wonder why you are selling yours?" Alvanley turned to ask her.

"I have my reasons," she answered evasively. She was already confessing enough.

"And I haven't offered a bounty for those. Understood," he said with a laugh. "You've already offered up the information I am after—or at least a good lie and quite the ruse, given that you've brought in the duchess. However, I'm not quite certain I believe you, W.G. Meadows. Not ten thousand pounds certain."

"What would make you believe?" Eliza asked calmly, carefully lifting the teacup to her mouth for a sip. Her hand did not waver, and she was proud of that.

"I think I should like to read about this little scene in your next column," the earl said.

"I'm afraid that won't be possible," Eliza said. The earl lifted a brow. "Mr. Knightly would read it, and he would not be pleased that I am here about this, to say the least. We run the risk that the column then wouldn't be printed."

"I concede your point," the earl said, sipping his coffee thoughtfully. "What about a different line entirely?"

"That should be possible," Eliza replied. "Nothing that would call too much attention. After all, as long as we three know it, it suits our purposes."

"If I were to see it in print in the next installment of 'The Tattooed Duke,' then I will have a bank draft ready by afternoon tea. Please do not call this early again."

"Perfect. What should the line be?"

Alvanley sipped his coffee thoughtfully. Eliza took deep breaths to quell her impatience. The earl picked up a book at hand.

"The poems of Byron," he said by way of explanation. After flipping through, he paused and said, " 'In secret we met, in silence I grieve.' "

Eliza smiled sadly at the line, all too fitting for her present circumstances. "Very well, Lord Alvanley. I shall see you Saturday next."

Chapter 41

In Which the Child Arrives

A drawing room across town

Althea had a talent for finding a man at his weakest, the way a lion could sniff out wounded prey.

On Saturday afternoon Wycliff received the note, stinky to high heaven with her perfume. *The child—your child—has arrived,* she wrote in her loopy, ladylike handwriting. *Do come at once. Ever yours, Althea.*

It was probably the last thing he wanted to deal with after the latest calamity in *The London Weekly.* He considered going at once, simply to avoid Eliza, but thought better of it. Give Althea an inch and she'd take an ocean. But it did not seem fair to keep the child waiting, uncertain. Lord only knew what she told him.

With his heart thudding out the beats of the word Timbuktu, Wycliff knocked on Lady Althea's door. Her butler answered and went through the ridiculous routine of checking whether the lady was at home to callers, when Wycliff could hear her ladyship haranguing the servants from the foyer. Something about the temperature of the tea.

After being kept waiting for fifteen excruciating minutes, he was admitted.

"Wycliff. Darling." Althea strolled toward him, her hand held out in greeting, her gaze fixed upon him.

Youthful folly, he thought, and that made him think of Eliza and her foolish marriage. He supposed, in some way, he understood her. Not that he wanted to.

"Althea," he said by way of greeting. He took her hand but would not kiss it. He thought of Eliza, the traitoress, and how he still wanted her. Duty impelled him to be here, but he did not have to like it.

The expedition! His better judgment reminded him. *Be nice!*

"My heart is warmed that you have found a moment for us in your busy schedule," she said. "You must be busy, being a duke, though I have no idea what occupies your days, since you do not frequent society . . ."

And then she turned to reveal the child. He was a pale, pudgy thing, with Althea's light golden hair, her blue eyes, and her scowl. His fingers and face were sticky with pastry. Wycliff's gut clenched. This was not his child. Couldn't be. Or was that wishful thinking?

"I'd like to introduce you to William. The little Lord Shackley," she said with a sparkling laugh. The boy, about ten years of age, showed the good sense to wince at the pet name from his mother.

Was it Shackley's boy? Wouldn't that be something—the name passing along with the blood? Wycliff looked up at the portrait of the late Lord Shackley hanging over the fireplace. His coloring was dark, his features strong. This was not his child either.

"William, dearest, this is mother's special friend. The Duke of Wycliff."

"How do you do?" the boy said politely. Then he ambled off to the tea tray and the stacks of pastries.

"William, do join us. I'm sure the duke wishes to become better acquainted with you."

"Indeed," Wycliff said. And this time he took a seat opposite the child. Althea sat next to her boy.

Wycliff had a father, barely. The man who had sired him lived in the same house, but his attention was always focused on mistresses or housemaids or anything other than a small boy who spent hours poring over maps and sneaking away from his governess to go exploring.

So he tried to connect with William, little Lord Shackley. He asked about school, studies, friends, travels, anything. He wanted to find some common point of interest with this creature who was supposedly his, sticky face and all.

"You needn't interrogate him," Althea said, miffed. "He's only a small boy."

Young perhaps, Wycliff thought, but not small.

"How old are you, William?" Wycliff asked the child in one last desperate attempt to make conversation and to find some bond between them.

"Ten." He spoke with his mouth full. Disgusting. Wycliff hadn't had the most attentive of nurses, but basic table manners had been a must. Cook had insisted upon it.

"When is your birthday?" Wycliff asked. Perhaps he might get the lad a present. Or a cake. Althea simply petted the child's mop of curls.

"August the twentieth," the boy answered solemnly. Then he licked his fingers.

"August," Wycliff repeated. Something didn't seem quite right about that.

"Wycliff, what are you about?" she asked. "Of course the boy knows his birthday!"

"Yes, but I did not know it. And now that I do . . ." He smiled, sadly for her. But his heart was lighter. "It comes down to simple mathematics, Althea. You and I were caught in September, and it was the last time we were together. I remember because we were celebrating my own birthday. I set sail a fortnight later, in October. According to the immutable laws of nature, the child would have been conceived in January. By then I was in Paris and packing my things for Venice. While my prowess as a lover is well known, even I admit I cannot perform the act from another continent."

"Well," she huffed, her cheeks reddening to match her lips. "Well."

Did she really not know that he hadn't fathered her child? Given the education provided to women, or lack of it, this was a possibility. Or was it a scheme?

Little Lord Shackley had been eyeing the pastry plate during this entire lesson on simple mathematics and procreation. Now he made his selection and merrily devoured it, oblivious to his mother's distress.

"I see I have left you speechless. I shall leave you to your privacy in order to recover yourself."

"You owe everything to me," she said in a low voice that sent chills racing up and down his spine. It was, in a way, the truth. "And I waited for you. Can you see how it looks to society—I have been spurned again and again by you. I can't bear it!"

"I'm not much of a romantic, Althea, but that is not a reason for marriage."

"But my money is?" she questioned, and he felt the sharpness of her words. "Don't tell me it hasn't crossed your mind. I know why you answered my letters. I've read the papers."

"I'll get my expedition. And I have no need of your money."

"This is not the end, Wycliff. I will not be made a fool by you," Althea said, with her painted red lips.

Oh, but it was the end. Wasn't it?

Chapter 42

In Which the Duke Calls Upon the Earl

Lord Alvanley was sipping coffee in his drawing room when Wycliff was shown in.

"I may have just met your nemesis, Your Grace," Alvanley remarked between sips.

"About yea high," the duke asked, holding his hand to chest height, "black hair, glorious figure? Sly, yet cheeky?"

"How interesting," Alvanley murmured. Then he reached for a cheroot from the box on the side table and offered one to Wycliff, who declined that, as well as the offer for coffee.

"Why would that be interesting?" Wycliff asked, having a good idea.

"Oh, merely that you think it's a woman," Alvanley replied easily. "Unless you are describing a man as having a glorious figure."

"Women are capable of the worst treachery, such as that of W.G. Meadows," Wycliff remarked. "And I'm not in the habit of commenting on men's figures, glorious or not. I'm here about your offer."

"Ten thousand pounds for whomever unmasks

W.G. Meadows," Alvanley confirmed. He lit the cheroot and exhaled a slow stream of smoke.

"Yes, that one. Or are you in the habit of offering vast sums of money for ridiculous things?" Wycliff asked.

"A man must keep himself entertained. I once wagered three thousand pounds on a raindrop race."

"What the devil is that?" Wycliff asked, and Alvanley smoked his cheroot and smiled as he explained: "Which raindrop would first reach the bottom of a pane of glass in the bow window at White's."

Wycliff was speechless.

"I haven't a wife to bleed me dry," Alvanley reasoned, which also explained that he was smoking freely in the drawing room, "or elder relatives to complain about how I spend my fortune."

"I won't feel guilty about accepting your ten thousand, then," Wycliff said. Because he would get this money. He knew the truth.

"Splendid. I should hate for it to be ruined for you," the earl said. "You do accept that I'll want proof before I merely hand it over."

"What did you have in mind?" Wycliff asked.

Alvanley sipped his coffee, pausing to close his eyes and savor the taste.

Wycliff didn't have any place to be, but the clock was ticking. Burke was probably charting his course or loading his ship right now. Lord only knew what else Eliza was discovering or inventing for her column at this very moment.

"See if you can get something published in the author's next column," Alvanley said. "A particular phrase, or story, that the author will unwittingly include so that you and I will know, irrefutably and in print, that you have identified W.G. Meadows."

Wycliff immediately saw that this would require Eliza's service in his household for at least another week. This didn't strike him as such a terrible thing. Torturous, yes. Dangerous, indeed. Fraught with the possibility of disaster, absolutely. But it was not a terrible thing at all.

"I suppose you know what you'd like it to say," Wycliff said. He took a deep breath and fought for patience as Alvanley took another luxurious sip of coffee. Good Lord, was there opium in it?

"There's a Byron poem I'm fond of," the earl said, gesturing to a book on his side table. 'We'll Go No More a-Roving.' See if you can get a line from it in the column."

"Agreed. You'll see it in W.G. Meadows's next installment of 'The Tattooed Duke.' I will call on Saturday afternoon to collect."

Chapter 43

In Which There Is Poetry

The conservatory

The duke called upon Eliza to assist him in the conservatory. Seedlings that had been collected abroad, having grown, now required transplanting into new, larger containers.

Of course he would ask *her* to assist him, of everyone else on the staff.

And yet, she knew the duke was not a fool. This must not be an innocent endeavor.

The conservatory was warm and humid. Outside, it was cold, wet, dreary England, with rain pelting the glass walls and ceiling. But inside, it was a tropical paradise. Eliza breathed deeply, inhaling the luscious fragrance of all the plants and blossoms. She loved this room, in a bittersweet way. She could only imagine what the rest of the world was like, and how much of it she was missing.

If only the duke would take her along . . .

The thought was sudden, unbidden, unlikely.

"Eliza." Wycliff turned, catching her eye from the far side of the conservatory. She waited as he walked toward her, weaving his way through this jungle of orange trees, ferns, and other vibrant greenery she could not identify. His gaze was intensely focused upon hers, demanding that she stay utterly focused upon him. She couldn't look away.

He wore his boots, breeches, and just a white shirt, rolled at the sleeves and stretched across his broad shoulders, left open at the collar, with a hint of his tattoos visible. As if he could not tolerate the slightest restraint. As if it wouldn't be long before the shirt was carelessly tossed on the floor and he worked in this hot room bare-chested.

Breathless. She was utterly breathless at the thought.

Wycliff pushed a branch out of his way, and she noticed that he had begun to wear his signet ring. His hair was pulled back and tied with a bit of leather.

She noticed his shirt, again, and that it was a bit damp and clung deliciously to his taut abdomen. He must have been watering the plants, she thought vaguely.

Still, he left her unable to take in air. There was something so raw and so strong about him. Like nothing could possible stand in the way of his deep, pure enjoyment of earthly pleasures. Something so capable about him—that he might single-handedly defend them from all manner of danger, survive on next to nothing, show a woman the greatest pleasure she'd ever known.

Eliza was stricken with both the urge to flee from danger and an overpowering desire to throw herself into his arms. In the end, she remained rooted where she stood. Wycliff stood before her. Her heart beat hard in her chest.

She loved him. She knew it like she knew the sky was blue, and like she knew the sun set each day and rose again in the morning. It was a simple, powerful fact.

"You requested—" she began, trying to explain her presence.

"You, Eliza," he said, in a warm, sultry voice. He took her hand and led her past trees and other plants. Her hand felt so small in his, and she felt so vulnerable as she followed him. Her heart skipped beats every time he glanced back over his shoulder at her.

He seemed to desire her, and she wanted him to love her. She wanted to hold his hand and explore the world. She tilted her chin up and gave him a sweet smile. She would win the money for him, for them. Knightly and *The Weekly* be damned.

"I require your assistance," the duke said. On the potting table before him was an assortment of small plants and containers and dirt. "I thought you might prefer this to dusting, or sweeping, or polishing the silver. But then again, who knows with women?"

"Saddler takes care of the silver," Eliza said. "No one else is allowed near. We might steal it."

"Well, I might sell the lot of it and sail to Timbuktu with the proceeds."

She smiled. In less than a week's time he'd have all the money he needed for his voyage, and he could keep the Wycliff silver collection. That is, if her scheme worked and Alvanley's word was good.

"What am I to do here?" she asked.

"Transplanting. Those little seedlings have germinated and outgrown their containers. They need more room to grow, otherwise they'll be stifled and die."

"And you didn't carry these seeds from halfway around the world to watch them wilt in your conservatory."

"Precisely. Here, I'll show you." Wycliff stood her before the table and came to stand behind her. From there, with her tucked up against him, and reaching his arms around her, he showed her how to remove the seedling, gently tease apart its roots and then replant it in another, larger pot where it would have room to flourish.

The rain fell outside, pittering and pattering on the glass ceiling above them.

She felt the rise and fall of his chest. She wished to fall back into his arms. The warmth of his body and the heat of the room were making her drowsy, languorous. When he stepped away to work beside her, she felt the loss of him intensely.

They were silent for a while, until he broke it.

"The child is not mine," he told her. Eliza slowly exhaled.

"You need not marry her, then," Eliza answered. She dared a glance at him out of the corner of her eye and saw that he was focused on the little green plants, which seemed so delicate and tiny in his large hands.

"Duty no longer impels me to," he answered. It wasn't a no. It wasn't quite a yes, either. It didn't matter, at any rate.

Liam. Brighton. What a mistake. Had she known then . . . had she just a bit of faith that great things were in her future, she could have waited instead of greedily snatching the first exciting thing to cross her path.

"What will you do?" she asked.

"You mean, how will I get to Timbuktu?" he said, and she nodded. "Perhaps my voyage will not look like I imagined it. Instead of a troop of soldiers, I could take only the essentials: myself, my wit, my weapons."

"But what of the estate, here? What about the tenants and the wages —"

"I am not sure if you are the angel or the devil on my shoulder," Wycliff said. "Tempting me into one thing, reminding me of a contradictory duty. You are trouble. But then again, most women are."

"Perhaps, but you seem unscathed as of late. In fact, you have been remarkably studious. In your library at all hours ... I wonder what you are reading?"

She noticed that he stayed there later and later each night.

He'd been in that locked room for hours, too. But she dared not mention that.

"I have taken to poetry, if you can believe it," Wycliff answered, and then he began to recite some lines: " 'So, we'll go no more a-roving/so late into the night ...' "

It was on the tip of her tongue to feign ignorance and ask who the author was, even though she was well aware that it was Lord Bryon. But it was hurting her soul to play the silly girl around this sharply intelligent man. And what did it matter at this point? As long as she managed the line "In secret we met, in silence I grieve" in her column, the money was hers to give to him.

So instead of asking who the author was, Eliza recited the next line: " 'Though the heart be still as loving, and the moon be still as bright.' "

"A poetry-reciting housemaid. Where the devil

did Mrs. Buxby find you?" Wycliff gave her a slow, lazy grin that warmed her up even more. For a moment the world beyond his gaze ceased to exist. Eliza thought of the pleasure he'd given her, and at the memory, heat pooled in her stomach, and lower.

"I hate that you are married," he said softly.

That sucked the air out right out of the room. Eliza imagined plants wilting in her hands. Wycliff's hands stilled, but he kept his gaze on the plants.

"Me, too," she said, and then she asked, "Does it have to matter?"

"If only I wasn't a run-of-the-mill Wicked Wycliff," he remarked. And then he recited a few more lines from the poem, " 'Though the night was made for loving, and the day returns too soon/Yet we'll no more go a-roving, by the light of the moon.' "

It made her lungs tight, in a panicked way, as if she needed him, loving by the light of the moon, to survive. What if he left for Timbuktu—without her? What if he sailed off and she had only a memory of what could have been?

If only, if only . . . if only a million different things. But life was the way it was, and certain things were as immovable as mountains. He was determined to be a better man than all of his ancestors. She was trying to show him that she was honest and faithful and true when it really mattered, so that when her disguise came to light, he'd know she wasn't a complete liar.

All they had was this moment, warm inside, and sheltered from the rain drumming on the glass walls and ceiling.

As they worked side by side, hands in the dirt and holding delicate little plants, Eliza wondered . . . if he knew, and if he didn't love her, what was she still doing here?

By all rights he ought to have sent her away long ago.

He must care for her. But then why could he not say it?

By the end of the week all the secrets would be revealed—let the cards fall where they may. She gasped for air, suddenly aware of the tension, and craving for the release. This unknowing could cease, this deception brought to light.

If she thought for a moment that she could tell him her schemes, she would have. But she'd heard his angst and frustration, and the scathing comments. He might storm away, and then she would never be able to fully explain her own hopes and dreams and needs.

When she won the money, she would give it to him for his own dreams. She just hoped they included her.

Chapter 44

Harlan and the Duke

Now this is more like it," Harlan said, exhaling a full stream of cigar smoke up into the night sky. A few stars peeked through the thick haze of fog.

"It's almost like being back out there," Wycliff said, although the roof now made him think of Eliza right here, and not some grand adventure out there. This was noted and pushed aside.

"Aye," Harlan agreed. He puffed thoughtfully on his cigar. They had come up to the roof after supper, rather than sitting in the stifling atmosphere of the library. Wycliff had been there all day, studying Arabic, reviewing the account books, and plotting his course. The mission would look different than he had planned.

In fact, all of his plans were now falling neatly into place. But still there were questions, unanswered. He sipped his brandy and asked one of the questions that had been nagging him for a while.

"Did you join Burke's crew yet?"

Harlan exhaled again, sending another puff of smoke into the air.

"I'm entertaining an offer," Harlan answered. "He recognizes my translation skills. He also has an expedition planned, and a departure date."

Wycliff felt his jaw clench, hard. Harlan, his supposedly trusty comrade, was defecting to his longtime rival. The lack of loyalty was breathtaking, save for one fact.

"And yet you're still here," Wycliff pointed out. Smoking his cigars. Drinking his brandy. Looking at the stars from the roof of his ancestral home.

"You did save my life. Once," Harlan remarked.

"When is Burke leaving?" Wycliff asked. He stared up at the few night stars and imagined a sky full of millions. His heart sang in its chains at the thought. But he couldn't shake the image of Eliza beside him, gazing up at a sky on fire with stars.

"In a few days," Harlan answered. "Which doesn't leave you much time. You could just marry Lady Althea and be done with it."

"I could," Wycliff said, but the words struggled in his throat, telling him that he absolutely could not. Not when she had tried to trap and outwit him with that child. Not when she was Hades' Own Harpy. Not when he still had another option.

He would get to Timbuktu. But would he get there first?

Harlan seemed to hear the struggle in his voice, and glanced warily at him.

"It's the maid, isn't it?"

"I might be able to come up with the necessary funds in time," Wycliff replied evasively. He found he didn't quite trust his old friend, not when he was likely to join a rival expedition. Harlan glanced at him curiously, and then taunted him.

"And then what—will you spend it on an expedition, or set up house with the little missus?"

Wycliff sipped his brandy, savoring the burn, and biting back words he was surprised to find at the ready. Timbuktu. Expedition. Of course. There could be nothing else.

"There's no missus. There cannot be. She's married," Wycliff said.

"That little housemaid has more secrets than you can shake a stick at," Harlan remarked.

"Aye," was all Wycliff could say to that.

"You know about her, don't you?" Harlan asked. "You're after the Alvanley money, yea?" Harlan fixed his good eye upon the duke. "I put two and two together. Good to see you're not so far gone that you can't recognize a woman's scheme when it's kissing you and talking honey mouth to your face," he said, using an Arabic phrase.

Wycliff stared at him, hard. His heart pounded heavily in his chest. The words made him dizzy with anger. His old friend thought him a fool, blinded by the charms of a treacherous woman. Worse: he knew that where he himself suspected a deep, dark, storming real love that could drown him, Harlan saw only an idiot in the throes of infatuation.

Harlan probably thought he wouldn't turn her in for the money. Little did he know.

Another sip, to give him pause before saying, "Yes. I know. Don't tell her."

"Oh, I won't say a word, old mate," Harlan said, taking a sip of brandy himself after setting the cigar down. "But I don't think it'll work out as you're planning it will."

"Whatever does that mean?"

"*Ties*, Duke; the kind of ties that keep a man on land, and get him thinking about heirs and spares and prudent behavior. Before you know it, you'll be cutting your hair, tying a cravat around your neck, and vexing over your reputation."

"You seem to have me mistaken for someone else," Wycliff replied.

"You seem to be refusing to admit that you're a man in love," Harlan said plainly.

"I told you, she's married." Wycliff nearly growled this unfortunate, immovable, impossible fact. He couldn't possess her—she wouldn't let him, so long as her husband might roam the earth. And if he couldn't have her, then he couldn't lose her.

"I hope you don't think that was artfully dodging the question," Harlan said with a snort, "because that just confirmed everything. You've gone and fallen in love with the chit."

After quitting the roof, Wycliff walked quickly through the halls on his way to the study.

He couldn't admit Harlan was right. Couldn't deny it either. That word rattled and banged around his head, knocked on his heart, burned in his gut. He couldn't admit to loving her, because then he couldn't very well turn her over to Alvanley for a cool ten thousand pounds, which he would then use to leave her. A man in love wouldn't do that. He needed to do that.

Wycliff entered the long corridor decked with the portraits of old dukes and duchesses and their dogs and children. They all smiled fondly down upon him, he knew, though he refused to look.

The trip to Timbuktu—and the respect and recognition for his own damned talents and not his lineage—was the summation of everything he'd ever wanted. Over the years, his heart beat for this. He inhaled and exhaled, each breath bringing him closer to his goal. Every shipwreck, plan gone awry, time in prison, night spent hungry under a big black sky, every wild beast hunted and every skirmish and fight with foreign tribes . . . he'd gamely taken all that on for a reason. For Timbuktu. For recognition. For his own damned sense of pride and honor.

Down the great staircase in the foyer he went, his boots pounding on the marble floor. He'd nearly ravished Eliza with a look as she scrubbed these tiles on all fours.

All of his plans, dreams, and quests quite nearly felled by a mere slip of a girl with a pen and feather duster. And eyes like the ocean that saw into his very soul. A pink mouth that gave him untold pleasure from her kiss. A quick mind that perfectly put into words what he was feeling.

Of all that he had seen and experienced in the world, there was nothing quite like Eliza. And he would turn her in, take the money and run. He had to. Or Harlan was right—he would never leave if he wrapped himself up in the ties that bind a man to land, to a future, to a woman.

Wycliff pushed through the heavy oak doors to the library. The last embers of a long-forgotten fire burned in the grate, and he put them to work lighting a candle, which he took to the desk. The book of poems lay open to that one particular page, tempting any spies. How Alvanley knew to name the line that so perfectly, gut-wrenchingly named this moment in his life, Wycliff knew not. That it was poetry pricked his male pride. For ten thousand pounds and a chance at his dream, he would survive.

Removing a fresh sheet of paper and writing things, Wycliff sat down to copy out Lord Byron's poem in its entirety.

> So, we'll go no more a-roving
> So late into the night,
> Though the heart be still as loving,
> And the moon be still as bright.
> For the sword outwears its sheath,
> And the soul wears out the breast,
> And the heart must pause to breathe,
> And love itself have rest.
> Though the night was made for loving,
> And the day returns too soon,
> Yet we'll go no more a-roving
> By the light of the moon.

He added *For Eliza* in his scrawl and signed it *Wycliff.*

He folded the page and sealed it shut with wax, pressing the signet ring into it so Eliza would know without a doubt that this was from him.

He'd recently taken to wearing the ring as a reminder of what he would leave behind—his inheritance, his reputation, his past, and one tempting vision of what his future could be. *Eliza.*

Funny how his heart still beat hard, with longing, given what he knew.

Treading a dangerous path, Wycliff returned to the attic and slipped the poem under her door.

Chapter 45

Deceiving Mr. Knightly

Offices of The London Weekly

There was the leaf of paper in Eliza's hand—the latest installment of "The Tattooed Duke." And then there was the one folded up and tucked into her bodice—a copy of Lord Byron's poem, handwritten by the duke himself and stuck under her door.

The one that might break Wycliff's heart, and the one that absolutely broke hers.

No more we'll go a-roving by the light of the moon? Eliza could take a hint. *And love itself have rest?* Rest, expire—she took that hint, too. Its meaning was plain to her: he might still care for her. Maybe. But it was, unequivocally, over. No more would they go a-roving. Loving. Anything.

It stung, like the prick of a wasp. Or like the snakebite Wycliff had once described to her. Or perhaps like a bludgeoning.

To make matters even more excruciating, this was the last meeting of *The London Weekly* that she was likely to ever attend. Knightly would find out soon enough about her deal with Alvanley. And then he would fire her accordingly.

It seemed she was in the habit of betraying the men she cared about the most. Funny, that.

This wasn't quite what she had in mind when she'd donned her disguise and got herself hired as a housemaid of the duke. Her intention had been to remain a Writing Girl, whatever it might take. And now she was walking away from it all . . .

"Well?" Sophie asked when Eliza slipped into the seat beside her.

"Yes, what is . . . I mean . . . how . . . Oh goodness. Where to begin?" Annabelle asked, flustered.

"For Lord sake, ladies, act normal," Julianna hissed, and Eliza thanked her.

"I can't. There is too much happening that I am too curious about!" Annabelle gushed, wringing her hands.

"Well here is something," Eliza said. She reached into her bodice—and then glared at another writer when she caught him eagerly watching her, or rather, her hand. "I have lost his affections, for certain."

"A poem," Annabelle said, eyelashes aflutter, when she saw what Eliza handed over.

Julianna snatched it away and read it quickly.

"No more loving. No more roving. I hope you were merciless in your column," Julianna said sharply.

"It should change once you have the money," Sophie said in a low voice.

"We ought to invite him to your birthday party, Sophie," Julianna said.

"He's already on the list, I think," Sophie responded.

"Did he reply?" Eliza asked.

"I don't think so. I'll send 'round a note tomorrow," Sophie said, and then she turned full force to Eliza. "*You* are attending, right? It is my birthday."

"If I can sneak out of the house," Eliza answered.

"Why do you not just quit?" Julianna asked bluntly.

"Because she is close to him when she is there," Annabelle said, answering perfectly for her. "And she may never see him again if she leaves. And when you are in love . . . well, just being near the person is a kind of warmth that is hard to forgo."

"Yes, what Annabelle said. Precisely," Eliza said. "Because any minute now he will turn me out and slam the door shut behind me. Until that happens, I'd like all my little moments with him, even if it's me pouring his coffee."

"I still think you should come to the party," Julianna said. "I have a dress to lend you," she offered. It would need to be hemmed, oh, a good seven inches. She could do that while sewing and sipping tea with Mrs. Buxby and Jenny. She realized then she would miss those two.

"I will attend," Annabelle said. "And I shall need a fellow wallflower."

"Nonsense," Sophie said. "Eliza will dance with the duke, and perhaps Knightly will ask you to waltz, Annabelle." Annabelle blushed furiously at that.

"Roxbury will dance with you both and flirt shamelessly," Julianna added.

"The flirtations of a rake are not quite as thrilling when the rake in question is madly in love with his wife," Eliza pointed out.

"Nevertheless you must come," Sophie said. "And if you could cause some sort of scandal with the duke—say waltzing together, caught together, etcetera—as a hostess, I would be much obliged."

"And I would as well, as a gossip columnist."

Eliza's two fabulous friends peered at her, smiling. She knew they meant well and wished nothing but the best for her. She knew they had adopted Knightly's credo. She also knew they possessed a security that she did not, with their handsome, wealthy, adoring husbands, as well as a wide circle of friends both haute ton and beau monde.

At the moment everything for her was utterly uncertain.

"This is her heart at stake," Annabelle chimed in, to her defense. "We mustn't make sport of it."

"Thank you, Annabelle," Eliza said.

"You're right," Sophie agreed. "But I still think you should risk attending, and I shall hope Wycliff attends. All sorts of romantic things tend to happen at balls, and I hope that it should happen to you." Sophie reached out and squeezed her hand, and suddenly everything was all right and she knew her friends only wanted true love for her.

"Ladies first," Knightly said, striding quickly into the room for the weekly meeting with his writers.

"Was Knightly invited?" Annabelle whispered to Sophie, who whispered, "Yes."

"Is he attending?" Annabelle questioned.

Knightly glanced curiously over at her, probably because she was talking and not paying attention to him, and most of all not sighing upon his entering a room.

"Yes," Sophie replied, again in a whisper.

"Then may I also borrow a dress?" Annabelle persisted.

"Yes," Sophie said again, biting back giggles. The entire staff was watching them now and the room had fallen silent.

"Ladies?" Knightly questioned, raising his brow.

"We are discussing our attire and other plans for a ball later this week," Sophie answered. Annabelle had gone mute. And pink.

"What rot," Grenville complained, to the surprise of no one. "That's why women shouldn't work. They distract the men from real matters of business by discussing—"

"Matters of courtship and thus marriage and creating the next generation," Julianna interjected. "Is there anything more noble than that?" she challenged. Eliza sighed. Her friend could never resist an argument. "No, I don't think there is. And we tend to such matters while also authoring the columns that make this newspaper a sales phenomenon."

"Speaking of that, Eliza, what do you have for us today?" Knightly fixed his piercing blue eyes on her. They hadn't exchanged a word—written or spoken— since the confrontation on Saturday. Her final words to him hung in the air: *I shall make it your problem.*

"More noble deeds, or nefarious ones?" Knightly asked coolly. He might as well have asked if she wished to continue writing for *The London Weekly*, so loaded was the question.

She smiled mysteriously and handed over the column.

Knightly took the page and began to read aloud: "'No one who had ever seen W.G. Meadows in her infancy would have supposed her born to be a heroine . . .'"

He paused and lifted a brow questioningly. Beside her, Sophie sucked in her breath. In this column, Eliza knew she was tiptoeing a fine line between writing about herself and Wycliff. And trying to please Lord Alvanley. She'd spent some very late nights spilling ink, burning her allotment of candles down low, scratching out sentences only to rewrite them.

Knightly continued:

> *"She was not remarkable in any way, and had little to recommend her. And yet, W.G. Meadows has captured the attention of London, feeding them tidbits of story like feeding a bird from her palm. Who is she? They wonder. The chatter is a low hum all over town. Lord Alvanley put a price on it, to the tune of ten thousand pounds.*
>
> *And this author has a tidbit of gossip well worth the price. The duke is known to resist all efforts to tame him; Lady Shackley knows this well. Her attempts to lure His Grace into marriage with a young pawn of uncertain parentage was thwarted by the duke's impressive deductive abilities. We cannot wonder at her desperate attempts to keep him; a woman is lucky to know a man like Wycliff, let alone possess his heart."*

"Are you saying that she faked a child so that Wycliff would be duty bound to marry her?" Julianna asked, in a dramatic gasp. It was unclear if she was aghast or delighted. Probably some combination.

"A pretend secret baby?" Annabelle questioned.

"Yes," Eliza affirmed. She offered up a silent apology to the duke and a prayer for forgiveness. She had to reveal the trick child to ensure that Knightly would print the column. It was a strategic blow to ensure a greater win. The loss of a battle to win the war. Or so she told herself.

"I *must* send her an invitation," Sophie murmured.

"And Eliza, you must ensure that the duke attends," Julianna added. "This could be just the scandal this season has been lacking."

"It sounds like we'll have a stellar edition of 'Fashionable Intelligence' next week," Knightly remarked. With that, he was off to the next topic and "The Tattooed Duke" was forgotten. Now all she had to do was wait for Saturday's publication.

And hope that her column was printed as she had written it.

And that Lord Alvanley's word was good.

And that Wycliff would forgive her.

And that nothing would happen between this moment and then to upset her carefully crafted plans.

Chapter 46

The Last of the Tattooed Duke

Usually, Eliza's first chore of the day was to start fires in the grates of the downstairs rooms. Today, the fires could take second place to *The London Weekly*, which she managed to snare first, before Saddler even had a chance to iron it. Quickly she turned to page two—page two! Oh, her heart still skipped a beat at that!—and skimmed the words to the latest and last installment of "The Tattooed Duke."

Eliza's eyes ran down the column, printed as she had written it, with the most important lines last.

> *Without the Shackley fortune, no more shall His Grace go a-roving. W.G. Meadows has shared much with London, and nary a line for the duke. To him, I say: in secret we met, in silence I grieve. Or perhaps, instead:*
>
> > *So, we'll go no more a-roving*
> > *So late into the night,*
> > *Though the heart be still as loving,*
> > *And the moon be still as bright.*

Her reign as W.G. Meadows was over because heiresses did not need to write for newspapers.

Wycliff did not wait for breakfast time to read this week's "Tattooed Duke." In fact, he did not even wait for Saddler to iron and press the "scandal sheet of Satan." He certainly did not wait for Harlan or Burke or even Basil to saunter in and avail themselves of his hospitality. He would not be a spectacle for their amusement.

He took the newspaper into the library. He turned to the second page.

Before he let his eyes find those cursed words, he paused. Everything depended upon this. The Wycliff estate, Timbuktu, Eliza . . .

He skimmed the column, skipping over words that did not suit him, seeking the particular line that would win the wager and determine his fate.

And then it was there: *No more shall we go a-roving. . .*

He tossed the newspaper aside and strode off to dress and to collect his winnings.

Chapter 47

The Great Reveal

Wycliff arrived with an issue of *The London Weekly* in hand. He was shown to Lord Alvanley's drawing room to cool his heels. Ten thousand pounds. He could almost taste it. He could almost feel the blistering heat of Africa and the glorious sensation of being out, alone, in wide-open spaces.

Alvanley's arrival was preceded by a maid bearing a tray of coffee things and a box of cheroots. She set everything up in a very particular way; it was clear she had learned her master's preferences and habits and took great care to ensure that everything was just to his liking.

This, of course, made Wycliff think of his own housemaid. His lovely, traitorous housemaid. He pushed those thoughts aside, though, because they were too complicated to contemplate and because Alvanley strolled in. He wore a silk wrapper, as if he'd just awoken.

It was two in the afternoon.

"Good morning," Wycliff said.

"Is it a good morning?" Alvanley mused. He settled into an obviously favored chair and poured a fresh, hot cup of coffee. Wycliff declined the offer of some himself.

"It is for me," Wycliff replied, and handed over the issue of *The London Weekly*.

"Mmm," Alvanley murmured, reveling in the pleasure of the first sip of his morning brew. Likely he would do the same in an hour or so, Wycliff thought, savoring the first sip of brandy for the day. Alvanley lit a cheroot and breathed deeply.

Then he reached for the newspaper, snapped it open to page two and began to read.

Wycliff did not see his face behind the sheets, but he would have liked to. Trails of silver-gray smoke rose up and faded away. Instead he had to content himself with the *sound* of a man reading. Save for the occasional *hmmm*, it was not illuminating.

But a moment or two later, one of those moments that felt like an eternity, Alvanley set down the sheet.

"You have satisfied our terms of the agreement," he said.

Wycliff nodded. *I know* seemed the wrong thing to say, at least until the banknote exchanged hands.

"However, we may have a problem," he said, and Wycliff suppressed his urge to growl with annoyance. *So. Damn. Close.*

The butler appeared in the entryway. "My lord, you have a caller. A female."

"That would be the problem to which I am referring," Alvanley said calmly. He reluctantly stubbed out the cheroot.

The butler stepped aside.

Eliza.

For a second Wycliff's heart stopped. When the

beat resumed, it was fueled by scorching, violent sparks of anger, sizzling and crackling.

Eliza.

He had suspected she was the author. He'd known. But her presence in Alvanley's drawing room was not just a confession—and judging by her wide eyes and softly parted lips, an unexpected one—it was an admission that she had done it for the money.

Fire. He felt like he was on fire.

He had suspected, but to *know* was another matter entirely.

All those moments they had shared—or so he had thought—were merely fodder. Every kiss, every glance, every minute on the roof sharing his bloody hopes and dreams and everything . . .

All those damned conversations where he railed against the author of "The Tattooed Duke," only to discover now that he'd been complaining to the authoress herself. In the flesh.

And she had gone and printed the damning details anyway, knowing full well the devastating straits it put him in.

He had suspected her duplicity; he had known deep down. But he'd ignored it because it was a truth he didn't like, because he might have been in love with her.

That was the kind of idiocy that would get a man killed in the wild. It was slaying him now.

"I trust you two are acquainted," Alvanley said cheekily, cutting through the thick silence.

"My housemaid," Wycliff said dryly at the same time as Eliza said plainly, "My lord and master."

"It all makes perfect sense now," Alvanley said. "I

was tremendously intrigued when both of you came calling to claim the prize. Brilliant, Eliza, if I do say so myself."

"Dare I say thank you?" she replied, but she was looking at Wycliff as she said it. He sneered at her, couldn't help it. But she remained calm.

"I'm not sure you could fall any lower in my estimation," Wycliff drawled. "Go ahead and take the accolades for your deception."

"I did it for you," she told him. There was a note of frustration in her voice, as if he was just supposed to see that this monumental betrayal—him, his privacy, his integrity, his pride all sold for ten thousand pounds—as a good thing. As a bloody *favor* to him.

"Did you? Really? For me?" he questioned sarcastically. He took a step toward her. Eliza stood her ground but she flinched. He knew what he looked like—some wild, heathen warrior clad in the barest trappings of a gentleman. She knew what lay beneath. Damn right of her to flinch. "Because if there is one thing you've learned about me, in all of your spying, it's that I like to have things handed to me. God forbid I earn something through my own hard work."

He did not want charity. Least of all from her.

"Allow me to explain, Sebastian—"

"You may call me Wycliff. Or Your Grace. Or if you were a proper maid you wouldn't even look at me."

"I'm not your servant anymore. I'm a writer, a published one, and a damn fine one at that," she snapped. Oh, the little bird was angry now.

"Oh, I'm sure Byron is cowering somewhere,

threatened by your talents. You write for a gossip-ridden news rag that sucks the life out of its subjects, merely for amusement and profit."

"We write what the people wish to read, or we are not published at all. I know that well, Your Grace, but I am also tremendously proud to have discovered a story to captivate Londoners. I am only sorry it came at such a great price to you."

"Was it worth it? Your little newspaper stories for my expedition, my reputation?"

"The story is not yet concluded, Duke. You may get your expedition yet, and who cares for your reputation when you are deep in the wilds of Africa, en route to Timbuktu?"

"That all depends, does it not, on the outcome of this wager," the duke said. "The neat sum of money for which you have thrown away love."

Her lips parted and no sound emerged. She blinked rapidly. Those eyes, those eyes . . . they would haunt him.

"Your Grace," she said quietly, "it has not escaped my attention that, as I have come to turn myself in, you are here to turn me in as well."

"There you have it, Alvanley. We have provided a dramatic scene in your drawing room, to entertain you at the start of your day."

"I am most obliged, I assure you," he said, the faint hint of a smile at his lips. Smoke curled around his hands, his jaw, and slinked up to the ceiling. "Bravo."

"I had not anticipated the performance," Eliza said softly.

"But you did so well playing the part of repentant

bluestocking," Wycliff said sharply. "The daughter of an actress—"

"You have absolutely mastered the role of haughty, impossible duke."

Alvanley cleared his throat. He put out his cheroot, took one last sip of coffee before setting down the china cup. Then he stood, clasped his hands behind his back, and addressed the two stubborn almost-lovers.

"Let us not avoid the facts. You are both here because I extended an offer of ten thousand pounds to whomever uncovered the author of 'The Tattooed Duke.' Whatever your opinions on the matter, Your Grace, I must extend my compliments to the lady: her column had me—an old bachelor who has known every amusement—riveted and enthralled. Of course, I must thank you for being so bloody intriguing as well."

"Thank you," they said in unison. They glared in unison, too.

Even Wycliff, still deep in the throes of hurt and anger, was able to see her pride. Rationally, he knew that it was quite the achievement and perhaps in time he would be amused to have played a part. But in the moment, he added *supremely irritated* to his list of bad feelings.

"In order to test this, I had requested that certain lines find their way into the printed version. Eliza, 'In secret we met, in silence I grieve.' Duke, 'No More We Go a-Roving.'"

At that, she gasped. "So that is why you left that poem for me. And spoke of it . . . I had suspected you knew, but I didn't realize you would scheme and use me as well. I thought it meant—"

"Perhaps it did," Wycliff retorted, because he was still angry. He was glad, at least, when Alvanley brought up the money.

"You both have satisfied my terms. I'm sure you are both wondering what I shall do about the sum offered," he said, and began to pace as he thought aloud. "I will not give you each ten thousand. That would be ridiculous. Do I divide it evenly? Or do I give it to only one of you?"

"Give it to the duke," Eliza said evenly. Then she turned to him, blasting him with the full force of her ocean eyes and rosebud mouth. He had to make the mistake of looking. "I did this for you, you know," she told him, and he suffered another flash of anger.

"I do not want guilt money, pity money from a *girl*," he retorted. It was damned unmanly to be so thoroughly trounced by a girl, and then saved by her! He would not have it. He didn't want her damned money or her pity, and he didn't want to assuage her guilt. No, she could keep every last farthing.

"What if it were a dowry?" Lord Alvanley questioned, and Wycliff answered him hotly.

"First, Lord Alvanley, with all due respect, the two of us are quite at odds, if you haven't noticed. Second, unless she were to add bigamist to her list of sins, marriage is out of the question."

"This is quite the dilemma," Lord Alvanley remarked. On that, they were all agreed.

In the end, because Eliza had been there first, it was decided she would collect the ten thousand. Stubborn to the point of idiocy, and enraged beyond reason, Wycliff refused to accept the money from her.

They might have had true love, had it not been for her rank deception.

He would not assuage her guilt, would not soothe her female-feelings, would not forgive her duplicity. Not even for ten thousand pounds. Not even for Timbuktu.

Chapter 48

In Which the Outcasts Become Sensations

Duchess of Hamilton and Brandon's birthday ball

That evening, Eliza made her debut as an heiress, for Wycliff refused so much as a penny, and Alvanley escorted her to the bank to deposit ten thousand pounds in an account for her. It was noted that she had been the first to approach Alvanley.

With ten thousand pounds to her name, the haute ton promptly forgot that she was the daughter of a playwright and an actress. It escaped their notice that they had not in fact made her acquaintance.

Not only had a new, pretty heiress come into their clutches, but a fourth Writing Girl had been uncovered. To add another layer of sweet, delicious scandal to the massive uproar unfolding, it was this young miss who had been the author of the column that had preoccupied Londoners and dominated every conversation for the past month. W.G. Meadows was a girl, who had turned herself in for a fortune.

It had been this young girl who discovered and informed them all of the duke's tattoos. Of his passionate nights in harems, of his frolics with nude, native women in Tahiti. It had been a girl who wrote of his brushes and battles with danger, and every other dramatic, scandalous thing.

Later they would wonder how, and why, and the full story would emerge, and the gossip would take a turn for catty. But for tonight Eliza was a sensation.

There was nothing quite like a lovely young woman with a sizable fortune and wickedness in her past, newly discovered by the ton.

The Tattooed Duke himself, contrary to all expectations, arrived at the ball.

Tonight, at the duchess's birthday party, the collective gaze of the ton was completely, utterly, and totally fixated upon the Tattooed Duke and his authoress. They made every effort to stay apart—save for scorching, meaningful glances from across the ballroom—while the hundreds of other guests made every effort to force these two together.

Lady Althea was in attendance, decked in a sinful shade of crimson, and looking like she had trouble on her mind.

Knightly was there as well, and his expression did not show him to be affected in the slightest by the defection of one of his prized Writing Girls.

The quartet of scribbling females were in full force at the soiree.

It was, in many ways, a typical ball—there was candlelight and laughter, silk and satin gowns, and men in black and white evening dress. The duchess served lemonade and champagne. The doors to the terrace were wide open. The orchestra played their usual tunes from behind a veil of potted ferns. But there was *something* in the air, a mood in the room, a sizzling undercurrent that might at any second become an explosion.

"I have never witnessed a scandal," Lady Charlotte Brandon, sister to the duke and sister-in-law to Sophie, remarked. "I should like to very much."

"I haven't either," Annabelle said. "And I would like to as well."

"Well, that will be easily remedied tonight," Julianna said, with a sphinxlike grin.

"No, it mustn't," Sophie answered. "Brandon will have my head if you do. He'll make a list of 'ways to prevent Charlotte from discovering scandals' or 'reasons why Charlotte should not be introduced to scandals.'"

Some busybodies hovered about, shamelessly attempting to eavesdrop on their conversation.

"I shall do my best *not* to cause one," Eliza said. And then she sipped her champagne, such a delightful drink. Her gown, loaned to her by Sophie, was the loveliest thing of pale blue silk, like the Tahitian sea in the duke's watercolors.

"If you're intent upon avoiding scandal, then you ought to set down that glass," Julianna lectured. "And do not accept another."

"Knightly is here," Annabelle said, apropos of nothing.

"So is the duke," Eliza said, sipping the champagne recklessly.

"Charlotte!" Sophie called out. "Where are you going?"

But Charlotte did not answer, for she had slipped away, lost in the crowds.

Wycliff saw her. It was absurd, really, the way he involuntarily sought her out and found her immediately in a room full of hundreds. But nevertheless he saw Eliza and felt a noxious combination of emotions: a hot surge of anger, stabbing pangs of hurt feelings—*Good God*—regret, for what he couldn't quite say, and lust.

But mainly anger. He was incredibly angry. Because he had quite nearly fallen in love with her—the purest of emotions!—and all the while she was lying to him. Very well, he had fallen in love with her. And he had to refuse her.

Anger. Absolutely.

He had returned to Wycliff House to find that she had packed her things and left. Just like that—gone. As if nothing had ever happened. No lust, no love, no laughter; just a house that felt tragically empty. Nevertheless—

He would not speak to her this evening.

He would not give the ton something else to talk about.

He would not participate in a scandal. Not any more than he already had.

Lady Althea slinked by, and he amended that last thought. Shackley money had worked before.

Eliza . . . Althea . . . Eliza . . . Althea . . . Eliza. . .

Wycliff glanced at the brunette who had come to stand beside him. She faced the ballroom, but the sidelong looks she gave him could not be missed.

"Pretend we have been introduced, if you please," she said. This was so they might be permitted to converse. And yet, to be fair, given their postures, it could not be definitively said that she was conversing or otherwise engaged with him. But her intentions radiated, and could not be mistaken. She meant to speak with him.

"Perhaps. If you actually introduce yourself," Wycliff replied. She heaved a sigh, the sort only young melodramatic girls did. The world over, it was exactly the same.

"My name is Lady Charlotte Brandon and I'd like to assist you in causing a scandal."

Wycliff choked on his champagne.

"I know, I'm extremely impertinent. And yes, my relations despair of me," Lady Charlotte Brandon continued. The name caught his attention, and significance dawned—she was likely close family, a sister perhaps, of the duke and this evening's host—who had married one of those nefarious Writing Girls. This Lady Charlotte was then likely to be a wolf in debutante's clothing.

"What if I do not wish to cause a scandal?" Wycliff asked. He continued, as did she, to face toward the dancers and pretend they were simply next to each other and had no greater connection than that. She was a young, presumably unmarried chit. He was known, an unrepentant sinner. This was not a good combination, the world over.

If he did not take care, they could be betrothed by morning.

"You do not wish to cause a scandal?" The young lady was aghast. And, he detected, supremely disappointed with him.

He watched Lady Althea, dancing, and had to admit that all that fiery, wild passion of hers when confined by the steps of a formal reel was a marvelous thing. She managed to positively hum and exude a potent energy so that it seemed this little dance could, at any second, with only the slightest provocation, turn into something much, much more wicked. Her dance partner quivered, likely in terror.

On the far side of the ballroom he didn't so much as see Eliza but feel her in the clench of his heart and the hair on his skin, which stood raised, alert, suspicious, aware. In the company of a tall, yellow-haired female, she seemed like any other wallflower, which is to say, sweet, innocent, and shy.

Oh, but he knew what Eliza was capable of. Days and nights of deception. Which was hard to keep in the forefront of his mind since she was not dressed as a housemaid and deferring to his wishes. No, tonight she was dressed as a beautiful woman—an heiress—who kept throwing glances his way from the far side of the ballroom. Quick, sudden, and piercing glances, like a spear thrown by a warrior hidden in a jungle thicket.

Eliza wore a pretty sea-blue gown that he was sure would set off her eyes in a bewitching way, if he were to get close enough, which he would not.

Danger! his every instinct warned.

Her hair had been done up in some elaborate manner composed of tendrils and wisps and sparkly bits—the language of feminine decoration was not one in which he was fluent. The whole thing probably took hours with hot irons and curling papers and other strange female contraptions. He could read that well: only a lady of means had time to waste on such frivolous pursuits as a fancy, complicated coiffure. Not, say, a housemaid who had only yesterday been dusting his library shelves and letting him believe she couldn't read the titles on the spines.

He could appreciate the overall effect of the silky, satin gown and the hair and the jewels. Eliza was a beautiful woman. Brilliant, daring, and deceptive, too. Wycliff recalled, forcefully, that he was angry with her.

But he couldn't deny she was breathtakingly beautiful. He caught himself wanting to know *this* Eliza—the smart, shrewd, glittery, literate version of herself.

"I could arrange a private meeting, if you wished it," Lady Charlotte said, the boldness of her suggestion barely undercut by the low tone in which she made the offer.

"Young lady—" Wycliff started, and realized how old and stuffy and proper that made him sound, when he was anything but. His hair was still long—when all the other gents had theirs cut short. He still wore an earring declaring his time as a common sailor—in a room of the most rarefied and refined who defined work as selecting menus with the help of a chef, or sleeping through sessions at Parliament. Under his evening clothes—a concession to the company—the inky black swirls and bold lines of his tattoos covered his chest.

He was not old, or stuffy, or proper.

"Lady Charlotte—" he began again.

"If you do not wish to cause a scandal, what about living happily ever after?" she asked in the manner of girls the world over, and their fairy tales. He scowled in annoyance.

"That would be my concern, not yours."

"If you insist, Your Grace," she murmured in a way that patently declared she did not agree one whit. "But I should like to introduce you to an acquaintance of mine. Her health is failing and she has a fortune to dispose of. Lady Millicent Strange and her daughter Araminta would be delighted for the introduction to you."

"Would they, now?"

"Yes, but you mustn't look closely at Lady Millicent's hand. It was bitten off by a wild boar, you see."

Wycliff bit back a grin.

"I must introduce you to my friend Harlan. His arm was badly mangled by the bite of shark. He lost his left eye in a freakish accident involving a spear, a tribal mask, and a kitten."

"Really?" Lady Charlotte asked breathlessly.

"It's as true as your Lady Millicent, her daughter Araminta, and the wild boar."

Lady Charlotte, rather than being shamed, smiled broadly.

"You are a man of sense. I am pleased," she told him.

They were then interrupted.

Wycliff's expectations of his reception this evening were low, and had already been surpassed when a man whom he did not know ambled over with two glasses of brandy in hand.

"The name is Roxbury," the man said by way of introduction as he held one of the glasses out toward him.

"Wycliff," he said, accepting and then sipping the proffered brandy.

"I know," Roxbury replied.

"Was it the hair? The earring? The tattoos that gave me away?"

"All that and the wide berth the entire ton was giving you. For a duke, to boot," Roxbury answered. And then he peered past Wycliff and said, "Well well. If it isn't Lady Charlotte!"

"Oh hello, Roxbury. Good evening to you," she replied ever so politely, when it seemed she'd been caught. The chit was bold.

"I hope you are enjoying this ball. Since it could very well be your last if you persist in associating with blackguards like this fellow," Roxbury told her. "I am given to understand that monasteries are not known for their parties. Or men. Which is where your brother is likely to send you if you cause more than the usual amount of trouble."

"Oh, bother that. It would take all the army and the cavalry to get me there. Instead, I shall run off to Timbuktu with His Grace. Fancy that! Me, a stowaway!"

Roxbury groaned. "I thank the Lord every day that you are not my responsibility."

"Perhaps I shall teach lessons to that baby you are expecting."

Roxbury paled. Lady Charlotte beamed. And then she strode off into the crowds.

Wycliff watched this exchange with an avid interest, piecing the pieces together as they bantered. Clearly, these two were close, their families, too. It was not the first time he had watched a scene like this and absorbed the familiar banter of loved ones. However, it was the first time that his scientific detachment failed him; he had never experienced an intense longing to participate until now.

"I myself have also been severely wronged by a Writing Girl," Roxbury said, once Lady Charlotte had left them alone. This piqued the duke's interest.

"They make a sport of us, then?" Wycliff asked, not sure if this diminished his anger—to be one of many—or inflamed it.

"Yes, they seem to. I think it's that natural feminine inclination to stir up trouble; witness Lady Charlotte. But Knightly spurs them along," Roxbury explained. Wycliff sipped his drink, thoughtful.

"I hope you got revenge," Wycliff said, and Roxbury laughed heartily, striking a dissonant chord of terror in his heart.

"Oh, I did. I shot him and married her," Roxbury said, traces of laughter still in his voice. "What is the saying—if you can't beat them, join them?"

"Or keep your friends close and your enemies closer," Wycliff remarked.

"Exactly. Marriage is the perfect solution," Roxbury replied. And then he frowned, "Although the rake in me thinks I ought to wash my mouth out with soap for saying such a thing."

"Marriage is an interesting tactic," Wycliff said benignly, and thankful that Lady Charlotte wasn't present to hear him say that. It was probably his only remaining strategy, if he wished to see Timbuktu.

"It certainly isn't boring," Roxbury said, sipping his drink. "It appears the ton is agog that you have come out this evening."

Wycliff smiled wryly. "I seem to be endlessly fascinating them—from a distance."

"Many of them are exceedingly dull and stupid, and one must be indulgent with them, as with small children. But come, I'll introduce you to some people worth knowing," Roxbury said, and Wycliff followed him in the direction of the card room.

They came face-to-face with Knightly on their way. In fact, this encounter occurred in the doorway to the card room—a particularly uncomfortable spot. The walls between the card room and ballroom were thick, forming an immovable barrier. Wycliff proved to be the same. Knightly had to face him or turn and flee. In front of everyone.

Wycliff was struck by the urge to make the man

squirm and sweat and otherwise wriggle like a worm on a hook. He recalled his own laughing retort to Knightly about having a housemaid write down his every word, and how remarkably close to the truth he had been. Knightly had sipped his brandy and likely thought him a fool.

And now that writer was ten thousand pounds to the richer.

"Knightly." Wycliff said this like a prelude to torture.

"Wycliff, Roxbury . . ." He said this coolly, as if he wasn't bothered one whit by an angry aristocrat, and one who'd already shot him, at that. Wycliff experienced a flash of jealously and a hankering for his collection of firearms.

"How are you enjoying this evening?" Wycliff asked him. Polite. Circuitous.

"I daresay it just got interesting," Knightly replied, "Although I suppose you'd like to hear I am not enjoying it in the slightest."

"So tell me, Knightly, do you plan to keep W.G. Meadows, our dear Eliza, as one of your *Weekly* wenches? Now that she's ten thousand pounds to the richer, what incentive does she have to stay?"

Knightly and Roxbury exchanged a glance that spoke volumes, and that irritated him. Especially since Knightly had looked extremely peeved verging on enraged at the mention of the loss of his author.

"So the cat is out of the bag. It was bound to happen," Knightly replied with a shrug. "But I wouldn't be so sure that the days of the Tattooed Duke are over."

"No, of course not. It seems nothing will teach you a lesson about using other people's lives and honor for sport."

That hit home.

The clench in his jaw was unmistakable, as was the narrowing of his eyes. Wycliff was even treated to a swift, sharp intake of breath.

In his periphery he saw that Roxbury's laughing countenance had gone serious and he, too, was nodding along. Another man wronged by a Writing Girl, indeed—and the man behind the women.

"I could start a brawl," Wycliff mused aloud. "Or, like an angry brute, give you a good pummeling out in the garden. Or perhaps even live up to the rumors and adopt the cannibal's diet. Or in proper English fashion, I might challenge you to a duel."

"Already been done," the two men said simultaneously.

"But I think I will leave you, Knightly, knowing that my revenge will not be so mindless and bloodthirsty."

"What is it you want?" Knightly asked, irritated. "If you want a bout of fisticuffs, then let us be one with it. If you are to enact some more subtle, devious form of vengeance, I'm sure that I deserve it and shall survive it. Do you want a retraction printed? I could devote an entire issue of the newspaper to detailing your noble deeds and calling W.G. Meadows a liar of the first order. But I assure you, the ton will still speak of your less savory aspects: the man captive in the dungeon, the cannibalism, the harems, the tattoos."

"What I want is what you have stolen from me. Your newspaper cost me my life's work. It cost me an expedition to Timbuktu. Your sneaky, conniving author even deprived me of the bounty on her pretty little head."

"You could marry her," Knightly had the *audacity* to suggest. Wycliff could feel his own jaw drop in shock. "The money would be yours."

Wycliff recovered himself after a hot sip of brandy and said: "If I were to marry a scheming, deceptive female with a fortune, I would have pledged my troth to Lady Althea Shackley weeks ago and be en route to Africa rather than here, in this bloody overheated ballroom, having this conversation with you."

What Knightly said next was something he hadn't seen coming. The words roared in his ears like cannon fire, and felt as such upon impact.

"But she's not in love with you. Eliza is."

Chapter 49

Secret Notes

Wycliff was ready to depart when the footman strode purposefully toward him, bearing a silver tray with a crisp, white vellum note folded and sealed upon it.

"Your Grace," he murmured, offering the sheet up like a sacrifice to a moody pagan God.

Wycliff took the sheet and unfolded it. The handwriting was that of a woman.

The duke glanced about the ballroom, wondering who wished to meet him in the library in a quarter hour's time, at midnight.

Eliza had resumed her wallflower status with the company of champagne and Annabelle.

"Is he merely an idiot? Or does he not wish to dance with me?" Annabelle mused aloud. She had engaged him in conversation and with hint after hint of her desire to dance. Knightly did not offer. "And if he does not wish to dance with me, why on earth not? I'm pretty, am I not?"

"You are beautiful, Annabelle. He is demented."

"I am inclined to agree with you," she agreed, her

voice dark. This was a first. Annabelle had always championed Knightly. Always.

Then the footman interrupted with a note on a silver tray. Eliza and Annabelle exchanged mischievous, wondrous looks before Eliza accepted the note and opened it.

"Who wishes to meet with you in the library at midnight?" Annabelle asked, reading the note over her shoulder. "It must be Wycliff."

"It could be anyone," Eliza pointed out, refusing to allow even a measure of excitement.

"Of course it could be anyone. But I am certain it is Wycliff. Or, it could be a trap of some kind. It could be dangerous," Annabelle said, grinning. "I shall go with you. For your safety."

"Annabelle, really—"

But someone bumped into Eliza at that moment, sending the paper fluttering off to the polished hardwood floor and her champagne spilling entirely down the front of her gown. Her pale blue silk gown.

"Oh, my apologies," the woman drawled. Eliza turned to see that it was none other than Lady Althea Shackley of the very loud, passionate love to Wycliff, of the funds for his initial voyage; Lady Althea of the fake child and the letters to the duke. Hades' Own Harpy.

"Allow me," Lady Althea cooed, barely managing to retrieve the note from the floor. Her dress was such that it did not encourage such an endeavor, but it was no match for her curiosity.

Lady Althea read the note, brazenly, and then glanced at the large clock above the mantel.

"You haven't much time," she pointed out. "It is nearly midnight and your dress is soaked in champagne. I suppose you might be able to do something, but you shall surely reek of wine for your interlude with your lover. But who knows, perhaps he likes it?"

Eliza's temper flared and she snatched the note back.

"Yes, but I suppose that you wouldn't know, Lady Althea, given that he's had the minimum amount of contact with you in the past decade."

Hades' Own Harpy drew in a sharp breath. Eliza stifled a *hmmph* of satisfaction.

"Do excuse us," Eliza said grandly, then walked away with Annabelle in tow. "I had to leave before she got the last word," Eliza explained.

"That was very well done of you. I'm quite impressed. Are we going to the library now?" Eliza smiled at Annabelle's use of *we*. She'd go alone, to Wycliff—it had to be he.

"After a trip the ladies retiring room, yes. Hades' Own Harpy is right. I do reek of champagne."

"It could be worse. You could smell of brandy." Annabelle wrinkled her nose.

"I wonder if the duke—and all men—would vastly prefer the scent of brandy on a woman, rather than floral scents and such."

"Perhaps that is what I must do to steal Knightly's attention . . ." Annabelle's pretty mouth twisted into a frown of sadness tinged with vexation. But at least she wasn't sighing anymore. "Oh! It's nearly midnight!"

Chapter 50

Midnight Rendezvous

It was nearly midnight. Lady Charlotte *might* have mentioned to Julianna that she had overheard of a clandestine meeting about to occur in the library. When the notorious Lady Drawling Rawlings, so named because of her ability to orate at great length, happened to notice the deliberate manner in which Julianna proceeded in the direction of the library and comment upon it, she *might* have fanned the lady's curiosity.

"Why do you not follow her?" Charlotte casually suggested. Really, anyone with an ounce of curiosity would do just that, without any debate. Lady Charlotte was itching to witness what Julianna was after, especially because she had a very good idea what it was. "I do believe I shall go."

Lady Rawlings narrowed her eyes.

"You could witness something inappropriate for young ladies," she scolded.

"Oh, I do hope so," Lady Charlotte replied pertly. And then she wandered off—giddy, positively *giddy*, in anticipation of the scene about to unfold before her.

It *might* include the Tattooed Duke, *might* include

a certain Writing Girl, *might* include champagne and romance and—Charlotte shivered with excitement—*might* include scandal. That is, if everything went according to her plans.

"Have you seen Wycliff?" Lady Charlotte's attention was diverted by a man to her left inquiring to another gentleman about the duke. "My cousin," he explained. She didn't stop to hear more. She knew very well where Wycliff was, but she wasn't telling. Not yet.

Charlotte was certain because she orchestrated the scene about to unfold—the duke, the notes, the setting, everything except some devastatingly romantic lines to sweep Eliza off her feet. But hopefully the duke could come up with those on his own.

Lady Rawlings fell in beside her. "You ought to have a chaperone," she explained. Charlotte smiled behind her fan. Perhaps Eliza and the duke would name their firstborn after her, in honor of her antics in bringing them together. It was a beautiful plan—the notes, the library, the secret midnight rendezvous—what could possibly go wrong?

The duke found the library easily. It was just steps from the ballroom. He found it set for a romantic interlude, complete with candles and bouquets of flowers pilfered from the ballroom. A bottle of champagne had been set out, along with two glasses. Someone had seduction in mind, and it wasn't him.

Was this Eliza's attempt to make amends? He poured himself a glass of champagne and wondered why that prospect induced a tightness in his chest, a dull throb in his heart. She was beautiful tonight. He reminded himself that she was treacherous.

The door opened. Slightly at first, as if uncertain, and then a woman slinked into the library and shut the door behind her.

"Wycliff," she said softly. A smile played on her lips as she surveyed the scene: a duke and all the instruments of a romantic proposal.

"Lady Althea," he intoned. Why did he feel a sudden avalanche of disappointment?

"Do you recall the time we made love on the carpet in Shackley's library? There was a roaring fire and wine while a thunderstorm raged outside?" As she painted the picture, Wycliff drank more champagne. The warning bells were beginning to sound.

"I do remember, particularly the friction burns on my back."

"Oh, Wycliff," she laughed, as if he were joking. But he wasn't. That was the first and last time he'd made love on a carpet without putting a blanket or fur down first. He drank again, to lessons learned the hard way. Then he refilled his glass.

"Are you not going to offer me some champagne?"

He did, briskly, as he told her, "Just so that we are clear, Althea, I did not set this up. I am not trying to seduce you and I have no intentions to rekindle our mad, passionate affair from ten years ago. "

And then he froze. Because there were voices in the hall.

Lady Althea heard them, too, if that wicked smile on her painted mouth was any indication.

"Whatever it is you're thinking, for the love of God, do not—"

Lady Althea then tugged down her bodice. He, foolishly, reached out to set it to rights. They were a tangle of bare hands and red satin and Lady Althea's exposed flesh when the door was flung wide open.

"Oh my goodness!" a gray-haired matron exclaimed. "Well I am shocked. I never! *Never.*"

"Oh my God," the statuesque stunner beside the matron gasped. He recognized her as one of the chits Eliza had been gossiping with earlier in the evening.

"I say, is that my cousin?" Another voice bumbled into the conversation. It could only belong to Basil. Wycliff groaned.

"Who is it? The Tattooed Duke?" a voice he didn't recognize piped up. In fact, more than a few voices piped up.

"This is not what it seems," he said, in the manner of many a Wicked Wycliff before him. Someone in the crowd snorted in disbelief, and frankly he didn't blame them one whit.

There, just off to the left, stood Lady Charlotte with her eyes wide in horror. When his gaze settled upon her, she had the decency to blush, bow her head and stare meekly at the floor. In an instant it was all clear to him: she had engineered this scheme from the notes to the "sudden interruption."

Wycliff weighed his options. He could expose her role in this ridiculous plot, which, if he remembered society correctly, would ruin her prospects forever. Or—

"Wycliff just proposed!" Lady Althea Shackley gushed. The crowd, now spilling into the library, gasped appropriately in shock.

His mouth fell open. His heart may have stopped beating, too. His lungs ceased to draw breath and part of his soul was paralyzed.

"I did no such thing," he said firmly. It was ungentlemanly, he knew, to disagree with a woman. But when such life-altering lies were on the table, exceptions were to be made. But his protest was no match for the growing din of a firestorm of gossip.

"What a romantic proposal!" someone exclaimed.

"The flowers are lovely, and the candles! He even thought of champagne."

Wycliff could not see who shouted out all of that damning evidence. He saw only Lady Charlotte, this time biting down hard on her lower lip. She at least had the decency not to look proud of herself.

She mouthed the words *I am so sorry.*

Damned chits. Their ideas of scandal and romance and midnight rendezvous.

Lady Althea chose that moment to drape herself across his person. He felt her touch like a boa constrictor, wrapping itself around the victim, chocking off their air supply. But he was a duke, a Wicked Wycliff, a man who had sailed around the world, survived deserts and jungles and other unimaginable hardships and adventures

He would not be felled by a woman, especially not Hades' Own Harpy.

Wycliff disentangled himself and considered his paltry options for escape. Rather than push his way through the throngs, the Duke of Wycliff strolled over to the window, opened it, and climbed out.

It was only when he'd walked a block in the cool night air that he wondered where Eliza had been.

Chapter 51

In Which Our Heroine Is Thwarted

The ladies retiring room

Oh, the indignity of it all burned. Burned! Eliza scowled. Furious, furious!

First, she and Annabelle found themselves locked in the ladies' retiring room.

No, first she was drenched in her own champagne, thanks to Lady Althea. Her new silk dress had been utterly ruined, despite her efforts to blot off the champagne.

"It's all right, you now have ten thousand pounds, so you can just buy another," Annabelle said in an attempt to console her.

"That wasn't how I planned to spend it. And I still have to leave the ball early or wander around in a wet dress. I'm not completely familiar with the rules of high society, but I'm quite sure that is not done." She couldn't greet Wycliff while in a wet dress and stinking of champagne!

"We'll just borrow one from Sophie. You'll be gone for a half hour at the least."

"Annabelle, I don't have the time. It's past midnight now!"

"Then we had better go. Never mind about your dress. I'm sure it will be dark enough."

That was when they discovered the door had been locked. From the outside. Or perhaps it was stuck, or secured shut. One thing was obvious: the door would not open. One thing was painfully clear: there would be no midnight rendezvous for Eliza.

"Oh, Eliza, I am so sorry," Annabelle moaned.

"Why are you sorry? None of this is your fault." It was the fault of Lady Althea. Or fate. Something was conspiring to keep her away from her true love.

"I mean, I'm sorry as in I commiserate with you. I suppose you might say 'commissorry,'" Annabelle said.

"Is that even a word?" Eliza asked.

"I think I just invented it," Annabelle said, smiling in spite of the circumstances.

"If only you could invent a way out of this retiring room."

Eventually they achieved escape by the utterly unremarkable method of waiting until another woman needed the necessary and opened the door from the outside. Eliza and Annabelle dashed out, walking at an exceedingly unladylike pace.

They were not alone. A steady stream of guests proceeded from the ballroom to the library. A Scene was most certainly in progress. The two Writing Girls arrived in time to hear Lady Althea (for it must be she!) announce, "The duke proposed!"

"Oh, Eliza!" Annabelle lamented in a tone of deep commissorry. But Eliza was already pushing her way through the crowds on her way out of the house. She wished only to be home, in her own bed at her parents' flat near Covent Garden. She wished to remove this sodden dress and wake up in the morning able to pretend for a moment that none of this—the column, the duke, the scandal—had ever happened. To pretend for one brief shining moment that she hadn't met the love of her life. And lost him.

To Hades' Own Harpy.

At that, Eliza began to cry.

She raised her hand high, to hail a hack. That overwhelming desire to be home clouded any common sense and judgment she might have possessed. She had loved, and had lost. Nothing else mattered.

That is, until she was grabbed, bound, gagged, and tossed into a carriage that swiftly took off at a gallop.

Chapter 52

In Which Our Heroine Is Missing

Library, Wycliff House

Those damned newspapers trumpeted his betrothal and impeding marriage—the one he had never proposed, never agreed to, and flatly denied. Wycliff tossed the news rags aside. He did not even bother with the dramatics of getting up from his comfortable upholstered chair by the fire only to storm the vast distance of six feet, furiously crumple the sheets, and feed them to the flames.

There was no reason to put on a performance when there was no audience, no sly housemaid discreetly watching him with her ocean blue eyes. Eliza was gone and he could feel her absence—as if the house were suddenly empty of furniture. It was that obvious. It felt that spare. Hollow.

He would become accustomed to it, and then he would leave. Alone.

Good riddance, he told himself. But the thought wouldn't hold; the feelings weren't there to support it. He missed her, in spite of all logic and reason.

Just because the newspapers said he was going to

marry Lady Althea Shackley did not mean that he would.

Perhaps if it had been an honest misunderstanding. Perhaps if lust had overpowered his wit and reason. Instead it was a plot by some starry-eyed society miss that had been hijacked by Hades' Own Harpy. He valued his freedom more than any pretense to honor or society's rules.

"Your Grace," Saddler intoned from somewhere in the vicinity of his left shoulder. The duke shuddered, which was damned undignified.

"Good God, man, announce yourself! Cease sneaking up on me."

"My apologies, Your Grace," Saddler said in the same monotone voice. "You have callers. Ladies. Three of them."

"Oh dear God," Wycliff groaned. In no way could three female callers mean anything good.

"My thoughts precisely, Your Grace," the butler took the liberty of saying.

"Is Lady Althea Shackley one of these ladies?"

"No, Your Grace. I believe they are the Writing Girls." Saddler uttered the name in the same tone and with the same face he might say *Lucifer's harem*. He did not hold "Satan's own news rag" and the women who wrote for it in much regard.

"Show them to the drawing room," Wycliff ordered. Because he was an adventurer. An explorer. And three Writing Girls begged the question: where was the fourth?

In the drawing room, three anguished faces peered up at him desperately. Much hand-wringing was in progress. Introductions were swiftly performed so they could get to the business of what was so devastating that they would ignore society's rules to call upon the likes of him.

Eliza was not among them. Why?

He schooled his features into a passive, bored expression. But there was a gnawing sensation in his gut that foretold doom.

"Your Grace, we are sorry to intrude, but an urgent matter has come to our attention," said the duchess, Lady Brandon.

"Eliza is missing," the blond one blurted out, mercifully getting straight to the heart of the matter. *It is not my concern*, Wycliff tried to tell himself. But the thought wouldn't take hold.

"We are not certain of Eliza's whereabouts and thought you might shed light upon the matter. Is she here?" Lady Roxbury asked briskly.

He let out a rich baritone laugh at that.

"Why, pray tell, would I know?" he asked. "Perhaps I have taken her captive as punishment for her brutal portrayal of me in the press, which has thrown innumerable obstacles to my life's work. Perhaps you suspect something more salacious. But if you haven't heard, I am betrothed. To Lady Shackley. But you," he said, focusing his gaze on the redhead, Lady Roxbury, "were present. And if I know women, there aren't secrets between them, so I can only conclude that you two also know as well. Or at the very least, one might assume that you Writing Girls read the newspapers."

"Lady Charlotte is very sorry," the duchess said. She looked truly pained about it.

"Yes, well, she'll get her comeuppance one day, and it will be entirely of her own making. Then you can be certain of one man who will not come to her rescue."

"Speaking of rescue, we are afraid for Eliza," Annabelle, the blond one, cut in. She seemed on the verge of tears. Horrors.

"That is why we are here," Lady Roxbury said.

"I told you, I don't know where she is." He was irritated. She was no longer his concern. For better or for worse. He scowled, wondering why it felt like *worse*.

"Which bring us to our second question," Lady Roxbury said.

"Will you help us find her?" the duchess asked.

Wycliff laughed, and again it was not a merry sound. Of all the women, all over the world, none had gotten under his skin and wormed her way into his heart the way this one had. He wanted to bark out a no and send these chits scurrying for cover. He wanted, desperately, to not give a damn that she was missing. But his pulse hadn't quite been steady since they said the words *Eliza* and *missing*.

This must be love, Wycliff thought, very reluctantly. Any notion of pride or right or wrong or anything—anything!—paled in comparison to one truth: his beloved had to be well. Eliza had to be safe. That was all that mattered.

Only now did he pause to truly consider life without her. Cataloguing insects without her banter. Hothouse work without hothouse kisses. What were his scandalous tattoos without her hands, her mouth, her touch, her gaze upon them? He thought of her gaze over the breakfast table (she should be seated at his side not serving him coffee). He thought of her first thing in the morning and last thing at night. He thought of this emptiness in the house, without her in it.

Wycliff even imagined arriving at Timbuktu—and turning to Eliza for a kiss of joy and triumph.

But her deception . . .

But she told his secrets . . .

But she used him . . .

But she was married . . .

But suddenly it didn't matter. At least, not enough.

There was not a second thought in his mind or a question in his heart: he would save her. He would make sure she was safe. He made no promises other than that.

Mrs. Buxby chose that moment to enter with a tray of tea.

"You rang for tea?" Wycliff inquired of his guests, who were making themselves right at home.

"I am with child," Lady Roxbury replied. "I constantly require replenishment."

"Then you might not wish to drink this," Wycliff told her. She lifted her nose at him and proceeded to pour a cup for herself. He bit back a laugh as she sputtered upon the shock of whiskey-laced tea.

"The ladies need fortification," Mrs. Buxby said defensively. "Especially if they are to search for Eliza."

"How do you know about that?" Wycliff asked.

"Oh for Lord's sake, Your Grace, all of your servants know everything! Any one of us could have penned that column. If we could write, that is."

In all of his years, Mrs. Penelope Buxby had been a kindly, sweet, tipsy old matron. She hadn't spoken to him like this since . . . since he was a boy sneaking out of the nursery in search of cake.

"Your are quite forthright today," Wycliff told her. "Have you been drinking, Mrs. Buxby?"

"Only tea," she retorted. One of the Writing Girls stifled a giggle. Mrs. Buxby said "Hmmph" and went off to eavesdrop from the hallway.

"When did you see her last?" Wycliff asked. She couldn't be very lost; Eliza was too smart for that. All he needed to do was help them remember some perfectly logical and safe location where she'd planned to be. Or was that wishful thinking? His heart pounded heavily in his chest. *Eliza, missing.*

"She and I were locked in the ladies' retiring room from just before midnight to quarter after," Annabelle explained.

"How does one lock oneself in a room?" he asked, leaning against the mantel and folding his arms over his chest.

"It was a nefarious plot," Annabelle said solemnly. "I dare not make false accusations, however—"

"Oh, it was likely Lady Althea did it to conveniently remove her rival," Lady Roxbury cut in. "That grand scene was supposed to be for you and Eliza, I am told." She watched him closely, searching for his reaction. He wouldn't give her one. But damn, how much simpler things would have been . . .

His heart beat hard. He thought about doing things on his time, not having his hand forced, of not bowing to society's whims and dictations. He was not that kind of man, which was why Lady Shackley would remain Lady Shackley.

"Lady Charlotte is extremely apologetic," Lady Brandon had to add. Again.

"Once you two managed to escape, what next?"

Wycliff asked, in an attempt to focus his thoughts and avoid the hurricane.

"We joined the throngs outside the library just in time to hear Lady Althea announce that you proposed. And then she fled. I tried to follow her—I got as far as the front door of Wycliff House. But then I lost her in the courtyard. There were so many carriages and drivers. It was so dark."

"Thus Eliza has been missing for nearly twelve hours," he concluded.

"I had thought she was with Julianna," Lady Brandon said. There were dark circles under her eyes. He only noticed this now.

"And I had thought she was with Sophie," Lady Roxbury said, wringing her hands. She, too, looked like a wreck of nerves and lack of sleep.

"Me, too," Annabelle said. "I thought she'd gone to change after Lady Althea bumped into her, spilling champagne down the front of her dress."

"We didn't notice until she failed to turn up this morning to discuss the ball, as we had planned," Lady Roxbury added.

"Has it occurred to any of you that she might not have wished to join you?" Wycliff asked.

"No. Don't be ridiculous," Lady Brandon retorted.

"We sent a man to inquire with her parents," Lady Roxbury explained. "And we have even inquired with Knightly. No one knows where she is."

"We thought that if she were not with you," Annabelle explained, "then that man Liam might know." When he appeared blank, she clarified: "The one you keep locked in the basement dungeon."

He heaved the sigh of a weary man plagued by females.

"First, there is no dungeon. Second, he escaped. Third, do you really believe all that rubbish when you write it yourselves?" Wycliff asked.

"Knightly wrote that column," Lady Roxbury said. "The one Eliza had turned in was too flattering, since she was trying to repair the damage she'd done to your reputation. Knightly wouldn't publish it. You should know that."

What else did he not know? He had seen naught but treachery, deception, callous disregard for his privacy. But what of her own dreams and demons? Wycliff realized there was so much of which he was unaware. The woman who could enlighten him was missing.

He glanced around at the three anxious faces.

"Your Grace," Annabelle said. "Eliza is our friend, and we love her, and we have good reason to believe she is in need of your help." Her cheeks flushed pink with emotion as she continued her impassioned plea: "If you have a shred of tenderness in that heart of yours, please do assist us. But if you do not, please cease wasting our time. If we should find her moments too late, I should never forgive myself,"

"I will help," he said quietly. The hurricane raged within. Eliza lost . . . what if they didn't find her? What if she were lost to him forever?

Anguish wasn't quite the word. Regret sounded too neat and tidy. There was a tremendous sense of loss. A hollowness that had always been there, that he was only now aware of when he realized the one thing—the one woman—who might fill it could have vanished without a trace. There was much to regret about their last encounters, for he had been cruel and merciless to a girl who had only been trying to survive in a world with all the odds stacked high against her.

No, anguish did not even begin to describe what he felt.

"Now where shall we begin our search?" Lady Roxbury said crisply.

A heart-wrenching silence descended upon the room, for not one of them had even the slightest clue.

Chapter 53

More Bad Luck

Earlier that morning

If this was the life of an heiress, Eliza didn't want it. Frankly, her accommodations as a maidservant at Wycliff house had been vastly superior.

They were at the docks; she could discern that much due to the salty sea air mingling with the stench of dead fish and unsavory characters. Seagulls squalled, disturbing the early morning quiet.

She was locked, yet again, in a small room. First the ladies' retiring room, now this. She knew it was locked because she heard the key turn and someone—that damned Liam, most likely—pushing a heavy piece of furniture against it. Given that her hands were also tied behind her back, it did not make sense why he did so. She was tired, scared, hungry, and in need of a bath. Above all she felt positively murderous to be kidnapped and locked up and sticky from champagne.

The room was dark—no windows, no candles—and light slipping through cracks in the bare wooden walls were all the indication she had of the time of day. She knew early morning light altogether too well from her housemaid days. Up at dawn, lighting fires and hauling buckets of water. She didn't miss it. But this was worse.

She'd spent the night sitting on the floor, leaning against the wall with her arms bound behind her stretched-out legs. Not the most comfortable position. She wondered about Wycliff; in all of his adventures he must have passed some deuced unpleasant evenings. He might have told her such stories up on the roof, or working side by side in the conservatory. If she hadn't been wretchedly married, he might have told her stories of his adventures as they lay entwined in his bed after a long evening of lovemaking.

Not that she would ever know.

Eliza heaved a heavy sigh that contained all the tears she wouldn't bother to cry; all the longing for a love that might, in another universe, have belonged to her; she sighed with the weariness of an abandoned wife in love again and unable to indulge; she sighed with weary remorse. She'd been so close to everything—true love, success, wealth. And yet here she was, held captive down by the docks.

She spent ten minutes raining down curses upon her awful husband. He was a cold she never quite recovered from, a plague that kept claiming victims, a pebble in her shoe that she couldn't shake out. First she muttered the curses: "Bloody jackanape, bacon-brained bounder, ugly loose-screw." Then she hollered them at the top of her lungs until Liam hollered for her to shut up.

She felt markedly better. But still captive.

Eliza considered her options. She could wriggle out of her binds, rubbing her wrists raw in the process. Or she could hope she might be rescued, festering in this dark, dank room for hours. Days. For as long as she might draw breath, which could only be hours, minutes. She knew not. Especially now that she had angered her idiot captor.

Sophie would think that she had gone with Julianna, who would probably assume she stayed at Sophie's, since that's where the party was. Annabelle wouldn't imagine that she could do something so utterly rash as walk into a London night alone. What the devil had she been thinking to do such a stupid thing? The truth was, she hadn't been thinking at all. One thought had stuck in her head, *Wycliff proposed!* in Lady Shackley's silky voice. Over and over. It was enough to make a girl mad. Or foolish.

The duke: he wouldn't notice her absence. Or care. He might even be glad that she wouldn't be around to write any other editions of "The Tattooed Duke."

Clearly, she would have to free herself.

But the sound of voices in the next room gave her pause. There was Liam, her long-lost husband. And someone else—a woman.

Chapter 54

Husband and Wife, Reunited

The door swung open and there he was. Eliza had caught glimpses of him on the street, in uneven light. First, the day she'd seen him outside of Galloway's pub in a wretched twist of fate. Second, the day he'd chloroformed her in an alley. Some way to treat a wife!

It was only now that she was able to take a good long look at her long-lost husband.

Time had taken its toll, but he was still a handsome devil with his tousled sandy brown hair and entrancing green eyes with the kind of lashes women always said were "wasted on a man." Liam hadn't shaved, so his jaw was scruffy. It made him look thoroughly disreputable, but in such a charming way. And when he grinned . . .

He was a handsome man. A sinning, lying, vanishing man. But it was his charm and his good looks that let him get away with God only knew what.

She remembered, vaguely, when those green eyes were fixed on her silly eighteen-year-old self. How was she to know it would come to this?

"Well, hello, Liam. It's been an age," Eliza said from her perch on the floor.

"Eliza. You look . . ." He paused, searching for the words

"Like I've been tied up all night and slept on the floor?" she supplied.

"I was going to say 'lovely' because that's what women like to hear, but if you insist . . ." Then he flashed that *forgive me darling* grin. She scowled.

"You were always so good at saying what women want to hear," she replied with feigned sweetness.

"I'm an actor," he said. As if she needed a reminder that he spun lies for a living.

"Playing the part of a good man. But once the curtain falls . . ." she said.

"I knew you'd be angry. But I thought your temper might have cooled in the past six years. Or was it seven?" Liam leaned against the door and made a slight effort to count on his fingers all the years between this strange moment and that long ago time. Brighton, a mere month after the wedding. One month of anything but wedded bliss—he drank, she was lonely. They fought.

One afternoon he'd gone out for a pint and never returned. She waited one week and hightailed it back to London and never looked back.

"What brings you back after all this time?" she asked. Was it a coincidence that he reappeared after she came into a fortune?

"Oh, I haven't been gone as long as you think. I've been in London for the past two years. Before that, traveling with the troupe. House parties, county fairs, and the like." Liam folded his arms over his chest. She would have liked to do the same, but her hands were tied.

"You've been in London for two years and did not contact me?" she asked.

"I had no idea you were in town. And no reason to seek you out," Liam said plainly.

"And you happened upon me outside of Galloway's pub," Eliza said, as she pieced it all together and cursed her luck.

"A coincidence I didn't think much of until I heard about Lord Alvanley's offer and put two and two together," Liam explained. "I saw you leave the offices of *The London Weekly* and followed you to the Duke's house. I was going to turn you in, but then it was all over town that you had won the money."

"And here we are. Shocking, really, that you should reappear now that I have come into a fortune," Eliza said dryly.

It was a challenge to seem commanding and imposing while tied up on the floor, but by God, she would manage it. She knew it, because Liam's eyes flashed with surprise. But then again, she'd been a meek chit when he knew her last. A lot had happened to her in seven years.

"If my knowledge of the law is correct, the fortune isn't yours," Liam said with a smirk.

Her jaw dropped. She hadn't thought of that.

"It's mine. As your husband. Your lawfully wedded husband." Liam smiled in a way Eliza imagined the devil would after some poor sap unwittingly signed over their soul.

It took a moment, a very long, excruciating moment, for the full meaning of Liam's words to sink in. The money wasn't hers; she didn't care about that.

It belonged to Liam; that burned. She had betrayed Wycliff, the man she loved so that she might set him free to explore the world. But the money wasn't hers to give and it now belonged to this shadow of a husband, this sorry excuse for a man, this lying charmer with a black hole in the space of his heart.

"I'll spare some to get you a new dress," he said, eyeing her champagne-stained and stinking gown.

Later, she would think of retorts, or recollect her urges to violence. But the brutal truth was still hammering away at her: she had betrayed the man she loved so she might set him free . . . and it was all for naught.

"Where have you been all these years?" Eliza asked.

"Around," he replied with a shrug.

"Why did you not contact me?"

"It's complicated," Liam answered. He couldn't look at her.

"It's my business to know," she told him. There was a hard edge to her voice. He looked up, shocked. No, she was no longer the girl he'd known.

"Actually, it's your business to withdraw ten thousand pounds. My ship leaves tomorrow morning," he told her.

"Where are you going?"

"America," he answered, shifting his weight from one foot to another.

"Why?"

"So many questions. You were always so inquisitive." And then he feigned her voice: "'Do you love me, Liam? What does this mean, Liam? Where are you going, Liam?'"

The memory of her younger self, foolish and in

love with a jackanape, added another layer of black to her mood. For no other reason that to vex him, and perhaps miss his escape to America, she would not make this easy for him.

"Well, answer the questions, then. I would like to know."

"To start, I thought we'd go to the bank and withdraw some funds. By some, of course, I mean every last farthing of that ten thousand pounds you just came by."

"And then what shall you do?"

"I'll probably take care of you so that the funds are rightfully mine, just in case anyone questions it. But they probably won't, because I am going to take the money to America. And before you ask why again, I'll just tell you. Because I don't have a criminal record in America. Because they don't care if a man doesn't have a title or a fancy name or nothing. I'm going to take your fortune and build a life for myself that I'd never have in England."

"Liam, you are most likely going to blow the lot of it on foolish wagers and loose women. You might spare yourself the sea voyage and do it here."

"And risk Newgate? I don't think so," he said vehemently. She resisted the urge to mention she'd once escaped from Newgate as part of a story. Always, the story.

"What have you done?" she asked.

"You should know that acting does not pay well. Crime pays more."

"Oh, well in that case I am consoled and forgiving," she said sharply. Liam pushed off the doorjamb and stepped into the room, walking toward her. Her heart started to pound. Would he hurt her?

He clasped her arm; his hand was warm. Then he gave a little tug. Her efforts to loosen the ties at her wrist had been successful. But now she'd been found out.

"Oh blimey, it looks like you've been trying to escape, Eliza," Liam scolded, as if she were a child caught trying to reach the cookie jar. He tied her bonds tighter.

"Now come with me, darling wife. We have a ship to board." Liam flashed that charming, devil-may-care grin. She scowled. He flashed a pistol, tucked into the waistband of his breeches. Eliza just sighed.

Chapter 55

At Last, a Clue!

The Writing Girls, their husbands, and Wycliff had all searched separate parts of London, questioned everyone they could think of. The day had been exhausting and now they all reconvened at Wycliff House with spirits dashed and strength reserves running low.

The husbands had joined them—the Duke of Brandon and Earl of Roxbury—both of whom were consulting with Bow Street Runners. Julianna discovered the locked doors and expressed her desperation to know what lay behind them. Even Knightly had been pried from his office, though he brought reams of paper to work on from Wycliff's desk. The one Wycliff had fantasized about bending Eliza over to ravish her. The one where he pored over account books, maps, and books, searching for a way out. None of that mattered anymore.

He looked around his study. It didn't escape his notice how loving the husbands were to their wives. They were doting, and attentive and present. It was something he had never seen in this house. It made him feel the pain of Eliza's absence all the more. What had he lost? The enormity of it was beginning to dawn on him, slowly and painfully.

A small army had been assembled. They had no known enemy or battlefield. But they had brandy for the gentlemen and Mrs. Buxby's whiskey tea for the ladies.

And then Harlan arrived. The hour was late, night was falling, slowly cloaking the city in darkness. If anyone had been inclined to depart, they would at least remain for Harlan's visit.

"I had come to say goodbye," Harlan said. He glanced around the room, obviously perplexed by Wycliff's sudden popularity with people of obvious quality. "I hadn't realized I was interrupting a party. Not much of a party, though. This is the most somber, depressing gathering of people I've ever seen."

"Goodbye?" Wycliff questioned.

"Burke's expedition leaves tomorrow afternoon," Harlan explained, brave enough to look him in the eye. Was he sorry? Wycliff thought probably not, in the same way that a lion wasn't sorry for devouring a baby gazelle. How could it be sorry for doing only what it needed to stay alive?

But still, his longtime comrade was leaving for a grand adventure. Without him. And he would remain here, his future utterly uncertain. It all hinged upon Eliza.

"*The Esmeralda*, at noon," Knightly cut in.

"How do you know that?" Wycliff asked.

"It's in the papers," the editor said witheringly. "Shipping news, page sixteen."

"Congratulations," Wycliff said stiffly, with a short nod to Harlan.

"Thank you," Harlan said, equally uncomfortable. "What has got everyone down? Something must be wrong. One could practically suffocate from the smothering air in here."

"You remember Eliza, Harlan," Wycliff said with a wry smile. "These are her friends—dukes and duchesses and earls and countesses. That is the damned man behind *The London Weekly*."

"And how fares Eliza, dare I ask?" Harlan queried.

"We don't know. She has gone missing," Wycliff explained.

"Indeed?"

"No, Harlan, I thought it would be a clever thing to jest about. Yes, really," Wycliff snapped.

"A lot of fuss for a housemaid, Your Graceship," Harlan said, looking suspiciously around the room. "But she never was just a housemaid, was she?" he asked with a grin that Wycliff couldn't return. She'd never been some housemaid; of all the things she'd been to him—confidante, lover—above all she had been the only good reason to stay in London. She was, as Harlan had so astutely pointed out, his tie to dry land.

Time passed and Wycliff was keenly aware that she'd been gone almost twenty-four hours. If there had been a trail to her, it was now cold.

He stalked over to the sideboard to pour a brandy. He needed to feel the burn, to feel something other than this overwhelming sense of drowning. Heart pounding, unable to breathe, choking for air, clawing for the surface that seemed just out of reach.

Where could she be?

What if they never found her?

What if they did? Dare he even consider that? He tossed back his drink and said to Harlan: "If you can be helpful, you're welcome to stay. Otherwise, you might want to enjoy your last night on the town with more lively, obliging company."

"Oh, I'm on my way to a houseful of fine English lasses, but first I think I'll tell you about something strange down at the docks," Harlan began, and he too poured himself a drink. He settled into a chair and slowly sipped his drink.

"Make yourself at home. Please, take your time, too. We have all night," Wycliff said dryly.

"As I have mentioned, I've been preparing our ship to leave tomorrow. Down at the docks. And maybe I wasn't watching every box of cargo. I might have been distracted."

"Harlan," Wycliff said, but what he meant was, *For the love of God, get to the damned point already.*

"The ship next to ours was also loading up. A man was boarding, along with a chit he held real close. I could have sworn it was Eliza. One of 'em looked remarkably like that fellow with the chloroform."

"Liam," Wycliff said, as if it were a dirty word.

"Aye. That's what caught my eye. Literally. One eye." Harlan flashed a grin at the ladies, who weren't quite sure what to make of this one-eyed man. Wycliff scowled darkly at the lot of them.

"And I thought, 'That looks a bit like Eliza. Harlan, why on earth would the housemaid be boarding a ship with such a shady character? She's naught but a sweet, innocent chit . . . It couldn't be her, but maybe it is.' Which reminded me that I ought to come say goodbye to you."

"Tell me you tried to get her," Wycliff said. His voice was tight.

"I didn't know it was her. It might not be. But now that she's missing and there's a chit who looks like her down at the docks, I thought I might mention it. But then again, who says she wants to be gotten?" Harlan asked, stopping Wycliff cold.

What if she wasn't kidnapped? What if she ran away? That was a question he would deal with when he found her.

Out of the corner of his eye he saw Lady Roxbury ambling toward the door. Her husband was a step behind her.

"Where are you going?" he asked.

"To the docks, of course," she replied, her tone implying it was a stupid question with an obvious answer. Of course a pregnant woman was going down to the docks at this hour, as darkness was beginning to fall.

Wycliff looked questioningly at Lord Roxbury.

"I have learned it's easier to chaperone her cork-brained schemes than try to reason her out of them. Women and reason; like oil and water. Besides, she's a crack shot."

"Are you certain that it's her?" the Duke of Brandon asked quietly. "We can't afford to waste time following false leads."

"We might as well," Wycliff replied. "We don't have any other leads to follow."

"What was she wearing?" Annabelle interrupted. All heads swiveled toward her.

"A light blue dress," Harland replied. "The color of the Caribbean sea. Which is why I wasn't quite sure that I recognized her. One doesn't always see servants all decked up. But then again, English customs are strange. Don't always add up to logic."

"Would anyone like to join me now?" Julianna huffed impatiently.

"We're not just storming off without a plan," Wycliff said. "That's where most expeditions fail. That cannot happen tonight," he added. And then they planned.

Wycliff and Harlan would go, of course. After some heated debate it was decided that the Duke of Brandon would stay to coordinate the Bow Street Runners, who would be called upon for reinforcements. Julianna would stay, given her condition, and Roxbury and Annabelle would stay to keep her company. Knightly would join, and call for Mehitable Loud to join them as well.

Weapons were selected, cleaned, sharpened, and loaded. A plan was sketched: they would stealthily board the ship, search for Eliza, remove her with all possible haste and delicacy. A scene was to be avoided.

"This is not how I planned to spend my last night on land, you know," Harland said. "The adventuring was to start tomorrow."

"Perhaps it'll only take an hour and you can have a heroic story to tell all the girls in the brothel," Wycliff replied.

"True. True."

"If we do not return within two hours, send reinforcements," Wycliff told the group that would be remaining.

"Go get our girl," Lady Brandon said softly as she squeezed her husband's hand for reassurance.

Wycliff nodded, but thought he'd go get *his* girl. Even if she was bound to another, she belonged to him.

Chapter 56

In Which a Rescue Is Attempted

The hour was now late, the sky dark. A thick, nearly full moon provided ample light, as did the light within pubs and brothels that lined the dock. But it wasn't much. The ship itself would be utterly dark; it wouldn't matter whether a man had one eye or two, it'd be impossible to see either way.

Wycliff, Harlan, Knightly, and Mehitable had come to rescue Eliza.

"I told you so," Harlan said, apropos of nothing.

"I beg your pardon?" Wycliff asked stiffly. He had one thought: *Eliza.* His every sense was on alert, as if he might be led to her by scent, or presence or just a feeling. Harlan was distracting.

"Ties. You're about to steal aboard a ship for a chit," he explained.

"It's the gentlemanly thing to do," Wycliff replied. But Harlan was right. At some point his heart ceased to belong to the wide-open world, and now belonged to a troublesome slip of an English girl. Oh, he still wanted to explore and to travel, but not with the same intensity or ferocity with which he wanted to find Eliza, love her, possess her, and be with her. He didn't give a damn about her long-lost husband or what society would say. He could not live happily without her.

"It's something for the Bow Street Runners," Harlan replied.

"I'm more suited for this task. I know my way around a ship in utter blackness. Plus, I know her," Wycliff said plainly.

"That ship is Burke's," Harlan said, pointing to one of the ships. "And the one right next to it, on the left, is the one I saw her board."

"*Spirited Away*. Departing for America," Knightly said.

"How do you know that?" Wycliff asked, once again surprised by the editor's knowledge.

"I read the newspapers," Knightly replied, as he had previously. "Do you not?"

"Only the bits with me in it," Wycliff retorted.

"Why is she on a ship bound for America?" Harlan wondered aloud.

"I can't imagine," Wycliff said. "She'd never mentioned a hankering to go. Never mentioned any plans."

There were a lot of things she hadn't mentioned, in fact. But that didn't signify now. Because even through the lies, he had known the true version of herself. And that girl wouldn't climb aboard ships to America late at night without telling those close to her.

His stomach knotted at the conclusion he was coming to: she had been kidnapped. He realized then he'd been holding out hope that she'd just run off of her own free will in a rush of anger. That meant she'd cool down and come back. But kidnapped . . .

He thought of the ten thousand pounds. She was an heiress. And thus a target.

There was activity on the decks, which meant they could not just stroll aboard and politely inquire if any heiresses had been brought aboard.

"It we wait until morning," Harlan suggested, "we could more easily slip aboard in the commotion of everyone boarding."

"I cannot wait," Wycliff said. It would be impossible. They paused, and he surveyed the scene and considered their options. He factored in the darkness, the men on deck, the likelihood that it was she on board and held captive. And then he formulated a plan.

"Harlan, Mehitable, I need you to cause a scene. Draw their attention so that Knightly and I can go ahead undetected. If one of you runs off, it'll draw the crowd and allow the other on board."

"You'd like one of us to be chased by an angry, drunken mob of sailors on shore leave?" Mehitable asked skeptically.

"You can do something else, but I need to get on that ship," Wycliff replied tersely. It wouldn't be easy with so many sailors and God knew who milling around.

Harlan shrugged in agreement. And then he shoved Mehitable. Hard.

"Oi! What the devil . . . ?" Mehitable drew up to his full height of six feet six inches.

"Ain't you gonna hit me back?" Harlan taunted. Even though he had one working arm, one working eye, and his opponent was twice his size.

Mehitable shoved Harlan, sending him stumbling back a few paces.

A few heads turned. Harlan called Mehitable unspeakable names. Mehitable replied in kind. Pushes, shoves, and punches ensued.

"A fight!" someone hollered, and a crowd began to gather. As anticipated, those on the deck of the ship rushed to the front to look down at the ruckus on the dock. Knightly and Wycliff would be able to sneak on the back.

They walked briskly, but did not run, toward the ship. Wycliff was annoyed to have a city boy like Knightly at his back. His expectations for the newspaperman's performance were low. But Knightly didn't complain about scuffing his boots and climbed aboard the ship with ease. He might not be useless.

They hesitated. A bunch of sailors were leaning over the side of the ship, watching Harlan and Mehitable hurl insults and punches at each other.

"She's probably in one of the rooms belowdeck," Wycliff murmured.

Down the dark, narrow, steep stairs into the belly of the ship they went. Wycliff first, with Knightly at his back. The ship groaned and swayed and one could hear voices somewhere—they were not alone on this ship—but it was impossible to discern where the others were.

"This is an impossible task," Knightly said under his breath.

"I know," Wycliff said, continuing to move forward. It was impossible. But it was unthinkable that he would not try. He thought of Eliza, laughing. Of that sly smile of hers. Of her quick wit and the way she felt in his arms.

Just to test the effect it would have on him, he

thought about "The Tattooed Duke," and her writing it. Would it send him into a rage? A dull ache, a slow burn? Wycliff discovered that he couldn't even hold onto the thought long enough to experience a feeling about it. He thought only of her, and wanting to hold her. The desire was overwhelming.

The minutes had gone by. They'd inspected nearly everything: the cargo hold, the kitchen, rooms, cabins, and hallways. They found nothing. Well, they found lots of things, but no Eliza.

"There you are, luv." A woman's voice cut through the silence. The men paused to listen. It was a welcome distraction from the terror of not knowing if Eliza was safe, after hours of searching.

"Did you bring supper?" a man asked, hastily adding "luv."

One could almost see her scowl from the other side of the wall, in the dark.

"I hope you're not going to be a bore for the whole trip to America," she said. "Because these quarters are too small for two, let alone one with a stick up his bum."

"We're eating, Maggie, must you be so vulgar?"

"Why are you saving so much of your supper? Did you sneak a stowaway on board or something?" Maggie asked. Wycliff's pulse quickened.

"Lord above, Maggie, just mind your own business," the man exploded. Wycliff and Knightly shared a look.

"I'm your wife. Your business is my business," Maggie retorted.

Hearing enough, Wycliff stepped forward to knock on the door. He heard the sound of frantic activity: wood scraping on wood, cutlery on pewter plates, hissed curses and conversation.

The door opened, and Wycliff knew he was in the right place. He recognized this unshaven man with the messy hair and the hard, cruel eyes. They'd met once before, briefly, in an alley off Fleet Street, after this bounder had plied Eliza with chloroform. In fact, Wycliff's fist was intimately acquainted with the man's face, but that was the extent of their involvement. The bloody cad had escaped him once before, but it wouldn't happen again. Not tonight.

Wycliff just hoped he wouldn't be recognized right away. He adopted the persona of bored, obtuse aristocrat.

"This isn't the ship to Boston, is it?" Wycliff inquired.

"No, New York," the man replied. Good to know.

"Ah, good. Then I am aboard the right ship. However, I believe this is my room," Wycliff said.

"I'm sure it isn't," the man replied, bored.

"The captain directed me here. Down the stairs, he said. Count the doors on your left. I'm looking for the seventh. Is this not the seventh?"

"I didn't count." The man was getting irritated now. Good.

"There is one thing to do, then," Wycliff said, becoming more cheerful as the other man grew less so. "Let's just see if any of these other rooms might be it."

"We have these two rooms," the man said sharply. "Don't look in those."

And that was all Wycliff needed to hear to know which doors to open. When the man moved to stop him, Knightly stepped out of the shadows to block him.

"What the devil! That's my—"

Wycliff pushed open the door. It flew open, slamming into the wall. His heart stopped beating, only to resume with a ferocious intensity.

Chapter 57

A Revelation

Eliza hated to say it, but being in captivity, such as she was, was bloody boring.

She'd spent the previous night and today in that dingy little back room. She had remained on high alert for a chance to escape as she was escorted to the ship. But pistols had been pressed into her spine every step of the way, and she knew those things go off at the slightest provocation.

That was not the escape she was looking for. They had all moved to the ship for the evening, since it would be harder for her to escape in the night, or so Liam told her. A woman's voice joined in now, no doubt the woman she'd briefly seen earlier, and again Eliza couldn't tell who she was or how she fit in with Liam.

She heard them eating supper. She smelled it. She was starving. Her hands were still tied. And she was tired from remaining on alert. And bored. She might as well just close her eyes and sleep now . . .

She could escape in the morning, on the way to the bank.

Suddenly, the door burst open and slammed against the wall.

She saw Wycliff.

She thought she must be dreaming.

"You can't go in there," Liam said hotly from the hallway. "That room is mine."

"This is the room for your mistress?" Wycliff questioned loudly. She wasn't sure what he was about. But he was here, and she trusted him. So she kept silent.

"Mistress? Mistress?" the other woman squawked. "I'm his wife! Not his bloody mistress. Why the devil would you think that—"

"Madame, it seems you and your husband have much to discuss. He is your husband, correct?" Wycliff inquired. Eliza suddenly was no longer bored. If Liam was with a wife . . . what did that make her?

"At the moment he is," the woman retorted. Her blond curls shook violently. "He might be my late husband before the night is out." No one attempted to talk her out of it. She pushed her way past the men and into Eliza's chamber.

"Do forgive me if I don't stand to join you, but I'm a bit tied up at the moment," Eliza drawled.

"Who the devil are you?" the woman asked. She set her hands on her hips. She was a full-figured woman, with pale skin and a mass of blond curls.

"I'm Eliza Fielding. Who are you?" Eliza asked politely.

"Maggie Fielding."

"I really don't think we need to have this conversation—" Liam started.

"Shut up, Liam." The women—the wives—snapped this in unison and didn't even bother to look at him.

"We cannot both be married to the same man," Eliza said matter-of-factly. Then she paused thoughtfully. "Well, actually we could, but then someone is looking at bigamy charges."

"Not if the second marriage was never valid," Liam said triumphantly.

Eliza's eyes connected with Wycliff's in an instant. She felt the intensity of his gaze in her very soul. Hope beat in her heart.

Do you know what this means?

The question was unspoken, but it was there in his eyes and hers. There was a chance . . .

And he was here, with Knightly! Two unlikely rescuers. She knew her eyes sparkled with happiness, even though she was tied up and held captive. Wycliff had come for her, and Liam might be a bigamist. What wonderful news.

There was nothing holding them back now. No silly technicalities, anyway. They could be together, freely, if they wished it.

Wycliff impatiently shoved Liam aside and pushed past the other Mrs. Fielding to kneel by Eliza and begin to work on her binds. He did so gently, without sacrificing speed.

"How long have they had you like this?" he asked in a low voice.

"Since after the ball," she replied. "Since your betrothal."

He swore violently. He kissed her wrists. He whispered, "I am sorry I couldn't find you sooner. And there is no betrothal."

Eliza smiled. Wycliff grinned, and held out his hand to help her stand. He didn't let go.

"What are you doing? Where do you think you're

going?" Liam interrupted, trying to intercept Eliza's liberation. Knightly yanked him back.

Somehow, in this awful, impossible situation, she felt love. And joy. She looped her arms with Wycliff and he pulled her close.

"Mr. Fielding, is it?" Wycliff asked casually. "It looks like we have you guilty of kidnapping and bigamy, let alone what other crimes you've committed that have you fleeing to America."

"Kidnapping? Bigamy?" Maggie echoed loudly. Liam cringed at the sound of her voice.

"Don't be ridiculous," he replied in the calm tones of a practiced liar. "It's not what it seems."

Wycliff turned to Maggie. "When did you marry this—"

"Jackanape?" Maggie said, echoing Eliza's own words earlier. "This lying bounder? Let's see . . . It was the summer after the great storm, and six months after my sister married. You were in town with the theater troupe. I daresay it was 1816?"

"And ours was in 1818," Eliza said. "I remember everything."

"Eighteen eighteen . . . that was the summer I was home with the fever," Maggie recalled. "and too sick to travel."

"We eloped," Eliza said, "and I just turned eighteen. I carried a bouquet of wildflowers." She had been idiotically giddy and in the throes of one's first, foolish infatuation. Liam was so handsome, and such a charmer. She imagined a life of travel around the country with the star performer. What foolish dreams.

"I signed. In the church. Before God," Maggie said. "You did, too, Liam Fielding. And from the sounds of it, within a year of our wedding you were marrying other women. There was the summer I was home caring for my sister during her confinement. Did you take another wife then, too?"

"While I am fascinated by this marital dispute," Wycliff drawled, "there is one point to confirm."

"We are not legally wed, are we, Liam?" Eliza asked. She tried not to sound too hopeful. Too utterly delighted.

"No. Sorry," he said with a shrug. "But that doesn't mean I'm going to let you go. Not with ten thousand pounds on the line."

"Do you hear that?" Knightly cut in.

They all fell silent. Off in the distance was a roar, growing louder. There were gunshots. And the unmistakable sound of shattering glass.

"It sounds like a mob boarding the ship. Makes our escape a deuced bit more tricky," Wycliff said, pulling Eliza close to him.

"This ship is not only transporting passengers," Knightly said in a lecturing tone, "but a significant shipment of gunpowder as well, which you would know if you read the newspapers. Therefore, I suggest we attempt escape."

Chapter 58

In the Duke's Bedchamber

Eliza closed her eyes and sank into the hot bath with a sigh of pleasure. She knew what it took to haul those buckets of boiling hot water from the kitchens to the duke's bedroom on the second floor, and Lord above, was she grateful to relax in the water after the dramatics of the evening.

Harlan and Mehitable's efforts to create a distraction were too successful. One dockside brawl devolved into a riotous mob. She, Knightly, and Wycliff managed a treacherous escape from the ship—only to have it explode once they hit the docks. They had managed to flee as the fire spread from one ship to another. The Bow Street Runners arrived with the Duke of Brandon. Order was restored. Arrests were made, including one Liam Fielding, thief, kidnapper, and bigamist. The fire was contained.

Through it all, Wycliff—Sebastian—never released her hand.

Now, Eliza opened her eyes when she heard the door open. Flames flickered in the fireplace. Candles wavered lazily in the slight breeze sneaking in through the windows.

"Well hello," he drawled, leaning in the doorway and indulging in a long, heated look. She slid lower in the bath, so the water covered everything up to her bare shoulders.

He closed the door behind him and came to kneel beside her.

"Wycliff, I—"

He pressed one finger to her lips, holding back hundreds of explanations and a thousand apologies.

"Your stories are your adventures. I understand. Now close your eyes," Wycliff said, succinctly, as he gently tilted her head back and poured water over her hair and lathered it up.

Eliza kept her eyes closed, holding back tears. Was this forgiveness?

"It's just as well," he continued. "I could never be content with some dull wife who stayed home while I explored the world. A wife ought to be by her husband's side."

She opened her eyes and turned to look at him through the steam rising up from the water.

"I thought I told you to close your eyes," he said. And she mumbled something about his overbearing, ducal demeanor, and he muttered something that sounded awfully like "impertinent chit."

She closed her eyes and a smile played on her lips. Wycliff poured more warm water to rinse her hair. She could get used to this attention. Did she dare?

"I am sorry, Wycliff."

"I'm not. Not anymore, at any rate. How was I to find you if you weren't right under my nose?" And with that, he dropped a kiss on her nose.

She parted her lips, wanting his kiss.

"I almost lost you—"

"Because of my stupidity," she muttered, sinking lower in the water. Note to self: do not rush into the London streets at night, alone.

"No, I was going to say that I almost lost you because I didn't see that you were giving up your dream for mine. I know you had to give up the Writing Girls and *The London Weekly* for the Alvanley money, which you meant for me. So I could leave you."

"It sounds very noble when you say it like that."

"Noble. Troublesome. Beautiful," he remarked.

"And not married," Eliza said, exhaling freely. It was so glorious to be free of tortured secrets and troubled pasts. To just be herself.

"For the moment," Wycliff said. She glanced at him, questioningly. Her heartbeat quickened.

But then he distracted her in a very Wicked Wycliff sort of way. He grinned, rakishly, picked up the bar of soap and began to lather it up, and then with silky, smooth, soapy hands began to caress her shoulders first, and then lower, to her breasts.

Eliza gasped as her nipples peaked under his touch. Her back arched as his hands dipped lower into the warm water, though never leaving her skin. Expertly, his fingers found the vee between her legs and began to stroke her there, slowly and gently at first and then with ever more intensity, always perfectly matching the pressure building within her.

She was light-headed from the hot water, from the steam, from his touch. Each stroke of his fingers brought her closer to the brink. Wycliff's mouth claimed hers and she let go completely, surrendering to that ever spiraling tension within, crying out in pleasure.

* * *

Wycliff watched her, luxuriantly draped in the bath. Her cheeks were the softest pink, her lips red from his own, her eyes deep blue, nearly black in this dim candlelight. He had almost lost her. He would not make that mistake again.

Offering his hand, he helped her stand, like Aphrodite rising from the sea, only more beautiful because she was *real* and she was Eliza—daring, intelligent, fiercely independent. He didn't want her to lose that, but he also didn't want to lose *her.*

The words burned on his lips. *Will you . . .* But her beauty left him speechless. Of all the sunrises and sunsets he'd seen, of all the sublime natural spectacles and stunning sights he'd witnessed on his travels, nothing compared to Eliza emerging from the bath.

Silently, he dropped to one knee.

"Wycliff?" she said, lifting one brow questioningly. She glanced around for a towel. She looked at him on bended knee before her. Little rivulets of water trickled down her soft pale skin. In that instant he was jealous of a mere droplet of water.

"Will you marry me, Eliza?"

Her lips parted in surprise but no sound emerged. With a deep breath, Wycliff forged ahead with the things he needed to tell her.

"I know that proposing to a naked woman is probably not done, and if I were at all a gentleman I'd wait until you were properly attired, chaperoned, and I was given permission from your father. But I cannot wait any longer for you. All over the world I have roamed . . . and my soul mate was right here. In disguise. But I see you now. You, the adventurous, reckless, loving, writing woman. I have fallen in love with you, Eliza. I want our adventures to happen together. So tell me, will you be my wife?"

There were tears in her eyes and a "Yes" from her lovely pink mouth.

His lips found hers. She closed her eyes. A kiss, heady and wanting. Eliza was achingly aware of how close she'd come to losing him forever, and she reached out, wrapping her bare arms around him and arching her back to push herself nearer to him. She felt him smile.

The duke pulled her flush against his taut abdomen and wrapped his strong, muscled, tattooed arms around her. For a second Eliza had to break the kiss to look at his arms, with all those jet black tattoos on his sun-browned skin contrasted against her own pale flesh. Everyone thought they knew about the duke's tattoos. But none knew them the way she did. None ever would.

"Kiss me. More."

His wish was her command. At his urging, she opened to him. Tongues tangled, she tasted him, he tasted her. It was bliss. There was no reason to stop now. So they didn't.

Hours might have passed. She didn't know. Time ceased to have meaning.

Somehow, they found their way to the duke's feather bed.

"I wanted you from the first time I saw you," she whispered.

"Mmm," he murmured. "And I distinctly recall ogling your bum when I first saw *you*." To prove his point, he clasped her bare skin, there. She gave a little laugh of pleasure, and then a gasp as he rolled atop her. The sensation of his weight was exquisite, but that didn't compare to his arousal, hard and hot, pressing against the vee between her thighs. She parted for him. It was instinctive. So was the desire, overwhelming, to feel him hot and hard inside of her.

Also instinctive was the "Please" she caught herself saying.

"Just you wait, Miss W.G. Meadows," he murmured, "it's my turn to torture you now."

"Just keep kissing me," she whispered.

"Oh, I will." In the dark, she saw the wickedest of grins. Heat pooled in her belly. She had no idea what he had in mind. But if that deliciously sinful gleam in his eye was any indication . . .

He propped himself up above her. She thought of her own words—a heathen warrior—and that made her blush. But not as much as her thoughts now: that he was some wicked God of seduction. She knew she didn't stand a chance of emerging unscathed from this encounter. But then again, she didn't want to.

He was hers. And she wanted to please him in a way that aroused and scared her.

He dropped another light kiss on her lips and then gazed down at her.

His chest was wide, muscled, and strong. She traced her palms over his tattoos. His skin was hot under her touch. When her fingers slid gently over his nipples, he gasped and shut his eyes. She did it again; he groaned. And again, and he said, "You'll pay for that."

He clasped her breast in his hand, and that alone elicited a sigh. His mouth closed over the center and she moaned. When his tongue flicked over the delicate nipple, she grabbed a fistful of sheets. This torture was repeated again, thank God, on the other side. By God above, she had no idea.

"More," she gasped. Where had this wantonness come from? He gave her more.

And then more . . . more than she had ever imagined. Truly, this had never crossed her mind. But as it happened . . . Eliza's grip on the sheets was firm, twisted, sweaty.

The duke kissed just below her breasts. She had no idea the skin was so delicate, so sensitive.

The duke kissed the soft pale skin of her belly; she sighed.

The duke pressed his lips to that spot where her thighs met her belly and then he kissed her inner thighs and she gasped. Her eyes flew open. In the candlelight, she saw his long dark hair, between her legs. Felt it brushing softly against the inside of her thighs. She fell back against the pillows. Shocked.

And pleased.

And shocked again.

Then the duke kissed her *there*, at that most intimate place. She couldn't help it. She gasped. And then moaned because his tongue flicked over an extremely sensitive spot. Then he did it again, and she moaned, and again and again and again.

She threaded her fingers through his long hair, needing to hold onto something. With her other hand, she firmly grasped the bedsheets. He loved her, with his mouth, in this wicked wonderful way.

Pressure was building within her. Vaguely, she was aware of her breath, shallow and panting. Then there was that ever-increasing pressure. She wanted to tell him to stop, she couldn't take it anymore, but found she couldn't move, or speak, or do anything but lie back and love every second.

When Eliza couldn't take it anymore, when she couldn't protest, when she had no choice but to surrender—she did just that. Waves of pleasure crashed over her and coursed through her. She cried out, again and again and again.

Wycliff collapsed beside Eliza, his love, his betrothed. Her lips were parted and a blush spread from her cheeks down to her breasts, to her belly . . . He felt damned proud to have given her that. His cock throbbed, hard with wanting.

She threaded her arms around him, pulling him close for a kiss. He rolled above her, his cock straining and pressing against the place where his mouth had been. He needed to be inside her, more than he had ever needed anything.

Her legs parted. He moaned.

Her hips arched. He bit his lip. Her little hands stroked his back. His cock strained against her. He murmured her name, *"Eliza,"* as he entered her, slowly at first. She pressed her palms hard against the small of his back, and he couldn't restrain himself any longer. In one strong thrust he was inside her.

Eliza, his love, gasped and writhed and moaned beneath him. He almost died from the all-consuming pleasure of that. But he didn't. He couldn't because it required all night to make proper love to a woman, from sundown to sunset, and he had only just begun. And then thinking actual thoughts became impossible. So he moved, slowly and surely and savoring the hot, exquisite sensation of being inside her. In and out, again and again and again and again and again . . .

Eliza wrapped her arms around him. And then her legs, dear God above. Her sighs of pleasure and moans of wanting were almost as intoxicating to him as the sensation of finally at long last being inside her. He had imagined this moment. Extensively. The reality surpassed it. Extensively.

His climax came on hard and fast, drawing a shout. He may have invoked God, or some deity or pagan idol. He may have called out for the devil. In an instant he knew true love and soul-consuming pleasure. And then he collapsed beside Eliza, his woman, and pulled her close. He would never let her go.

"I love you," he gasped.

"I love you," she whispered.

It was the last thing he said to her that night, and the first words he spoke in the morning—and each night and morning ever after.

Fashionable Intelligence

By A Lady of Distinction

THE TATTOOED DUKE, TRIUMPHANT

At last, the infamous Tattooed Duke has returned—triumphantly—from his expedition to Timbuktu. His Grace, Sebastian Digby, Duke of Wycliff, is the first European to travel to this ever-elusive city and return. He was not without competition; the duke's longtime rival, Monroe Burke, engaged in an extremely competitive race to Timbuktu with the duke after the loss of Burke's fully stocked ship in an explosive dockside melee. But that was two years ago—old news, you'll agree.

Congratulations are in order to both gentlemen (yes, gentlemen, however wicked and disreputable they may appear to be), for I am informed that these two brave explorers put aside their rivalry in order to enter this fabled city together. The race, dear readers, resulted in a tie, with the safe return of both adventurers. Congratulations to those who wagered accordingly!

And what of the Duchess of Wycliff, you wonder? This intrepid heroine was with her husband every step of the journey, in corsets and skirts to boot. (Did she wear proper ballroom attire in the wilds of Africa? We must ask . . .) Did we expect anything less than an adventure of historical significance from one of *The London Weekly*'s own Writing Girls? Her exclusive reports of her thrilling, dangerous, nearly disastrous, and ultimately triumphant travels will soon appear in these pages.

If that is not enough to satisfy your curiosity, London, then plan your visit to the British Museum where the Wicked Duke of Wycliff will display all manner of treasures from his travels, which have spanned the globe from Tahiti to Timbuktu. I am told that these magnificent items have never before been displayed in England and the exhibit has been in development for years. His Grace had kept them under lock and key in his Berkeley Square residence (much to the vexation of his wife, who, like this author, cannot bear to leave a door locked or a secret uncovered).

Now, for the really delicious gossip. This author has it on good authority that the duke and duchess are settling into their Berkeley Square residence, preparing their next great adventure: a family of their own.

Next month, don't miss these exciting new love stories only from Avon Books

A Week to be Wicked by Tessa Dare
When a confirmed spinster and notorious rogue find themselves on a road to Scotland, time is not on their side. Who would have known that in one week such an unlikely pair could find a world of trouble, and maybe . . . just maybe . . . everlasting love?

The Art of Duke Hunting by Sophia Nash
On a ship in a storm-swept sea, a duke with no desire to wed and a countess who swears she'll never give her heart away find desperate passion. But they must forget their moment of folly, for if the *ton* were to learn their secret, all their fondest dreams could be ruined.

Confessions from an Arranged Marriage by Miranda Neville
It happened the usual way. He had no plans for marriage, she abhorred his wastrel ways...but a moment of mistaken identity, an illicit embrace, and the gossiping tongues changed everything. Will their marriage be one of convenience . . . or so much more?

Perilous Pleasures by Jenny Brown
Lord Ramsay has long awaited his revenge. But when the daughter of his sworn enemy is delivered into his hands, he isn't prepared for the vulnerable, courageous woman he finds. As passion burns as bright as a star—Ramsay and the bewitching Zoe will be bound together in a desperate struggle that can only be vanquished by love.

REL 0312

*At Avon Books, we know your passion
for romance—once you finish one of our
novels, you find yourself wanting more.*

May we tempt you with . . .

- **Excerpts** from our upcoming releases.

- Entertaining **extras**, including authors' personal photo albums and book lists.

- Behind-the-scenes **scoop** on your favorite characters and series.

- **Sweepstakes** for the chance to win free books, romantic getaways, and other fun prizes.

- Writing **tips** from our authors and editors.

- **Blog** with our authors and find out why they love to write romance.

- **Exclusive content** that's not contained within the pages of our novels.

Join us at
www.avonbooks.com

AVON   *An Imprint of HarperCollinsPublishers*
          www.avonromance.com

Available wherever books are sold or please call 1-800-331-3761 to order.

978-0-06-209264-9

978-0-06-208478-1

978-0-06-211535-5

978-0-06-204515-7

978-0-06-207998-5

978-0-06-178209-1

Visit www.AuthorTracker.com for exclusive
information on your favorite HarperCollins authors.

Available wherever books are sold, or call 1-800-331-3761 to order.

ATP 0312

*G*ive in to your Impulses!

These unforgettable stories only take a second to buy and give you hours of reading pleasure!

Go to *www.AvonImpulse.com* and see what we have to offer.

Available wherever e-books are sold.

AVONIMPULSE

IMP 0811